TALES

OF THE

AL-AZIF

A CTHULHU MYTHOS ANTHOLOGY

EDITED BY MATTHEW DAVENPORT

& C. T. PHIPPS

Taking a deep breath, I gritted my teeth and reached for the handle that would release the lid of the glass case. A lot of the more dangerous artifacts protected by wards such as those etched on the glass over the *Al-Azif*. Those protections were supposed to stop anyone from taking the artifacts except for the dean of Miskatonic University.

While I was currently holding that title, I had done very little to embody it. Sometimes magic cares about how you act as well as who you are. As I grasped the handle, a tingle of energy rushed up my arm. My vision clouded with the silhouette of a large man. The shadow thing raised its arm toward me and my mind flooded with waves of nausea. Fear followed, and doubt.

No sooner had the doubt entered my mind than my own spirit rebelled. If Miskatonic had been any other university, then I would have been a failure as a member of the administrative staff. Miskatonic wasn't like any other University, though. Miskatonic University was the leading research center and central hub for all knowledge regarding the occult and things beyond the veil. That difference was enough to change my role as the dean from one of administration to the guardian and protector of that knowledge.

It also meant that I was directly responsible for the protection of our world from the beasts beyond the veil. In that regard, I faithfully embodied the title as fully as any who had held it before me.

And much more than Brandon Smythe ever had.

The fear and nausea fell away, and the shadow creature faded from my view. The latch on the glass case turned in my hand and I was able to lift the glass.

Sitting in the middle of the shelf was the *Al-Azif.*

CONTENTS

ABOUT THE AUTHORS

DAVID J. WEST

David J. West writes dark fantasy and weird westerns because the voices in his head won't quiet until someone else can hear them. He is a great fan of sword & sorcery, ghosts and lost ruins, so of course he lives in Utah with his wife and children.

DAVID HAMBLING

David Hambling is a journalist and author based in Norwood, South London. His fiction, starting with a collection, The Dulwich Horror & Others, explores the Cthulhu mythos in his own locale. His novels include the popular Harry Stubbs adventures, also set in the 1920s, and he has previously contributed to ST Joshi's Black Wings of Cthulhu collections.
He can be found at: https://www.facebook.com/ShadowsFromNorwood/

MATTHEW DAVENPORT

Matthew Davenport hails from Des Moines, Iowa where he lives with his wife, Ren, and daughter, Willow. When his scattered author brain isn't earning weird looks from the ladies of his life, he enjoys reading sci-fi and horror, tinkering with electronics, and doing escape rooms.
Matt is the author of the Andrew Doran series, the Broken Nights series (along with his brother, Michael), The Trials of

Obed Marsh, and Satan's Salesman among other titles. He's also a self-styled student of the Cthulhu Mythos and exercises that influence in his stories and as an editor at the blog Shoggoth.net.

You can keep track of Matthew through his Twitter account @spazenport. Matt occasionally updates his blog at davenportwrites.com.

DAVID NIALL WILSON

David Niall Wilson has been writing and publishing horror, dark fantasy, and science fiction since the mid-eighties. An ordained minister, once President of the Horror Writer's Association and multiple recipient of the Bram Stoker Award. He lives outside Hertford, NC, with the love of his life, Patricia Lee Macomber, his children Zane and Katie, occasionally their older siblings, Stephanie, who is in college, and Bill and Zach who are in the Navy, and an ever-changing assortment of pets.

David can be found at: http://www.davidniallwilson.com Or Connect on Facebook at http://www.facebook.com/David.Niall.Wilson

C.T. PHIPPS

C.T Phipps is a lifelong student of horror, science fiction, and fantasy. An avid tabletop gamer, he discovered this passion led him to write and turned him into a lifelong geek. He is a regular blogger on "The United Federation of Charles" (http://unitedfederationofcharles.blogspot.com/). He's the author of Agent G, Cthulhu Armageddon, Lucifer's Star, Straight Outta Fangton, and The Supervillainy Saga.

THE SKULL ON THE DESK

by C.T. Phipps

"You are going to get yourself killed, Abdul Al'Hazred, and everyone will remember you as a madman," my uncle, Abbas, said.

The sun was beating down on our heads and we'd been riding our horses for hours. We were well provisioned and had just left a camp of Banu Ua nomads when their questions about where we were going had grown too close to the mark. It was said that they murdered anyone who attempted to loot the ruins of the Rub'al Khali or "The Empty Quarter." I did not consider myself a looter but a man of philosophy.

Nevertheless, I'd pushed us to an unhealthy degree and wondered if I was putting our lives at risk. It was not yet eleven in the morning, and when we reached noon, I did not know if I could stop myself from pressing further. If it was not for worry that our horses might pass out and strand us there to die alone and forgotten, I'm certain I would not have stopped.

I snorted and looked over at Abbas. "They already consider me to be a madman, Uncle."

"You are not helping your case," he said. "I have indulged you far too much over the years. Your obsession with the idolaters of the past has blinded you to what is important in life. You should be putting your third child into a second wife's belly."

I shook my head. Women had never interested me, or boys for that matter, but I had long been cursed with a temperament unsuitable to the rest of the Caliphate. I had questioned everything my tutors taught me and my father. I dare not ask Allah to bless his soul given my blasphemies, and had been smart enough to beat prudence into me when they'd claimed I was an atheist. I was not, I just did not believe in the gods they did. I did not share the faith of my countrymen and could not believe in a benevolent all-powerful being who looked over our world. I *did* believe there was something beyond this crude physical matter, though, and that it was the duty of all righteous men to seek its secrets the way the ancient Greeks had. Had Socrates not believed in an Unknown God that was better and more interesting than the naked stone statues his people had prayed to?

"You do not indulge me," I said, more amused at my uncle's chidings than annoyed. "My father left his entire fortune to me. You live off my largess."

Money was unimportant in the grand scheme of things, a belief my father and uncle had continually bemoaned. What good was currency when the universe was vaster and more exciting than anything that could be bought with gold or silver? What purpose was the gathering of wealth when we would all die one day and be food for insects? Better to devote oneself to unlocking the secrets of the world than fretting over petty things like the price of rugs. Ironically, though, it was the wealth my father had gained haggling over every coin that allowed me to pursue my research.

Abbas snorted, unhappily. "I may have a habit of overindulging in ways that are not forbidden, but at least I do not waste a vast merchant empire's funds on pottery, clay tablets, and scrolls."

My uncle did not believe and that was a good thing. Well, perhaps it was better to say he believed in the common ways of the locals. His dreams were not filled with stories of ancient Dagon and the city of R'lyeh where he dwelled with Dread Koo'toolu or of the idiot god Azazel-Thoth who lived at the center of the universe (if such a place existed). No, his dreams were untroubled by dark, unseemly shapes that flapped wings on invisible winds while whispering of worlds beyond this one.

Half of my father's employees had abandoned me, forcing

me to buy slaves to replace them, and I'd had to whip one to death after he'd sought to exorcise me with a cat. I still remember how I'd slept peacefully for a week thanks to his savage's prayer to Allah, Bast, Nodens, and a host of other strange deities. Most would have appreciated such a thing, but I lived for my strange mind-bending dreams.

"I have retrieved relics and wonders from the ruins of Babylon, spoken with the mystics beneath Memphis, and learned long-forgotten languages," I said, defending my studies. "Thrice I have been invited to speak with the wizards at the Umayyad court."

I did not mention that I was now banished from the court on pain of death. The old vizier, a Greek Christian heretic hated by all but the Caliph, was thought to have been dragged off to hell when tricked into walking onto an Elder Sign claimed to be given to the new Caliph by an angel. The new Caliph, despite his learning, believed more like Abbas and said that I was a damned fool who had sold his soul to Iblis' Nyarlathotep. As if I would be wasting my time with fools like him if I could garner that being's attention!"

"And what has it gotten you?" Abbas asked.

"I just said—"

"They burned down our warehouse in Baghdad," Abbas said, shaking his head. "I tried to arrange three marriages for you and each family turned me down when I said it was for you. Our reputation is worse in every town we visit. Only Christians, Jews, and heathens from Cathay will deal with us in some places."

I frowned. I didn't want to admit to my uncle that there had been material cost to my actions beyond even what he knew. The family fortune had been halved by my actions and halved again. This might consume the whole of my remaining funds. If we found nothing here, then I might be forced into the streets. "They are fools."

I would do anything to continue my research. I would find a way.

"You are not a wazir, Abdul," Abbas said.

"What?"

"A wise man, a wizard, a sorcerer, whatever you want to call it," Abbas said, shaking his head. "I know what you have been chasing this entire time and it does not exist."

I turned around and snarled at him. "You know nothing."

Indeed, if he knew my true purpose here, he would not only turn back, but run screaming from house to house that I was an enemy of God.

He'd have been right to.

"You talk of speaking with wizards and the courts, but I know a man who can pull a snake from his mouth as well as make a camel disappear, none of which actually uses real power. There is no such thing," Abbas said, clearly disgusted. "You have been chasing children's fantasies and ghost stories for your entire adult life and it is time for you to grow up."

I could not tolerate his words, they were too close to the truth because I was chasing real magic out here in the desert. The power of the real gods, not the ones prayed to my countrymen. Beings I hated and envied in equal measure.

My hand moved down to my scimitar. "Apologize now or—"

"What? You'll kill me? Your own flesh and blood? We are alone in the desert and almost to the point we need to turn around! Let go of this madness!"

I spit three curses at him and galloped off.

The endless dunes confused and frustrated me, and the Nameless City was no closer than it had been hours before. The heat, and my abusive treatment toward the horse, who had trusted me to get us both through the journey safely, seemed likely to be my undoing. I, who had raised natural forces like the heat and the weather, above any theology or god, was threatened with dehydration and exhaustion, with none of the water I had expected to find in sight.

I proved to be a greater fool than my uncle. The heat got to me, and my horse collapsed, leaving us both exposed to the noonday sun. I had devoted so much of my time to the study of ancient civilizations and languages that I had never learned the proper way of surviving in the desert. In the end, my horse died before me and I was left to a slow, lingering death under the burning heat of the sun.

Perhaps that would have been a fitting end for me in my desire to prove Allah false and the universe ruled by more unforgiving forces. I'd made the mistake of believing this made my quest righteous when truth had no favorites. The universe did not care if the insects or humans (was there a difference?) knew what gods ruled over its physical laws. It simply was and the whole of humanity was an infection growing in the wound that was life on Earth. I would have laughed but my lips were cracked, and my throat was far too dry.

I only lasted the night before I fell to unconsciousness and expected death. My dreams, at least, were still a place of refuge and I saw things that enticed the imagination even as my upbringing made me recoil. I saw the obsidian-skinned face of the Black Pharaoh in the stars above, looking out over a vast kingdom of a million celestial spheres. I saw men shaped like beetles, worms, gnats, fish, and slime praying to things I could only make out the indistinct hideous shadows of.

I saw the early Earth receive falling stars containing these monstrous things—beings that were miles-tall and half as wide—shaping reality with thought. There were no humans in this world, and for a moment I believed that the tales of my faith would prove true. These were the jinn and efreeti, creatures created long before man. They were nothing like us, though, and as far superior to us as I was to a locust. I saw these beings war with flower-headed fleshy things and each other, destroying the world multiple times until they went into a terrible slumber.

Dead but dreaming.

Why are you showing me this? I begged the Black Pharaoh.

The Black Pharaoh did not give me an answer, though, instead gesturing to another sphere. Many other spheres in fact. I saw races on dying worlds drawn to the Earth. Fungus from Yuggoth, goatmen from Leng, shapeshifting centaurs from Kastro'vaal, and hive-minded insects from Callisto. They came to pay homage to these great old beings that settled on our world. It sickened me to realize that we were a destination for a pilgrimage by the universe's other races. Religion and truth were not enemies and the only thing different for enlightened beings was what forces one humbled oneself before.

Do you still wish to know the truth? The Black Pharaoh finally spoke to me. *Even though the truth will bring you nothing but misery, despair, and madness?*

Its voice was like a lion's claws on my soul, tearing away my sanity with each syllable. As a child I had often torn the wings off of insects to amuse myself. It reminded me of how I felt realizing that as such a mighty being had deigned to notice me.

"Yes!" I shouted, suddenly feeling like my throat was healed. "There is nothing man was not meant to know, no truths that I fear, and no greater thing than to know the unknowable! If madness be my punishment, then let it be the madness of the enlightened among the ignorant!"

One of my tutors had told me of the scholar Plato among the Greeks. My tutor, an obese debauched man named Duhat, had believed them to be the greatest civilization of all time. I had ignored most of what he tried to teach me, but one story remained stuck in my head. Plato had spoken of a cave where all of humanity was imprisoned, and the only things the prisoners knew of the outside world were shadows cast upon a wall. Then one poor soul had wandered out of the cave and been exposed to the beautiful, yet terrible, world beyond. When he returned and tried to enlighten his fellows, they had ostracized and killed him. I did not know if the latter part was an invention of Duhat's or not, but I preferred to be the man who had seen the true world than the disgusting fools in the cave.

Is the madman the one who denies the truth or the one who proclaims himself the sole holder of it? Does any of it matter since truth is a concept of humans? None of life matters except to the beings who recognize facts and interpret how they makes them feel.

Silence! I snapped, only to reel back in horror at the realization I'd addressed a god with such insolence.

Instead, Iblis'Nyarlathotep just laughed. *You address only yourself.*

I pondered those words and interpreted their meaning. *Yes,*

I am a god or, at least, their prophet. I must write my own holy book to guide the feeble masses from Plato's cave. Madman or genius, I will be the father of a new religion.

Or many. You will find the answers you seek in the Al-Azif.

The Book of the Insect?

The Book of Lies, the Black Pharaoh said. **The remnants of a dead civilization that sought to save itself but could only shift its fate to another damned, doomed race. Despite the fate of its authors, that book contains the names of many Great Old Ones and true gods, or at least true, as any such being worshiped by mortals may be.**

Show me this book! I will do anything! I must know!

I promise you, Abdul, you will know more about everything than any other man of your race has ever learned. It will merely cost you knowing yourself.

That was when I awoke.

Air entered my lungs and I felt like a new man. I soon found this to be literally true. I turned to see my corpse lying beside me on a stone slab. The two of us were in a pyramid-shaped chamber with multiple stone slabs, like altars. Light was provided by organic crystals growing along the walls and bathing us in an unnatural blue-green light. I was relieved to find that I was intact, with two hands, two feet, and smooth brown skin. My manhood was intact, apparently even my circumcision undone. The Abdul Al'Hazred beside me looked like he'd died of dehydration, however, and was little more than a skeleton.

I felt, given the circumstances, my next actions were quite reasonable.

I screamed.

A woman entered the chamber, but not like any woman I had ever seen. She was dressed in a shockingly immodest style with only wrap around her breasts and a loincloth. Her hair hung down past her shoulders and her skin was black like the Pharaoh's, yet her eyes were of the clearest blue. There was a vague sense of the old Egyptians about her, but I also sensed that she was something else. Whatever soul, if such a thing existed, emanated behind that gaze did not feel in any way human. It was as if a pagan goddess was gazing upon me or one of the creatures I'd seen in my vision.

"Away woman, with your nakedness!" I said, covering myself.

The woman seemed annoyed rather than apologetic. *You will find no one here believes or shares your social values, Abdul Al'Hazred. I suppose you are not as enlightened as you think you are.*

I heard her voice in my mind. It was melodious but inhuman, sounding like a choir of pipes rather than an utterance of words.

"What are you?" I asked, stunned. "How do you know my name?"

We are the Yith, the woman said. *We read your memories while transferring your mind to a clone. You are an important historical personage of this reality's time period.*

"A c...lone?" I asked, trying to understand. I felt like a foolish, ignorant child compared to her.

You would call it a homunculus. We took samples of your essential salts and used them to grow you a new body before transferring your soul into it. That is the closest approximation I can make of the science involved to your frame of knowledge.

Her words angered me. "I can learn anything you can teach me."

Why would we do that? the woman asked.

I had no answer for that. Why indeed? Most beings were motivated solely by their own self-interest. It was one of the reasons I hated my fellow man. "Why save me in the first place?"

You are a source of information we are collecting about humanity's extinction.

I blinked and stood, no longer caring about my nakedness. "Extinction? What do you mean?"

Humankind is not the first intelligent species to have evolved or existed on Ketra'goo'an, what humans call Earth. The Yith, my species, inhabited it sixty-five million years ago before an extinction-level event forced us to move our consciousnesses to the far future. As part of our efforts to gather and preserve knowledge, we have charted and catalogued the period between those two times. I am wearing the body of a woman of this time period while her consciousness is safely stored in the past. Many of your greatest scientists, philosophers, or thinkers were either my race or beings who learned from them.

I found myself stunned and fascinated. Here was proof positive of the Earth being far older than so many theologians claimed, yet a part of me had enough lingering loyalty to my species to be appalled. "Is there no way to stop the death of my race?"

The woman stared at me with her empty, ancient eyes. *Your race has already died. Time is not a progression. All that is happening, has happened, and will happen at once. Consciousness is a movement along a pre-arranged set of events. Events may change based upon which reality in the quantum frequency you are inhabiting but—*

I felt like my head was going to explode.

I am distressing you. I shall stop.

"No!" I shouted, raising my hands in the air. "You mustn't! I must know more! This is why I have come to the Nameless City! To discover the secrets of the worshipers of Acheron, Baalzebel, and the Lords of Locusts!"

I had lied to my uncle, who I expected to be either dead or safely on his way back to Baghdad in order to loot my fortune. I had told Abbas my goal here was to investigate a city consumed by a sandstorm in order to find a cache of gold that had been hidden away by the pagan idolaters who once inhabited it. I'd used golden fish I'd bartered from the cult of Dagon along Egypt's shoreline to convince him or at least incite his greed. Abbas had insisted on melting down the sacred relics of the ugly, foul-smelling people in order to make coins, but I'd convinced him to help me. He never would have agreed to come if he'd known my true purpose.

The *Al-Azif.* The Book of the Insect.

It had been ages since the oceans had drunk Atlantis and the rise of the sons of Aryas. The ancient times had passed with the Israelites putting to sword the Canaanites, Stygians, Philistines, and worshipers of Set-Yig. True magic was a thing of the past and I'd been able to find only a few scattered fragments of the *Book of Eibon* that served as humanity's sole insight into not only the truth of reality, but the art of manipulating it. It was said that the *Al Azif* was the last relic of unfathomable power to be had by those brave and deranged enough to read the secrets of devils.

The woman looked at me curiously. *The mutated humans who inhabited this world, possessed by brain parasites containing Callisto consciousnesses, have been purged. The advanced life-forms of their world worshiped Yog-Sothoth, the collective consciousness of space-time, and do not respect the proper flow of history. They were attempting to alter the flow of events in order to guarantee their ascension in this planet's future. They would replace both my race and the hybridized offshoots of humanity's future evolution with their own descendants.*

I barely registered anything she said after her first sentence. "The Nameless Ones are all dead?"

It was like a blow to the chest and I almost murdered the woman where she stood. This had been my last chance of discovering the secrets of the universe. The Nameless Ones were said to be walking corpses full of scarabs that knew the true names of the wind, fire, earth, and water.

I did not believe in superstition, but I'd seen a fakir put a scarab it claimed to be from the Nameless City into a child's mouth and the boy then speak great wisdom about magic, gods, science, and the future. I had sat down at the feet of the hybrid being and learned of countless fascinating things, including the location of this city. The price had been high, at least for the boy, with the scarab eating its brain after a few hours but I felt it well worth it. Sadly, the scarab died not long after I slit the throat of its owner in my attempt to acquire it.

So, the woman replied. *You wish to see the Al-Azif? Your mind practically screams in lust for it.*

My gaze met hers. I wondered if she knew how much I was willing to do to achieve greater knowledge. She'd dangled a carrot in front of me and there was only one response. "Yes. Take me to it. Now."

The *Al-Azif* hovered in the air at the center of a chamber that had been a temple for once-human creatures. It was a towering pyramidal edifice built around a single central chamber that seemed infused with unearthly alien power.

The chamber had no seats, but dozens of rows of black stones were arranged in a circle around the blue nimbus engulfing the *Al-Azif*. My mind briefly conjured the image of hideous desiccated corpses, riddled with otherworldly vermin, shambling forward to offer prayers to the unholy thing. The *Al-Azif* itself appeared as a vellum book very similar to the kind produced by the Caliph's scholars. I had expected it to look much older but a part of me realized that it was not a book made of pages and ink. Instead, somehow, it appeared thus to me to aid my understanding but was more like an information source incarnate.

"Beautiful," I whispered, walking forward. The Yith woman had provided me with a robe and sandals that lent me a false sense of decency and modesty as I approached the object of my search. "It is everything I could have imagined it to be."

The Al-Azif has been a plague upon your race since its arrival on your world sixteen million years ago, the Yith woman spoke. *The Ixtol, as they called themselves, devoted themselves heavily to the worship of the Great Old Ones and constructed machines to channel the power of the mind. They derived the secrets of Azathoth, Nyarlathotep, Yog-Sothoth, and the Sleeping Ones.*

"They were wise," I said, slowly approaching the book.

They were fools, the Yith woman said. *They conjured things that they could not put down and warped themselves trying to become more than they were. Eventually, the planet Ixtol, that you know as Callisto, was scoured of all life. Their Priest-God sought to preserve himself and his people. He poured their consciousness into an artifact that he believed would eventually possess lesser beings.*

"So, he sought to do exactly what your race did," I said, not afraid to show my contempt. I was right outside the nimbus of blue light now.

Yes, the Yith woman did not deny it. *But they wished to destroy a sentient species to do so. Your species. Which is unforgivable.*

I did not see the difference between what she said the Nameless Ones had planned for humanity and what her people had done to the residents of this city. The Yith had, indeed, purged the city of all life. I could find no trace of the Nameless Ones as we passed through courtyards, streets, and palaces on our way to the *Al-Azif*'s location. There were no signs of men, women, or children (if the Nameless Ones could be said to have any). Instead, they were empty, but curiously alive with lights, and strange metallic sounds that emanated from each building. I did not see any other Yith, but statues made of living metal shaped as animals or hovering cones moved about the place.

I tried to touch the book, but my hand was shocked when I reached for it, causing me to pull back. "Sorcery!"

Science, the Yith woman replied. *Though the two words are merely variations on the method of using the will to create an effect.*

"You say the Nameless Ones tried to alter time?" I asked, unable to comprehend such a thing, no matter how I tried.

Yes, the Yith woman said, walking beside me. *They provided advanced knowledge to species unprepared for its use. The so-called Sorcerer Kings and mutant civilizations of the past owe much to their influence. Not all of them, though, because the other species of humanoids on your world, like the Deep Ones or Ghouls, have their own origins. Indeed, it was the Deep Ones who destroyed the early civilization on your island of Crete to prevent the extinction of mankind. In time, the Al-Azif will be used as the basis for your book—*

"I must read it," I said, looking at her. "Now."

That is not how it should happen. We have done our best to repair how events are meant to flow in order to facilitate an optimal timeline for our—

I grabbed her by the throat with both hands then threw her against the blue nimbus, causing her to utter an involuntary cry of pain. I gripped her and slammed her head into the nimbus repeatedly. After the first few blows, there was a sickening crunch. I threw her lifeless corpse to one side.

Good, the *Al-Azif* spoke in my mind. **You are worthy.**

I looked at the book and reached for it. "Yes, I am. Are you… are you the Black Pharaoh?"

A mocking, hideous laughter answered me and I closed my fist tightly at the mockery. The fist passed through the blue nimbus without difficulty.

"What is so funny?" I asked, my voice taking on a dangerous edge.

I am Vhourvath, the voice spoke. *First and last among the Ixtol.*

"So you're not Nameless Ones after all," I said, grabbing hold of the book.

What followed was an agonizing sensation, like fire burning through my body and brain. It felt like I was burning, inside and out, but I saw no wounds or flames. Falling to my knees, I clutched the *Al-Azif* to my body despite the fact it was the source of my agony.

Your mind is a black, swirling storm of chaos. I cannot take your body, Vhourvath spoke to me.

"What?" I called out, sweating from every pore. "You wanted to *steal* my body?"

I didn't know why the thought was so shocking to me. I had always admired the glorious amorality of the races I'd read about. How they were wild and free, unshackled by notions of good or evil. Yet, it was *offensive* that they dared treat me with the same disdain they treated other humans.

The Yith or something else has blocked my passage. You are useless to us.

I felt another burning sensation across my body and realized the Nameless Ones were trying to kill me with pure pain. Dropping the book had no effect and I thrashed on the ground and held my head with both hands. "I can help you! I can give you bodies! Worshipers! Whatever you desire!"

The pain stopped.

What do you want in return? Vhourvath asked, sounding almost human in its suspicions. *Your species evolved to be as selfish as any other.*

I needed several breaths to calm down before I answered. "Knowledge."

Power it is.

With Vourvath's assistance, I made my way through a strange series of portals that carried me across the desert back to civilized space. What followed was close to a decade of studying the *Al-Azif* and bartering with its deranged occupants. I was forced to flee from the cities I dwelt in many times, the missing children and dead priests inevitably creating a panic among the foolish locals who did not understand the importance of my work.

My uncle abandoned me, having informed on me to imams and wazirs both, and causing the Caliph to call for my head. There was a substantial price on my life throughout all the lands the Prophet had united through his faith. Many times I was forced to fake my death or use the powers now at my disposal to protect myself. Whole villages ended up carried away by byakhee or swallowed up by blood-drinking Cthonian horrors. I could not control the terrible things the book allowed me to conjure, but I could summon them and sometimes even turn them against my long-dead insectoid patrons.

I lived thus until I completed my life's work, the *Necronomicon*. I compiled it from secrets I learned from the lips of mummified skulls, from eaten brains, and from drug-induced visions. The *Al-Azif* had aided me in my work, but was not the sole source of my knowledge. Indeed, by the year 730 of the Christian Calendar, I had surpassed Vhourvath and created a text that had been copied hundreds of times by my followers. It was the new Quran in my mind, and would usher in an age of horror and wonder once all mankind had embraced it. My book's existence caused certain challenges, though, that needed to be dealt with.

You are a fool, Abdul Al'Hazred, to believe you can simply tuck me away in a chest, Vhourvath whispered as I carried the book through the underground tunnels my followers had dug beneath Damascus.

"You have become...inconvenient," I said, thinking about the near miss I'd had in Samarra. Hundreds of my scarab-eyed slaves had been blasted to dust by a wizard who had conjured the power of a golden-eyed god named Kthanid.

Many of my followers, from the fallen Byzantine knight

Lord Wilfred Whiteley to the debased medusa Marcia, had been slain by these cults of the Elder Gods. They had the means to track the beings I had helped the book to "rebirth" in the bodies of my former race. I had no loyalty to the Nameless Ones, any more than they had loyalty to me, but they had become useful servitors. Most of them were all but mindless without their master and obeyed whomever claimed to represent their eldritch gods. I had better servants now. Humans who believed I was a true mouthpiece of the gods and were pledged to live for great Cthulhu the way other fools did for ⊚Īsā ibn Maryam or the Prophet.

You think you can simply hand me over to the dogmen and I will disappear from your life? You are as much a fool as the zealots you claim will be spared when the Great Old Ones rise.

The ghouls underneath Damascus were a nation unto themselves and had agreed to bargain with the *Al-Azif* for more of its secrets. I was growing older, and while not even as old as my uncle Abbas had been when he'd first joined me on my quests for forbidden lore, I was already pondering the means to escape my impending death. I did not trust the immortality of the Nameless Ones, who promised much but simply moved around one's corpse like a beetle did its shell.

"It is my destiny to live forever," I said, simply. "You who act as a superior species have had millennia to destroy my race. Instead, all you have done is create a few failed civilizations and vermin-oriented cults. I am done with you. When people think of the texts that answer the questions of the cosmos, they will think of my book, not yours."

You still think with your pedestrian human mind. It hurts to even lower myself to speak with you as if you were an equal rather than a slave-tool made by Elder Things to supplement their shoggoths. What have I devoted to your race? Twenty thousand years? It is a pittance of time to manipulate your species to become slightly more useful for the hour of mine's rebirth. You are nothing more than cattle we have husbanded as food.

I had gotten used to Vhourvath's delusions of grandeur. I

had once thought the Nameless Ones to be a superior species, but years of exposure had made me realize that both species were equally pathetic and insignificant. The Nameless Ones were but one of a million races in this star cluster alone, and the universe would not mourn their loss any more than it did my race.

"My race is still alive," I said, feeling strangely defensive about a species I'd long held in contempt. "Yours is but copied information in a reliquary. You're not even the real Vhourvath, just his memories and personality stored along with those of his servants."

Reality and dream are one. When you learn this, you will truly be dangerous. But the hour of your end is almost upon you.

I ignored him. I would live forever, no matter the cost. I saw that the end of the cave contained a half-dozen dead ghouls. The furred, wolfen-faced beasts had been shot with Cathay crossbow bolts and their throats cut with scimitars. Dozens of smooth stones were spread around their bodies, each etched with a heinous Elder Sign. I could not see beyond their bodies for a moment, because I had to avert my eyes from that twisted star. It seemed to contain all that I despised in the universe, despite being nothing more than lines carved in rock.

I held tight to the *Al-Azif* as my vision cleared, seeing four masked men in robes, the Elder Sign hanging from their necks on leather cords with weapons drawn. Their eyes were crystal blue and contained an inhuman intelligence. They were not what surprised me the most, however. There, looking like a sheep in a pack of wolves, was my uncle, Abbas.

Time had not been good to the once overfed and healthy man. Most of Abbas' hair had fallen out and his face was gaunt. There were deep wrinkles under his eyes. Liver spots dotted his neck and he'd lost perhaps forty pounds. He was sixty years old but now seemed like a man approaching eighty. There was none of the warmth or faith in his eyes, either, but instead the paranoid look of a man who'd been exposed to the horrors beyond, and without the strength to embrace their gifts. He held a copy of the Quran indicating that he still clung to the beliefs he'd tried to instill upon me, but his expression was one of dread and hopelessness.

I fell back a step and lifted my right hand, making a pair of horns with my fingers. "You! You cannot have my book!"

It was a ridiculous statement and I wondered why I made it. If the Yith desired to retrieve the book, they were welcome to have it. I had bargained, manipulated, and tricked every secret I possibly could from Vhourvath. Indeed, I had exceeded him as both a magician and master of the arcane.

You are a primitive creature with an ape's mind. You cannot begin to know the secrets of the Ixtol.

I scoffed at his taunts, focused instead on the assassins before me. They were not moving forward but instead keeping their distance. This gave me hope I might conjure flame, lightning, or a host of flesh-eating bugs against them. The real magic, imposing one's will upon the universe through dreaming, was not simple. Every syllable of the inhuman tongues I'd learned to mangle the words of seemed banished from my lips. The Elder Signs prevented my speaking, the words lodging in my throat as if the sun was burning away my saliva.

"You have done terrible things, my nephew," Abbas said, his voice weak and broken. "You have consorted with devils and sent many souls to hell. I have followed you and your cult, trying to help those who would unmake this hideous religion you have created, but it is too large. Slaves and sultans worship your evil gods. I beg of you, surrender, and let us try to make right what you have done before both of us are judged."

My uncle advanced, but it was not with weapons or even his fists. Not that he looked like he could wrestle a girl fresh into maidenhood. Instead, there was only love and pity in his eyes. I saw that he blamed himself for not steering me from my path, and had genuinely tried to make amends for what he perceived as my moral failure. I rewarded him for this by bashing his head in with the *Al-Azif*, splattering the book with blood and brain matter. It was as heavy as a stone tablet in that moment, then light as a dream the next.

The four Yith came at me, but I hurled the book toward them and ran in the opposite direction. I did not know if they were a species that would take revenge for one of their number being murdered, but did not wish to risk it. Instead, I simply ran in a crooked path underneath Damascus' busiest streets. I knew these paths well and had used them to visit my acolytes. Many a second or third son, sometimes a female babe, had been offered up for the favor of Cthulhu's Chosen.

Climbing up a rickety wooden ladder, I exited into the back of a lamp shop and pushed through the crowding shoppers into the broad daylight of an open market. That was when I saw dozens of blue-eyed Yith staring at me through those eerie eyes. They had known where I was going to be!

I hissed and cursed before raising my hands in the air. "Ph'nglui mglw'nafh Cthulhu R'lyeh wgah'nagl fhtagn." *In His House at R'lyeh dead Cthulhu waits dreaming.* None of the insects around me understood what I said, but I then began to chant their doom. I called across space and time for the dark things to come forth and kill every man, woman, as well as child in the city. The Yith inhabited the bodies of men, regardless of their true nature, and would die confronted by a creature that ate consciousnesses as well as flesh.

I laughed.

Right up until a small boy deposited a rock covered with an Elder Sign at my feet.

The thing that ate me before a horrified crowd of onlookers was both invisible and uninterested in the other residents of Damascus.

It also took over an hour to finish.

Death was not a release.

I was disappointed that oblivion did not greet me. I felt caterpillars crawl in and out of my eye sockets while flies flew around inside my brain cavity. I was trapped inside a bleached yellow skull, the flesh of my body having been eaten away by the centuries that had passed. One of my followers had retrieved some of my remains, and then used my own principles of sorcery to bind what lesser men would call a soul.

Yet, in my followers' stupidity, they did not copy it precisely. Imbeciles like Baron Randolf of Dunwich, John Dee, Lady

Johanna De la Poer, and the blood-drinkers Solomonari of Romania introduced errors where I had created perfection. Hundreds of variants of the *Necronomicon* spread throughout the world, their truths watered down and poisoned with the religions or suppositions of fools. The cult of Cthulhu spread, turning science into religion, and became the hidden faith of millions, in defiance of my wishes, but I could do little. I had become a toy for whatever wizard used me to consult with them or their descendants, and who knew me as a mere curiosity.

Despite my wretched state I remained aware of two facts. One, the *Al-Azif* was still out there and had not remained with the Yith for long. I maintained some small connection to the accursed tome due to my long use of it and felt whenever a mortal of enough will or knowledge tried to harness it secrets. Two, the Great Old Ones would eventually arise and destroy the world that the Nameless Ones sought to colonize.

It was a petty revenge, unworthy of a great wazir such as myself, but one had to make do with what one had. The Yith had tricked me. They had seen how the *Al-Azif* would interfere with their preferred timeline while knowing it had always been my destiny to bring horror to the world through forbidden knowledge. They had sent their enemy down a path to his doom (or was it our doom?) by giving me a silver key to open the door to hell. I knew my own fate as well as that of the human race's, but it would be centuries before I could divine that of the artifact. No wizard or priest would lend me their power to learn the truth, even if they craved the book for themselves.

Instead, one writer in the New World was the answer to my last desire. The storyteller had a mind with a strong will as well as powerful abilities as a dreamer. Sitting on his desk as a gift from Aleister Crowley, who knew his wife Sonia, I was able to briefly steal his potential while inspiring him with tales of the weird as well as macabre. I used him to peer into the future as well as the past to know what fate met the *Al-Azif* after it left my hands. I could not see all its past, mostly the last century before and after my time, but what I glimpsed amused me terribly.

Tales I will now share.

A MANUSCRIPT FOUND IN CARCOSA

A Porter Rockwell Adventure

By. David J. West

Ayesha pulled the covers up over her chest and nestled her head into the imported goose feather pillow. Their house, on the exterior, appeared to be a traditional Muslim one but the interior contained a variety of objects from all around the world due to her grandfather's exotic interests. Moonlight splashed against the wall through the open window where a warm breeze fluttered the curtains. The room was cast in various shades of grey and inky blue from both the moon and a few dim city lights.

The soft sounds of her parents preparing for bed downstairs was comforting. Somewhere in the hot dark below her window, a hawker called and bid guests enter the hotel next door. It was a familiar enough sound, for Cairo was still a bustling city with folk coming from all over the world to witness the wonders of the past and intrigues of the present. What would the future here yet hold, she wondered?

Ayesha was almost asleep when fear crept in and knelt upon her bed. She couldn't fathom what was causing the sudden anxiety, the very panic that gave her chills despite the night heat and blankets. Then the slightest whisper of movement caught her eye. A tiny spider danced across the bare stucco wall. It made its way toward the ceiling corner directly across from her where the shadows lingered.

Ayesha watched it almost casually, unperturbed at its

presence yet wondering what caused a garden of fear to sprout all around her. It was no threat, so tiny and fragile in its own way and yet, she could not take her eyes from it as it meandered closer and closer to that dark corner opposite her. Were its legs growing longer as it grew closer to that space? Was it a trick of the shadows casting eerie light on those thin spindly appendages? It looked like it was expanding.

Certain that the dark was playing tricks on her, she watched in disbelief as the tiny abomination seemed to grow larger with her every heartbeat. It reached the corner and the shadows lengthened in rapid succession. Her eyes grew wide in fright and terror took hold of her heart, gripping it in an icy vise despite the heat of the summer night. The drum of her heartbeat threatened to explode out of her chest. Surely the thunder of it must be waking her parents.

The legs widened, and the misshapen body stretched and took on the form of liquid shadow, roiling blackness that coalesced into the form of something caught between the shape of both spider and man. It seemed to melt, drizzling down the wall, until its legs reached all the way under the bed. It seemed a dreadful combination of animal, insect, person, and living darkness. Some terrible thing that did not belong in this universe and existed by its own laws—like a nightmare or jinn.

Then it forcefully peeled itself from the wall and ceiling, with an audible rip. Glaring red eyes winked into existence and pierced her soul. The misshapen head elongated, twisted like it was cracking its own neck and, turning back, brought itself to face her, looming ever closer. The creature's empty soulless eyes stared malevolently into hers.

The long arms reached but did not grasp her on the top of her frozen limbs but instead seemed to grasp her from beneath and rise inside her body. The cold touch seeped up from beneath the bed first as if tarry liquid were filling the room and rising over her flesh, penetrating her skin, muscle and bone.

Petrified, Ayesha tried to shout to her mother, to her father, or even her grandfather but no words came as the shadowy arachnid thing squeezed his shadowy fingers inside her mouth. She felt her soul sucked into oblivion as if her body had become heavier than iron, and she sank into the bed, only to be swallowed by the dark. All that followed in her mind was the chittering of insects then nothing.

The airship lifted off and soon London looked like a set of smoky building blocks far beneath them. The final passengers to board, a pair of Americans, a beautiful young woman with platinum blonde hair and a brute of a man. They had purchased their tickets just as the guidelines were being released and were making their way to the dining car. Walking was uncomfortable as the airship leaned slightly upon takeoff.

The young woman, a Ms. Elizabeth Dee, wore a dress and jacket that were, by Victorian standards, nothing less than scandalous. Though they were perfectly modest, it was entirely too tight compared to the voluminous evening gowns that the rest of the women aboard were wearing. She received more than her fair share of stares from the other passengers but her intimidating escort made those sidelong glances seem inconsequential.

Porter Rockwell was dressed like a frontiersman, for indeed he was, with dark leggings, tall boots and a scuffed black coat with more than a few bullet holes revealing his white linen shirt beneath. He had a brace of pistols leering over the top of his vest and a gold chain pocket watch as well as a long bowie knife at his belt. Yet the most noticeable features were his beard and long unkempt hair flooding out from beneath his slouch hat. His presence made the other passengers naturally quite nervous. Most assumed he was an actor since there was no way they would (normally) allow an armed cowboy to walk around like it was Buffalo Bill's Wild West show. Security had taken one look at him and decided to leave him alone as there was a shadow of something else in his eyes. Something that gave him a freedom of movement unparalleled in most places because most people simply didn't want to approach him.

"Do you need anything, Miss Dee?" asked the maître d.

"I should like to see the menu," Elizabeth said, flashing a smile.

"Dinner will be served at six o'clock Greenwich mean time.

So, I'm afraid you will need to wait."

"That's fine," Elizabeth said. "I'm not hungry anyway, but my bodyguard, Mr. Rockwell, would like to see your wine list."

"Whisky," Porter corrected.

"For you, I will see what I can do," he said to Elizabeth. "I imagine there should be some spirits available even at this hour." He then vanished as swiftly as possible.

This was only Elizabeth's second time in an airship and the novelty of looking out the windows was still fresh. But after some few minutes of watching, the clouds rolled in and disguised any possible features from her view. She fished in her purse and pulled out the yellowed envelope that had set them on this adventure. "I'm still excited. I am literally on top of the world."

Her companion grunted, as he put his hat over his eyes in a vain attempt to sleep until the bar was open.

"Porter, do you know anything about Egypt?"

He pretended to snore.

"I know you're not asleep." She slapped him across the knees with the envelope.

"I know it's got sand, mummies, and pyramids and that's all I know about it," he said from beneath the hat. Most of that he'd learned on their trip to London, visiting the museum with his companion. She had an immense love of old cultures and weird esoteric practices. It seemed all the rage in the British Empire now. Personally, it came off like graverobbing to Porter.

Elizabeth read the curious letter again.

Greetings and Salutations, Miss Elizabeth Dee

Please pardon the intrusion from a stranger, but I have acquired a rather curious artifact that I was told you may be the one person able to ascertain the hidden knowledge contained therein. It came in a box that has seen much harsh wear and the only inscription that can be read is upon the outside of the package which reads, A Manuscript found in Carcosa. *I don't believe I have ever heard of the place and most of the locals go batty when I try to get more information from them. In any case, I have strayed from my point.*

I was told that you are something of a metaphysical savant, an expert in such things and that your amazing talents might help to get to the bottom of this wonderful mystery. If you should agree to come and look at this manuscript, the Royal Society and I would be most delighted. I have already arranged passage aboard the soonest departing airship from London, The Victoriana. I do hope I am not being too forward with you. I do understand that a certain Mormon gentleman is accompanying you, a guardian perhaps that will establish that our intentions here in Cairo are of the most honorable and sincere.

Please do come and help alleviate our insatiable curiosity. A reward of some five hundred pounds will be yours for simply looking at the manuscript and giving us your noted opinion.

Thank you, most sincerely,

Sir Arthur Brummell of the London Royal Geographical Society,

Cairo Antiquities Division

She folded it and put it back into the envelope. "It does seem to be a bizarre coincidence, my receiving this invitation right when we were ready to leave London and return to the States. And so much money for just looking at it."

"Don't much believe in coincidences," Porter growled from beneath his hat.

"What do you believe in?"

"Always having a backup," he said, as he reached into his vest and produced a dented flask. He shook it and popping the stopper revealed it was empty. "Sometimes I don't follow my own gospel well enough though."

She snorted a laugh. "You are the holiest man I know."

He smiled and tucked the hat back over his eyes. "Wake me when the bar is open."

Elizabeth shook her head and pondered. It was a long way to Egypt but the airship would make that go by quick as anything.

They landed in Cairo late the next day. The warm atmosphere washed over them with a dazzling aroma. People hawked their wares to passengers as they disembarked, and servants did their best to keep the hollering merchants and pick pocket children away from the wealthy European tourists with shouts of, "Emshee" or "Allah yahanen aliek!"

"What does that mean" Elizabeth asked a porter.

He gave her a confused look, then understanding the question said, "Emshee is the most valuable phrase you will learn while in Cairo. It is *Go Away*! Use it liberally while you are in our city and forced to deal with the many beggars and tramps."

"And the other I am hearing?'

He smiled. "That is *May God Give You Pity*. It is the politer brush off for the beggars."

Elizabeth and Porter found themselves among the last of the passengers to exit. A very thin man in a dark coat and jacket, despite the heat, was waiting for them with a small placard that read, Ms. Elizabeth Dee.

"I am Elizabeth Dee," she said.

The thin man had a pencil mustache and eyes half-hidden behind thick lenses. He bowed and fumbled over himself saying, "So pleased you could make it, Ms. Dee. I am Archibald Leech, Mr. Brummell's assistant. And I am to escort you to your quarters for your stay here in Cairo and then on the morrow take you to meet Mr. Brummell and examine the manuscript."

"We won't be meeting him tonight?" asked Elizabeth.

"I'm afraid not. He had some, uh, business to take care of and begged me to represent him well and offered his most sincere apologies. He plans to meet you tomorrow in time for tea."

Porter scowled and gave Elizabeth a look of displeasure at this development. She merely shook her head and smacked him across the chest. "Not everything is trap."

"No, but it ain't the best way to make introductions."

"Most people these days in positions of importance have go-betweens and of course things do come up."

Porter looked at the carriage that Mr. Leech had directed them toward and he spit after taking a long gander at the horses. "You need to feed them better."

"I beg your pardon?'" stammered Leech.

"You heard me. They aren't getting enough grass or water. Look at the veins standing out on their legs."

"I am assured that Mr. Brummell has the very best men taking care of his horses."

"Mmm hmm," grumbled Porter. He then leaned in close to Elizabeth, "If a man can't take care of his horses, how do you suppose he is gonna take care of anything else?"

She rolled her eyes. "Please, can you just give someone a chance, who may not know as much about horses as yourself?"

He grinned at her, and his eyes sparkled the message of *Not Likely* loud and clear.

Once they were in the carriage, Leech directed the driver to carry them through the city. The setting sun cast red light across the clouds and the darkness of the land lay in contrast to the fading glow of the sky. Palms were silhouetted on the horizon with the towers of the citadel and the jutting pyramids granted an exotic flair to the evening.

"This place is amazing. I've never seen such a strange city," said Elizabeth in awe, as the carriage rolled through narrow side streets and cobbled avenues.

Porter watched, but more out of the habit of being alert for danger than any appreciation for this ancient land.

The stars had just winked into existence as they came to a stop outside a large manor house with a multitude of dark shuttered windows. An entryway with a small gabled roof overhead, held by carved pillars granted a cosmopolitan look while still holding onto the glory of ancient Egypt.

"Are those real?" asked Elizabeth as she ran her bare hand across the hieroglyphs that covered the wide sandstone pillars. "They are!"

Leech looked at her in wonder. "You can read those?"

"No," she said shaking her head, "But I could feel their age, their story."

"Ah, Mr. Brummell went to great expense to bring those all the way from Elephantine for the hotel. He hoped it would be attractive to the mass of incoming investors and government types."

"Who?" Elizabeth asked, shaking her interest away from the wide pillar.

Leech answered, "The Khedive government is greatly in debt to both the United Kingdom and France. We are going to be receiving the Suez Canal and other tokens on behalf of this debt and as Mr. Brummell says that will bring in the bureaucrats and so forth to help manage things. White man's burden and all that, don't you know."

"So, I won't be able to see the manuscript until tomorrow?"

"I'm afraid not. Mr. Brummell keeps it locked up very tight. I have only seen it once myself. It made me quite uneasy. Too many flies."

"What?" asked Porter jerking to attention.

"I swear, the one day I could see the manuscript, we were upstairs in Mr. Brummell's study and flies were swirling about me. There had been none in the room before. We shut the windows and doors but it only seemed like there were more of them after that. I could do without such queer nonsense."

"You don't think it is something special?"

"I don't know what to think of it. But I will tell you this. I do hope you can help translate it and get Mr. Brummell to think of other things. He has become obsessed with it as of late and not a one of us in the hotel have had good dreams since it came inside. I keep dreaming that I am a spice merchant during the plagues of the Exodus and my mouth keeps getting filled with flies." He shook uncontrollably at the thought. "And the locusts, well I am not going to talk about the locusts. Disgusting insects. To think some peoples use them to clean the flesh off bodies."

Porter grimaced and looked to Elizabeth as if to say, *Really?*

She declined to even look at Porter and again rapped him across the chest. "So, the hotel is open for business and yet the guests all complain of sleeping poorly?"

"They do. We have yet to have much in the way of people who stay the night. I have taken to finding excuses to sleep at my cousins some few blocks away near the embassy. I sleep much better."

"How many people are here now?" asked Porter.

"Well, Mr. Brummell of course, his cook, the two maids, though I understand one is about to quit, Jennings the butler, Hatfield the gardener, and a dozen or so Egyptians that are the cleaning staff."

"All of them sleep poorly now?"

"All the ones I have spoken with. It has been hard to keep

help these last few weeks. The Fazir family, stays only because they have nowhere else to go and Mr. Brummell pays them quite well."

"I should like to speak to them," said Elizabeth.

"They are just the hired help," said Leech. "They know less about their lands and history than a schoolboy. Ignorant savages just like most everyone in this dreary city. They have no respect for legacy."

"Why are you here then, Mr. Leech," Elizabeth asked coldly.

"I was tasked with serving Mr. Brummell's father when I was a lad. It was either that or Australia, and frankly, I'm not sure I made the right choice, but here we are." He paused warily. "Please don't tell him of my complaints."

"I won't," said Elizabeth, "but I'll thank you not to refer to the people here as savages, at least not in my presence."

Leech gulped and looked from Elizabeth to Porter who just shrugged.

Leech had a pair of boys take their luggage and follow them inside. An ornate red rug caught their eye as it led inside a large gallery of a room, with expensive paintings upon the wall and several leather sitting chairs positioned around the room. Ornate metal squares were affixed to the ceiling in a beautiful intricate pattern. A peacock strutted casually beside marble statues and ferns. A lit gas chandelier hung from the ceiling, casting a wavering glow over the decadent splendor of the room. Leech clapped his hands and an older Egyptian gentleman with a bushy gray beard and turquoise turban appeared from behind a desk. His dark eyes beamed with delight when he saw the two strangers. He clapped his hands together saying, "I am Mustafa, at your service, gentlewomen and mens."

"Good day," answered Elizabeth.

"Yes, Good day, jolly day, welcome to the House of Aram-Bey!" he shouted jovially. "For how long shall you be joining us?"

"These are the guests that Mr. Brummell spoke of," said Leech.

"Oh," the desk clerk's demeanor changed sharply, and he was no longer the boisterous showman. "You have their keys then? We are done, yes?"

"Yes," said Leech scowling.

The desk clerk vanished behind a curtain.

"You see the type of help we have then?"

"I don't suppose you ask him to behave that way for guests do you?" asked Elizabeth.

"Well, I don't. But yes, Mr. Brummell likes the help to be animated, as it were. It grants the visitors a bit of needed flavor. They all remember Mustafa's mannerisms."

"Are there any other guests here?"

"Alas no, word has spread throughout the quarter that we are cursed. The servants spoke of it first before they quit *en masse* and soon enough the whisper campaign began and we have had no new guests checking in."

"And don't you think there could be something to these allegations?" asked Elizabeth.

"No, they are just superstitious sav—people," he corrected himself.

"Why do you think Mr. Brummell asked us here?"

"I believe he said you could read a multitude of dead languages. At least that is what we were told through some of his associates in the Royal Society. Is that not the case?"

"I'll see what I can do," said Elizabeth. "But I do hope you will try to keep an open mind to things beyond your basic senses."

Leech harrumphed at that. "I am a man of science. Such flights of fancy have no place outside of children's books."

Elizabeth looked to Porter who shrugged.

"Hey Leech, where can I get some whisky?"

"Sharia law is here in the city, no one brews it if that's what you are asking."

"Well where do I get my liquor then?" asked Porter getting rather uncoiled.

"I am sure I will be able to secure you some spirits in due time."

"Don't take too long," urged Porter.

Leech flared his nostrils and slightly bowed his head. "I will have Mustafa show you to your rooms. I would encourage you to get a good night's sleep and enjoy your time here before Mr. Brummell approaches you with the nonsense of the manuscript."

He then showed himself out, as Mustafa, who had just passed through the velvet curtain, stood by with his arms folded across his chest.

"Follow me," he said.

Elizabeth and Porter followed him as the silent boys struggled behind with their luggage. Porter wheeled and took up both bags from the two boys with ease and shushed them away by tossing a silver dollar across the red carpet.

Mustafa who had not turned around to see anything could hear the two boys struggling to get the coin. "You gave them too much, they will become enemies now because they cannot share so much money. Greed destroys friendships."

"You saying I shouldn't have given them anything?"

"No, just not that much. A penny each and they would still have felt like kings and remained friends."

Porter at the foot of the stairs stomped his booted foot upon the tiles and both boys ceased their struggle to look at him. "Bring it back."

They still tugged at one another but the boy that had the best grip on the coin led the way back to Porter.

"Hand it over."

The boys reluctantly did so. Porter reached into his coat pocket and found two pennies. He tossed them each one and they smiled in wonderment at their new-found wealth.

"A cheap peace is better than an expensive war," he said to Elizabeth.

Mustafa led them up two flights of stairs to their rooms. They were across the hallway from each other. At the far end of the hall, a door opened and a young woman with her face half hidden by long black hair looked at them before ducking back inside her room.

"Many other people on this floor?" asked Porter.

"Just the other servants, few of them as there are. That was Ayesha. She and her family have dwelt here for some time. They clean and cook for both the hotel and Mr. Brummell." He unlocked their doors then handed each of them their key.

"Inside you will see all the latest comforts. Cairo is becoming quite the cosmopolitan city. Mr. Brummell has left nothing to be desired."

Glancing inside there were fancy four poster beds, chesterfield leather couches, a writing desk, multiple lamps and sconces for light as well as beautiful paintings of the Egyptian countryside.

"If you need anything, simply ask," said Mustafa with a wave of his hand.

"You seem like a man who knows things. What else can you tell us?" asked Porter.

Mustafa gave a low chuckle. "I know many things, but you must ask the right questions." He bowed, turned and left them to their rooms.

"What do you think?" asked Elizabeth.

"This is a mighty strange place, and we haven't been told half the truth by anyone yet. Something is going on beyond just a strange book, I'll wager."

"That was my thought exactly, but I'd like to reserve judgment until I can see the book for myself and speak with Mr. Brummell."

Porter grunted and strode into his room. He glanced in the closet and under the bed.

"Not nice enough for you?" Elizabeth teased.

Porter grinned, "I don't know that I have ever slept in so fine a bed."

"Well, I'd say you have earned it."

"Thanks. Not sure how much I'll be able to sleep just yet, when my mind is still wondering on this strange new land and the curious goings on. But I'm sure gonna try. Holler if you need me." He then shut the door and Elizabeth heard his heavy boots stride across the floor.

She closed her own door and went to the window. The bright moon hung over the city. It looked magical. The silver light washed over the city and, in the distance, cascaded over the pyramids, granting them a surreal warmth. Then why did her room suddenly feel so cold?

Instinct welled up in her and she began a spell of protection, a ward of light over her room and that of Porter's as well. She felt the energetic walls come up and push back against an unseen force that sought to invade her private sanctum. It felt heavy, dark, and oppressive. It felt hungry. Something banged against the invisible shield. It hit three times, but sensing that the field would not allow passage, it—whatever it was--moved on. Elizabeth sensed the dark presence fading away.

Elizabeth carried her lit candelabra into the hall and knocked on Porter's door.

He grunted something from within.

"It's me," she said.

"Come in," he said.

She turned the handle and slid inside.

Porter who had been worrying at a bottle, looked her up and down. "You're in your night shirt."

"I was about to go to sleep and something tried to get into my room."

His six-gun was out in a heartbeat and he made for the door.

"No," she said, tugging on his sleeve. "It's gone and it wasn't a man or anything."

"Animal?"

"No. Something etheric. Something intangible. My magical ward blocked it from entering the room, but I wondered if you sensed anything odd."

Porter shook his head. "No, but this is a mighty big city full of strange things, so if I did, not sure I could chalk it up to anything supernatural or just plain weird. Like this bottle for instance"

"Well, I'm going back to sleep but just wanted you to know."

"Uh, huh." He was focused on the bottle again.

"Let me," Elizabeth said. She took the bottle from him and knocked the marble in the top into the wider chamber in the neck. "You can thank me later, but it's not alcohol. It's called a soft drink. I had one on the airship when you were asleep."

"Not alcohol?" he asked, his face contorted in disgust. But then he took a long pull and was visibly delighted at the flavor of the sparkling brown liquid. "It's sweet but good."

"Good night, Porter." She closed the door.

"Good night," he hollered after her and then downed the rest of the bottle.

In the morning they had breakfast alone and by almost noon, Elizabeth was concerned over where their host was. Porter, unlike his usual suspicious self, was uncaring about the debacle and found himself snoozing in a huge velvet chair in the lobby. Elizabeth read the local English paper twice over by the time Mr. Leech arrived. His face was ashen, and he rubbed at his spectacles nervously.

"I have terrible news," he said.

"What is it?" asked Elizabeth.

Porter blinked awake from beneath his slouched hat.

"Mr. Brummell has taken quite ill. I'm not even sure he will last the afternoon. We rushed him to the hospital a few hours ago and a very renowned surgeon from London, named Black is looking him over, but from what I overheard it doesn't sound well at all."

"What does he have?" Elizabeth asked.

"They think it is some kind blood disorder. I have never seen Mr. Brummell in such a state. He looked like he had seen a ghost. He looked so drained and weak."

"Is there anything we can do?"

Leech shook his head. "But he did ask to see you. The hospital staff said he was not to be disturbed by anyone, but he took my hand and insisted that I bring you to him. He said it was most important."

Elizabeth looked to Porter and then nodded to Leech. "Well then, please take us to him."

Leech whispered to an orderly, who gave a silent nod and led them to the rear of the hospital and then up three stories of an incredibly steep staircase. The orderly glanced at the hallway before urging them to hurry and enter Mr. Brummell's room.

The window was open and a breeze blew hot winds and a white curtain over his pale body. A fragment of sheet hung over his waist and his bare chest was blistered with sweat. He didn't appear to be over fifty years of age with a trim mustache and goatee just beginning to turn salt and pepper grey. But his eyes were haggard and sunken with the crow's feet denoting a man of many years' experience.

He struggled to rise upon his elbows but could not and fell back down upon his bed with a hushed cry of pain. He coughed once then swallowed and said, "Forgive my lack of attire and the situation. I assure you I am not contagious with malaria or anything."

Porter rolled his eyes at Elizabeth.

"I understand," said Elizabeth. "What did you need to speak to us about? Under your condition, we could have waited to meet."

Brummell shook his head. "This couldn't wait I am afraid. I think the manuscript, the book, brought something into my hotel. I think it is something malevolent. We must find out and eliminate it if such is the case. I need your help in deciphering it."

Elizabeth shot a concerned glance to Porter.

"I was told that you could read and understand such things. That you have an uncanny ability," he paused and coughed again.

"What happened to you?" she asked.

"I believe I was attacked by an entity associated with the book, or perhaps by one that does not wish the book to be read."

"What kind of attack," asked Porter.

"I was in my study, at my desk, reading when my lamp flickered because a flurry of moths suddenly swarmed the flames, suffocated it and the light went out. But the room also went cold despite this dreadful heat. Then I felt legs crawling on me, all over me."

"A person?"

"No. Insects. They were in my clothes. Centipedes, flies, moths…I don't know but I was surrounded by them in the darkness. I cried out, but my voice went hoarse as something took me about the shoulders and I felt the wind of its breath upon my neck and it bit me. I went faint and hit my head on the desk as I fell. Then I awoke here. The doctor says I have a blood disorder and hit my head from a swoon, but I know better. Something bit me and I have become infected with an enchantment, a curse related to that necrotic manuscript from Carcosa. I know it. Some demon bit me. Personally, I know the book is not from Carcosa originally. It's from Callisto and shows all the signs of it."

Porter tipped his hat back and furrowed his brow.

Brummell pursed his lips and acknowledged Porter's dubious look. "It is all right if you find it hard to believe. I didn't believe it myself at first. I was fascinated just to have my hands upon a curious manuscript, something that I could lay hold of and use to ingratiate myself amongst the other member of the Royal Society. I didn't believe in curses nor all the wild theories of the diggers and Egyptians that helped me procure it."

"Where did you procure it? I have never heard of a place called Callisto," said Elizabeth. "Well, aside from the moon of Jupiter."

"There isn't as far as my knowledge," Brummell said before continuing as if this odd fact was irrelevant. "The locals think it's from many places and tied to folklore ranging from the legend of the Mad Arab Al-Hazred to the Nameless City in Saudi Arabia. There's claims this book was by ghouls in distant Carcosa for the past millennia."

"Carcosa? I've never heard of such a place either."

"I don't know that there is such a place in our world. Rumor is that it is in the fringes of a nightmare, a lost city of the dead and dreaming."

Porter shuffled in place then attempted a yawn to mask his doubt.

"Mr. Rockwell, I was told that your involvement with Miss Dee is not without curious and even supernatural event. Why do you question these things given all you have experienced yourself?"

Porter shrugged. "Let's just say, I wait and see before I believe everything I hear."

"I assure you I am not lying. There is something otherworldly about this book."

Elizabeth asked. "When can I see it?"

"I will have Mr. Leech take you to my residence. It is near

the hotel. He will get you into my study. The book is there. I had it locked in a trunk. He knows where I have hidden the key."

Leech interrupted. "Perhaps you could just tell them where the key is, M'Lord. But perhaps I am not needed to be involved in this at all. Sir?"

"I need you to assist them," said Brummell sternly.

Leech hung his head.

"If he is afraid, perhaps…" said Elizabeth.

"I am not afraid," countered Leech, "I just have a lot to do to ready Mr. Brummell's affairs."

"Nothing is more important than this," said Brummell. "Something is out there, and the book is key to a greater mystery that must be solved. Lives are at stake, not including my own."

"What do you mean?" asked Elizabeth.

Brummell coughed and said, "I know something was affecting the servants. They said there was a curse and I did not believe them until it befell me. They warned me that something was feeding upon our energies, that there was a dark host that drained folk in the night. I thought it superstitious nonsense. I thought I was above their fears, that such a thing could not touch a man of science and meaning. I was so very wrong."

"I need to know where you found the book," said Elizabeth.

Brummell hung his head. "I told everyone that we found it digging in the desert near Rafai, but that is not true. I was with a caravan, I wanted to find Irem of the pillars. A trio of blue-eyed Bedouins came upon us and said they wished to sell some artifacts. I looked over their wares and could see that most of them were fakes. But one of them produced the manuscript from his saddlebags. He claimed his people had retrieved it from Carcosa and much blood had been spilt acquiring it. He also added that it was destiny that the book enter the world again."

"Destiny?" Elizabeth asked.

Brummell gave a brief shudder. "I'll never forget it. It was covered in flies. At first, I thought he had a raw piece of camel, but then I realized it was a book. The strange characters on the cover caught my eye and I thought I had seen them before in a dream. I was instantly obsessed. I offered him a princely sum and he didn't even bargain with me. He was happy to be rid of the thing. I lied and told the Society that I had dug it up in Rafai. I don't know that they believed me but whenever I showed it to anyone they were fascinated. The writing was at times clear and other times strangely unknown, almost as bizarre as that book discovered by Voynich, but in any case, it was mine and I alone tried to decipher it. Always it teases at meaning. Sometimes as I read passages, flies or beetles would land and give credence to a perceived thought or maxim, then as they strode like conquerors on a battlefield I would read a new decipherment. It's all confusing unless you see it for yourselves. I have no explanation, only questions and nightmares."

"Then I suppose you had best let me see it," said Elizabeth. "But what about you? How are you feeling? Do you fear that whatever attacked you will come back?"

"To finish the job," joked Brummell. "Perhaps, but this is more important than just me. This is proof of a dark conspiracy upon our world, a proof of sinister events at play from ancient times that seek dominion in our world. I have studied Von Junzt and I think this relates to some of the unspeakable cults that he has mentioned in times past."

Elizabeth looked concerned as Brummell took on a wild-eyed frenzy.

"Are you familiar with the Mad Arab Abdul Al'Hazred?"

"I'm not. At least until you mentioned him earlier," she said, lying. All true magicians knew of him and his work. He was not a name to drop lightly, though.

Brummel smiled at the opportunity to educate her. "I think the manuscript is something he found. Perhaps the origins of all his later writing, including his most infamous."

Porter interrupted. "What does a long dead Moslem have to do with all this?"

"He wasn't a Mos—" Brummell fell back into his bed in a coughing fit.

A nurse looked inside the room then vanished. A doctor and two orderlies abruptly entered. "Who are you people? I gave strict orders for no one to be here! Get them out of here!"

The two orderlies were broad, strong Arabs and made as if

they would enjoy assaulting the strangers.

Porter eyed one of the orderlies with menace, tapped his forefinger on the butt of his pistol and the man backed down.

The doctor noticed but had more gravitas. "You must leave," he insisted.

"He doesn't have malaria," said Elizabeth.

"Oh really," snapped the doctor. "I suppose you're an expert on infectious diseases of the mind?"

"I thought it was a blood disorder?"

The doctor took her by the arm and escorted her into the hall. Porter followed, ready to strike a blow.

The doctor shut the door and said urgently, "He hit his head. He has been jabbering nonsense since his servant brought him in. He does have a blood condition, but it is not serious. His madness is. He was screaming all night that things were crawling on him, and I must tell you there wasn't a roach in the place. He is mad and needs rest and relaxation. Are you family?"

"No."

"Then I'm afraid I must ask you to leave and not disturb him again. I need your cooperation to cure him of these delusions."

"I do want to be informed of when he can have visitors again," said Elizabeth.

"Certainly. Give me proof of your business with Sir Brummell and I will accommodate you. Until then, get out."

Porter was ready to launch an assault, but Elizabeth took him by the shoulder and they exited. Leech was not far behind. On the street he got the door of the carriage and jumped in after them.

"Listen," he said, "You don't need me to show you where the key is hidden. The globe in his study is hollow. He keeps his scotch in there. The key will be on a chain."

"Scotch?" questioned Porter.

Leech continued, "The key will open the big sea chest that he has against the back wall. The manuscript will be inside in a tight silk bag. Look at it but be aware of the insect problem that comes with it. I would have netting with you if possible."

"You're not coming with us?" asked Elizabeth.

He shook his head. "You don't need me for any of this. I'll see you into the house but then I should go and prepare his affairs. Sharks will come calling if they think he is on deaths door."

"You don't think he is, though, do you?"

"No," said Leech. "I know he is."

Leech met the housekeeper and introduced them and then promptly left. The housekeeper, an older woman who was half Egyptian and half English, bid them welcome but disappeared back into the kitchen, leaving them to search out the study themselves.

It was a dark room as the curtains were drawn tight over the only window. Elizabeth drew them back and was met with a handful of buzzing flies leaping awake from the movement. They divebombed at Porter.

Porter swatted at them with his hat. "How many more are there?"

"You should see this," she said.

Porter came closer to the window. The sill was dark with dead dried bodies of flies. There must have been hundreds. Enough to coat the entire bottom of the sill with a blanket of black bodies.

"Let's find that key."

"Way ahead of you," said Porter, as he took hold of a large globe and pulled the top off. Inside was a trio of bottles of liquor, a small wooden chest and gold necklace with a key. Porter tossed the key to Elizabeth and then popped the cork from the bottle of whisky.

He guzzled mightily.

"I found the trunk," said Elizabeth.

"Good," muttered Porter. He opened a second bottle.

"Perhaps you should pace yourself with our host's spirits."

"Uh huh."

Elizabeth turned the key and the trunk's lock popped back. She lifted the lid and inside the spacious thing was only a black silk bag. She reached down and grasped the book within. She brought it up, put it on the desk, and loosened the drawstrings, opening the bag. She pulled the book out of the bag and her fingers almost felt an electric shock at touching the thing. Black leather with curious glyphs across the cover fired the imagination. What kind of leather was it? How long ago had the faded gold paint been brushed across the hoary old surface? What secrets did it contain? Some part of her could feel the book's appearance was not its true self but, try as she might, she could not pierce whatever glamour covered it. Indeed, she could feel the book actively resisting her attempts to pierce its secrets as if it had taken one look into her soul and decided she was not the kind of person it was looking for. Despite this, she opened the book. Crude ink was scrawled in think blobby lettering along with bizarre drawings denoting man and beast and worse.

"It is mostly Arabic, but at times it seems to borrow from other languages as well. Here is a stanza in Latin, Hebrew here, and scrawled hastily in the corner is a note in Sumerian cuneiform."

"Can you read it?" asked Porter.

Elizabeth shook her head. "Not much from my humble learnings, but I could use my gifts to divine a translation of intent. My only worry is that if it is a truly evil book, I'm not sure I want that voice in my head."

Elizabeth was understating matters and worried she'd revealed too much. There was a malign intelligence in the book and she wanted to divest herself of it. Another part dismissed her worries. Old books, like many things, carried psychic impressions of their previous owners and it was entirely possible she was just getting a false reading. It was one of the perils of being both psychic as well as a sorceress, however mild in power, that everything seemed to contain a trace of the macabre.

Porter grunted at that.

"Wait," she said, then leaned down close to the book and blew. A large black beetle was walking across the page and went flying from the book. "Did you see that?"

"A bug?" questioned Porter absently.

"Yes, but I thought it was part of a word. I could have sworn

I read that Hebrew glyph as a warning. But without the beetle it reads as a sign of opening. The opening of keys and doors."

"That's vague," Porter drawled.

"Not really. It speaks of the openings of portals, dreams, and other worlds. Keys and gates." It was familiar language to Elizabeth from the various occult societies and books she'd read, often from people who had read books about or influenced by the *Necronomicon*.

"Like I said, vague," Porter said.

Elizabeth gave him an exasperated look for that remark and went back to reading. Several times she had to wave flies away that landed and seemed to place themselves only on the letters and ink spots rather than anywhere upon a blank section. "Curiouser and curiouser."

She perused the book for another minute while Porter made himself comfortable in the fine leather chair. He propped his hat down over his eyes and put his feet up on the ottoman.

A scream from downstairs jolted both from their respective reveries.

"That was the housekeeper!" said Elizabeth.

Porter was up and at the door, hand on his pommel.

"Let me see what I can see," said Elizabeth, drawing upon her powers.

"No time," said Porter. He opened the door and looked. Seeing nothing, he poked his head out.

"*Ah shazah!*" cried a veiled man, as he swept his scimitar toward Porters neck.

Elizabeth flexed her power and sent a shockwave blocking the scimitar from reaching Porter's neck and sending the would-be assassin flying over the stair rail. "I told you to wait."

"All right, how many more are out there?" asked Porter, with a drawn revolver.

"At least three. Downstairs with the house keeper."

"Who are they?"

"I don't know."

Porter stepped out into the hall and looked over the railing. The first assassin was sprawled across the floor, red leaking from a broken neck and crushed face. Another darkly clad assassin was mounting the stairs, brandishing a long-curved knife. Porter leveled and shot the assassin in the chest. He tumbled back down the steps.

The housekeeper screamed again.

Porter made his way down the steps and saw the third assassin holding a blade to the housekeeper's neck.

"Give us the book!" demanded the assassin.

"Like hell," growled Porter, taking aim.

The housekeeper screamed.

Only the eyes of the assassin could be seen. His gaze was determined and cruel. He shouted again, "Give us the book or we will kill her!"

Porter's own gaze narrowed, and he took the shot, placing a bullet between the eyes of the assassin. The dead man's eyes reeled upward, and his body crumpled and fell as the housekeeper fainted. It was far from his first hostage situation and he'd always found the best way to deal with such things was to get rid of the hostage taker. After all, you couldn't trust a man who hid behind women to keep his word to do no harm once he got what he wanted. A noise alerted Porter to a fourth man in an adjoining room. Dashing in, Porter saw the assassin as he leapt out a window into the alley outside.

Porter glanced out the window and spotted the man fleeing to the right. He followed out the open window.

"Porter, wait!" cried Elizabeth, as she reached the threshold.

"I'm gonna get some answers!" he called, as he dropped to the cobbles. He raced after the fleeing assassin.

Elizabeth stuck her head out the window and watched as both men disappeared around a corner into a crowd of passersby.

The housekeeper was screaming again but this time it was a different tone relating to just waking up and finding herself beside the gory body of her would-be killer.

"Easy there, it's all right. You're safe," said Elizabeth, trying to calm the woman.

"You should have given them the book," said the exasperated woman. "The Mahdi will not be pleased."

"The Mahdi?"

"Yes. These were his men."

"You don't sound too upset that we saved your life," said Elizabeth somewhat perplexed at the housekeeper's attitude.

"If I had been slain, I would have gone to paradise."

"Regardless none of this is your doing. It's not right."

"Isn't it? I have been a party to these doings for some time," said the housekeeper.

Elizabeth was taken aback. "What can you tell me?"

"The book is powerful and does not belong in a foreigner's hands. It should go back to Carcosa and only the Mahdi can do that. Until then, it will be a plague upon us."

Elizabeth didn't know what to think about that. She hoped Porter was all right chasing after unknown persons in Cairo, but until she knew where he was, she would continue trying to read the book and learn more about its mysteries. It was the strangest thing, though. The paper didn't really feel like paper and she could understand the text like it was English. Stranger still was that it hadn't seemed strange when she had been reading it.

Porter was disoriented by the city, its loud calls and the buzzing murmur of the crowds as they gossiped, cried out and bargained with one another. He might have lost sight of the assassin completely but the man's dark clothing and keffiyeh stood out from those of other men on the streets.

The assassin rushed toward the citadel and Porter guessed that the man hoped to lose him in those tall minarets. He wanted to take a shot at him and wound him in the leg but with the chaos of people moving in and around the retreating assassin, even Porter didn't want to take the chance of a misplaced shot.

The assassin turned once to catch a glimpse of Porter closing in. He hurried into the dark tower doors of the citadel and vanished into shadow.

Porter slowed his pace and kept both guns out and trained on that column of black. He took a deep breath and kicked sand into the entrance. There was no sound, no shuffle of feet within.

He frowned and took off his hat and tossed it just inside the door.

Nothing.

Porter cursed under his breath. He had hoped someone might play their hand and lunge at it as the battered woolen thing whisked inside. Now he would have to go into the black and get it.

He rolled inside suddenly with both guns trained outward, ready for anything.

Nothing.

The inside was a long hallway of innumerable pillars. A faint trace of dust revealed the fleeing tracks of his quarry retreating in a straight line further into the palpable gloom.

He watched, wary as a starving wolf, and followed. Slits of daylight poked through crumbing tiles in the roofline and granted some reproach against the dark. Something scuttled not far beyond and Porter kept his pistols trained on the pillar as he rounded it, expecting an ambush, but it was a groveling old beggar.

The old man kept his hands up and then pointed toward the far end where the assassin must have passed by moments ago. Porter didn't trust the old man, but there was naught to go on.

Porter stepped, and the floor fell from beneath his feet. Sand and carefully arranged tiles dropped into darkness. He lost a gun as he grasped the edge from which he had just stepped.

The beggar was there, revealing himself as the assassin, if not another of the brotherhood. He tore away his false beard and crude mask and gloated over the dangling man a long kris dagger in his fist.

Porter still held one gun in his other hand and swinging it up he shot the assassin square in the chest.

The assassin cried out and fell back, his foot just beyond reach.

Porter swung a leg up to the lip of the pit and grasping the assassin's foot, pulled the man into the pit behind him. It was a long way down but at last he heard the body hit the floor.

Taking a long breath, Porter watched and waited to see if anyone else would come at the sound of the pistol's report. He didn't have to wait long. A pair of men appeared, dressed much as the others had been. These men brandished both knife and sword. Porter ducked around the side of a large pillar and came at them from behind, getting the drop on them and knocking the men into each other.

"Who are you working for? Why do you want that damned book?"

The assassins didn't speak but looked to each other as if questioning their own resolve. They each shouted something in Arabic that Porter couldn't hope to understand and launched themselves at him. Two bullets and two dead men later, Porter looked over their corpses. He could find nothing to tell who they were or what they wanted. They were too zealous to be simple robbers. They must be a part of some kind of cult but which one? He traveled a little farther in the direction from which the assassins had come.

A doorway of solid wood waited patiently at the far end of the hall.

Porter made ready and kicked the thing in. He rushed in with his six-gun in one hand and bowie in the other. One man waited for him, seated at a table, an oil lamp and scroll before him.

The bearded man looked up from his scroll. He appeared neither surprised nor worried at the sudden intruder. "You are not English."

"No. I'm American. Who're you?"

"My name is of no consequence to you."

"Not what I asked," growled Porter waving his pistol at the man.

Unconcerned the man sat back in his chair and said, "You would not know my name if I told you."

"Yeah, well, I am concerned with you and yours attacking me and my friends. I've already put about six of your goons in the ground, so you better talk."

The man smirked. "The English have killed many more of my countrymen than you, and I would not talk to them. Why should I talk to you?"

"Smart guy, huh? Look, your men attacked me and a lady friend. One of 'em asked for a book. Why don't you tell me about that?"

"The book does not belong in the hands of any man. I mean

to take it back to the dark lands and the cavern dwellers below. It should not be read by living men."

"Might be I agree with that, but you gotta let me know why I should trust a bunch of fanatics."

The man stared shrewdly at Porter, then said, "I dare speak of this to you only once, as we are each warrior brothers under the skin. Long ago, before Muhammed brought us the Quran, men and ghouls worshiped the same gods. When man rejected the Great Old Ones to follow Allah, the ghouls felt we were apostate and deserved punishment. Allah in his wisdom has granted men the dominion of the earth, but not of the whole earth, there are dark places, haunted places like this Carcosa, where the Great Old Ones still hold sway and council and these places can never be wiped clean. You should leave these lands and never come back. I leave you now. Aleikum Salaam." He then stood up to walk away.

"Not so fast," said Porter. But the sound of men moving behind him caused him to turn about. When he looked back, the man was gone.

"Are you the man firing shots in the dark?" asked a voice, holding a lantern.

"That'd be me," answered Porter. "Who're you?"

"Cairo police."

Elizabeth read more of the book and wondered at its curious meanings. She forced herself to reread passages and committed several to memory despite the headache and knots in her stomach that it had given her. The book seemed to be teasing her with its secrets and many times, what was on one page didn't seem to be there anymore when she went bac to consult it. Even so, there were genuine secrets here, perhaps more than she'd ever encountered in any book she'd read on the occult.

"Yog-Sothoth knows the gate. Yog-Sothoth is the gate. Yog-Sothoth is the key and guardian of the gate. Past, present, future, all are one in Yog-Sothoth. He knows where the Old Ones broke through of old, and where They shall break through again. He knows where They have trod earth's fields, and where They still tread them, and why no one can behold Them as They tread. By Their smell can men sometimes

know them near, but of Their semblance can no man know, saving only in the features of those They have begotten on mankind. It is through Yog-Sothoth's truck with mortal races that his children were spawned and marauded through the ages. One of which brought death and ruin to the home of the Ixtol, forcing them to become as words in the aether to escape."

Yog-Sothoth," she murmured under her breath. "I don't think I want to meet him or any of these Old Ones."

She glanced at the window. It was already dusk. Time seemed to have vanished as she had been reading. Moving away from the book seemed to ease her headache and her stomach relaxed as well. It certainly did not feel like she had been there reading for very long, but hours had passed in moments. She almost felt as if she had been in a daze, a hypnotic trance. She rubbed her eyes and gave herself a sharp slap to surprise herself awake. Where was Porter?

Elizabeth went to the window and scanned the streets of Cairo. The bustle of folk moving to and fro gave the illusion of a river in torrent. One dark stone seemed immovable against the current. A lone man clad in a black kaftan stood staring up at her. She did not care for his gaze and drew the curtain shut with a shudder. She reinvigorated her magical wards about the house and noticed that while they had not been broken or banged upon as they had the night before, she had the distinct feeling that something had been gnawing at them surreptitiously along the edges like a rat in the walls. Nothing before had ever had the power to go unnoticed and yet weaken her magic. Sending her etheric signal outward, she expanded it greatly, hunting for the source of her troubles.

A wave struck a tangible shape, like a man, but not a man. It had too many arms or appendages. It struck back with its own sorcerous intent and their wills clashed upon the cosmic field of battle, unnoticed by most of the folk in Cairo.

The psychic repercussions of the conflict would be discussed by the holy fakir's in their hashish dens for years to come. Anyone with a sprig of spiritual sensitivity felt the waves of etheric tension as they rocked against the two forces of chaos and order.

Whatever the many-limbed thing was, Elizabeth could tell it had exquisite power and yet it was not material. It was a phantasmal force and it wanted her and more importantly the book. Dark forces seemed to come at her from multiple directions like the legs of a spider but could not penetrate the ward of astral protection that enveloped her and the house.

Creating a knife of spirit vapor, Elizabeth drew in as strong a point as she could manage and drove it at the center of the dark creature.

Stricken by the pointed attack, the cosmic spider shrunk away, as the psychic knife penetrated the many layers of its defenses. Elizabeth pushed and felt the tip of the knife cut into a noncorporeal organ. Suddenly, the thing fled and Elizabeth fell to the floor in the office, as her own determination on the astral plane made her dizzy and nauseous. The thing was gone.

She knew it had never really been there where her own sight could see it, but she still rushed back to the window and threw back the curtains as if expecting to see a trail through the sky demarcating its retreat.

The dark man still stood on the corner, watching. He looked up at her and gave her a nod, then turned and was lost in the crowd. It looked like he gave her his approval. He wasn't a dark sorcerer sending a bound Thugee demon after her? Cairo truly was a strange place.

Deciding that since Porter had not yet returned, she felt for him across the astral plane and discovered that he was still in the city, apparently awake and sitting in a large room, surrounded by other men. He must have found one of those secretive bars and was drinking again. Fine time for that! He was supposed to be helping her, not getting drunk.

Elizabeth was angry. She would not send for him. She could take care of herself. But the book? It wasn't safe here anymore, that much was certain. Already men had broken in and attempted to steal and even threatened her life, Porter's, and even the housekeeper's. She would take it with her in secret and keep it safe in her room as she studied it more tonight. Wrapping that thing in her shawl, she then managed to fit it into her bag and folded it under her arm as unsuspecting as she could. She locked the door to the study and went downstairs.

The housekeeper was dozing upon a couch and Elizabeth decided not to wake her as she let herself out the back door. It was a short walk back to the hotel and no one need suspect she had removed the book at all.

Back at the hotel, Elizabeth went up the stairs to her room. She opened the door to find the skinny dark-haired girl Ayesha there. It appeared to Elizabeth that the girl had just stood up as if she had been looking beneath the bed.

"What are you doing here?" asked Elizabeth, surprised at someone being present in her room.

"I'm the maid servant. It is my duty to clean the rooms. I have just finished, begging your pardon," said Ayesha.

"That's fine. I'm sorry if my tone sounded rude," said Elizabeth. "It looked like you were searching for something. I have no valuables.'

"I would never," cried Ayesha. "Please don't tell the master that I was doing anything of the sort! I would lose my livelihood and be forced into the streets."

"No, girl, no, don't worry," said Elizabeth taking her hand. She realized the absurdity of calling Ayesha 'girl'. She was likely as not near the very same age as the Egyptian. "Can you answer my questions about this place?"

"Perhaps," said Ayesha cautiously.

"Do you know Mr. Brummell well?"

"Yes," she offered slowly.

"Is there anyone that would wish him harm?"

Ayesha's eyes darted toward the door and she looked out, then shut it softly. "There are many who would harm the English master if they could, both some of his countrymen and some here in Cairo. He has delved too deeply into their business says my grandfather. That's all I know."

"Could I ask your grandfather about that?"

"He would not answer you. You are a white devil. Begging your pardon but you are English or American and a woman. He would not answer you. I don't know that he knows anything beyond rumors anyway. He is a fantastic storyteller, but such talk is beyond his usual domain."

"Thank you, Ayesha," said Elizabeth. "I am sorry I startled you in your duties."

"It is fine," said Ayesha, averting her eyes. "I must return to my side of the hotel now, before I am missed."

Elizabeth nodded and let Ayesha pass her to the threshold. The door was still cracked open and Elizabeth heard the thump of a body hitting the floor. She rushed to the door and saw Ayesha sprawled motionlessly across the carpet, a section of her upper torso raised by the shadowy hands of something almost invisible.

It looked like heat waves manifesting from nowhere with an indefinable shape, but there was no denying the soulless eyes that glared hungrily. Elizabeth knew it was a creature of the book and a malevolence no human mind could comprehend.

Porter sat all day in the prison cell full of the vilest characters that Cairo could imagine or import. It seemed that most of these had at least one thing wrong with one of their eyes and judging by their continual scratching most had venereal issues.

Porter kept to himself as best he could but it was crowded and since he had been taken into custody, no one had spoken English to him. Several of the other men imprisoned begged for something, but Porter didn't know what to say beyond "Emshee" to the ones who appeared to have the plague.

"You. American!" barked one the guards. "Come with me."

He unlocked the cell door and held it open only just wide enough for Porter to slip through. He then slammed it shut just as one the other prisoners attempted to follow. He caught the man's fingers in the door and chuckled as the man shrieked in pain.

"This way. The captain wishes to speak with you," said the guard, leading Porter down the corridor.

He was shown into a bare room with a table and two chairs.

"Sit," said the guard.

Porter sat and the guard closed the door and left. Almost immediately the door on the opposite side of the room opened and another man in a red jacket beckoned him to follow.

Porter grumbled but stood up and followed the man. This

one was English and dressed in a military uniform. Though Porter didn't now the man's rank since he was unfamiliar with their insignias.

"I take it you had enough time in there?" asked the soldier.

"I've had more than my share of time behind bars, thanks," answered Porter.

The man grunted and bid Porter follow him down a long corridor, then up several flights of stairs. He then held the door open and spoke to the seated man inside, "Here is that American who was chasing after the Mahdi's men."

A man seated at a long mahogany desk stood up and came forward. He had massive red sideburns just beginning to hint at grey that met at a mustache. "I'm Lord Meriwether. I understand you shot several of the Mahdi's men. Good show!"

Porter nodded sheepishly. "They tried killing me first. I was just defending myself. Do I need a lawyer?"

Meriwether shook his head. "No, no. This isn't an inquisition, sir. I'm congratulating you for killing some of the rogues. Have a seat. Cigar?"

Porter looked about the room. There were stacks of books, numerous animal trophy heads mounted on the wall, and several curious items on a cabinet including a shrunken head.

"Ah, that is my other trophy collection. That head you see there, was a friend of mine, I took back his head from some savages in the Isthmus of Darien. Of course, I never told his widow I had it. Would have shocked the poor woman to death. It was better to tell her that he simply died of disease in the jungle."

"Uh huh," murmured Porter.

"Well," said Meriwether, as he lit Porter's cigar. "We are men of the world. Let's get down to business then."

"All right," Porter said softly. He noted peripherally that the military man behind him was joined by another two men.

"You successfully followed the Mahdi's men to one of his numerous hideouts. You killed what, six of them, Stone?"

"That's right, he got six," answered Stone, the red jacketed soldier.

"And even helped flush the rascals from the Citadel. We

have never been able to follow them to roost like that. Always lose them in the hustle and bustle. But we did successfully follow you and therefore since you cleared the way, we got a stronghold of theirs done away with."

"You're welcome," said Porter, wishing they would get to the point.

"Yes, well," said Meriwether, puffing on his cigar. He didn't seem to know what to think of Porter's gruff answers. "You don't know the situation down here do you? The troubles we are having with the revolutionaries and Islamicists?"

"Nope."

"When you went into the Citadel, did you get a chance to speak with the Mahdi? Did you see him?"

"Can't say that I did, no," Porter answered, seeking what the line of questioning was after.

"Perhaps it's for the best. The man is a hypnotizing charlatan. Lies for a living, don't you know. He has an army of zealots who would die for him with a motion of his hand, or worse they kill for him. An army of assassins who think they will go to a paradise replete with seventy-two beautiful virgins if they do his bidding."

"That so?" questioned Porter, blowing a ring of smoke. "Might be I need to rethink my religion."

Meriwether cocked his head at that remark.

"Not really," Porter answered. "I'm Mormon."

Meriwether chuckled at that, though a little unsure if Porter was still joking. "The Mahdi is a fanatical leader. He keeps trying to assassinate our people and even those of the established Egyptian government. Why, he has made attempts on my life a dozen times now I should say."

"Rough."

"Yes, quite. In any case, he is also a black magician or at least that is what he would have his people believe. He seeks some old magical book that old Barty Brummell has gotten a hold of. And now the poor chap has been poisoned just so that the Mahdi's people will believe that he has put a curse on him."

"Is he still alive?"

"Who, Barty?"

"Yeah," said Porter, turning in his seat to look at Stone and the others. "Do these guys have to stand behind me like that?"

Meriwether puffed on his cigar, "No, no, of course not. Stone, Williams, Leech, move around will you."

"Leech?" said Porter, realizing that one of the men was Leech the assistant of Bart.

"My apologies," said Leech, "But I was trying to stay undercover as it were. I am an agent of Her Majesty's government and am doing whatever it takes to keep the peace. And Leech is not my real name, but it will do for now."

Porter grunted at that. "Seems things would be a whole lot simpler if folks just spoke truth the first time."

Meriwether grunted and puffed again on his cigar. "Yes, well, we both know the world doesn't work so simply. I advised Brummell not to bother with contacting your young friend, Miss Dee, about coming here to translate for him. We have top men that can do that work as well back at Oxford."

"Seems like he sure thought he was up a creek unless Elizabeth could help him out," said Porter.

"Whatever the book says is irrelevant. But we don't want it getting into the Mahdi's hands and increasing his sphere of influence over the rebels."

"Yeah, what do you want me to do? Get me and Miss Dee to leave?"

"On the contrary, I want you to stay on. I could use your help in dealing with the Mahdi and his men. I can make it very worth your while. You would be doing Her Majesty's government a monumental favor and we could reimburse you handsomely."

Porter rubbed his thumb and forefinger together. "How handsomely?"

"Perhaps, a hundred Guineas? A day?"

Porter's brows piqued. He made a show of counting on his fingers and nodding to himself as if he were adding it all up. The Englishmen looked consternated at the display. "All right. I'm interested. What do you need?"

"Get us the book, before the Mahdi steals it again. We don't want any harm coming to your young friend Miss Dee either. Once we have the book, I'd like your assistance in rooting out his next spider-hole and helping to take him alive if possible."

Porter rubbed at his jaw and asked, "Why didn't Leech here turn the book into you earlier before any of this happened?"

Leech gulped. "Mr. Brummell didn't fully realize what he had and frankly I did not either. Once we guessed at what it might contain, he sent for you and Ms. Dee. I tried to persuade him to turn it over to the Society at large, but he declined. He wanted to see what Miss Dee might say. That's when he was poisoned."

Meriwether interjected, "Mr. Brummell was a high-ranking member of the Society. We trusted his judgment but now that he is gone, we must soldier on without him as it were."

"He's dead?" asked Porter.

"Afraid so," said Meriwether. "But as I said, things were moving apace of another. It was too convoluted to keep track of. Now, we must do the best we can. We need to take the book out of the equation. Return it to us and we can have specialists look it over and take it away from the Mahdi's dark design."

"I can do that. I'd better be getting back to Elizabeth pronto then," said Porter.

"Good show," said Meriwether, clapping Porter on the shoulder. "Leech will go with you. Oh, and no need to tell Miss Dee about his secret assignment, agreed? No need to worry the fairer sex."

"Sure," said Porter, as he helped himself to a handful of Meriwether's cigars and put them in his coat pocket. "When do I get my guns returned?"

"I have them," said Stone, stepping forward and handing the gun belt over.

"Thanks," grumbled Porter, as he put the gun belt on. He checked the revolvers for ammunition and then felt the comfort of the bowie knife as it slid up and out of the sheath. "Just checking."

"Of course," said Meriwether.

They shook hands and then Leech led Porter to the door.

"Godspeed," called Meriwether after them.

Leech led the way down a flight of steps and out a rear entrance of the police station. The government agent had a carriage waiting.

With twilight fast approaching, Porter was anxious to get back to Elizabeth. He was irritated that he wasn't getting the full story from the government types and was glad he had chosen in the beginning to keep some things to himself. He had always been suspicious of government types but until they had anything concrete to give him concern, he would take their money and see about helping with the book. It had to be best to keep it away from the crazed cultists.

He just hoped that nothing had happened to Elizabeth while he had been imprisoned.

The demon gripped Ayesha about the arms and held her up like a shield in front of Elizabeth.

"Let her go!" she commanded.

"She is mine!" roared the demon, though Elizabeth knew the words were an echo of its dark intent rather than the girl's.

"I command you to let her go!"

The demon chuckled and let go of the girl with only one of its many arms and took a step toward Elizabeth, still dragging the girl behind itself. The thing seemed immaterial, just a shadow brought to life and yet Elizabeth could hear the bizarre steps of the thing as it approached. There was a sound like paper tearing as each footfall hit the ground and then was raised in its approach. It made her nauseous.

Winds blasted at Elizabeth's hair as the dim red eyes of the shadow beast flared.

Elizabeth's protective ward flexed as the thing reached the invisible shield. It slammed three fists against it.

I will get in, it spoke directly into her mind. *It is inevitable. I will tear you apart, just as I did that foolish scribe in Damascus. No one may command me and live.*

"Who?" Elizabeth found herself asking. Somewhere in her mind, Elizabeth saw what the demon referenced, a wizened old man with ink staining his fingers. He strode through the streets of a city in broad daylight when the demon struck, yet invisible, and ripped him limb from limb in front of a horrified crowd. It took great pleasure in that, striking down the man who believed he was its master.

Al-Hazred tried to command me, but I showed him at the last. I always prevail in the end.

"Not this time," shouted Elizabeth as she threw a beam of light straight at the demon's heart, and like a rushing of waters, the light surged and slammed into the spidery chest of the demon. The magic she wielded was of the small gods of the Earth but it was real sorcery and a cleaner source than Abdul Al'Hazred's and his ilk—or so she hoped.

The demon dodged sideways and went through a wall then back up through the floor, dragging and banging Ayesha's body behind it as it came on from new directions. The girl's body couldn't pass through the walls but since it retained its grip on her, she was flung all through the corridor like a rag doll.

Ayesha's grandfather was at the top of the stairs. His wide eyes fixed on his granddaughter. "No! I command you in the name of our Prophet to let her go!"

These words meant nothing to the demon, but it gave curious heed to his walking stick.

The old man twisted the knob on the top and a light shone from the amber jewel attached there. "Feed, feed, feed, but not here and not upon this one. You must go to the house Aram-Bahksh. Feed upon his bones and soul. Go now! I command you!"

Elizabeth noticed a strange sign carved into the yellowed stone. Whatever the glyph was, it seemed to hold some sway over the insectoid demon.

Hissing, the demon dropped Ayesha and stepped backward through the wall, vanishing.

The old man rushed forward and grasped Ayesha in his arms. "I have you my child. You are safe now. I have banished the Invisible Beast. It will not return tonight."

"Tonight?" questioned Elizabeth. "What about tomorrow?"

It was then that Elizabeth realized her powers were still growing. She was speaking Arabic fluently despite having no previous knowledge of the language. Her ancestor John Dee had said magic was in the blood, *her blood,* and that her powers would continue to grow, but she had not expected it to be quite this soon. A part of her worried that reading the *Al-Azif* had enhanced her in ways that tainted her connection to her ancestors and their patrons.

The old man wheeled and glared at Elizabeth. "Go away, infidel harlot. This does not concern you."

"I beg to differ. It most certainly does concern me. I stopped that thing from taking any more bites out of your granddaughter and from what I understand, it was violating her before I came to Egypt. So, it concerns me very much."

"I don't speak to loose women," he snarled beneath his breath.

"You have it all wrong, old man. I am not that kind of woman, and I am here to help. You have powers with that staff, and I have powers in my blood. I can help, but I need answers."

The old man gave a crooked smile. "Nonsense. You cannot help us. Only those who remember the old ways can do anything."

"But you said you have forgotten most of them and that your father knew more than you," said Ayesha weakly.

"Aye, that he did, but I can still send the thing away. You must stay close to me, so that I can keep sending it away when it returns," said the old man.

"That's your solution?" scoffed Elizabeth. But the old man ignored her.

"That is all that can be done anymore," said the old man sadly, as he ran a caressing hand over Ayesha's face.

"There has to be a better way," said Elizabeth.

"You know nothing," snapped the old man. "The monster will plague our family until our dying day. Perhaps on the other side of paradise we will be free of it, but here and now, this is our fate. We must accept it."

"But why, grandfather?" Ayesha cried.

"It has always been like this," he explained gently, rubbing his hand over her head, but glaring daggers at Elizabeth. "Our family has always been in league with such forces. We have served the sultans, viziers, even Saladin himself and before that perhaps even the great pharaohs with our skills. But there is always a price. No one living remembers how to cut us loose of the ties that bind, both blood and spirit. The demon must feed and without anyone to direct it, it will return to those of the blood it can commune with. It was hungry and your little frame was the tastiest, I suppose."

"No," she shook her head, tears welling in her eyes. "Not just me. I don't want it feeding on anyone."

"Little fool," he said. "It must feed, like the lion and the mosquito. It needs bloody sustenance and I cannot stop that any more than I could stop the Nile. It must feed, better for it to feed on an enemy than one of our own. That is what is right."

"No! Send it back to where it came from," begged Ayesha.

He frowned and said, "No one can put it back. It will never go back once it has been to our world."

Elizabeth crossed her arms unconsciously, while building strength in her mind and her magical wards.

"Soon enough, it will feast upon this white woman and be satisfied for a very long time," said the old man, pointing offhandedly toward Elizabeth. "No great loss for there to be one less breeding cow of the English."

"I can understand you," snapped Elizabeth. "I hear your words as if they are my own. I can summon the light of Elysia's seven stars."

The old man wheeled to face her. "So, you have talents, good for you. But the demons of the doorway will take care of you soon enough."

"No, grandfather, this must end," said Ayesha, pulling on her grandfather's sleeve.

He pulled away. "Nothing ends. It is a wheel that must travel on."

"Open your eyes, I am here to help," said Elizabeth.

"No! You're just an interfering foreign she-devil. The demon will take you by rights!" cried the old man, as he raised his staff malevolently.

The yellow amber jewel that crowned the top of his staff suddenly exploded with a boom of thunder.

The old man wailed at the loss of his enchanted stone.

Porter was at the bottom of the stairs. His Navy Colt's blue steel barrel was smoking like a dragon. "Looks like I'm just in time."

Elizabeth shook her head. "You have no idea what you've done!"

"How was I to know?" growled Porter, "It looked like he was about to hit you over the top of the head with it!"

"Well, he didn't and now we don't have anything that can banish that shadow demon," said Elizabeth.

"Sure, we do. You just do your thing like you always do and send it away," he said, waving a hand as if shooing flies.

Elizabeth strode to the hotel lobby. "I have tried. It keeps coming back. It's attached to that book somehow, I think. Either that or it's just searching for anything related to Al'Hazred's legacy. But it also seems to be attached to Ayesha and her family. That old man you almost took the head off is the girl's grandfather. He seems wrapped up in black magic. He isn't much of a sorcerer, but that gem you destroyed could banish it. I'm not even sure it was the gem itself, though, it had a curious glyph carved into it. I sensed something primeval and powerful about that sign."

Porter added, "There's some powerful symbols out there all right, I've seen more'n a few myself."

"Would you remember them if you saw them?"

"I suppose," he said, with a shrug.

Elizabeth drew a pad of paper from her purse and attempted the squiggly hooked-cross, saying, "I think their ancestors were magicians in league with whomever wrote this book; however long ago that was."

Porter chewed the edges of his beard that curled into his lips as he watched her draw. "That looks mighty close to something I saw in an old tomb in California not too far from Sutter's Mill way back when."

"To what purpose?" she asked.

He scratched at his beard. "I don't recollect a lot from that time frame, but me and an Indian gal name of Bloody Creek Mary ended up going into a cave after a fool partner of mine. We thought there might be some treasure or gold in there. But there weren't no gold, just a bunch of big-toothed monsters. We eventually got out and sealed the door and it had that peculiar sign on it. The way those things were," he shivered, paused and had a faraway look in his eye.

Elizabeth had never seen Porter show fear before. His reaction gave her more pause than words ever could.

Porter came back into the present. "Well, I reckon those things could have torn that stone door off that mountain no problem, just flung it away like a river in flood, but they didn't. I think that sign kept them bound up. Like they couldn't pass it. I was forced to vacate the premises and lose all interest in my bar there not long afterward for unrelated reasons."

Elizabeth continued, "I think signs like this can have power over things from other worlds. Perhaps it can both banish and invoke and even damn them."

"That I don't know," he said, fishing through his vest pockets.

"Well, it's not your specialty is it?"

"Nope," he said, taking a pull from the flask.

"Honestly? At a time like this? I can't have you getting soured on me. Besides, where were you all day? I sensed you sitting with a bunch of men earlier. In a bar getting drunk?"

He frowned, but more so at the empty flask than her words. "I wish. I was in the Cairo pokey. They nabbed me for using up a few more of the them cultists.

"I haven't told anyone about them, but now that you mention it, the bodies were gone and I was so obsessed with reading the book that I didn't even ask the housekeeper what happened to them. Everything happened so like in a dream that I didn't even think of the bloody carnage wrought there."

Porter grunted suspiciously.

"Then?" she prodded. "How did you get out of jail?"

"Well, funny story regarding that book. I got some fellers that want us to hand it over to them for safe keeping. They say it will be better staying out of the hands of the Mahdi."

"How is any of that funny?" Elizabeth asked.

"Guess you had to be there," Porter answered with a shrug.

"Yes, but who were these men?"

"English authorities. Seems that cultist prophet, the Mahdi wants to kick them out and reinstate the Caliphate. He had his charms."

"You met him?"

"Well, yeah, almost killed him after I took out six of his boys, but he vanished right when the law arrived, and they got the drop on me first, so he's gone. He wants the book and then the English tell me they want the book. So far the only folks who don't really want it are us."

"What did he look like?"

"Who, the Mahdi?"

"Yes," she said, exasperated.

"Dark hair, long nose and pointed beard. Penetrating eyes. Pretty tall too I reckon."

"I think I saw him watching the house," she said.

"When?"

"It was several hours ago."

Porter pulled his gun and moved toward the front door.

"It's not like that," Elizabeth broke in, taking his arm. "I think he knew I was battling with that shadow demon. I think he approved when I sent it away."

"How can you tell?"

"Well, he nodded at me."

Porter's brow furrowed in confusion. "Nodded at you? From where? Was he in the house?"

Elizabeth pointed out the window toward the street. "No. He was watching from the street corner. I saw him through the window. Not here but at Mr. Brummell's. But I am sure he was looking at me and he nodded. I know it sounds crazy, but I'm sure of it."

Porter exhaled deeply and said, "It does sound crazy, but considering everything else we've been through the last little while I'm gonna believe you're right. What next?"

"I had better renew my energies into shielding the entire hotel," she said, as she moved her hands in an interlocking wave, summoning her powers.

"You do that," said Porter, slumping down onto a love seat and striking a match to enjoy one of Meriwether's cigars.

She closed her eyes and concentrated, murmuring her own soul song and prayer, creating an invisible shield to protect the hotel. After a long moment she stopped, and said dejectedly,

"It's not working in so large an area."

Porter perked up. "Why not?"

"There is something inside, linking to the darkness, like a magnet drawing a lodestone."

"Can't you cut that line?" he asked, glancing about the room as if he could see what she spoke of, while knowing full well he could never see the myriad magical things she dealt with daily.

"It doesn't work like that," she said. "I'll have to decrease my radius and keep outside of that drawing."

Porter nodded amiably. "All right then, what now?"

"I shall have to focus on a smaller area that we can control."

Porter held his hands up signaling to the whole of the lobby. "How about just this?"

"Perhaps, but it would be best if we had the household inside the circle of protection with us. Especially Ayesha."

"After all that caterwauling after I shot his walking stick, I don't think that old man is gonna take too kindly to being a part of this."

"Whether he likes it or not, I need to make sure Ayesha is protected."

"Well," said Porter with a grin, "There she is."

Ayesha was slinking down the stairs. She slowly approached Elizabeth and said, "Thank you for all you have tried to do for me, but it is of no use. So long as my family is linked to the book and that Invisible Beast, it can lay claim upon my body. You had best leave the book and depart this cursed land before anything more happens to you."

"Is that how you feel? Or is that your grandfather talking?" asked Elizabeth pointedly.

Ayesha lowered her head. "It is true, they are my grandfather's words. But you have been kind to me and I would not like to see any harm come to you."

Leech appeared behind her and said, "Well, I've calmed down Mr. Al-Hazred, but he is still quite concerned over the destruction of his property."

Porter snorted. "Self-defense, besides he was raising that pig pole too close to my gal Friday's noggin."

"Gal Friday?" Leech looked confused then glanced up the

stairs toward the glowering old man. "Yes, well, despite our previous arrangements we don't need you causing a ruckus here with the natives."

"What's with you, Leech? You jump ship faster than a honeymooning sailor in port. First, you're Brummell's man, then Meriwether's and now it's like you're that old codger's whipping boy? What's with you?"

Leech pulled at his collar. "I'm afraid I don't know what you're referring to. I am my own man. Just doing a job, is all. Now, about that book?"

"Don't you fret about it, *Leech*," growled Porter.

Elizabeth came between Porter and Leech as Ayesha retreated. She suddenly met Ayesha's gaze. "Wait. Your surname is Hazred? Al-Hazred? The book is your ancestor's doing, isn't it?"

"No, not my ancestor but of his cult! We are the last descendants of his first followers," shouted the old man as he descended the stairs. "The *Al-Azif* is our master's property and we must have it back! It was stolen from us by ancient blue-eyed devils and now Englishmen who serve the King in Yellow seek after its truth and power, but it is not for the likes of them! It belongs only to the true faithful of the Great Old Ones!"

As he came down the stairs, Elizabeth realized there were too many feet beneath the old man's robe. Multiple protrusions made two or three steps for every regular footfall. Here and there a small hint of an oily green appendage revealed itself. If he had ever been human it was a long time ago and his congress with unnatural things had left him as much thing as man.

He grinned hideously at her utter horror, things moving underneath the skin of his sagging mask-like face. "I am now as my father wished to make me. More perfect than human, I am created and bound in the image of greater things to come." He tore away his robe revealing a lower portion of his body resembling nothing so much as a giant praying mantis crossed with an octopus.

"You're a monster!" Elizabeth cried.

Ayesha hid her face saying, "You spoke of sacred things, but all the while you hoped to make me a mother of abominations like you!"

"Your grandfather is gone. He was a husk and I have claimed his husk. Without his staff, he was helpless before me," proclaimed the old man, his voice losing its accent and becoming something otherworldly. His posture also changed, becoming more animal like, as if he had just expelled the last of the human within him. "You will be the mother of a great brood and be unto a queen of the desert. Through you the Ixtol will live again. Vhourvath commands it."

"Like hell," muttered Porter, as he pulled the trigger. Click, click, click. His gun did not fire. "Damn, Meriwether! They gave me one good shot and duds!"

Elizabeth warped her powers to create a shield of protection, between herself and the monstrous sub-human spawn of an otherworldly horror.

"Foolish mortal. When you destroyed the Elder Sign on the staff, you opened the door for us to take you all!" His body further contorted and transformed before their very eyes. Bones snapped and cracked at unnatural positions. The upper portion of his body, seemingly a human insectoid centaur of sorts had its skin sloughed off, revealing the upper portions of a Mantis creature replete with massive pincers.

Elizabeth sent a massive cosmic blast of energy at the thing. It was as if a powerful wind struck and sent it back a step, but no damage was done.

Ayesha screamed.

"My master, what am I to do in serving you," asked Leech, in a semi-catatonic state.

"You are no longer needed, traitor," spoke the Mantis, as its pincers snapped and separated his head from his shoulders. A fountain of blood covered the pale tile floor.

Porter threw his useless gun at the monster. It struck the thing in its large compound eye, but it snapped its head back sideways and lashed its long forelegs out to attack both he and Elizabeth.

Elizabeth's shield sounded like a gong had struck and she

held her ears as one of the pincers raked the near transparent walls.

Porter dodged backward and had his shirt shredded by the serrated pincers.

"Your etheric powers won't keep me out," said the Mantis. "I am traveler of two worlds. I will enter the other and get you on the inside. You can't keep up your defenses for both."

Elizabeth's mind reeled at the implications that her magical defenses could be making her vulnerable in the nether worlds, but before she could think, Porter was running away and out of the lobby. Had he gone mad? She felt nearly insane herself at this horrific transformation and possession. She felt the book in her handbag, it pulsed like a beating heart and her stomach threatened once again.

"Porter! Don't leave me!" she cried.

But he was gone. Ayesha had fainted and was sprawled across the floor.

The pincers raked over the shield again, so loud this time that her teeth rattled.

Gunshots rang out.

Porter was back!

No, it was English soldiers spilling into the hotel and flanked by a portly looking man, who seemed like a general. "Fire again! Take the demon down and the witch too!"

"What? I'm not with that," she said.

"I know who you are," said the general. "And if you're not with us, you're against us."

A raking pincer clawed across her shield, just as the sparking of bullets crossed and ricocheted over it. Soon, one thing or another would break through her defenses.

More gunfire and smoke filled the room. Elizabeth thought she would go deaf. Then she realized the gunfire was coming from another direction.

Men in turbans and dark khalats' flooded inside and took the fight to the soldiers. Gunfire echoed back and forth and still the demon tore at her shield to reach the precious book. She thought to cast it away from herself so that she might have a spare moment to flee, to run and escape the incredible thundering carnage. But amidst the smoke and gunfire and hideous cries of the Mantis, that seemed impossible. She flexed her shield in her anger and pushed back against the general and the demon both. Elizabeth cried aloud and felt lightning dance from her fingertips and shoot across the room.

Everything went still.

Smoke was blinding. A small fire burned in the far end of the room.

The shooting stopped. Men from both sides lay destroyed over the lobby floor. The general had met a bloody fate but whether from a bullet or the demon she was not sure.

There was no movement. She glanced around but lost track of where Ayesha had fallen.

A massive pincer caught her across the waist. Pressure squeezed and threatened to rend her apart.

"Give uz tha boook," clicked the Mantis demon, less intelligible than ever before. It had more legs than it had just moments before.

Elizabeth tried to create a protection ward but the Mantis squeezed her even tighter. She thought she might pass out from the pain.

Porter roared and leapt from the top of the balcony, knife in hand. He landed on the abdomen of the Mantis and brought the blade down sinking into the back of the thing a dozen times as it let go of Elizabeth and tried to shake him off. Green ichor flew from the raised knife right before it would plunge down again. The monster reeled and twisted and still the tenacious wild man attacked.

More of the dark clad men of the Mahdi entered the hotel and surrounded the demon. Porter was finally flung away as the thing twisted about until it could get to its feet.

The Mahdi himself stood there with a rifle and his men opened fire on the thing. Elizabeth covered her ears despite how terribly they were already ringing. After emptying most of their ammunition from their cartridge belts, the mantis had stopped moving. They threw torches upon it and anything else that might burn.

"Come with me. Your part in the *Al-Azif's* destiny is over," said the Mahdi as he led Elizabeth and Porter from the hotel. Someone had grasped Ayesha as well and carried her out.

Black smoke billowed from the hotel and dark clouds loomed on the horizon.

"The revolution has begun," said the Mahdi. "Tonight, I throw off the yoke of the Nameless Ones and tomorrow I will throw off that of the English. I have become very fond of this time and place. It is the least I can do before I leave."

Porter rubbed at a sore shoulder and just looked to Elizabeth.

"What do you want?" she asked.

"I must take the book away from those who would use it to open a gate to other worlds. Those men who came belonged to the King in Yellow and sought to manipulate the gates for their own ends. They had no idea of the danger they could have unleashed. The book has a role to play in the world but not to bring about its destruction. That will come from other sources."

"What did they almost do?" Elizabeth asked, confused.

Mahdi did not answer for a moment. "You should never call up that which you cannot put down. Please, give me the book."

Elizabeth glanced to Porter and he nodded. She reached into the handbag and gave the cursed tome to the Mahdi. It was during that moment she noticed he had the most peculiar crystal blue eyes. Still, she trusted him to keep the book safe since only a madman or an alien would want to see it unleashed upon the world.

The Mahdi bowed and took the book, then he and his men vanished into the gathering darkness.

"Thanks for coming back," she said.

"I never left you, "I just had to get at it from a better angle. I knew you could hold it off a little while."

"How did you know you could hurt it?" She asked.

"This knife was blessed by a holy man a long time ago, kinda like me. I figured it would do the trick." He said, still rubbing at his sore shoulder. "I need a drink."

Elizabeth agreed.

THE BOOK OF INSECTS

A Harry Stubbs Adventure

By. David Hambling

"Man may learn from the animals, for they are his parents; but the animals can learn nothing useful to them from man. The spider makes a better web than man, and the bee builds a more artistic house".
—Paracelsus (Theophrastus von Hohenheim), 16th cent.

"God has an inordinate fondness for beetles."

Evolutionary biologist JBS Haldane, on being asked by a group of theologians what one could conclude about nature of the Creator from a study of his creation.

I record these events for a posterity which might be able to make use of them. There is a time for everything, according to the prophet, and I can only hope that these words survive until the day that they may be properly understood and acted upon. The effort may be entirely wasted; my experience in this matter suggests that no warning, however stern, can prevail against the siren song of heart's desire. The *Al-Azif* has an unmatched power to tempt and corrupt those who are open to corruption.

All of which is a way of saying that I am more than relieved to have shed the burden of that unholy book. As to how it came into my hands in the first place, I can claim little credit. Practically the entire thing was the work of Captain Cross, from the planning through to the execution. My part was as a supporting member of the cast, no more than a henchman, albeit a useful one.

The book is undoubtedly still out there, and still working its mischief on any who cross its path. What follows may assist in identifying the signs it leaves, and perhaps in mitigating its most pernicious effects. My fear is that it may, like an insect which grows from grub to larva to adult, become capable of greater levels of destruction.

It was characteristic of the Captain that I met him entirely unexpectedly, and that after an unpromising start he recruited me swiftly to his cause.

I always arrived in my office at 8:30 prompt. Lantern Insurance occupies a spare room in a building otherwise given over to a concern selling cheap crockery sets by post. Lantern Insurance was something of a phantom; I was the only employee, and I had no proper work to do as such. I was just waiting for my elusive employer, Miss De Vere, to hand me an assignment.

I put my time to beneficial use though. I was making progress on two correspondence courses, as well as getting through some background reading on relevant matters. I also found time to carry out a few debt collections on behalf of my mentor Arthur Renville.

I was on good terms with the packers. They were all female and, as groups of women do, they had decided that a man on his own needed looking after. They were very kind with cups of tea and acted as unpaid receptionists—though perhaps the real pay was the interest that my peculiar customers added to their workaday routine.

Miss Hodges saw me as I arrived. She stood up from her sawdust-filled crate, a saucer in each hand.

"There's a visitor waiting for you in your office, Harry," she said. "A gentleman -- I think."

She did not sound entirely sure on that point. My throat tightened. I had been waiting for a letter, a telegram, a messenger, from my employers. Now, it seemed, one had arrived, and I was to be given my mission.

I was surprised to find a shaggy, crumpled character in my seat, with one booted foot up on the spare chair. He was of middle years, his tawny hair unkept, and his beard ragged. He looked exactly like one of those celebrated musicians who are known as virtuosos, whose passion for their art is expressed as personal untidiness.

I had the impression that the stranger had spent the night here. A bulging carpet bag in the corner, the sort carried by travelers, strengthened this presumption. His walking stick was propped up on the desk by him. The one thing which was not shabby was his coat, which fell about him in rich blue folds, and was spangled with bright brass buttons. I learned later it had belonged to a captive Austro-Hungarian General; Cross had received it in part-payment for a book. As with so many things pertaining to the Captain, it was a long story.

He seemed to be drowsing, and my sudden entrance must have been something of a surprise. I have been called a gorilla, a bruiser, an ogre and other descriptions not entirely flattering to my vanity. A career in boxing and the loss of half an ear had not improved matters. My not inconsiderable bulk, in combination with facial features decidedly unlike those of any matinee idol, has often persuaded debtors that my arrival was the signal to settle their accounts.

But this intruder was far from awed by my towering over him. Rather, he was indignant.

"Who the devil are you?" he demanded, thrusting his hands into his pockets in an oddly menacing gesture.

I knew at once that this man was nothing to do with my employers. He was as surprised to see me as I was to see him.

"My name is Harry Stubbs," I said, with dignity, removing my bowler and hanging it up. "May I enquire who might I be addressing?"

"Where the hell is Skinner?"

Skinner was my former partner, a quick and capable man, if not overly honest, whose comradeship I missed greatly.

"I'm the sole proprietor of the enterprise at this juncture," I said. "Mr. Skinner departed some time ago."

I was not about to give any details to a stranger. The man

scowled. His scowl was directed not at me but at the world at large.

"Damn, damn, damn," he said, and banged a fist on the table for emphasis. "God-damn!"

"May I ask as to your business here?"

"I wanted Skinner, for three reasons," he said, weighing me up on each point as though I might be an acceptable substitute. "Firstly, he's a top man when it comes to ferreting out books. Secondly, he understands a few things about the world that others who have not experienced them do not. And thirdly, he has an account at Rosebery's, which I sorely need at this point."

Rosebery's is a local auction house in Norwood. As he spoke, the stranger swung his foot down awkwardly from the chair with a hollow thump, holding it with both hands. It was an artificial leg—and in a flash, I knew who he was.

"You're Captain Cross!" I said. "Skinner mentioned you."

"I should imagine he did," said Cross. "Did he mention he owes me money?"

Skinner had spent no little time in tracking down old books. By his account he had traipsed around innumerable antiquarian booksellers in the largely vain pursuit of obscure and frequently non-existent volumes. Skinner was not a devotee of the written word, and had little respect for the mainly bespectacled, milk-drinking, bicycle-riding individuals he encountered on the way. There was one notable exception in this characterless bunch: a man who was sometimes a rival, sometimes an ally and always a drinking companion. Captain Cross was a kindred spirit to Skinner, a buccaneering ex-soldier who looked on booksellers the way a privateer looked on Spanish treasure galleons, swooping down at the first sign of a prize. He and Skinner had undertaken some very successful joint enterprises.

I remembered the name because another Captain Cross had been a famous highwayman in this neighbourhood a couple of hundred years back. His modern namesake had something of the same freebooting style about him. Cross had a nose for sniffing out books, an expert eye at valuing them, and a neck-or-nothing attitude which saw him slapping down money and clinching the deal while others dithered.

I recalled also that Cross was not a man to trifle with. On one occasion, Skinner and Cross had been robbed at knifepoint in an alley in Sydenham. Or rather there had been an attempted robbery. Cross had whipped out a gun and shot the hat clean off their startled assailant's head before he could move a muscle. The robber, understandably, had fled. I thought that sort of trick was confined to circuses and boy's adventure stories, but Skinner swore to the tale's veracity.

"Are you still in the same line of work?" I asked. "Locating books?"

"And in hot pursuit of the biggest catch yet," he said. "Problem is, I haven't a bean, and Rosebery's won't extend credit to the likes of me. I came to beg assistance. And I assure you it will be worth your while."

If the book was truly valuable—and Cross was only interested in the very cream—then he would need some finance, however good a bargain he was getting. Lantern Insurance did have an account at the auction house, and I could have offered to help. This was not the sort of business that I should be getting involved in though. It was at best a side-track.

Cross sensed my reluctance.

"If you're really a friend of Skinner's, then maybe he told you about our little escapade on the trail of a little-known work by an old Arab called Al-Hazred," he said.

Of course, I knew the work he was referring to. I knew also why he was circumspect in discussing it.

"I have some experience regarding the same book," I said. I recalled only too well a certain grisly, not to mention fatal, incident in the Shackleton case, and a page torn from an old grimoire.

"In that case it might interest you to know that I'm on the trail of the original," said Cross, and there was fire in his eyes. "Not a translation or a copy, but the original work, written in Al-Hazred's own hand, more than a thousand years ago. The actual *Al-Azif* itself."

This was a trump card and Cross knew it. He had gathered from Skinner that Lantern Insurance had no great interest in old books per se, but that our attention was drawn by the occult, of circumstances that smacked of uncanny forces intruding into our world. From what I knew of Al-Hazred, anything pertaining to him was of the greatest interest. If the *Al-Azif* was one-tenth as dangerous as I suspected, then it must be secured at all costs.

I was trying to frame a reply, thinking that I should contact Miss De Vere and get her to advise my exact course of action -- but Cross was already reaching for his stick with one hand and a battered, wide-brimmed hat with the other, climbing awkwardly to his feet.

"I thought that would pique your interest." He grinned wolfishly, his long coat flapping about him, as though he was a bird about to take flight. "Come on, Stubbs, to the bidding—we haven't a moment to lose!"

What could I say? I was swept into the chase.

Rosebery's is a Fine Art auction house, where paintings and sculpture are the usual order of the day. Books occasionally pass through their hands, usually books related to art. I would have walked there, as it's only a short way down Knight's Hill towards the library. Cross however was not so mobile and preferred not to hobble more than a short distance, so we hailed a cab.

The main hall was sparsely attended that day. We had no difficulty gaining admission and acquiring a bidder's card. The place was more genteel than a street market, but it still had that air of hushed excitement, of hidden treasure waiting for he who could identify it among all the trash. The auction was underway, but they were only up to Lot Twenty-Five, a gloomy old painting of a ruined church. I would not have given you two bob for it, but bidding was already up to two guineas.

Cross went through the catalogue minutely, his finger tracing the lines of text describing the lot he intended to bid for. Only after he had satisfied himself did he look around to see who else was in the hall. There were the usual nodding grey heads, but Cross's gaze darted across the hall to a trio all dressed in black. At first I thought the tallest, who had shoulder-length hair and blue-tinted glasses, was a woman, then I realized it was a male. He might have passed for a Romantic poet. He had one arm draped around a shorter person with dark cropped hair, who on closer inspection proved to be female. The third member sported a short red beard and his gender could at least be assigned without difficulty.

"Masculine women and feminine men," said Cross as they looked daggers at him.

"Who are they?"

"Anarchists," he said. "Anarchists with a decidedly unhealthy interest in the *Al-Azif.* The tall one is Cameron. He's the leader. The woman is Parker, she's his right hand. The other one is just a minion, but still dangerous. Keep an eye on them."

I was only familiar with anarchists from the newspaper headlines. They had a reputation as bomb-throwing extremists intent on bringing down the government, and every other government. They were not the force they used to be though. Progressive politics had moved on since the War, and with the success of the revolution in Russia most of the former anarchists had defected to Bolshevism or other groups. But there were still some die-hards who committed the occasional atrocity and kept their black flag flying.

"What do they want with it?"

"They have a lot of funny ideas, those people," he said, speaking in an undertone. "They think it's a great undiscovered political tract."

"But what is it really?" Since it was effectively my money that was being staked, I felt I had a right to ask.

"The term 'Azif' applies to strange sounds in the night; in this case, the nocturnal sounds of desert insects," said Cross, in the same low voice. "In one sense the whole thing is complete gibberish—'gibberish' also being an Arabic word, from the alchemist Jabir ibn Hayyam."

Cross was already showing his tendency to get side-tracked, but he recovered himself.

"The story goes that Al-Hazred wandered in the desert and took down the meaningless sounds, believing they were some kind of divine message. A sort of blasphemous parody of the Koran. Luckily for him, people took it as a joke, and they started laughing at him and calling him 'Al-hazred the mad' when he preached his new gospel in the bazaar. People found him highly amusing, and they encouraged him to expound his philosophy for small change. He's lucky they were so starved for entertainment in those days, or the imams would've stoned him to death."

This did not make much sense to me. From what little I knew, Al-Hazred's work was supposed to contain occult wisdom, not transliterated insect calls. The story I'd heard was that the *Al-Azif* had been found in a nameless city and was the basis for the *Necronomicon*.

"So this priceless book is just nonsense," I said.

"Yes and no," said Cross. "It looks meaningless, but they say the reader can find anything in it he wishes, the answer to any question. Good gibberish has that quality—you can read anything into Nostradamus. Or the Chinese I Ching."

"I'm not so sure that latter is nonsense," I said. I had once encountered a Chinese gentleman whose skill with oriental divination was uncanny to say the least.

"When the *Al-Azif* is consulted there appears to be a process of rearrangement of words," said Cross. "The description reminded me of a device called a Zairja, an Arabic astrological instrument comprised of rotating metal discs. You turn them according to the question and read off the answer."

"So it's not a book in the normal sense?" I said, trying to picture the thing. It sounded more like loose leaves which were shuffled like a deck of cards.

"Hard to say until we find it," said Cross. "They say he wrote it, or found it, on the wing-cases of beetles, but perhaps he pasted them into a book."

"Surely not."

"Well, there are a lot of conflicting accounts. I managed to trace the book to Egypt, from where it apparently fell into the hands of the Mad Mahdi. The fellow who staged a revolt in the Sudan against the Egyptians in '81. When he died his followers took it back across the Red Sea to Arabia..."

"Lot Forty-Nine," announced the auctioneer. "A collection of miscellaneous Arabic books belonging to the Hon. Robert Entwhistle, principally comprising specimens of the Koran, the earliest dating from the mid-Eighteenth century." There was a pause while two porters in brown coats brought in a crate, laid it down on a table and opened one side to reveal the books piled untidily inside.

"This Entwhistle was the Assistant Commissioner of Aden," said Cross. "He was given the *Al-Azif* as a present for adjudicating a dispute between two bickering tribes."

My knowledge of world geography is hazy, but the pink areas on the map were beaten into me as into every English schoolboy. Aden is a British possession on the Southern tip of Arabia, and an important naval port.

"You mean they gave it to him as a bribe?" I said.

"Far from it. You see, it was the losing side in the dispute that gave it to him. Someone from the other tribe warned him the book was a trap, containing a deadly scorpion within its pages."

"What did he do?" I pictured the Assistant Commissioner finding some means of opening it from a distance with strings and rods. Or maybe he just invented an excuse to ask some underling to do the job while he waited in the next room.

"He did what any well-trained civil servant does when faced with a difficult problem," said Cross. "He filed it away for future attention and forgot about it."

"Shall we start at one guinea?" suggested the auctioneer.

Cross raised a hand fractionally.

"I have one guinea," said the auctioneer. "Do I hear one guinea ten shillings?"

"Yes!" called out the long-haired anarchist, waving his bidder's card high in the air.

"Amateur," muttered Cross, and caught the eye of the auctioneer who was already glancing in his direction. The auctioneer registered his bid.

Another man was also bidding against us. I believe I recognized him as the proprietor of a second-hand bookshop in Tulse Hill with a rather select clientele.

The bidding progressed in small increments. The long-haired man seemed untroubled, but his companions became agitated when we reached four guineas. At five guineas the three of them put their heads together for a brief consultation, and they gave up at six guineas, ostentatiously walking out after their last bid was topped.

The bookshop owner went ten shillings higher but was soon persuaded by Cross's fierce look that he meant to win this one and damn the consequences. The other man smiled wryly, convinced no doubt that he had forced Cross to pay over the odds, before dropping out himself.

"Sold to Mr. Stubbs," said the auctioneer. Cross was empowered to bid on my behalf, but the bidding was in my name.

"That went higher than I thought," said Cross. "But it's a bargain. I think maybe we'd better secure our loot sooner rather than later though. I don't trust those three."

We hurried along to the sales room where successful bidders collected their purchases. As Cross had suspected, the anarchists were there before us. The two porters in brown coats cowered in a corner, while the female anarchist pointed a pistol at them and her two colleagues were struggling with the crate.

Cross reacted instantly. His stick clattered to the ground as he reached into both pockets, and with the speed and skill and skill of a Western gunfighter, drew out two guns, both of them considerably larger than the pocket automatic wielded by the anarchist.

"Why don't you three scuttle off now," said Cross pleasantly.

The woman turned to aim at Cross.

Cross fired. The report of the weapon caught me by surprise. Not a single, sharp snap, but a prolonged rattle in which multiple reports reinforced each other, battering my eardrums.

The wall next to Parker exploded in a shower of plaster dust as the bullets stitched a line across it, momentarily obscuring her. I was so deafened I was not even sure if the anarchist fired back, and then Cross's second burst of fire obliterated my hearing again.

The room was full of smoke and dust. The anarchists were fleeing through an open doorway. Cross, though following them with the point of his machine-pistol, let them go.

I leaned down to pick up Cross's walking stick for him. It was a heavy blackthorn item, with elaborate brass fittings.

Cross's guns disappeared back into their pocket-holsters and he took the stick back with a nod.

"Everyone sound?" Cross asked the porters. "Good, good, good. Stubbs, take charge of the booty. Gentlemen, thank you, we can take it from here."

The porters looked around in wonderment, more bewildered by the eruption of gunfire than the attempted robbery. As I was myself. But I hoisted the crate on my shoulder obediently as Cross led the way out through a gathering crowd, drawn by the sound of shooting.

"Small spot of bother," Cross explained as we passed. "Attempted robbery thwarted. All in a day's work. You have Mr Stubbs' address for any enquiries. Or if there's a reward to pay! Cheerio now."

The auctioneers gaped open-mouthed, too taken aback by this display to try and stop us. The two porters had become the center of attention, and as we left they were explaining about the attempted robbery.

"You can't just go shooting people," I said.

"There's no closed season on anarchists," said Cross. "I like to bag a brace of them before breakfast. Speaking of which, I haven't had any yet. Where do they hide the taxi-cabs around here?"

There was one nearby, and I instructed the cabbie to take us to the Electric Café. Partly because it was a good place for Cross to find a late breakfast, but mainly because he had some explaining to do. A shooting incident would not go down well, and I wanted to get our story to Arthur before anyone else did.

The Electric is Arthur Renville's base of operations. Arthur's business is usually conducted in the hours of darkness and concludes with breakfast at the Electric. He needed to know about Cross before things got out of hand.

"Mr Renville is a consignment man," I explained to Cross. "He deals in shipments of goods that have been written off for insurance purposes and cannot be disposed through the regular retail channels. He co-ordinates the activities of a large number of freelance individuals, and as a consequence he has a role in regulating activity in Norwood and the surrounds. Unofficial commercial activity, that is."

Arthur had been my patron for years. I owed him a good deal in many ways. It would be neither fair nor accurate to say that Arthur headed an organized crime syndicate, and I would never put it in those terms. But certainly, every criminal in the area was affiliated with him one way or another. The police might never stir themselves enough to find out what had happened at Rosebery's, but Arthur would know it within the hour. And if Cross's presence was deemed to be bad for business, so much the worse for him.

The Captain twigged readily enough that Arthur was a man to be placated if he wished to continue operating in Norwood.

Fortunately, Arthur was in a mellow mood. There was no frantic activity around him, just a couple of associates idly chatting over tea and cigarettes and plates scattered with the bony remains of kippers. Business seemed to have been concluded. I lowered the crate in a corner and introduced Cross. Arthur invited us to sit with him while his companions politely excused themselves. I took a deep breath.

"There has been an unfortunate incident as Rosebery's," I said. "Mr. Cross was obliged to fire warning shots at some anarchists who were attempting to appropriate some goods—"I indicated the crate which I had left in the corner—"which we had just purchased, a lot which we believe includes a priceless book."

Arthur's eyes narrowed. He looked as though someone had just tried to pass him a cargo of rotten fish.

"Shooting—anybody hurt?" He said. "Have the police been on the scene?"

"No casualties whatsoever," said Cross. "Rosebery's aren't likely to draw attention, and there won't be many bluebottles buzzing round that one. Nothing to upset yourself over."

His cheery expression was not echoed in Arthur's face.

"I don't know who you think you are," said Arthur. "But I'll have you know that sort of wild behavior won't wash in Norwood."

"It's a free country," said Cross. "I can go where I please."

I had warned Cross that a conciliatory attitude would be needed. In his natural buoyancy he had disregarded my advice. It does not do to intrude on Arthur's territory and shoot the place up, even in self-defense. Much worse is answering back when called to account.

Arthur's face was granite.

"You can indeed go where you please," he said, slowly and evenly. "But you won't be going anywhere if Stubbsy here kicks your crutch away." It was a low blow, and well-aimed. Cross was as sensitive as anyone about his disability. And he understood that he had transgressed.

The room suddenly seemed very quiet indeed. Every pair of eyes was fixed on Cross.

"I assure you, it was purely self-defense," he said at last.

"Show me what you shot them with," Arthur ordered.

Like a boy handing over a catapult, Cross slid the weapon out of his pocket and placed it in front of Arthur. It was not the usual service revolver, the common weapon in such circumstances, but something more specialized, something you would only see in the hands of a professional.

"German," Arthur said. "Mauser, with a bespoke extended magazine by the looks." He ejected the remaining bullets from the clip one by one, and they rolled around the table. "What does it hold, eighteen, twenty rounds? That's a lot of mess for somebody else to clear up. I hate mess. And look, you've got the front sight filed down, for a quick draw. Who even carries this sort of weapon?" He looked up at Cross to confirm that his words were having an effect. "Other pocket, if you please."

Not much gets past Arthur. Cross, even more sulkily, placed the second weapon on the table. It was a bulky, single-shot weapon with a barrel shaped like a bell.

"A flare pistol?" said Arthur, raising his eyebrows. He broke open the action to extract an outsize cartridge. "What's this all about then?"

"Three reasons," said Cross. "Firstly, the large barrel scares the hell out of anyone you point it at—it's like looking down a railway tunnel. Secondly, that's not a flare, it's something rather more tactical. Thirdly, sometimes a thirty-calibre Mauser won't cut the mustard."

"You're not shooting big game here," Arthur told him. He hefted a weapon in each hand. "And you don't carry machine-guns around Norwood, Mr Cross. It's not Chicago. We can't have loose cannons."

"No," said Cross.

"I'll just take charge of these here loose cannons for the time being," He passed the pistols to a confederate and they disappeared behind the counter.

"I am awfully sorry," Cross said, looking after them. He sounded contrite.

"These anarchists, now—what are they doing here?" asked Arthur.

"They were after the same thing as Captain Cross," I said, "I don't think there will be any further incidents."

"As a matter of fact," said Cross, apologetic, "it's a little more complicated than that."

"Please elucidate," said Arthur.

"Of course that crate does not contain the actual *Al-Azif,*" said Cross, appealing to Arthur. "Rosebery's aren't amateurs. They'd spot an eighth-century original a league off. They wouldn't leave it in a collection of miscellany and list it at a guinea. Any work that old is worth a bundle."

"If the *Al-Azif* isn't in it, why did we just buy it?" I asked.

"Heave that crate up on the table and I'll show you."

They cleared the table of teacups and ashtrays and I placed the crate in front of Cross. As we looked on he rummaged through the contents with practiced skill, sorting the books into piles as he went.

"Here we are," he said, finally pulling out a small ledger from the depths of the crate. "The plum in an otherwise undistinguished pudding. Entwhistle's catalogue of his collection."

He opened it to show listings and descriptions in squiggly Arabic and neat English of all the books that Entwhistle had been gifted in his role as Assistant Commissioner. Cross leafed briskly through it before pouncing on the third page.

"Hah! I knew it."

He ran his finger under the entry as he read it out:

"No. 272—Al-Azif—'book of insect calls' (??), manuscript, Coptic binding, author unknown, date unknown (poss 14th century from cover?). Legibility poor. Numerous marginalia. Binding very poor condition. Insect damage. Donated 1882 by Emir S.E. Estimated value unknown. Loaned WA 1884. See Notes."

Cross explained that every gentleman whose library runs to more than a few hundred volumes, and which contains valuable books, keeps a written record of what has gone where to prevent anything being overlooked. Like Boots Lending Library, but on a smaller scale. It was the presence of exactly this ledger that he had been checking for so fervently in the auctioneer's catalogue.

"Just as important is that we now have full legal title to the *Al-Azif*," said Cross. "It is part of the collection which we bought, even though it was not physically present, on account of having been loaned out. We may not have it, but we own it."

"Is that so?" Arthur asked. Legal title was the sort of point that interested him greatly.

"That particular point was decisively settled by Fisher versus Tailor, 1865," Cross said. "Not the first time I've been on this merry-go-round. All we need to do is show the loanee our receipt and he's obliged to hand it over, by law."

"But until then," said Arthur, "We can expect further trouble from these anarchists of yours. So who might the borrower be when he's at home?"

"It's a Professor Walter Armstrong of South Norwood," said Cross, reading the notes. "Shouldn't have too much difficulty tracing him."

Forty years seemed like a long time, but Cross seemed entirely confident that the Professor would still be present with the book to hand.

"Armstrong…and this book is priceless, you say?" Arthur asked, shooting a look at Cross.

"Utterly," said Cross.

I doubted whether Arthur believed that any commodity was priceless. His honor and his good name were priceless, but no physical object merited the same evaluation. He was clearly impressed by Cross's conviction though, and perhaps even

Arthur was a little taken by the man's style. Calculation would be the main factor though; Arthur would have determined that the anarchists were as unlikely as Cross was to abandon the quest. It was to minimize the chance of any further disturbance, rather than in pursuit of monetary gain, that he decided to permit Cross to continue and even to assist him.

"Mario," Arthur called over to the proprietor, who had been hovering at a discreet distance. "Two Full English for these gentlemen, at your earliest convenience." I had breakfasted earlier, but I was ready for a little something, and the prospect of rashers of crisp bacon with runny egg yolk made my mouth water. "And get your boy to nip next door for Sammy, we have need of his services."

Sammy was the neighborhood tobacconist, and as with most such establishments his shop was a clearing-house for local gossip and rumor as much as it was for cigarettes and pipe tobacco. If you wanted to pass the time of day chatting about football or politics or the weather, he always had the latest information at his fingertips. But he excelled when it came to local news and events, and his proximity to Arthur's base of operations benefitted both men. Sammy possessed a compendious memory, and after years in the area he was a great repository of information. Not much that was newsworthy went on without him knowing about it. With Sammy you got not just the bare facts known to the public, but the story behind the story.

The man himself arrived a minute later, a benign, silver-haired chap. He saluted Arthur and me, accepted the offer of a cup of tea, and looked on Cross with keen interest.

"Sammy," said Arthur. "The name professor Walter Armstrong just cropped up in our conversation, and for some reason it rang a bell. Wasn't there some scandal with that man—Balham was it?—that he was wrapped up in? This was years ago."

"You'll be thinking of Durham," said Sammy, as though it happened last week. "Scarlet Durham, Durham Scarlet, that whole business. Armstrong's son-in-law he was. Twenty years ago—twenty-three years ago if I remember right."

The qualification was quite unnecessary. Sammy's memory was as reliable as an almanac. His eyes travelled from Cross to the books, now relocated to a side table, and the empty crate with Rosebery's stamp on it. He said nothing. Sammy listened more than he talked.

"Is he still with us?" Arthur asked. "Old professor Armstrong, obviously, not Durham?"

"Professor Armstrong, the noted authority on insects." He paused, as though consulting a mental filing cabinet of obituary notices. "I think he's still with us, though he's never been a well man. He had an attack of apoplexy and was left paralyzed years ago. I reckon I can lay my hands on a current address in two shakes, if you need it."

Sammy's shop had a telephone kiosk crammed in one corner, and he kept a telephone directory, local maps, trade directories and various other reference works for his clientele. He was a dab hand at finding things, even when the searcher had only the haziest idea what they were looking for. And he learned a lot in the process.

"When you've finished your tea," said Arthur. A cup had been placed before Sammy with two complimentary custard creams tucked in the saucer, a mark of his good standing. "Mean time, maybe you could refresh our memory of what happened with Scarlet Durham."

Sammy was a natural performer, who was never happier than when he had a tale to tell and an attentive audience.

"This was back before your time, Harry," he started. "Year of Our Lord nineteen hundred and two. This Durham was something of an entrepreneur, a self-taught inventor. A tinkerer. Dyes were the great thing then. There were lots of new chemical dyes coming out of Germany, bright colors—well, you're used to seeing people dressed up in every color of the rainbow these days, but back then anything that wasn't brown or grey turned heads.

"If you could come up with a new shade, one that was properly fast and would stand washing, you could make your fortune.

"Durham dabbled in dyes. He had a lot of failed experiments

behind him. He was just a Sunday-afternoon potterer, and the Germans have all these huge industrial laboratories, what chance did he have?

"Well, out of the blue he announces that he has a new dye— Durham Scarlet he calls it—redder than a ripe tomato. Secret formula, he says.

"As a publicity stunt he books a box at the opera, and he shows up in a bright red suit, with a bright red shirt and a bright red tie. Red top hat, gloves, you get the picture. Sort of thing you would expect from an American inventor, not a British one. It was quite a sensation. By all accounts he was the most striking sight there, and everybody was talking about him.

"Durham went with a gang of friends, sporting red ties and waistcoats and similar garments, but Durham was the only one with the full fig. Well, they quaffed a few bottles of champagne, and enjoyed being a spectacle, all those ladies with opera glasses peering at them in their finery.

"Halfway through the opera, the place is warming up, as such places are wont to do, and the supply of cooling champagne has run low. Our Mr Durham starts sweating and appears uncomfortable. His friends say he was surreptitiously scratching himself all over his back.

"Then something snaps and he lets out a cry and gets to his feet, flailing about, and shouting "Get them off me!"

"His friends restrain him and pin him to the floor, but during the struggle Durham gets even hotter and more agitated. Perhaps at the start he was just trying to get outdoors to the cool air, but by the end he is writhing like a madman, screaming and howling so loud that even the diva on stage gives up and falls silent.

"All eyes are turned to the box where Durham is struggling against his friends. He throws them off, and with a shriek to chill you to your marrow he takes a flying leap from the box and lands—*splat!*—on the stage. Breaks his neck and dies on the spot in front of a thousand spectators.

"Afterwards, when they examined the body, they found great red welts all over him wherever the dyed cloth had been in contact. The heat of the opera house had brought about a violent allergic reaction. An unexpected side effect of Durham Scarlet.

"There was enough to keep the newspaper sketch men in business for a week just in the manner of Durham's dramatic departure. Not least the question of whether it was suicide or accidental death, given that these are two very different cases when it comes to whether his life insurance pays up.

"Now, the twist is this: it turns out Durham Scarlet is a variety of cochineal, an extract from the shells of beetles. You see, Mrs. Durham was the daughter of a professor in the study of insects—your Professor Armstrong, as it happens—and the recipe came through her. It was a recipe she found in one his old books of insect lore. It seems she had been trying to help her husband. Only she wound up killing him instead.

"Well, that was enough to start an even bigger round of newspaper headlines. There have been enough poisonings, but this was the worst of the lot. People said she was fed up with him wasting all his time and money on useless inventions and wanted to put an end to him before they ended up in the poorhouse.

"So, what everyone is asking is whether she knew this red dye recipe was poisonous? Was she really trying to help him make his fortune, or do away with him?"

Everyone's head around the table shook in unison as we waited to hear the answer.

"And that's what we never found out," said Sammy. "Because when the original recipe was produced for the court, it was so smudged and faded, and in such a strange language that nobody could make out exactly what it said, apart from some of the ingredients and the word for red. And they had to get a Latin teacher in to explain that much."

"That's a charming and very moral story, isn't it?" said Arthur.

"Reminiscent of the death of Hercules," said Cross. "His wife was tricked into giving him a shirt that poisoned him."

"I couldn't help but wondering whether this old book—the one with the recipe—might be the same as the old book you're looking for."

Arthur was aware of the scope of my activities. While he

professed skepticism about anything out of the ordinary, preferring to believe it was all in the mind, he knew that men had been killed over this sort of thing. And he recognized funny business when he saw it, into which category this case squarely fell.

"Very likely," said Cross.

"Thought so. That's the thing about books," said Arthur. "Once you open one, you never know what's going to come out. You two watch yourselves when you go talk to that professor now."

I had left a message explaining the situation with Miss De Vere's answering service. Her telegrammed instructions were admirably terse:

GET BOOK SOONEST STOP
INFORM IMMEDIATELY WHEN IN POSSESSION STOP
DO NOT REPEAT DO NOT OPEN BOOK STOP
ENDS

That was unambiguous. And at the same time Arthur had assigned me to the task of looking after Cross and keeping him out of further trouble, so I was committed to the search for both personal and professional reasons.

Arthur had arranged a car for our convenience, and as a way of keeping tabs on Cross. I did not drive and Cross could not, so we had been assigned a driver, a lean, tough-looking individual, a member of Arthur's extended band who I had not met before.

"Name's Bear," he said with an unmistakable American drawl, leaning over the seat and extending a hand to exchange a firm handshake. He had the dark complexion of one who has spent a lot of time outdoors.

"Like Chief Running Bear?" I asked. I could easily imagine him as a Sioux warrior astride a pony with a bow and arrow.

"Hell, no," he said, laughing. "I'm just another paleface. Plain ol' Donny Bear."

"Family changed it from Bauer, I expect," said Cross. "A

German name."

I gathered that Cross had no love for Germans, but Bear was untroubled.

"Maybe so," he said. "Matter of fact it was Germany that brought me here -- I came over here to help you boys fight the Germans. First AEF unit in France, under Pershing."

"You lot took your time coming," said Cross, but he shook Bear's hand warmly. "BEF under Haig. From '14."

"What made you stay in Europe?" I asked.

"I always wanted to see Sherwood Forest," Bear said. He made a face. "See something good here instead of just ruin. Flat bust that was. I guess I wound up here in a different band of merry men instead."

"Life is full of disappointments," said Cross. "We press on."

"Amen to that," said Bear, starting the motor.

En route I restored the Captain's arsenal, which Arthur had left in my keeping. I reminded him of Arthur's stipulation that he must ask my permission before firing another shot. The anarchists were likely to be around somewhere, and Arthur had a slight preference that Cross should shoot them rather than vice versa, so long as he was not involved.

"You go unusually well-armed for a man in the book trade," I said as Cross methodically fed bullets into the Mauser's clip.

"Three reasons," he said. "I often carry a great deal of cash—it's the only way to seal a bargain quickly. Secondly, a man who walks with a stick, as I do, is a magnet for robbers. And thirdly, running away is not an option open to me. So you might say my extra arms make up for my deficiency in legs."

"Very good," I said. "But dangerous."

"It's a dangerous business," he said. "I can lend you a weapon if you like. You can't take on those anarchists with your bare hands. They're all armed to the teeth."

"No thank you," I said.

"How about you, Bear?" he asked.

"I don't think Mr Renville would be too happy about me packing a rod," said the driver. "But I guess I won't need one. I'm just the lookout and getaway driver."

In the event there was no sign of an anarchist ambush. The

professor's bungalow was on Alleyn Avenue. The door had a brass knocker in the shape of a honeybee on a flower.

"Norwood used to draw quite a few of them," said Cross. "It was the wildest woodland close to London. They used to discover rare beetle species here. I assume that was what drew the Professor."

I was waiting until my watch showed the appointed hour of two o'clock before knocking.

"So, was he paralyzed shortly after he brought the book back?" I mused, not having the mental agility to do sums in my head.

"Yes—dashed odd coincidence, wouldn't you say?" said Cross. His tone said that it was no coincidence at all.

I knocked twice.

"Gentlemen," said a manservant, opening the door. He maintained a poker face at the sight of the two of us, a giant and a tramp. "The professor will see you in the drawing room."

I had expected insects in the house of an entomologist, and I was not disappointed. Framed specimens lined the walls of the hallway, in a scene reminiscent of the Horniman museum's splendid collection of beetles, butterflies and other small invertebrates. The drawing room was similarly decorated.

A shriveled old man in a bath chair cocked his head as we entered. A blanket was tucked around his legs, and his hands lay in his lap like dead spiders. The nails needed cutting. His head, with a faint halo of silver hair, was enormous compared to his shrunken body, and his face was remarkably smooth, giving him the look of a grotesque baby.

A sort of high table on tripod legs supported a glass of yellowish liquid with a drinking-straw at the level of his chin.

"We shan't trouble you for long, Professor," I said. Years of experience in the field of debt recovery have persuaded me of the value of brevity. I had the receipt for the book ready in my pocket, but I doubted there would be much argument with a man like the Professor.

"Please," he said, in a voice thin and reedy but still quite distinct. "Do sit down. I'd like to talk with you."

We sat awkwardly side by side on the overstuffed horsehair

sofa while the professor inspected us. There was a newspaper on the coffee table. Either his servant read the news to the Professor, or perhaps he folded it up and placed it on the small table where the Professor could read it.

"Insects can re-grow limbs," he said, looking unabashedly at Cross's artificial leg. "Something else in which they surpass mankind."

"No doubt," said Cross.

"I always knew someone would come for the book," the professor said at last. His voice was feeble, but his mind still seemed sharp. "Sooner or later. But it's been a good long while. What do you want it for?"

"I find rare books for a living," said Cross. "And the *Al-Azif* is as rare as they come."

"You look the type." This was stated as an observation.

The rugs I noted, were ragged around the edges, showing signs of moth damage. The flooring beneath was riddled with woodworm. The professor must be indifferent to this decay around him.

"It's a unique text," said Cross. "The only book I know dictated by insects, if you believe that story."

"I believe it," said the professor.

"So it really is just a hundred pages of 'bzzt bzzt bzzt, click-clickety click'," said Cross. "No wonder his publishers never commissioned a second volume."

Cross was fishing for information. The professor was happy to oblige, but not in the way he expected.

"Have you ever listened to a telegram being sent?" asked the professor. "Click clickety click."

"That's a code," said Cross.

"Listen to a cricket on a hot day and count the chirps you hear in fifteen seconds," said the professor. "Add thirty-seven and you get the temperature. Insects use codes too."

"I never knew that," I said.

"Insects have no intelligence," said Cross.

"Of course not," said the professor. "Nor do telegrams. But they carry distilled wisdom within them. Al'Hazred took it down, even though he had as little understanding as the insects."

"I look forward to seeing this book," said Cross.

"I wouldn't advise it," said the professor. "The man who gave it to me said there might be a scorpion in it—even though scorpions are not insects—"

"Aren't they?" I asked.

"They're arachnids. But the book is far more dangerous than scorpions." Something glinted beneath his brows.

A beetle, black and shiny, emerged from a crevice in the coffee table, executed a zig-zag path and disappeared. The table must be rotten inside to have beetles living in it. Everything in the house was rotten.

"Dangerous—how?" asked Cross.

"Dangerous for the ignorant," said the professor. "But you don't have to open it. I can share with you the best it has to offer. I started writing a monogram on the *Al-Azif*—you would not believe what the ink looks like under a microscope—but I soon gave up. I never wrote another word, because I found what I wanted."

"What's that?"

The professor inclined his head and coughed, very deliberately, twice, on to the high table in front of him. "Look."

On the surface were a pair of fat, wriggling maggots he had coughed up. They were huge, the size of the last joint of my little finger, off-white with black dots for heads. They appeared to twist and look up at us. I could scarcely believe my eyes.

"The secret of immortality," the Professor said. "The alchemy of insects. When parasitic wasps lay their eggs in a host, its bodily functions are arrested. The secret of my good health. I'm perfectly fit, never had so much as a head-cold. I haven't aged a day in the last forty years—and I never will. A gift of the Children of Callisto and their leader." He seemed surprised by our hesitancy. "Go on, take one—swallow it. Immortality."

"They said you'd had a stroke of apoplexy," said Cross.

"Not a stroke—a symbiosis," said the professor, with the air of one boasting about having found a rare bargain. "My little guests keep my body in a condition of perfect stasis. I will outlive every man alive—and their children. Perhaps I will outlive mankind itself."

I was at a loss, but Cross spoke up.

"Tithonus," he said. The professor looked puzzled, and Cross went on. "In Greek mythology, Tithonus was the lover of the goddess Eos, who asked Zeus to make him immortal. Zeus granted her wish, but Tithonus still aged, and became ever more withered and feebler, until Eos could no longer stand him. Eventually, according to the story, he became a cricket."

A slow smile spread across the professor's face. "Lucky man. Maybe I too will become an insect myself, in the end," the Professor said. He cocked his head. "One of the rulers of the world. Perfectly adapted. Much better than—apes."

He looked at me as he said this last word, but I'm sure he thought of everyone the same way.

"Immortality gives one a perspective," the Professor mused. "Insects rise above the world of men; the book of *Al-Azif* allows us to join them. As a treasure for the wise—but a trap for fools. "

"We'll just take the book," said Cross. "If you don't mind."

"You want to make money?" asked the Professor scornfully. "My son-in-law, that fool Durham, just wanted money. He got his dye—and he died from it!"

The professor wheezed unpleasantly in his mirth. I brushed at my ankle as I felt something crawling on it. The professor looked down at the maggots and up again at us, as if not quite able to believe our folly.

"You'd rather have money than immortality? You idiots," the Professor said, and bent his neck to lick up the maggots again with his tongue. "Still, you can take the book. I don't need it."

"And where is the *Al-Azif*, Professor?" I asked.

"My daughter, my unfortunately widowed daughter, has it." There was no paternal warmth in his voice. No more, perhaps, than beetles express about their young. "My man will give you her address."

That would be the woman who married Durham, and who may have encouraged him to seek out what he needed in her father's book. We should have thought of her first. The *Al-Azif* was unique, never copied, and might be something that defied conventional wisdom about what books were. It was a living thing, this object, and seemed to drive people mad when they had it. The *Necronomicon* had a similar reputation but there were hundreds of people who'd studied it with only a handful becoming bug-eating nutters like the Professor.

"Thank you very much for your help, Professor," I said, rising to my feet as Cross did the same.

"Idiots," said the Professor again, looking up at us. "Rushing around uselessly. People think the mayfly has a short life because the adult form only lives for a day. What they don't consider is that the larvae live for years, quietly biding their time in the water. Others may while away centuries, snug in their underground cells."

"I didn't know that," I said.

He shook his head. "Insects know that the secret of life is just—living. I read the newspaper, and it's all people arguing about trivia that nobody will remember next month, never mind next century. The insects have been here millions of years— millions! They have perspective. Or rather, *we* have perspective. You keep rushing around."

This strange little man was completely assured of his superiority over us, over all mankind, I wondered what would happen if you cut open that withered body. Would writhing maggots come spilling out of the incision? Or was if just a hollowed-out shell, as dry and papery as a wasp's nest?

Was he immortal, or was that an illusion fostered by the things that burrowed through him, which would last only until they finally ate too much into his vital organs? I very much suspected the latter.

"I'm afraid rushing around is my job," I said.

"That book will kill you," he said with a malicious smile. "Both of you."

"Don't worry Professor," said Cross, tipping his hat. "I know how to handle books."

It was a jolly evening at the Conquering Hero, as Saturday nights generally are, Saturday being payday for most working men. The pub was full and the entertainment was correspondingly boisterous. This was no time for solo singers to show off their

skills with poignant airs of love and loss and longing. It was a
night for celebration, and we roared out songs that practically
drowned the old piano: patriotic songs, drinking songs and
music hall numbers. We were so loud you could hear the echoes
from the street outside when the singing stopped.

At some point in the proceedings someone passed me a
glass of whisky, bellowing that it was from a fan. I could not
see the donor to salute him, but it was not the first time that
someone who had followed my boxing career had been moved
to stand me a drink. Beer is my preferred tipple, but this was
good whisky, as far as I could tell, though in truth I barely
noticed it.

I did not appreciate that anything was amiss for some time
afterwards. It was only when the outside air struck me that I
felt I was not quite myself. Usually, the draft of cool, fresh air
after the smoky fug of the pub is a tonic, but this evening I felt
dulled even as I walked home. I put my feelings down to more
drink than usual, but I was not halfway there when I stumbled,
then stumbled again. I looked down at the pavement, with the
accusatory glance of a drunkard who thinks he has been tripped
up deliberately. My unsteadiness was getting worse rather than
better. Now that I stopped to notice, my legs were half numb.

A car was moving down the curb fifty yards behind me.
When I looked back a minute later it was still there, going at
walking pace. I put two and two together: they had drugged me.
By that time every step was like walking through quicksand.
I held on to a pillar box to recover myself, but the quicksand
was rising. I looked back to the car. It had stopped, and the
doors opened. Men wearing black advanced towards me—one
with long dark hair, one with a red beard. Then the quicksand
engulfed me, and I slipped away.

After an ellipsis of unknown length I was revived by the
shock of cold water. My mind was not fuzzy at all. If anything I
felt refreshed, though the sensation of water running down my
shirt collar was rather disagreeable. I tried to move an arm and
found I was bound fast—tied to the thick wooden chair I was
sitting on.

I was in a dark room, an underground room I felt sure,

because there were no signs of windows. The ceiling was so low that, if I had been able to stand up, I could have touched it easily. Instead there were posters, mainly red and black, with slogans about the proletariat and freedom. It must have been a storage cellar, now turned into an anarchists' lair.

Facing me across a table was the woman I knew as Parker, and her partner, Cameron.

They were still dressed in black; almost a uniform. Her outfit was not without feminine touches and her eyes were rimmed with kohl. He still wore blue spectacles, and from this distance I could see that they were faceted, the light from a single bulb above the desk glinting off surfaces in turn as he moved. There was an empty water glass in his hand, and I deduced that he was the one who had just revived me.

I had never read much about anarchists. My knowledge went little further than Mr. Verloc in Joseph Conrad's *The Secret Agent*, which is a fine tale if harder going than my usual fare. In that account the anarchists placed great faith in the notion that that if you blew things up they would be rebuilt better next time. But then throwing bombs is more fun than attending committee meetings.

"Mr. Stubbs," said Cameron. "My apologies, but this was the only way we could talk to you."

"The accepted procedure is to visit my office during business hours," I said, just for something to say while I assayed the situation. It would not hurt to stay polite.

I was bound with a stout cord, evidently a single piece. Forget what you have been told about strongmen snapping such bonds by flexing their mighty muscles. The correct technique, which has been perfected by Harry Houdini, is to alternately flex and relax your muscles to create some give in the rope; that way you can eventually get enough room to wriggle out. I was tied tightly though.

My arms were tied together in front of me, and I was fastened to the chair at several points. It was an elaborate and thorough job by someone. I guessed they must have secured a prisoner for interrogation before.

"We prefer not to be shot at again by your associate," he

said.

"Cross is a lunatic," added Parker. Her accent was neutral, difficult to place. Perhaps English was not her first language.

"As well as being a liar and a traitor and a thief," said Cameron. "Whatever Cross may have told you, we are not the villains of the piece. He betrayed us."

"He hasn't told me anything," I said. My wrists between us, and I could not very well move them without Cameron noticing. Instead I turned my head for the first time, left and right.

The first thing that caught my attention was a display of pistols on the wall. They were not simply in rows but arranged in an elegant triple fan. A way perhaps of reminding followers of their power and purpose.

"We asked him for help," said Parker. "Since he is such a renowned book finder. Unfortunately, he's also a crook."

"That's why he tricked you into buying it for him," said Cameron. "He just wants it for himself. He'll cheat you too, when it suits him."

They did not interrupt each other or complete each other's sentences, they shared a common view. They reflected each other like two mirrors, multiplying to infinity, swamping everything else in their own world. Anything else outside their world was beneath their interest.

"Maybe so," I said. "I only met the man today, I don't know him."

"He must have told you we're anarchists," said Cameron. "We are motivated by ideology. We go through all this," he gestured at the walls around him, "risking arrest, being shot at by reactionaries, giving up our time, our money, our lives, all for the cause of a better world."

Cameron was by no means shy about the sacrifice has was making, but he did not look to me like a man who had suffered. He finished by wrapping an arm around Parker's waist, as if emphasizing that she was one with him in this heroic mission.

"Whereas Cross is just working for personal gain," Parker said, spitting out the last two words.

It would not be wise to argue back in this situation; and in any case what he said about Cross was substantially true. He never claimed to be working for any cause higher than his own private benefit. Whether he had indeed betrayed the anarchists I could not guess.

"If you're so high-minded and full of benevolence, perhaps you might demonstrate it by untying me," I suggested.

Cameron held up a hand, indicating that I must be patient a minute yet.

"Please, let us explain why we need the book," said Parker. "As Kropotkin himself says, insects have a perfect, egalitarian society. All goods are shared equally."

"There is no idleness, no accumulation of personal wealth," said Cameron. "Insects have no shame, no guilt, no social convention—there are no insect police, no prisons, no laws. Perfect freedom, perfect justice, perfect equality. Perfect anarchy. That is the society we aspire to."

"It might work very nicely," I observed, "but for the fact that human beings are not insects."

They both smiled the same smile, as though they had just scored a point over me.

"Moses went into the desert, and he heard the message," said Cameron. "'Look to the ant and consider her ways'."

"Jesus listened to it for forty days and forty nights," said Parker. "But he only caught part of it. Mohammed too, got his dictation from the same source, with enough power to conquer half the world. But only Al'Hazred managed to take it down flawlessly."

"He was mad," I said, also doubting Jesus had listened to bugs for the Sermon on the Mount.

"Madness probably helped," agreed Cameron.

"This is not just speculation," said Parker. "We know. The book has already given us so much."

"Let's show him," said Cameron.

"We will show you something incredible," Parker told me as Cameron went to a niche in the wall which resembled an altar, approaching it with something like reverence. "A man of your caliber, in your profession, must have known some astounding things in his time. But this is going to be the most astounding thing you have ever heard of."

I was in no mood to be astounded, but anything which increased the delay and gave me time to think was to the good. I affected a polite interest.

From inside the niche, Cameron withdrew an inlaid wooden box about the size of a cigar box. He opened the box and solemnly withdrew a strip of thick brown paper.

He held up the paper before my eyes. It was antique, there was no doubt of that, as thick as pasteboard and brown as leather. With some difficulty, because the light was so dim, I could see a single world scrawled in dark brown ink. The lettering was jagged and entirely uneven, it looked more than a little like insects crawling across the page.

"This is a line from the *Al-Azif*," said Cameron. "Just one line."

I strained to make out the letters. There might have been a capital C, a tiny z or the number two, followed by a capital H, and e or a three. No words that I could recognize, but it seemed to be in Roman rather an Arabic script, which was itself curious.

"It's a bookmark from Entwhistle's library," said Cameron. "It must have been damp; and the words transferred themselves on to the bookmark before it fell out."

"I'm sorry not to be more impressed," I said. "But I don't see..."

"The letters change," said Parker. "The words are slowly mutating. HOLE becomes HALE and then HATE and MATE. It tells you things."

Perhaps one of the letters was slowly melting into something else; but the light was bad and it was not easy to tell, nor was Cameron holding it still enough to be sure. I must still not have looked sufficiently astounded.

"Don't you see—the whole book is continuously writing itself!" said Cameron. "It's alive!"

"Like a swarm of ants foraging, foraging over the entire field of written knowledge," said Parker. "It generates every possible truth and assimilates it, learning and gathering over the centuries..."

They were both transported, but one blurry line at a time seemed like a slow way to gain knowledge. I could not even feign being impressed. That slow mutation suggested the *Al-Azif* would be a difficult book to copy; by the time you finished, half the world would have changed. Maybe they were right in the bugs which seemed to be called by the object contained something of the book itself. Was it haunted? It would explain a few things, but haunted by what?

"He's too stupid," said Cameron, losing patience and reverently replacing the relic in its cigar box.

"This one line has taught us more than you can imagine," said Parker. "We have learned more biochemistry than every university in Europe. As you will shortly witness for yourself." That had an ominous ring to it. Cameron meanwhile was bending over and retrieving a key to unlock a desk drawer. "This new knowledge has enabled us to consolidate our control of this group and absorb a number of others in just a few months."

"And that's why you want the *Al-Azif*," I said. "More knowledge and more power. Paving the way to a paradise of human insects."

"Exactly," said Parker. "Helping humanity become as perfect as insects."

This yearning for the supposed natural innocence of insects seemed a deal more fanciful than wishing we were back in the Garden of Eden. I was not at all sure what they meant. Were we to change our political organizations to that of the hive and the nest or did they intend actual physical transformation? H.G. Wells wrote a book, *The Island of Doctor Moreau*, in which a misguided scientist attempts to turn animals into people using surgical techniques. The society of animals does not last long, nor does its creator. The story is not, for my money, one of Wells' better works, being too much of a simple morality tale and tending rather to satire. The central idea though is made surprisingly credible, which I suppose is Mr. Wells' genius. Perhaps it might be possible to blend humans with insects, though even Dr Moreau would have hesitated at that degree of nightmarish hybridization. Surely such a thing was madness.

Cameron had returned, and they seemed to be waiting expectantly for a response. If they were expecting me to ask for an application form so I could join their group, they were disappointed. But perhaps that was not their intention. Maybe they just wanted me to applaud their genius now they had shown off their cleverness.

"Now that we've explained our reasons," said Parker, leaning closer to me for the first time, "will you tell us where the book is? We can pay whatever you like."

Her long nails were painted black. They looked like claws.

"What with? You couldn't even outbid me at Rosebery's," I reminded her.

"We can get money," she said. "Say how much you want and we'll raise it."

Anyone who reads the papers knows anarchists are notorious for bank robbery. I had no doubt that was what they would have done.

"Why didn't you offer money to Cross?" I asked.

"We did!" protested Cameron. He was holding a bundle wrapped in a white cloth which he passed to Parker.

"That was what we were doing when he betrayed us," said Parker.

"I can't say I entirely trust your sincerity with the financial offer," I said, indicating my bound hands. "Under the circumstances."

"We do understand," said Cameron. "But you must appreciate that you absolutely will tell us everything you know."

Parker had unwrapped the cloth and placed four stoppered glass vials in a row on the table top in front of her. As he leaned close, she kissed him on the cheek and they smiled at each other. I sensed the unwholesome excitement between them.

Parker gestured with a silver hypodermic. "The wisdom of insects, in liquid form."

The two of them giggled at that. They were like children looking forward to a game.

"Have you ever been stung by an insect?" asked Cameron.

The question was needless, but it was as well to play along. "Who hasn't?"

"This chemical is the sting of the ant," she said, tapping the first vial with the needle. It was a cloudy, muddy white. "Sharp and unpleasant. It's a jab that hurts out of all proportion to its size. Not the worst pain you'll ever experience, but one you would prefer to avoid. It's nothing though, compared to the distilled sting of the wasp." She tapped the second vial, this one a mustard yellow. "That feels like a white-hot knife stabbing through to your marrow."

"The effects are quite something," said Cameron. "That's why we have to tie you up so thoroughly, so you don't damage yourself or anything else."

"I've had wasp stings," I said.

"It also paralyses on the central nervous system," said Parker. "It was a derivative of the wasp venom in your drink that knocked you out so thoroughly. A strong man like you, rendered completely powerless by an insect."

Their self-satisfaction appeared to be boundless.

"But the sting of the bee is as to the sting of the wasp as the wasp is to the ant," Parker continued, indicating the third vial, which contained a muddy brown liquid. "This extract is simply excruciating. It causes the body to swell and puff up, the breathing becomes labored, the heart pounds..."

From her tone she might have been recounting happy memories rather than a most vicious torture.

"It can be fatal," said Cameron. "If a person is weak or the dose is too large. We will have to calculate your dose very carefully. About how much do you weigh?"

"What about the fourth vial?" I asked.

"The sting of the scorpion is beyond words," said Parker. The fourth vial was a vivid, pillar-box red. "The pain alone will kill you. And you will do anything, tell us anything, to end that pain. You will beg me to shoot you."

"The scorpion is not an insect," I said. "It is an arachnid, a relative of the spider. It has eight legs rather than six."

The two of them exchanged a look.

"You're right," she said. "It's not really from a scorpion, it's an extract from a type of beetle."

I deduced then that the red liquid must be the famed Durham Scarlet. For all the good that information would do me.

"The pain it produces is genuinely astonishing," said Cameron. "Men who only grit their teeth and grunt even at the bee venom lose all control with the fourth sting. The pain is invariably fatal. It's a grisly business."

"You've tested it?"

"On police spies," said Parker. "Agents provocateur."

"Traitors," said Cameron. "Guinea pigs."

"It never fails," said Parker. "We always get the information we want. And the result terrifies the others who witness it."

They were like two children, wrapped up in their own game. A game that was deadly to others; they had no empathy for anything outside their own charmed circle of two. Anarchy meant license to do what they wanted. And I could see how their ruthless approach, and their collection of torture-drugs, might have helped them dominate and absorb other groups to consolidate their power.

"It's an astonishing achievement," said Cameron, seemingly irritated by my lack of enthusiasm for their ingenious implements of torture. "With just four bottles of chemicals we can surgically extract the truth from the most hardened criminal or the most devious traitor."

A traitor being, I suspected, anyone in the group who disagreed with them. And what information might they have gleaned to blackmail or coerce others?

"The judiciary, the detective service is obsolete," said Parker, brandishing the needle. "This is the way to get to the facts. Spies and secret agents are redundant."

"Except that no civilized nation would ever use it," I said.

"Typical bourgeois mentality," said Cameron. "The Ixtol have a society based around concepts which would make Karl Marx drool with envy."

I had no idea who the Ixtol were and, honestly, didn't particularly want to know.

Parker opened the first vial, drew back the plunger of the syringe to load it with a suitable dose, her eyes bright with anticipation, and passed it to Cameron. He was smirking now, chuckling to himself. This was their little game, one they had invented, and they certainly enjoyed it.

"You're going to tell us everything," he said.

This was, not to put too fine a point on it, a rather ticklish situation. Story-book heroes may be able to free themselves with a single bound, but I was not so fortunate. I had neglected to secret a sharp blade in the lining of my jacket—not that I could have accessed it without being seen even if I had such foresight. The man who tied me up was at least a Boy Scout in his knowledge of knots and they could not be unfastened by my teeth or any other means.

The cord was a stout one, and if I am strong I am not nearly strong enough to snap an undamaged rope.

Furthermore, I was being watched closely and they had plenty of weapons to hand. They could go to the wall, select a gun or two and shoot me dead a dozen times while I was still grunting and struggling to free myself.

There was, however, one factor which gave me some grounds for optimism.

Rickety chairs are the bane of a man of my weight. I always prefer to sit on something substantial when available. I had no immediate knowledge of the chair I was tied to, but I had been making a close inspection of the chairs on which the other two sat, on the assumption that they were of the same general design. I did not believe they kept a special chair reserved for captives.

It was an ordinary dining-chair, past its best, the sort that would have been demoted to use in another room. It was, however, a good quality piece, and that worked to my advantage. The fashion in furniture is to make them as fine and delicate as possible, not massive and heavy. In the past, this had meant at least one embarrassing incident when a chair let out a loud crack when I sat on it. It also meant that the article to which I was now bound would not long survive rough usage.

I intended to give it some very rough usage indeed.

During the conversation I had been testing the extent of my movement. My feet were firmly on the floor. It would have taken a much larger piece of furniture to keep me off the ground and I was able to throw myself forward so the chair tilted up on its front legs, then project myself upwards and backwards so that it landed with all my weight on the rear right leg.

Now, this whole plan could easily have gone awry. If I had

been tied to it differently, then the loss of that leg might simply have meant I was left lying on the floor still fastened to the chair. But the leg and its attendant cross-strut snapped clean off, splitting the seat from the back and freeing the rope that had been looped around them. This gave me enough freedom to straighten up. Rolling awkwardly, as I was still attached to the remains of the chair, I rose to my feet.

"Don't be—" Cameron started to say and then I threw my hands up and shattered the light bulb. The room was plunged instantly into coal-cellar darkness.

I was still tied up and it would take some time to free myself, but I reasoned that absence of light would impede them a deal more than it impeded me. The darkness would be my shield.

"Secure the pistols," said Cameron. "I'll get him."

Cameron's only weapon was that loaded hypodermic, but he was completely free and dealing with a man bound hand and foot. He could stab me any number of times and the best I could hope was to land an awkward, double-armed blow.

I shuffled back, working furiously to free my hands. I had located the end of the cord, but it could not simply be pulled free. It needed to be worked over and under and through knots.

The two of them were moving about. I could distinguish Cameron's stealthy footsteps, and the swish as he lashed out at the air in front of him in a wide arc. With my bound arms I could not even grapple effectively, and I needed to deal with that sting of his.

His arm brushed my shoulder. I hopped away as he struck at where I had been. My back struck the wall and I retreated along it.

"Where are you?" he muttered. Unfortunately, struggling out of ropes is hard to do in complete silence and he started to close again. He moved cautiously, not wanting to give me the chance of knocking him down with a lucky blow.

"I have the guns," said Parker, and there was the metallic click of a hammer being pulled back.

"Good," he said. "Get ready."

Ready for what? The loose end of the rope was coming away now, several feet of it, and I was just seconds away from freeing myself. Unfortunately, I did not have those seconds.

There was the rasp and flare of a match and the whole scene was illuminated: Cameron barely out of arms reach, a lit match in one hand and the hypodermic in the other. Parker stood across the room holding a pistol in a two-handed marksman's stance.

I ducked and whipped at Cameron with the loose end of the rope. He cried out as the match flew into darkness; the syringe fell to the floor with a metallic tinkle as I whipped him again.

A flash of orange light accompanied the crack of the pistol. The bullet passed so close I felt the passage on my cheek. There was a second and a third, and pings as the rounds ricocheted off the solid cellar wall and floor.

"Hold your fire!" shouted Cameron. He sounded scared.

I kicked a leg free of the bindings. Now I could move. I dashed across the room as fast as I dared, holding my hands in front of me, and a door opened ahead. There were men on the other side—more anarchists, alerted by the gunshot, outlined by the light behind them. I was not stopping for anything. I ploughed through them like an express train, almost tripping over the rope that flailed around me.

"Out of the way!" shouted Parker behind me, but she could not get a clear shot before I found the staircase and bounded up it.

The exterior door was bolted but not locked, and I was through it an on to street in a trice. I did not recognize the street. A car skidded to a halt next to me and a back door was flung open. My first thought was that it was more anarchists and I was done for, until a voice shouted from the back.

"Hop in, Stubbs!" I heard a voice shout. It was Cross and looking very pleased with himself. Bear slammed the accelerator down and we sped past the anarchists as they spilled out on to the pavement. By the time they realized I was in the car we were out of shooting range. They were lost to sight as we rounded the corner.

"That was a damned close-run thing," Cross said, helping untangle the rope from my wrists. "A kidnapping, I take it?"

"They drugged me."

"Took you, but they couldn't hold you," he laughed. "Amateurs."

"How did you know to look for me? And where to look for me?"

"My lucky stars," he said. Cross rolled up his sleeve to display a tattoo which might have been a pattern of interlocking stars. "This was done for me in Istanbul by an old Kurdish witchdoctor whose life I saved…he insisted on it. The thing gives me pins and needles whenever there's something up, and it started itching like fury this evening. "

He rolled his shirt back and buttoned it.

"I thought my life might be in danger, but that made it fade. Then I concentrated on you, and it blazed."

Under other circumstances I would have suspected he was pulling my leg, but Cross was in deadly earnest.

"How did you find me?"

"Well, I rousted Bear here, then I'm afraid I got myself in your landladies' bad books," he said. "I raised merry hell until she answered. When I persuaded her to look in your room, and you weren't there, I knew that they must have taken you."

It was a fair enough inference; I'm sure my landlady would have told Cross how unlike me it was not to be back fifteen minutes after closing time. That did not explain, however, how he knew where the anarchists were based.

"Oh, I visited their lair once before," he said. "They insisted in blindfolding me to take me there. But on the way back I counted the turns, and I formed an idea of the location."

"You met with them?"

"Cameron wanted to hire me. But I didn't like the cut of his jib. I told him I'd think about it, or they'd never have let me go. The one good thing was that it gave me a pretty good idea of where they lurked. We've only been combing these four streets five minutes, and who should pop up but Harry Stubbs?"

This indirectly confirmed what Cameron had said. The anarchists had been doing business with Cross before, and there had been a rupture between them.

"Road hogs," complained Bear as a vehicle came past us behind at speed. "And at this time of night—"

There was a tremendous smash and the car lurched sideways as the other vehicle pulled into us. Bear, a seasoned hand at managing his machine, kept it under control with almost miraculous skill. Rather than ploughing into a lamp-post, the car regained it's position in the road and the other vehicle skidded and fell back.

"Damn," said Cross, holding on to a leather strap with one hand while feeling in his pocket with the other.

"He did that deliberately!" said Bear, looking left and right as he glanced back at the vehicle pursuing us.

The streets were empty, and we could only see our pursuers intermittently as they passed under the wide-spaced street lights.

"Make for the police station at Rochester Row," said Cross. "Next left."

The wheels screeched as we rounded a corner. Our pursuer had the advantage of a more powerful machine. On the long straight stretch that followed the dark car gained with the inexorability of doom, until it almost filled the rear window. Cross had wound down his window and held the Mauser ready on his lap.

A dark, round object sailed past—for a moment I thought it must be a pigeon in flight, then there was a flash and a boom, and the windows on my side were starred with shrapnel. The bomb had missed its mark by some ways. The scars on the window were long gouges pointing backwards.

"Permission granted," I said to Cross, and in an instant, he was leaning out the window, firing back at them: a series of aimed, single shots rather than the rapid-fire burst.

I could not tell if his shots were having any effect, but there were orange flashes of answering fire from the other vehicle, which had fallen thirty yards behind.

Bear swerved left and right, trying to make a more difficult target. This also made it harder to gain distance on our pursuers.

Killing us would achieve nothing, in fact it might leave the anarchists even further from their goal, since we were their best lead. A bullet bounced off the metal roof inches away from my head and a second later a wing mirror exploded in a shower of glass.

"This is senseless," I said, as we screeched around another corner.

If we could get more of a lead we could pile out of the car and make a run for it. The night was dark, and if we disappeared down an alley we could lose them soon enough. But this was a stratagem which called for two good legs, which one of us conspicuously lacked.

"Sense goes out the window when the shooting starts," said Cross, dropping his gun into the footwell.

The Mauser has an internal magazine. It cannot be reloaded quickly and easily , and especially not in the dark inside a speeding car rocking wildly from side to side. Cross extracted the flare pistol with his left hand, passed it to his right.

"What do you say?" he asked. "In for a penny, in for a pound?"

"Permission granted."

Cross leaned out the window, then immediately drew in again, putting a hand to his forehead. Fresh blood poured down from his scalp. For a moment I thought he was mortally wounded, but he swore, dabbed at the injury and winced. Then he gritted his teeth, leaned out again and took careful aim.

There was a muzzle flash like an artillery piece, and behind us there was a gout of orange-yellow flame and black smoke. The car behind swerved, bucked as it hit the kerb, then flipped over and skidded along on its side in a shower of sparks, vanishing into the dark between street lights as we sped away.

"Amateurs!" Cross yelled at our receding opponents.

"You got them," said Bear.

"Actually, I missed," said Cross ruefully. "The driver panicked. Still, same result."

His head wound was superficial, if messy, but Cross played it up, and insisted that we stop at the home of a doctor friend who lived nearby.

"Is there really a doctor friend of yours here?" I asked, ringing the numbered bell.

"Yes, but although a doctor of philology," said Cross. "He owes me a favor." He removed the blood-soaked handkerchief from his head and replaced it quickly. "He'll get us some clean bandages. And some decent French brandy if we're in luck."

I could not believe that anyone would answer the door at

this hour, but a balding, spectacled man in his shirtsleeves opened.

"Oh, it's you," he said, seeing Cross. "Got anything good for me?"

"Only a head injury," said Cross.

The other man looked disappointed, but not altogether surprised.

"I was hoping you'd found that Sofian Codex at last. I suppose you'd better come in." The doctor of philology opened the door wider to admit us and ushered us a narrow staircase. Books were stacked on every stair, leaving a narrow passage. "Cross, you can clean up in the bathroom, it's the first on the left. Don't go getting blood everywhere! Now, I wonder where I left that bottle?"

Cross' plan was to spend the night here. His view that it would not be safe to go back to Norwood, given that the anarchists knew our car and could probably find out where I lived without too much difficulty. I was inclined to agree. Of course, Arthur could raise a scratch force ten times that of our opponents at the drop of a hat, but the last thing Arthur wanted was a pitched battle. He would thank me more if I did not bring trouble back into Norwood. Bear was of the same mind.

The philologist was hospitable enough, and he and Cross happily chatted about obscure books. He was indifferent as a host though, and the accommodation he offered was somewhat basic. Cross and Bear were able to clear space on sofas by removing the books piled on them. None of the furniture was large enough for me, so I stretched out on the floor with a blanket over me and three rugs for a mattress, with a pile of books for a pillow. Surprisingly enough after the excitement I drifted off easily into a deep sleep, lulled by gentle waves of exhaustion and brandy.

Apparently, I snore.

Mrs. Durham had agreed to see us the next day. According to Sammy she had lived a quiet life since her widowhood, with few interests outside her home. She was financially secure. Her husband had evidently not run through the entirety of his fortune, and despite of the manner of his death she had collected on his life insurance. She clearly had good lawyers.

Mrs. Durham's house was less inviting than her father's. It stood behind a brick wall nine feet high, topped with jagged broken glass which were a good deal less ornamental and more brutal than the traditional row of iron spikes.

"She's a woman who likes her privacy," observed Cross.

A housekeeper admitted us through the front gate and down a long path to the front door. She was a slim, sober woman in her forties, with the smart but unbending air of old-fashioned help. A crucifix showed conspicuously at her throat. She did not indulge in small talk but led us with professional courtesy. The garden had received little attention, and the flowerbeds and shrubbery were becoming overgrown.

"Madame doesn't usually receive visitors," said the housekeeper, taking our hats and coats. "Madame is not at all well."

I am sure that Cross wondered, as I did, that her unwellness would resemble that of her father, or whether it might relate in some other way to the book.

"There's really no necessity for her to see us at all," said Cross. "It's merely a matter of collecting an item—a book of her father's."

"Yes, sir. Madame does understand that," she said. Was there a slight shudder at the reference to Professor Armstrong? "But sir, Madame wishes to speak with you."

"You wouldn't happen to know if the book is in the house?" I asked. I was not expecting an answer, but if the reply was in the negative then it might save us a wild goose chase.

"The book is in her possession," said the housekeeper evenly.

She led us to an upstairs bedroom and paused outside.

"Madame is sensitive to light," she said.

She knocked twice. After an indistinct reply she opened the door.

The room was curtained and shuttered, but a nightlight on the bedside table shed a pool of illumination. It was barely enough to make out the silhouette of a figure propped up in bed. She did at least seem more substantial than her father. The room was filled with the scent of patchouli, or something very like it, which filled your sinuses.

"Please," said a voice. "Sit down."

We took the two chairs, placed some distance from the bedside.

"We've no wish to inconvenience you, Mrs. Durham," Cross began.

"You want to take the book," she said. Her voice was steady enough, but oddly without character. I would not have known whether it was male or female.

"As I mentioned in my letter, my business partner and I have purchased the book," said Cross. "Your father merely had it on loan."

"Why do you want it?"

I was starting to see better in the semi-darkness now, and I could make out the old woman's white nightcap and the outline of her face. She was propped up on a mass of pillows; her arms and everything else were invisible under the quilt.

"It's a unique volume," said Cross. "There are no copies. Plenty of collectors would give their eyeteeth for it."

"It's the devil's book," she said tonelessly.

"We were very sorry to hear about your husband, Mrs. Durham," I said. "We understand the book may have painful associations for you."

She was silent a moment. Overcome, perhaps, by emotion.

"You know about that. And you've seen my father. What more proof do you need that it's the Devil's book? Beelzebub, he's called, the Lord of Flies. God of buzzing insects. The book is his bible, a book of evil temptations."

The dark was too profound to get more than the faintest suggestion of her features. I could distinguish out the grey hair, and the dark ellipses of eyes, but no hint of expression.

"His words, maybe," said Cross, "but legal title to the book is ours. We will debate with Old Nick if he cares to bring an action."

"You can debate with my solicitors instead," Mrs. Durham said.

Now it was Cross's turn to be silent.

"Be reasonable, Mrs. Durham," he said. "The law is plainly on our side. You've no case. Perhaps we can recompense you in some way for the book?"

Her head turned, her whole upper body turned as she shifted to point the blank spaces of her eyes towards us.

"Just go away," Mrs. Durham said. "And leave me the book. It's the Devil's book. It can do nothing for you. For anyone. You know about my father, my husband. There were others... before them."

"I'd have thought you'd be glad to be rid of it," said Cross, in a last attempt.

The quilt rustled as she shifted beneath it, turning away from us.

"Go away," she said. "Write to my solicitors if you must. But I warn you, I'll fight you—and you'll be sorry if you win."

"I think you've made that abundantly clear," said Cross.

The housekeeper had been waiting on the other side of the door and opened it to escort us out.

"Mrs. Durham seems very distressed about the book," said Cross. "Perhaps it might improve matters if we were to take it out of her hands."

"She won't give it up," said the housekeeper, with finality. "Not for anything. She asked me to refer you to her solicitors, Latham and Rowe of Norwood, for any further communication."

"She's just making trouble for herself," said Cross. "If you could persuade her to do the decent thing then we'd be very grateful to you. And it would be for her own good, nobody wants to go to law."

He laid great emphasis on this latter point.

"Oh dear," said the housekeeper, with a catch in her voice. "I so wish I could help you. I really do. I wish she'd never seen that accursed book. But it's much too late."

We were at the front door now.

"It *is* the Devil's book," she said, pausing with her hand on the door knob. "Please don't come back."

Cross turned and stood for a moment contemplating the door after she had shut behind us, leaning heavily on his stick.

"Damn," he said.

"Not what I hoped for either," I said.

Bear brought the car down the street as soon as he saw us. Cross could walk with the aid of his stick, but it was plain he did not much like it. He eased himself into the back seat.

"The old lady didn't cough up?" asked Bear, seeing our expressions in the rear-view mirror. "That's too bad."

"I felt I was in Little Red Riding Hood," said Cross. "Talking to her in the dark. 'Grandma, what big ears you have'."

Perhaps unconsciously he rubbed at this forearm. His star tattoo must be itching from the encounter.

Skinner had always remarked that with women, you could never tell what you were getting. What with corsetry and padding, some of them were upholstered like armchairs. The shape of the body underneath might bear no relation to the external form. And with paint and powder and artful use of lighting, even a woman's real face was to some degree a matter of speculation. However, the widow Durham presented a more extreme case than Skinner might ever have encountered.

"From the way she talked, she must have first-hand experience of the *Al-Azif*," I said. "And she's none the better for it. She wants to stop others doing the same. What if she decides to destroy it?" I asked.

He shook his head.

"Not possible. It's been tried many times." He laughed at my look of disbelief. "The Inquisition ordered it burned in Malta in 1534. According to one account, the words came out of the burning pages like a swarm of angry ants, spreading the flames and causing great consternation to those who witnessed it. One friar was burned to death. They don't know what happened afterwards, but the *Al-Azif* turned up a few years later in the library of the Grand Master of the Knights Hospitaller, in Valletta in Malta, about half a mile away."

I could picture the words settling on another volume, like a swarm of bees occupying a new hive, settling in and rearranging themselves into their cells, shifting around slowly and ceaselessly.

"She might just throw the book into the Thames in a

weighted sack," I said. "But I suppose someone has already thought of that in the last thousand years."

"Whatever they tried, it didn't work," said Cross. "The Mad Mahdi, pious Muslim that he was, wanted to destroy it, and his advisors should have been experts on Arabic occult matters. Despite their best efforts the book is still with us, and I doubt that Mrs Durham can do anything except try to stop anyone else getting their hands on it."

"So, we have to resort to the law," I said, though I knew already that Cross was not the type of man who placed great store in solicitors.

"No, for three reasons. Firstly, the law is slow at the best of times. Secondly, Mrs Durham's budget might stretch to a great many lawyers. And thirdly, I'm damned if I'll put up with a lot of legal evasions, obfuscations and obstructions just to get a book that already belongs to me."

"Law's a waste of time," said Bear from the front seat. "Why don't you get in there and grab it? She's just an old lady."

"Capital idea," said Cross, warming at once to Bear's forward approach. "I was thinking that stealth and the cover of darkness might be preferable though."

"We're not exactly the ideal squad for burglary," I said. Cross's single leg was a hindrance, and I am not built for shimmying up drainpipes. I doubted whether Bear's duties would extend to anything criminal. Arthur was sensitive about that sort of thing.

"I wasn't proposing gymnastics," said Cross. "You may not have noticed, but there are no alarms, and no dog. Nor a telephone. Someone with your beef ought to be able to force the side gate and one of those sash windows without too much effort. How difficult can it be?"

"If she wakes up and decides to shoot the burglars, then it might be decidedly uncomfortable."

"Shoot the burglars?" scoffed Cross, looking to Bear for support. "I've never heard anything so ridiculous. She's the middle-aged daughter of a professor, not Annie Oakley."

"I know tough old dames back home who'd shoot you dead," Bear offered. "Over here, they're real genteel."

"Quite so," said Cross. "If she hears anything going bump in the night she'll hide under the covers and wait for us to leave."

I could have cited any number of reservations. But the fact was, I did not have anything superior to offer, and there was something to be said for swift, decisive action. Now that she knew we were after the book, Mrs Durham might take steps to conceal it—or have the volume placed in a safe deposit box at her bank. Even Cross might baulk at robbing a bank. If we acted promptly, say tonight, then she would be unlikely to have any new measures in place.

"What about the housekeeper?" I asked. "She looked like an alert type."

"One of us should keep an eye on the place," said Cross. "See what happens this evening, Maybe the housekeeper lives in, but I'm betting she has a home of her own and she'll go off duty after she gives the old woman her supper."

"I'll take the first watch," said Bear.

There was no formal agreement, but I had been democratically outvoted. The plan to rob Mrs. Durham had been settled.

While Bear watched the house and Cross occupied himself browsing in a library, as good as place to avoid anarchists as anywhere. I visited a friend who is a carpenter by trade, and who was obliging enough to lend me a pry-bar whenever the occasion arises. He has a pretty fair idea of what I use it for, but he has little sympathy for those who end up being pursued by debt collectors. And I always stand him a drink in return.

"I never borrow money," he informed me cheerfully as he handed over the instrument. "It only leads to trouble in the long run."

"I had observed the same myself," I said, feeling the solid weight of it in my hand. The pry-bar is a J-shaped length of good Sheffield steel, and a very useful implement too for gaining entry. "If I might ask your professional opinion..."

"Ask away, Harry my boy."

"Can you pry open a sash window?"

"Depends," he said at once. "If all it has is a catch, then that'll give way first and you're in. Some of them have bolts on the outer side rail though. If you try to force that..." he sucked on his teeth. "You'd get in, if you've got enough leverage and push hard enough, but you'll wreck the lower frame. That'd be messy. It'll make some work for me the next day."

"And break some glass panes in the process?"

"I reckon so." He nodded slowly. "Real burglars take a razor blade and a chisel. They cut out the putty from one of the panes and ease the glass out in one piece, so they can reach through and open the window. The real clever ones put it back afterwards so nobody knows how they got in."

"How do you know this?"

"You ain't the only one who borrows tools from me," he said, and winked.

I managed to get a few hours' sleep that evening. Cross might prefer to stay awake the whole time, but I am not at my best at two in the morning and being fogged with lack of sleep is no way to start an important operation.

Bear had fulfilled his promise of keeping watch. He reported that the housekeeper had left the place at seven, locking the gate behind her. The light in the old lady's room had been extinguished at ten; since then, all had been quiet and dark.

He stopped the car at a distance he described as 'a block away' from the house. It looked different in the dark; bigger, for a start. He offered round a thermos flask of hot coffee, sweetened with whisky.

"You know the story of the Monkey's Paw?" I asked.

"Seen a couple of stage productions," said Cross, wiping his mouth on the back of his hand. "Why?"

"I'm beginning to think the *Al-Azif* grants its readers wishes in much the same way as the amulet in the story," I said. "That's why things always turn out badly."

Bear was looking at me quizzically, and although he was only the driver I explained how every wish was twisted: when a man wishes for a sum of money, his son is killed in a horrible accident, and the compensation is the sum he asked for. When he wishes for his son back the boy returns but as a walking, mangled corpse.

"Deliberate, demonic malice is one explanation," said Cross.

"But it may be simpler than that. You see, I knew a major who had an Italian batman. The batman was always eager to please, but he always managed to get the wrong end of the stick. When the major asked for water and a brush in the morning, he got a bucket of cold water and a scrubbing brush instead warm water and a shaving brush. When called for hot water for tea, it was never more than lukewarm. The batman was doing his best, he just never understood properly what was called for."

"I see," I said. "And you think that an insect intelligence might have even more trouble than an Italian figuring out what was really wanted?"

"I was thinking about old Al'Hazred and what happened to him. He wanted to prove the power of the book to people in the marketplace—and he died in front of their eyes, screaming that he was being devoured." He squinted down the dark street, as though trying to make out Al'Hazred's last moments. "Maybe not the sort of proof he was after, but I wonder whether anyone ever checked the body to see if he was eaten up by insects from the inside rather than invisible demons from the outside."

"If even he couldn't control it…"

"Nobody can," he agreed "But—and I am anticipating you here—we don't know what Mrs Durham was seeking when she opened the book, so we can't tell what it might have done to her. But I assure you that I am not taking any chances. If she has been affected by the book, I have a way to keep her at bay."

"You think she might be dangerous?"

"Didn't Skinner drum it into you," he said. "Women are always dangerous."

"Lavender oil," said Bear from the front seat. "Old-fashioned remedy to keep bugs away. Fleas and ticks too, when I was in the Army."

"Rustic remedies aside," said Cross, "I was thinking of this." He drew out a piece of thick white paper with a curious pattern inscribed on it. "You know how gamekeepers will nail the body of a dead hawk or fox to a gatepost? Well, as I understand it, this is more or less the same thing for the *Al-Azif.*"

"What is it?" I asked, taking the sheet.

"A sort of sigil. It might have originally escaped from the

Al-Azif, but it's been neutralized—killed. If you mark a window doorway with it, it's supposed to have a repellent effect. 'Exclusion principle' according to the geometrist who told me about it. Well, I used it once, a long time ago—seemed to do the trick. Up to a point. That's another story!"

Cross's plan was to pen the old lady up in her bedroom while we rifled the house. Which was a sound enough plan, except for the possibility that the book was in the bedroom with her. The Captain, ever the optimist, said we could cross that bridge when we got to it.

He made me copy out the sigil several times until I had it exactly. The inscription had to be made just so, looping back on itself. Being more mobile, I was the one who would have to chalk it on her door.

A silence settled over the car, not broken until our driver spoke up.

"There's a full moon behind those clouds," he said, leaning forwards for a better view. "You boys stay on the other side of the street or it'll light you up when it comes out. I'll wait back here, but I'll be ready when you holler."

"What do your lucky stars say?" I asked Cross.

He touched his forearm. "Proceed with grave caution." He retrieved his stick and opened the passenger door on his side, gesturing me to do the same.

We stopped half way, altered by a noise outside the house. But there was nothing more after half a minute. Presumably a cat on its nocturnal perambulations; hardly enough for us to retreat or call off the operation.

The wooden side gate was, of course, locked. I inserted the thin end of the pry bar through the gap between the gate and the gatepost at the level of the lock. The gate was not a tight fit—they seldom are—and with one quick movement I forced it open. The wood gave way easily and there was little sound.

"Good work," murmured Cross, and we hastened through into the garden.

The moon was out now, painting the lawn silver, with black shadows so dark they might have been cut out with scissors. The shards of glass along the top of the wall shone like ice. I felt like

I was under a spotlight as we crossed over the lawn to the lee of the house. If I had been more alert to my surroundings and less concerned about moving swiftly before I could be observed, I might have noticed something to my advantage. But it was not to be, and the whole drama played out to its bloody finale.

I had turned down the offer of tools other than the pry bar, on the grounds of lack of expertise. This was not the time to be learning new techniques. I would pry the window open, one way or another, and live with the consequences.

I had not informed Cross of the possible risk if the window was bolted. He waited expectantly beside me as I inserted the bar and applied a little leverage. I was going to gradually increase the force, listening for sounds of any strain that might presage breakage, but to my surprise it opened at the first effort. There was not even a catch to force; the window had been left open.

"It's open," I said quietly, levering it up far enough to get my fingers under and slide it up carefully, so as to avoid making any sound.

"Lady Luck is with us tonight," said Cross.

I hooked the pry bar back over my shoulder under my jacket.

I went first. My entrance was by no means graceful, and for getting through even a large sash window is a feat akin to a large dog jumping through a small hoop. I achieved it with a minimum of fuss and rearrangement of the furniture on the other side, a low table being the only obstacle.

Cross passed his stick through, then accepted a hand as he hauled himself after me. He was more mobile than I expected; he might have a paunch and only one leg, but there was a deal of power in his remaining three limbs. I wondered again if this was a sensible plan. If we had to egress at speed, we would be sunk; but Cross was not a man who would accept being cut out of the action.

None of the curtains were drawn, and the large windows admitted enough ghostly moonlight to illuminate the place fully, except where it was blanked out by shadow. The only sound beyond our breathing was the steady ticking of a grandfather clock in the hall.

"Go," said Cross, and soft-footed as I could manage I crept into the hall and up the stairs. One step creaked horribly as I trod on it and I froze in place. A minute passed and there were no sounds from upstairs to show I had been heard, so I carried on more slowly.

I was grateful for the thick carpets. The bedroom door was exactly as it had been previously, and with the greatest delicacy I could muster I recreated the mark that Cross had shown me. This was surely the most dangerous part, as Mrs Durham might easily wake to scratching at her door. But either she was a sound sleeper, or was so scared that she made no sound, and I completed my handiwork without any interruption.

I arrived back to find Cross exactly where I had left him. He had not dared move until the charm was in place. I did not place so much trust in magical protection as Cross seemed to. But it would be better to have it than not.

"To work," he said, and the yellow beam of his torch splashed across a low bookshelf. He scanned the titles individually, unhurriedly, but shook his head.

There were more caches of books along window sills and under tables, but nothing that even approximated to what we were after. The kitchen yielded, predictably enough, a shelf crammed with works relating to the domestic arts.

Cross opened the hall cupboard; not a very likely place for books. In addition to the usual coats, hats and boots, there were several other objects I could not easily identify.

"Well, well, well," said Cross, brandishing one.

"What is it?" I asked.

He turned it around, and I saw at last it was an artificial foot. He picked up another: a whole leg. Mrs. Durham had a considerable collection of prosthetic arms and legs of different shapes and sizes.

"There's some fine craftsmanship here," he said admiringly. "Money no object for her."

They were obviously custom-made. Cross examined them with interest. It was not just the idle curiosity of one who has personal experience, more of a professional study.

"Specimens of all four limbs," he remarked. "Catering for

amputations at different joints. Some of them have been used, but not all."

"What does it mean?" I asked.

"Unless she's able to regrow them like an insect, I'd guess that Mrs. Durham currently has a severe shortage of natural extremities. Something has eaten them away, gradually, judging by the varying ages of the replacements."

"The *Al-Azif* is playing tricks on her," I said.

Four steps led down from the hall to an L-shaped room, what some might have called a vestibule or ante-room leading to the dining room, conservatory and back parlor. The walls were decorated with fish in glass cases and the heads of stuffed animals, but what arrested us was the form sprawled in the shadows. Cross saw it at the same time as I did. His light clicked on, and the yellow circle captured a prone figure.

At first, I thought it must be Mrs. Durham, who had fallen down the stairs and injured herself. For some reason I even thought that we were responsible, that she must have heard us breaking in and was fleeing when she tripped and fell. I was wrong on both counts. The body was not Mrs. Durham, nor was it an accidental fall.

"Recognize him?" asked Cross.

The man was dressed all in black, but it was the red beard that finally clued me. This was the third anarchist, the one who had been in Rosebery's, bidding against us for the collection of books. His face was unnaturally pale. The pallor of death.

Cross moved the light across the body, across his chest and abdomen and down. There was no sign of any blood or any injury until we inspected his legs. A slender rod, something like a quill pen without the feathering, projected from below his knee. Cross tapped it gingerly with the end of his stick; the quill was embedded firmly in the man's leg.

"A poison dart," he said out loud. "Or something of that ilk."

He flicked the beam of the light around, perhaps looking for the source of the lethal instrument, but there was no tripwire or other indication of a booby-trap.

Noises reached us from outside, and Cross snapped the

light out at once. The kitchen door opened, and then sounded like a drunken man staggering around, bashing against the furniture, followed by a peculiar tappety-tapping sound and scraping.

The sounds were getting closer.

Cross moved swiftly and quietly, back into the hall and up the stairs to the landing. I was right behind him.

"If she's down there," he said, "then she can't be up here. We can search the bedroom."

"What if that's not her down there?" I asked.

"I'd rather take my chances with her than whatever that is," he said.

The bedroom door was not locked. I opened it as quietly as I could. Cross had his Mauser drawn. You could tell the room was unoccupied even without being able to see. There was no sound of breathing, and it did not have the feel of human presence. After a moment I clicked on my torch, shining it at the wall and half-covering the light to reduce the chances of waking her.

We were the room's only occupants. On the bedside cabinet were a grey wig and a nightcap. Beside them was something which might have been a funnel made of pale wood and which I had not noticed there before.

The quilt had been thrown aside, revealing a deep depression in the bed. A quantity of stuffing had been removed to create a deep nest or hollow in the mattress. I tried to visualise the size and shape of the person who could occupy it and appear to be human when covered with bedding.

Speculation was futile. What we needed was to find the book. There were a number of religious and inspirational works on the dresser and in a corner shelf. While we were engaged in searching there was a sound from the stairs, and Cross's gun was again in his hand, but the muffled noise quickly receded again.

I was looking through the wardrobe when I heard a sound from Cross. The bedside cabinet yielded a volume of unmistakable antiquity. It was surprisingly small, and the cracked and stained cover bore no title, but there could not be another like it.

"Jackpot," said Cross, slipping the book into an interior pocket. "You might wish to egress via the window, but I'm afraid I'll be taking the stairs."

I had considered the possibility of avoiding the staircase and whether a rope could be improvised by knotting the bedclothes as they do in films about prison escapes, but Cross has firm ideas of his own physical limitations.

"I'll come with you," I said.

I opened the door and listened. Stealthy as cats, we slipped out on to the upper landing, and stopped again to listen.

I moved to go first, but Cross held up a hand and went instead. The expedition was his idea, and he meant to lead it and take the consequences. Such was his sense of honor in spite of the tactical disadvantages of a man who walked with a stick being in the lead.

Walking downstairs in dappled moonlight was not so easy. For one thing, the light sometimes seemed so bright that it left you dazzled and you could not see where you were putting your feet in the gloom. And we stopped at every slightest sound, as though in a children's game, ready perhaps to dash back upstairs if we were found out.

We reached the hallway and stood there a moment with bated breath. It was not easy to tell in the gloom, but there was no sign of the dark outline of the anarchist's body.

Something was scraping and tapping outside. A shadow moved across the frosted glass window beside the front door. It was moving too fast and was too indistinct to make it out properly, but it was not a human being. Even if it had once been human.

Cross nudged me and we both fell back towards the kitchen. There was another exit there, and it would put the house between us and whatever was out front.

The kitchen was black as pitch, the high windows facing in the wrong direction. The door was locked, and I fumbled around for a key on shelves and ledges by the door, felt around and found the key dangling on a string.

I was just fitting the key into the lock when the front door opened, and something came in.

The kitchen door was still open behind us. Cross moved to close it, but it took him longer to cover those three steps than the thing took to cover twice that distance across the hall.

No light fell directly on it then, I did not get much sense of what the creature looked like, except that it was big and low, and it undulated as it moved like a series of breaking waves. Cross tried to close the door with both hands, dropping his stick in the process, and the thing reared up and slammed into the door on the other side with a hollow boom.

Partially closing the door shut out most of what little light there was; I turned on my torch, and the circle caught Cross struggling with something as shaggy as a bear. Instead of letting go of the door with one of his hands, he shoved the creature back with a foot.

That was a mistake.

Even as I recognized the thing as an immense grey-green caterpillar, bristling with long quills as sharp as thorns, Cross impaled his foot. Two of the quills had run right through his boot at different angles.

I seized Cross's stick, and, like a boatman pushing off, gave the thing a mighty shove. Cross roared, and his false leg with the boot on detached itself as the creature toppled backwards. Cross slammed the door and held on to it. A second later the creature thudded against the other side, its many legs rattling against the wood.

"Leave me!" Cross shouted. He was holding on to the door hand with one hand—there was no bolt or lock and fumbling into this pocket for a gun with the other, while trying to keep his balance on one leg.

"We're leaving together," I told him.

"Impossible," he said. "Save yourself, I'll hold it off at long as I can."

"Out of my way," I said. I had hauled a substantial wooden drying-rack from its cubby hole, and I shoved Cross aside to wedge it firmly under the door handle. It would hold for a few seconds at least, perhaps more.

"Harry," he said hopelessly. "I can't make it—"

His words were cut short as I leaned over and hoisted Cross

over my shoulder in a fireman's lift. Cross was not a small man, and he was by no means underfed. He was the heaviest man I ever carried, but I am used to loads. I was hauling a sheep carcass on each shoulder in my father's shop when I was fifteen, and the howitzer shells I lugged about in the War were heavier than those. I thought I should at least be able to stagger for a hundred feet with Cross, given the added incentive of that thing behind us.

"My hat," said Cross and for some reason I stooped and picked it up before flinging open the door to the garden and loping awkwardly down the path. It was easier than I thought, though it would be very easy to overbalance as I lurched dangerously with every overburdened step.

I made it down the path, in and out of the beams of moonlight bright as searchlights, flung the garden gate open and charged through. I ran into and practically knocked over the man who had been waiting on the other side.

There was an astonished pause as I took in the situation. There were half a dozen of them all told, mainly couched furtively in the shadows.

"It's Stubbs!" snapped a female voice. I recognised Parker.

There was nothing for it. I hit the man next to me squarely on the solar plexus, and even as he folded over I threw a quick left at the jaw of another who another who was raising a pistol.

If I put Cross down he could never escape. I could hardly fight with a man over my shoulder though, and my tactics from here on were shaky to say the least.

Another anarchist was too far away to reach, but I unhooked the pry bar from my other shoulder and threw it. It spun through the air and struck his forehead, so he reeled backwards.

A shot pinged off the wall beside me. It was answered by a burst of gunfire from under my arm. Hanging upside down from my shoulder, Cross was nevertheless endeavoring to return fire.

I turned around to give Cross a clearer field of fire. There were a mixture of gunshots and running feet as the anarchists scattered while I lumbered down the street away from them.

I doubt whether I could have made it very far before one of them shot us, but there was a hefty boom and shattering of glass behind me as Cross fired his flare pistol into a parked car. The thing burned furiously, putting a wall of smoke and flame between us and the anarchists. The car itself did not explode, but the risk that it might probably deterred the anarchists from approaching it.

I was daring to hope we might be getting clean away when someone stepped out from behind a tree twenty feet ahead of me with a gun in his hand.

"Stubbs," he said, squinting as he tried to make out what I was carrying.

It was Cameron. I felt Cross move and heard a metallic click. He was out of ammunition.

The anarchist leader raised his pistol.

Cameron's shadow leaped out beside him and he turned to see the source of the light. There was a rush and a thump, and he was flying across the bonnet of the car which screeched to a stop inches from me. Cameron hit the ground heavily, his gun clattering across the pavement. He may have been still moving, but he was out of the fight.

As in all the best Westerns, the cavalry had arrived in the nick of time.

Bear had left the doors unfastened and they swung open. I bundled Cross inside unceremoniously and followed him in. This was not such as easy feat as the car was already in motion, accelerating and turning wildly.

I do not rightly know what happened after I lost sight of that scene. I had the impression of some commotion on the far side of the burning car. The anarchists had encountered the thing that came through the garden gate just a few seconds behind us, and that was keeping them occupied.

In any event, Bear was able to drive off without a scratch, though he had left something of a dent in the bonnet where he had struck Cameron. Cross was not so lucky; a bullet had creased his shoulder and he was swearing freely as he clambered up from the footwell into the seat.

"It's not serious," he growled at me when I asked. "But it's bloody painful all the same."

"Whoo-ee!" said Bear. "That was kinda close."

"You took your time coming," said Cross. That seemed a little unfair considering he had saved our bacon.

"They jumped me while I was waiting for you," said Bear. "One of them was in the car, keeping me covered. But when you all came out and started shooting he got distracted. I bet he never knew what hit him."

"Good work," I said.

"Did you get the book?"

"We surely did," said Cross, using his handkerchief as a pad to hold to the wound. "It cost me a leg, and a good boot, a bullet hole in me and in my coat, and some wear and tear on my nerves—but we did indeed get it. Damned unfair I have to be the one getting hit again. Stubbs is a much bigger target."

"That reminds me—permission to fire granted retrospectively," I said.

"Thank you kindly," he said.

"Was that thing a… a caterpillar?" I asked.

"Mrs Durham had plenty of reason to regret her life," said Cross, nodding. "I think she wanted another chance. She wanted to be young again—but for insects, being young means something rather different."

The newspaper reports the next day talked about a disturbance and damage caused by hooligans letting off fireworks and deliberately setting a car on fire. This was accompanied by the usual diatribes about the poor morals of young people these days.

Any investigation would surely have turned up plenty of evidence of the action, but in the absence of any serious crime, or witnesses, neither the police nor the gentlemen of the press troubled themselves much over it. The anarchists retrieved their casualties, which is commendable in a group which might be expected to lack espirit de corps.

Mrs Durham retreated to her lair, back behind her high walls. Without the *Al-Azif* she had no chance of reversing its effects. However, it is highly doubtful whether anything else she brewed up with its help would have left her in any better condition. The book had passed out of her possession forever.

I would never invite Miss De Vere to anywhere as vulgar as the Electric Café. In truth the proprietor and the customers might be flustered to find a woman in their midst, and a beautiful one at that. Lyons Corner House was not much better, but at least it was the sort of café frequented by ladies, some of them from the better classes.

Miss De Vere was resplendent in a shimmery outfit of oyster grey. She was the most glamourous figure in the room by some margin; necks craned as other customers tried to take discrete looks. With her looks and American accent, people probably thought she was a Hollywood starlet, with her bodyguard. Around us, the waitresses bustled and the clientele sipped tea and attacked their cake with tiny forks. I had almost finished mine, but the cup in front of her was untouched and she wore an expression of bored irritation. But she kept turning the diamond bracelet on her wrist around and around.

She was untroubled about the Professor and Miss Durham, almost amused by what had happened to them. Without the book, she did not believe anyone could replicate what had happened to them. She was equally unconcerned about what Cross knew. Apparently, she was already aware of him, and saw him as a clownish but occasionally useful contact. She noted the address of the anarchists' lair though, and I had no doubt that she would arrange a police raid and retrieve the bookmark in the aftermath. Miss De Vere was always careful about loose ends.

It was the location of the Al-Azif itself that troubled her. And she was not patient.

"Did you know that the Mad Mahdi died of typhus?" I said. "That was what put an end to his whole crusade. But what interests me is that typhus is a disease carried by insects. So what I was wondering was if one of his followers opened the book and – "

She cut off my wondering with a look.

It was one-minute past ten by the clock over the counter.

"I don't care if he's dead and his brain riddled with maggots," she said. "I care if you can't find the book. Why did you have to give it to him?"

She could not understand that, as Cross had assured me his

client would only need it for a short time before giving it into my care for keeps, I had not hesitated to let him take the *Al-Azif*. He explained that his client was aware of the danger, but that she was entitled to make her own decisions. In any case, he gave his word to return it, and, him being an officer and a gentleman, I could hardly doubt his fidelity. He had seemed very confident that at all events he would not be harmed himself. He simply wanted the book for his client.

I was on the lookout for Cross' blue coat, but the next person to enter was a messenger boy in a bottle-green uniform, cap pushed back on his head. He stood in the middle of the tea room for a moment, peering around as if through a thick fog, unabashed by the looks he was getting. He was on an important mission; they always are. His eye lit on me and a smile broke across his face. Someone must have given him a verbal description of my appearance and he was gratified to identify me so easily.

"Mister Stubbs, ain't it?" he said, with the casual air, just short of insolence, native to all messenger boys. "Parcel for you. An' I should tell you that clock's two minutes fast, so I'm not late actually."

He thrust a brown paper package, fastened with twine, into my hands, then waited with an expectant air. I fished out a coin for him. In my relief I overtipped him with two shillings. He blinked exaggeratedly, grinned and pretended to bite the coin to see if it was real.

"Thank you sir," he said, and doffed his cap cheekily to Miss De Vere. "And very pleased to meet *you*, Miss."

She ignored him. Her eyes were locked on to the package, which was of a size and shape to suggest a small book. I duly unwrapped it and found, not only the volume I had expected, but a long strip of newspaper and a letter.

Dear Stubbs,

Book enclosed as per agreement.
Client acted as expected, in spite of l warnings, cautions, &c.
Enclosed cutting buries what happened in half-truths. Amateurs.
Expect you can piece it together easy enough.
Am now in funds and hurrying to Alexandria post haste as have
just been advised Sofia Codex found there!! Don't intend it will get
away from me again. I am one step ahead of the Turk this time.
Great pleasure doing business. Best regards to Skinner if seen --
remind him he owes me.
Yrs in haste,

Capt. X

I don't think he had previously mentioned this Turk, or
anything to do with Alexandria, but the Captain lived in the
midst of his own torrent of adventure and was doubtless bound
for new perils and prizes.

I had almost expected Miss De Vere to snatch the book as
soon as I unwrapped it, like a cat after a mouse. Instead she
asked me something quite unexpected.

"What's the clipping?"

It was from yesterday's paper, I could not tell which one, but
it was one of those newssheets which specialized in sensational
crime stories. And this time there was a tale which did not need
any of their usual embellishments or suppositions, with violent
and bloody death in a fashionable hotel in the heart of London.
We read it together.

Miss G was a lady from a good family with considerable
academic achievement but rather plain looks. The death of her
parents had left her comfortably off, but in spite of her sound
financial situation she had failed to attract a husband. This was
perhaps in consequence of her apparent preference for dashing
young officers rather than the staid landowners, respectable
clerics or older commercial gentlemen who would be her more
natural mates.

Miss G had even been to university, and it was in this that I detected the roots of the tendency which proved fatal. Somewhere in her career she must have come across accounts of the *Al-Azif* and its miraculous powers. That in time had led her to seek out Cross and offer him an extravagant sum to locate the book. The offer had been made some time ago, but he had never forgotten it, and when the anarchists unwittingly passed him the clue he needed, Cross had succeeded at last in delivering the book to her.

Miss G had not needed the *Al-Azif* for long. It seemed that, like everyone else who wanted it, she had a single purpose in mind. I can only guess as how she deciphered it, or how she found what she wanted. I suspect though that the book responds quite rapidly to a powerful will, and the recipe may have appeared in plain English the first time she opened it, the letters shaping themselves before her eyes.

Miss G would not be the first person to seek for a love philter, though in her case the results were more dramatic than most. Her target was a cavalry lieutenant, an outstanding horseman and polo player of some repute who was much sought-after ornament on the capital's social scene. According to the newspaper report, Miss G had met him twice before. He had made a lasting impression; his framed photograph was found on her dressing table. It seems doubtful if the Lieutenant, who had relations with a a number of debutantes, had noticed the dowdy middle-aged woman in these encounters. However, when they met again, seemingly by chance, outside a saddler, he had been unable to take his eyes off her. The friend who was with him was puzzled by his behavior, finding in Miss G nothing much to look at, and her conversation no more than banal. The one thing he did notice about her was a scent, not quite like any perfume and yet not like anything else either. Cross had scribbled a note in the margin: "CF Spanish fly—beetle extract."

The Lieutenant had sent his friend off to his club, saying that he would join him later for cards. This he never did. The couple were seen walking round Green Park, arm in arm; an acquaintance of the Lieutenant's assumed that he was accompanying his aunt. The Lieutenant and Miss G went to a restaurant where they took a private room. A waiter, bribed no doubt by the newspaperman, said that the couple drank champagne freely but ate only a few bites of the meal they ordered, and held hands the entire time. They were clearly romantically involved, which excited some comment among the staff.

Afterwards the pair repaired to a nearby hotel, which the newspaper tactfully left un-named, and checked in to adjoining rooms with a connecting door. The normal rules of decency had to be observed, even if the two made little attempt to hide their growing physical intimacy.

A certain amount of sound is normal in hotels, though the night porter had that he had never heard quite so much noise made over quite such a prolonged period even from the honeymoon suite. It was not until the next morning that the horror of what had occurred became apparent. The Lieutenant's lifeless body was found, the sheets soaked in blood from a most terrible wound to his neck which had killed him. Miss G was discovered nearby, naked and bloody but uninjured, in an advanced state of shock and hysteria.

The version of events preferred by the police was that the Lieutenant, after too much to drink, had lured her into his room and assaulted her. Miss G had chanced to pick up a razor or similar instrument and, in defending herself from his advances, had by luck fatally slashed his throat. This newspaper mocked the police's account, attacking it on all points. A bellboy who had seen the body said that the wound was not the clean one that would have been left by a sharp instrument but looked more like the work of a wild animal. The Lieutenant had been savaged so viciously that his head was barely still attached to his body, and moreover there were clear bite marks on his face and shoulders.

Some were puzzled that the Lieutenant, a powerful and athletic man, should be unable to fend off a small woman, even one driven by vampiric fury. But the extent and nature of the wounds suggested that they had been carried out over a prolonged period, and that the Lieutenant had been a willing participant throughout.

Cross had scribbled something in the margin here: "CF certain species of mantis. Also Black Widow (tho' spider not an insect)." Miss G's mental state was uncertain. It seemed likely that she would be in an institution for some time, if not permanently.

"She got what she wanted," concluded Miss De Vere. "She got her heart's desire. I guess he did too. Romantic, wouldn't you say?"

There was laughter in them, a dark laughter, in her blue eyes. Now the book was here her mood had lightened.

"You had better take this," I said, handing her the book.

"Don't you want to find out what it could do for you? Just take a little peek?"

"No, thank you," I said. The book didn't feel like a book. It felt like a living thing and every part of me was repulsed by it except a small curious bit. A part I hated.

"Smart," she said.

She weighed the book in her hand like someone trying to guess what a parcel contains by shaking it.

"You're not going to read it," I said.

"Of course not," she said. "You know Americans. I'll wait for the movie."

Then Miss De Vere slipped the *Al-Azif* into her handbag.

"Will you destroy it?" I asked.

"When the time is right," she said, standing up. I wondered if this meant that she lacked the means to do it, at least for the time being. By Cross' account the *Al-Azif* would take some destroying. "But first, there's a university in New England that is interested in old books—a little bit too interested in the wrong sort of old books. I'm going to lend it to them, see what happens."

She waited to see how I would object, but there was no point in rising to this sort of baiting.

"Have a pleasant journey, Miss De Vere."

"So long, Stubbs."

A faint whiff of perfume trailed behind her, then Miss De Vere and the book were gone. I breathed considerably easier. Perhaps I would have been tempted to open it, if the book had stayed in my possession. Cross, for all his mad dashing about, was a man who was satisfied with life. All he wanted was to be on the trail of the next rare find. I doubt whether it would have occurred to him try to do anything about his lost leg, and in any case he was wise enough not to meddle with the *Al-Azif.*

I would not claim to be quite so wise myself. That book had a way of getting through to people. Perhaps, as Cross thought, it was just an ignorant servant that tried to do the right thing. I was not so sure, and I suspect it manipulated people for its own unguessable ends, carrying out its own experiments with us. I did not wish to become an experiment. Temptation was gone from me, and the cursed book was bound to another continent.

I ordered another pot of tea and some crumpets to celebrate.

ANDREW DORAN AND THE CRAWLING CAVES

An Andrew Doran Adventure

By. Matthew Davenport

Miskatonic University, Massachusetts

I had maps and historical texts stretched out in a mess across my desk. For the first time in as long as I could remember, I looked the part of my title as dean of a prestigious college.

Slamming my hands down in frustration, I shouted, "Are you sure that your dad's journal said South Africa?"

My assistant, Nancy Dyer, came into my office from the adjoining room. She threw her father's journal onto my desk.

"For the last time, you know that I can't read the journal anymore."

Nancy's father had written his journal under the influence of an ancient alien city. Nancy had only been able to read it while she was under the same influence.

Walking to where the journal had landed, she pulled a folded sheet of paper from it and held it up to me. "That's everything I was able to translate, and yes, the directions very specifically state that the *Book of Eibon* is in a pyramid in South Africa."

I didn't even look at the sheet of paper in Nancy's hand.

"There are no pyramids in South Africa." I was getting annoyed and not for the first time.

"Dad was a geologist, not a historian," Nancy said. "You're the historian; figure it out."

As frustrated as I was, Nancy had made a valid point. I wasn't just a warrior against the misuse of the occult, I also carried a doctorate in anthropology. Instead of alleviating my distress, the thought only served to annoy me further.

"If that book falls into the hands of the Germans," I explained through gritted teeth, "the end of the world will be the only positive outcome."

"Then," Nancy replied, "get to work." She scooped up one of the books of maps and took it over to the chair that I had once thought of as Leo's.

Leo had been my friend and assistant, and after he'dbeen mortally wounded, I had helped him make the transition to another universe. It was a place where he could continue to survive and build a life for himself. He lives in the Dream Lands between our reality and the veil, and his chair in my office has been inherited by my newest assistant.

Giving up on my previous line of thought regarding the location of the *Book of Eibon,* I grabbed Nancy's translation from the desk and unfolded it. I read it without really paying attention as another idea floated into my mind.

"South Africa is believed to be where modern man took his first steps. That's where humanity as we know it today was born." I paused as thoughts started to coalesce. "But we know that humanity was aware of the ancient gods in those days as well."

"So?" Nancy looked up from the book of maps.

This time gave the translation my full attention. "Maybe this isn't about a pyramid as we know it, but more of a tomb."

"Like a cave?"

I nodded. "Like a cave."

At that moment, Carol Berg, my secretary and nagging office wife stepped into my office.

"Shit," I said with mock exclamation. "You found me."

Carol flashed a sarcastic smile that showed a sharper set of teeth than the usual person was known to have. She was a Wendigo, but despite that, she was the best administrative assistant that Miskatonic had ever had on staff. It helped that she had outlived most of the staff by over a century.

"Charming as usual," she sighed and set the mail on top of the maps spread across my desk. She eyed the mess and raised an eyebrow. "I won't even ask if you've signed the renovation contracts yet."

I had been stacking books by the door that needed to be returned to the catalogue. She picked up the stack easily with her inhuman strength. "There's a letter from your sister in that pile."

"My sister?" I was surprised. I hadn't heard from my sister in almost as many years as it had been since I had originally left Miskatonic University. Around that same time, I had been involved in events that had devastating consequences for our family. I was unsure of my sister's thoughts on the subject. I never reached out to her out of concern it might cause problems. I didn't know if she needed space, or if she would blame me, so I chose to remove myself from the equation. I hadn't received a letter from her since.

"You have a sister?" Nancy tossed the book of maps at Carol's feet. The secretary sighed and picked it up..

Much like the rest of my life, the topic of my family was a convoluted mess that had become mired in the darkness beyond the veil. They were my proof that Miskatonic University's stance on meddling with the darker arts couldn't be done without paying a cost.

Fortune favors the mundane, though, and my sister, thus far, had managed to avoid having anything to do with my world.

"Yes," I answered Nancy's question. "We don't talk much. She's a school teacher in upstate New York." I grabbed the pile of mail and dug through it until I found the letter. It was a plain envelope with my name written as "Andy Doran." The return address was in Harrisville, New York, and had my sister's name above it.

Nancy was quickly looking over my shoulder.

"Mary Doran?" Nancy smirked as she read over my shoulder. "I'm in suspense. Open it and let's see what your mysterious sister has to say."

I had to admit that I was curious too. I tore open the end of the envelope and let the letter fall out.

Andy,

I know we haven't talked since what happened with Mom, but this letter isn't for catching up. I need your help.

The mountains have swallowed the people. That's what everyone is saying. Over the last year, men, women, and children have gone missing from the village of Harrisville, where I teach. The children are the latest to start disappearing and were what galvanized my interest in this mystery.

Where Harrisville is located, near the end of the Adirondack Mountain range, many wild theories have been made and have gained fuel as rumor. They've muddied any real facts that I've managed to gather. The rumors range from cults in the foothills to the very mountains themselves seeking vengeance on the locals for some imagined atrocity.

All of the rumors, and one discovery, are strange things.

Occult things.

Your thing, not mine. Until a week ago.

Last week, one of my students who had gone missing a month ago, returned. He wasn't himself and he mostly spoke in tongues that I didn't recognize. The few things that he said in English only served to add fire to the rumors or confirm that there is something cult-related happening.

While I stated that I didn't recognize most of his words, one language did sound familiar as what I've heard of it has forever been etched into my mind. They were the last words that I heard Mom speak in that damned language you taught her.

If that wasn't enough to convince me to write you, the boy's next words were. He began chanting the name Al-Azif.

While we are a small town of mostly loggers and farmers, we know who to call when strange words need to be researched. We called the anthropology department at the nearby State University of New York in Potsdam. They told us that Al-Azif is the name of an ancient book currently in the possession of Miskatonic University.

I called Miskatonic and was proud to hear that you were recently given the title of dean. Congratulations. While it pleased me to hear of your success, I was equally displeased to hear that no one knew how to get a hold of you.

Whatever our disagreements, Andy, I need your help. Adam, the boy, hasn't eaten since his return. I've been working with Potsdam to research this Al-Azif cult and what they could possibly want, but information about the Al-Azif is almost impossible to find. You're the only person I know who understands anything about this occult stuff. Please come and help us.

Love, Mary

Underneath her signature was the address and phone number for Harrisville Central School, where she worked.

I set the letter down on my desk and contemplated it. I didn't stop Nancy from picking it up and reading through it.

When she finished, she passed it to Carol before asking, "What happened with your mother?"

I shook my head and pushed maps off my desk until I found the phone. "Nothing worth rehashing right now." Rage suddenly flooded my mind as I realized that, once again, a powerful tome was at fault for putting those that I cared about in danger. "Not while both the *Book of Eibon*, and now the *Al-Azif* are threatening more lives."

I dialed the number at the bottom of the letter and waited for someone to answer.

"Hello," came the sharp, yet pleasant, voice on the other end of the call. "Harrisville Central, this is Barb speaking."

"Hi, Barb," I said, "This is the dean from Miskatonic University in Massachusetts. I'm trying to reach Mary Doran."

The call was short, but Barb had confirmed most of what I had already feared. I hung up the phone and turned to face Carol and Nancy.

"They haven't seen her in a week. They think she's been," I hesitated before using Barb's words, "swallowed by the mountains."

"Like the rest of the missing?" Nancy asked.

I nodded and focused my attention on Carol.

"Where is it?"

Carol knew what I was referencing and answered quickly. "It is in the armory. In the locked corridors. Only the dean, you, are physically allowed to retrieve it."

I grimaced at that. The locked corridors were magically warded against intrusion on a level that made the rest of the armory look like an open field. Retrieving the *Al-Azif* might be more difficult than I had previously thought. Of course, since when has retrieving a book been a simple matter for me? "First, I'll get the *Al-Azif* and then I'll go find my sister."

"Wait," Nancy's face furrowed with concern. "Where's what? The *Al-Azif*? What is it?"

I sighed before I explained. "There are a lot of answers to that question, and while I don't think any of them are correct, I don't think any of them are wrong either. Historically, it is the book that the insane Abdul Al'Hazred wrote when he was dying in the desert."

Nancy shook her head, "No, that's the *Necronomicon*."

"Yes and no," I answered. "The *Necronomicon* is the final draft. The *Al-Azif* was written by a man who claimed to hear the words of the universe in the chirps of the desert bugs. Either that or it was the book which Abdul Al'Hazred used to write the *Al-Azif*. When you accept that, the next question you have to ask is how someone wrote an entire book while they were in a desert with no supplies."

"Alright, how?" Nancy asked.

I shrugged. "You don't do the writing. A lot of the theories out there are centered around the book being alive. That if you listen to the chirping long enough, you start to understand the language of the insects, and if you can truly understand the language, maybe you can ask them to write the words for you." Nancy's face showed that she wasn't understanding, and I didn't blame her. N nobody truly understood the *Al-Azif*. "Insects have been here since the dawn of time. They have seen everything and Al'Hazred briefly understood the secrets of our reality, and many more, when he wrote that book. It's distilled power in an alien language that no one can understand. I've heard stories that it works like a kind of misunderstanding granter of wishes, offering you what you want, but twisting it into something horrible."

Personally, I didn't entirely believe my own theory. Abdul Al'Hazred had become a figure of myth over the centuries and that was not including the fact he wrote about aliens, gods, spirits, ghosts, and ultraterrestial beings. Distilling fact from fiction was often an exercise in futility. Not that I didn't stop trying.

Nancy's eyes lit up. "Like the Monkey's Paw?"

I didn't know the reference. "Maybe, I don't know, but that's just one myth of its power. I've heard others say that book itself is a conduit to all of space and time, existing outside of it as a vast intelligence. There have been stories of rulers using it for guidance, getting prophetic messages from the future about crops or approaching armies. Other stories say that it is an avatar of the Crawling Chaos, Nyarlathotep, spreading god-like power like a disease that consumes its host."

"Which is it?" Nancy pressed.

Carol answered, "Everything I have ever heard says that it is all of those things. It isn't a book, like the *Necronomicon*. The *Necronomicon*'s power is in the knowledge that is learned from it. The *Al-Azif* is power itself. Power with a mind."

"And you're just going to take the *Al-Azif* with you to save your sister. Right into the hands of the monsters who want it?"

"If they want the book, then it might be the only thing I have to bargain for my sister." I held up my hand as Nancy started to point out an obvious concern. "Don't worry, I'm not going to give them the book, not even for family, but if I don't have it with me, they'll know."

"Are you going to use it?" Nancy's concern was evident.

Carol answered for me, and for a moment I saw a foreign emotion cross the Wendigo's face. She was afraid. "You don't use the *Al-Azif*," she answered. "It uses you."

"I'll get the truck," Nancy said as she stood.

"No," I said before Nancy could leave the office. "You're not coming with me."

"Excuse me?" Nancy crossed her arms. "Evil cults have kidnapped your sister and are going to leverage her to get a powerful book from you and I'm not coming with you?" Her brow furrowed as she glared at me. "You're crazy if you think you're going alone."

"No, I'm delegating authority." I pointed at her father's journal. "Our time is running out and we need to find the *Book of Eibon*. You're the leading authority on understanding his work." I held up my hand as she started to argue. "And this is a family matter. I have to go, but you need to figure out where that book is hidden."

"I can't figure this out on my own," Nancy countered.

I shook my head. "And you won't do this on your own." I nodded toward Carol. "If the answers are anywhere, they are in this university. Carol has been here for a long time." I ignored my secretary's glare and continued, "If anyone can find those answers, it's her."

"I would thank you, Dr. Doran, but I am not sure if that was a compliment or an insult."

Winking at Carol, I said, "A compliment, of course. I am an archaeologist. The older you get, the more I care."

Carol rolled her eyes and turned toward the door. "Come with me, Ms. Dyer. I will show you where the books regarding South Africa's prehistory are located. One was actually annotated by your father."

Nancy hesitated before following Carol. "Are you sure?"

I smirked. "If I know Mary, she's already subdued the cultists with her stern look. I'll probably be saving them."

She gave me a half-smile and turned to follow Carol to the library.

The Armory, Miskatonic University

The first time that I had stepped into Miskatonic's secret armory, I had been impressed. The armory is a vast catalogue of occult artifacts from all over the world. Some were powerless and simply used during rituals by occult groups. A dagger from the Esoteric Order of Dagon, or the paintings from the deplorable Richard Upton Pickman fell under that label. No power to them but such dark terror associated with them that removing them from the public sphere was deemed the only safe action to take.

Then there were the other artifacts with aspects beyond the understanding of normal men. My pistol and sword were both such items. While I had yet to learn the history of my monster-killing gun, I had recently had the chance to come back down to the armory and read the provenience card. The 1840 non-commissioned cavalry sword that I carried was known as the Blade of Captain Fitz. The card didn't speak to the history of the sword, so much as to how it was made, but I knew something of Captain Fitz from my studies and was able to fill in the gaps. Captain Arlington Fitz was the leader of the First Regiment of the United States Esoteric Cavalry. The USEC was the government's answer to the encroachment of the occult on their New World.

They had my job.

The provenience card only had the following to say:

Forged in the fires from another world and with metal found in a crater in Montana. It was blessed by American Natives to corrupt the beasts of other worlds.

Properties: Nothing foreign to this plane of existence can withstand the touch of this sword's blade.

All of the artifacts in the armory had similar cards, although most of them recorded a vague list of properties or were only labeled with "Unknown" and the year that it was entered into the armory.

Thousands of artifacts and weapons filled the shelves and lined the walls of the armory, but unlike the first time I'd visited, I wasn't particularly impressed by the sight.

Instead, as I walked the aisles lined with the most dangerous artifacts of the Earth's history, I only saw the thousands upon thousands of items that weren't there. Every day, more pieces of alien technology, of spirits from beyond the void, and from history's dark past, passed into the wrong hands, and when that happened, people died.

Or worse.

Miskatonic's armory had become for me a monument to the amount of work I still had left to do.

I felt the energies of the things calling out to me. They begged to be used, promising me the fortunes of entire kingdoms for only a moment of contact. Knowledge has always been the truest of powers, and my knowledge of the truth behind these articles protected me from succumbing to any of their false promises. Not everyone would have been so strong, and I feared the day that some hapless student of the university stumbled upon the secret entrance to the armory and managed to make it past the wards.

I turned off of the center aisle and made my way to the nearest wall. The books in the armory were locked in glass cases along the walls, and I didn't need Carol's great memory to know that the *Al-Azif*, the oldest and possibly most powerful of any of the books, would be in the back.

The further in I went, the more stained and aged the cases appeared.. The final case, in a poorly lit corner, was covered with protective inscriptions and housed only one book.

The *Al-Azif* was an ancient tome and looked the part, but even its weathered brown pages and rotted brown cover didn't speak to the book's actual age. The provenience card was barely legible. It read:

Collected by Brandon Smythe on a trip to Norwood, London. 1925. Properties Unknown.

Taking a deep breath, I gritted my teeth and reached for the handle that would release the lid of the glass case. A lot of the more dangerous artifacts protected by wards such as those etched on the glass over the *Al-Azif*. Those protections were supposed to stop anyone from taking the artifacts except for the dean of Miskatonic University.

While I was currently holding that title, I had done very little to embody it. Sometimes magic cares about how you act as well as who you are. As I grasped the handle, a tingle of energy rushed up my arm. My vision clouded with the silhouette of a large man. The shadow thing raised its arm toward me and my mind flooded with waves of nausea. Fear followed, and doubt.

No sooner had the doubt entered my mind than my own spirit rebelled. If Miskatonic had been any other university, then

I would have been a failure as a member of the administrative staff. Miskatonic wasn't like any other University, though. Miskatonic University was the leading research center and central hub for all knowledge regarding the occult and things beyond the veil. That difference was enough to change my role as the dean from one of administration to the guardian and protector of that knowledge.

It also meant that I was directly responsible for the protection of our world from the beasts beyond the veil. In that regard, I faithfully embodied the title as fully as any who had held it before me.

And much more than Brandon Smythe ever had.

The fear and nausea fell away, and the shadow creature faded from my view. The latch on the glass case turned in my hand and I was able to lift the glass.

Sitting in the middle of the shelf was the *Al-Azif.*

I had brought a satchel from my office with my Colt .38 inside it. Lifting the flap , I used it to slide the book into the leather bag without touching it. I secured the flap, closed the case, and turned back the way I'd come.

With the *Al-Azif* in my possession, it was time to make my way to upstate New York.

Harrisville, New York

It took me the rest of the morning and some of the afternoon in Leo's truck before I reached the small village of Harrisville. The roads took me through the countryside of multiple states, but it was New York's Adirondack Mountains that captured my imagination the most. On each side of the road, hills sloped toward the sky. They were covered with pine trees whose trunks were almost red, and the green of their needles were hidden beneath a fine dusting of snow.

Even with the snow, the roads were excellent for driving, and I found myself reminiscing about my friend and his old truck. Calling it Leo's truck wasn't accurate. This truck belonged to Miskatonic University and said so in faded paint on the side. When Leo had first arrived in the United States, he quickly saw the value of having a vehicle to aid me in my missions and had appropriated the machine from the groundskeepers at the university.

My friend wasn't dead, not in the conventional sense, but at the same time that's exactly what he was. The spiritual idea of death is that our souls leave this plane of existence and travel to another for an eternal rest. In the most basic of ways, that's exactly what Leo had done. As his body had lain, bleeding out, I'd helped him move the essence of what and who he was to the Dream Lands, a plane of existence shaped and controlled by the thoughts and dreams of not only the living, but of every mind that has ever existed. It's both alien and familiar and time does not exist there in the way that we would think of it. Leo was in a new home of eternal rest and I was left in this world with a bodyto bury.

Unlike the others who I had lost over the years, I could still reach out to and, in a way, visit my friend occasionally, but it was dangerous. The odd physics of his new world, and the issues around how they experience time there meant that every time I tried to visit, I was forced to leave my body unattended for an unknowable amount of time. Every trip to the Dream Lands, I risked returning to my starved and forgotten corpse.

As I drove through those beautiful mountains, my mind drifted back to my sister, Mary. I tried not to dwell on the last time I'd seen her, and instead focused on memories of our childhood. In one way or another, my role has always been that of explorater, and protector.. I thirst for learning more, and using what I learn to protect those I deem to need protection. Mary was never needy. While almost a decade younger than me, she came to my aid more than I ever came to hers. I left home for Miskatonic when she was just getting into high school. I returned as frequently as I could to check on her, but never for her sake. I missed my sister and enjoyed our talks. It was those frequent visits home that led to the events of the last time I saw her.

I hoped she'd have forgiven me by the time I found her. Harrisville was a small town on the Oswegatchie River nestled in the foothills that marked the northwestern end of the

Adirondack Mountains. It was mostly made up of loggers and workers of the talc and zinc mines. The local school was a three-floor brick building in the middle of town. I parked Leo's truck on the road and left the satchel with the *Al-Azif* and my pistol in the cab.

I entered through the double doors; the administrative office was immediately on my right. As I stepped through the office door, I couldn't help but feel like Gulliver on the island of Lilliput. I hadn't attended this school, but most schools tend to give adults that awkward feeling. It's a place built for shorter people and, while I wasn't an exceptionally tall member of my species, I felt every bit of my stature.

The office had a green metal desk in the front and a side office with the closed door. Behind the green desk sat a sharply dressed young woman with brown hair. Her nameplate read Barb Scanlon.

"Can I help you?" she said, in a pleasant tone.

I extended my hand and shook hers. "Yes, I'm the dean of Miskatonic University in Massachusetts, Doctor Andrew Doran. I called this morning."

Barb's eyes lit up when I said my name. "Doran? Is Mary your...?"

"Sister," I answered.

She gasped loudly and put a hand over her mouth. "Oh my, and you heard about Mary from me?" She stood and patted my hand that was still on her desk with both of hers. "I am so sorry. I had no idea."

I did my best to react politely, but it was an awkward approach. Pulling my hand back, I said, "You were fine. It's alright. I'm just here to follow up on any more details you might have about her disappearance."

"There's not much to tell, I'm afraid," Barb explained. "Ever since that boy came back, she hasn't been coming in to the school. All of her time has been spent searching for answers."

It didn't surprise me that Mary had skipped work to hunt for answers so much as it surprised me that she was the only one. "People are disappearing from your town and only my sister thought to go look into it?"

Barb shook her head. "Not at all. The rangers have been organizing careful searches of the areas people where have gone missing." She sighed. "But when Adam came back, the organized searches weren't enough for her. That's when she went missing."

"Do you know where she was last seen?" It felt like Barb wanted to gossip more than help me, and I wasn't having any of it. "Can you tell me anything that can help me find my sister?"

The secretary's mood shifted from sympathy to impatience, which I thought was uncalled for given the fact that I was the one with family missing.

"No, I don't know where she went missing, but I'm sure the ranger station between Pitcairn and Cranberry Lake, east of here, would have some idea. Ms. Doran was organizing her searches from there." Barb started scribbling on a notepad as she continued. "That's all that I know."

"What about the boy, Adam?" I pulled the letter from Mary out of my pocket and held it up. "My sister wrote me and said the he was still alive, but not doing well. Has that changed?" The letter disappeared back into my pocket before Barb could grab it. The last thing I needed to be explaining to a local was that my sister thought the occult and magic were at play here. It would either serve to fuel the superstitions and rumors or it would cause the school secretary to decide I wasn't worth taking seriously. Either way, I didn't need my investigation crippled before it began.

"Adam Mitchell is still very sick." Sympathy filled her eyes. "That poor boy hasn't spoken more than gibberish since he came back."

Remembering what my sister had written about the *Al-Azif* and Adam's gibberish, I was interested in speaking with the boy. "I'd like to wish his family well. Where can I find him?"

"Adam's parents surrendered to his illness and have left him with Dr. Kellogg. Adam was taken to Dr. Kellogg's clinic," she leaned back and pointed over her shoulder toward the wall, "just down the street from here."

Barb gave me the very simple directions to Dr. Kellogg's clinic, which also happened to be his house. I thanked her for her time and headed back to the truck. While there, I grabbed the satchel but removed my gun from it. I didn't think I would need it when I was visiting with Adam Mitchell. Whatever was happening to the boy hadn't had any ill-effect on the rest of the village, so I was willing to bet I would be safe.

With that consideration in place, the satchel was still coming with me. I had a feeling it would be best to have the *Al-Azif* close at hand when I met the young Mr. Mitchell.

I left Leo's truck parked at the school and walked to Dr. Kellogg's house. Barb's directions had been incredibly easy to follow. They consisted of walking north until the first intersection and taking a left. The house that Dr. Kellogg used as his home and clinic was only one house down from the corner.

It was a two-story home on a hill raised up from the level of the road. I took the stone steps up to the porch and noticed that his last name was carved into the stone of the top step. The porch wrapped entirely around the house and had no furniture, aside from a bench on each side of the large front door.

On the door hung a wooden sign on a rope that read, "Open." I took that as an invitation and walked into the landing and makeshift waiting room for Dr. Kellogg's clinic.

The waiting room was empty. There weren't any nurses or patients. Instead, there was a sign-in sheet at the reception desk, and a series of chairs were lined up against the walls of what appeared to be an old-fashioned drawing room. Behind the stairs that led to the second floor was a door. I walked over and leaned in. There were voices on the other side. Not seeing any other options, I knocked.

The voices fell silent before the door opened to reveal a fully dressed elderly man sitting on an examination table and a middle-aged man standing at the door. The middle-aged man was obviously the doctor, as he had a white coat and a stethoscope around his neck.

"Can I help you?" Dr. Kellogg asked.

I addressed the man on the table, "Sorry to interrupt." Returning my attention to Dr. Kellogg, I introduced myself. "I'm Dr. Andrew Doran of Miskatonic University. When you have a moment, I would like to discuss one of your patients, Dr. Kellogg."

Dr. Kellogg shook my outstretched hand "Call me Scott. I'll be out in a minute." He then shut the door.

Less than a minute later, the elderly man exited from that same door and thanked Scott before leaving me alone with him.

"Doran, was it? Any relation to the school teacher?" He shoved his hands into the pockets of his lab coat after hanging the stethoscope on the banister.

"Yes," I answered. "She's my sister. I've come here to find her and maybe help with your town's situation."

Scott nodded. "I'm sorry about your sister. I guess you're here to meet with Adam then?"

I nodded. "Mary sent me a letter before she went missing and mentioned that he might be a clue to all of this."

The doctor sighed and started up the stairs. "Let's get this over with, then. He's upstairs."

We climbed the stairs to the second floor and passed two doors before stopping near the third.

"His condition hasn't improved," Scott explained in a whisper. "If anything, the symptoms have grown worse. He might not talk to you or make sense when he does."

"What are his symptoms?" I asked.

His shoulders sagged with the weight of the boy's prognosis. "Erratic heartbeat, strained breathing, clammy skin, no appetite, loss of memory, he's delirious at best, and he's been experiencing seizures."

"Seizures? Like epilepsy?" I asked.

Scott nodded. "His symptoms are consistent with extensive brain damage and some sort of infection. We've got him on a steady stream of medications, but nothing seems to be working."

I nodded and placed my hand on the door, but Dr. Kellogg stopped me, grabbing a bottle and a handkerchief from the nearby console table.

"He's been emitting a heavy smell," Scott explained. "I encourage you to splash this with some perfume and wear it."

He then proceeded to demonstrate, tying the handkerchief around his head, covering his nose and mouth. He looked like he was going to rob a train. I replicated his actions, then he opened the door.

The smell wasn't the first thing I noticed, but that was only because of the draft that struck us as we entered the room. The first thing that I noticed was the almost complete darkness. Before my eyes could adjust, the smell hit me.

The doctor hadn't been entirely forthcoming when he'd mentioned the symptoms Adam was experiencing, and the smell gave away another that hadn't been mentioned. The boy reeked of rot and death. Whatever he was experiencing, he was either dead or dying from it.

That was a problem I had discovered when dealing with the medical profession. As long as a person was moving, doctors always assumed that the person was still alive. Unfortunately, it was difficult to explain the matter of darker possibilities to a man of science. Even corpses can move, and just because a person is dead doesn't mean that their body is. How do you explain to a doctor that flesh is just a vessel, and when the person passes on, their body can become a home to something else? Something worse.

Dr. Kellogg stayed by the door as I approached the bed in the center of the far wall. Adam Mitchell lay under a set of heavy blankets, shivering.

"His seizures happen more frequently in the presence of light," Scott explained. "We haven't seen much improvement, but we've tried keep him comfortable."

Adam's body was doing more than shivering. He seemed to be in the throes of one of his seizures as I approached. I stepped forward, grabbed the blanket and pulled it back.

Even in the dim light, I saw how gray his flesh was. I was no doctor, but the seizure was also not what I'd expected it to be. Each limb twitched individually and without any rhythm. As my eyes adjusted, I noticed lesions all over his flesh. They were dry, and each one was a dark red. They didn't seem to be healing at all.

I decided to check on Adam's heartbeat. I reached forward and grabbed his wrist, feeling for a pulse. The moment I did, all of his seizing stopped.

Adam's other hand shot forward and grabbed my wrist like a vice. Heat radiated off of him. Slowly, his head turned toward me, and his eyes opened.

They were gray and seemed empty.

"We know you, Doran," Adam spoke with the voice of a child, but behind it were a series of clicks and hums that reverberated. "You stink of the book. Of the *Al-Azif*."

Scott Kellogg was suddenly at my side. "This is the most we've heard him say."

"You have not used the *Al-Azif*," the boy sounded curious. "Why?"

"That's hardly fair," I answered. "You know me, but I don't know you. Who are you?"

"We are Adam, but we are *more* Adam. Why haven't you used the *Al-Azif*?" he repeated.

I pulled against the grip, but Adam didn't want to let go. "What do you mean by 'use the *Al-Azif*?' How can it be used?"

Adam's gaze never wavered from mine as he explained. "Since the Mad Arab first asked for understanding, people have asked, and the *Al-Azif* has provided the answer. You have the book but have asked for nothing. If you ask, it will provide."

At what cost, though, I thought. *Lives are the fuel for black magic and this book may be the root of all.*

Twisting my wrist, I decided to look at Adam's. In the dim light I almost missed the black mark, no bigger than a fingernail, across the inside of his wrist. I looked closer and saw that it was a tattoo of the word, "more". As I stared at it, it seemed to move very slowly up his wrist and toward my hand.

I twisted my arm quickly toward the point where Adam's fingers touched and broke his hold on my wrist.

"What do you care? What does a little boy from Harrisville care about the *Al-Azif* or a dumb dean from Miskatonic University?" I demanded.

"The *Al-Azif* will help you get your sister back. You only need to ask." Adam's non-answers were frustrating me.

"Where did you learn to be 'more Adam'? Where is my sister?"

Adam's seizure was starting again, but slower than the last time. "The foothills. The forest. There are people there who are looking forward to your arrival." Adam's eyes closed, and the seizure resumed at its full pace. His eyes drifted shut and it was obvious that the conversation was over.

Scott was staring at Adam in shock. I turned to him and immediately asked, "The foothills? What are those?"

"He means the Adirondack Mountains, more specifically, the foothills of them on the southeast side of town, toward Cranberry Lake." He said, but it was obvious as he stared at me that his mind was elsewhere. "It's where people believe the disappearances have been happening."

"That's where I need to go, then." I started toward the door but was stopped as the doctor grabbed my wrist.

"That's the most he's said since we found him. Who are you and what the hell is the *Al-Azif*?"

I sighed and pulled my arm from his grip. "Mary believed that the disappearances were related to it. It's an ancient book," I hesitated before adding, "that some people believe holds magical power."

I didn't like leaving Adam in whatever condition he was in, but there was nothing I could do for him. There was a slim chance that if I could find whoever had done this to him, I could reverse it, but I wasn't holding out hope. While many had tried, there was no reversing death, and I was willing to bet that whatever had been answering my questions wasn't Adam. Adam wasn't home anymore.

Before I left the clinic, I pulled out my map and asked Scott Kellogg where exactly I might find the foothills of the Adirondack Mountains.

Dr. Kellogg's directions led me through the village of Harrisville on Route 3 and east. I passed a sign that read "Village of Pitcairn," but there were almost no houses or signs of life. I spent another twenty minutes on Route 3 before I was at the place that Dr. Kellogg had indicated marked the stretch of land where the people of the area were thought to have disappeared.

The forest was thick on both sides of the road and sun was

setting. It had been a long day, but I wasn't about to surrender to exhaustion yet. If whatever was inside of Adam had decided that I was worth meeting, perhaps they would come out and greet me. Aside from stomping into the woods in the dark, I had no other ideas, so I got comfortable in the truck and kept my eyes on the dark forest.

Dr. Kellogg had explained that not everyone had disappeared from this spot, but most of them had. There were nine people that were known to have disappeared, including Mary. She'd disappeared while searching for the same thing that I was. Adam and his family hunted near here, and Adam had disappeared while scouting the area. Three more had vanished in these woods as well, but the rest had been scattered, with at least two having been taken from the middle of Harrisville, or at least that was the last place anyone had seen them.

It wasn't guaranteed, but if I was going to find whatever was taking everyone, this was my best bet. I sat there for three hours after dusk before I pulled out the flashlight and stared at the satchel holding the *Al-Azif*. It was another ten minutes before I opened the bag and shone the light on the ancient tome.

It could have been nerves, but I thought I saw it writhe under the glare of the light. I seriously considered destroying the thing at that moment, but I couldn't deny the explanation that I had given Nancy for why I had brought it with me. If I destroyed the *Al-Azif*, it could hurt my chances of exchanging it for Mary. I was hoping that I wouldn't have to trade the book for her, as I don't think anyone should have the kind of power that the *Al-Azif* is rumored to contain, but I couldn't destroy that option.

The book's power was another consideration. Was it even possible to destroy the *Al-Azif*? It throbbed with eldritch energy in a way that the *Necronomicon* never had. Even though I felt its power, I couldn't sense how that power would manifest itself. Adam had implied that it worked like a genie's lamp, but I knew from the history of the *Al-Azif* that it was more than that. It's sordid history included stories of resurrection, predictions of the future, and glimpses of parallel planes of existence. All of them had gone astray.

My theory was simple. I believed the *Al-Azif* to be the living embodiment of universal understanding. As humans in our world, we believe that we know how the universe works, but we haven't cracked the cover of that book. When Al'Hazred became lost in the desert, I think he found the secret language of how the universe works, and in his maddened state he put it into this text. By that reckoning, this wasn't a granter of wishes or a weapon, it was just a book that had all the knowledge of the universe available to it. With a book like that, that was also potentially alive, you could ask it for the answer to any question and in knowledge there is power. Hesitantly, I pulled the book out of the bag. A tingle of energy moved up my arm and I was flooded with a unique sensation of ... recognition.

I opened the book without thinking.

The pages of the *Al-Azif* were entirely blank. I flipped through them until I finally located a dark mark in the middle of the book. It was a black dot no bigger than the head of a nail. I stared at it a moment before I noticed that it was moving. As soon as I noticed that small movement, it exploded into a new shape and formed words. I started and almost dropped the book.

I noticed immediately that it was the same style as the writing on Adam Mitchell's arm.

When the words had finished forming, they read:

DR. DORAN
GO TO THE RANGER STATION.
TRUST BEAR.
-J. H. BOOTH

The words disappeared just as quickly as they had appeared, returning to the small dot on the page.

The potentially evil book with magical powers had just given me instructions. I wasn't sure if I should trust it or not, but nothing else seemed to be happening.

Unfortunately, I didn't know where the ranger station was or why I should trust a bear.

Too many questions. Was someone trying to help? Did I just

receive a message through the book, or was someone trapped inside it? How long had the message been there? If someone sent me a message through the *Al-Azif,* when did they send it? I didn't know anyone named Booth, but in the circles the *Al-Azif* might travel, people could know my name..

I had told Nancy that it was possible the book existed outside of space and time. If that was the case, was Booth someone I would meet later on my journey? Was Booth someone I could trust?

It didn't matter. I had run out of leads. I closed the book and tossed it back into the bag. That was when my light caught something else in the satchel.

Words.

I didn't recognize the language, but words in the same style of writing as those in the *Al-Azif,* simply penned in a different language. Adam Mitchell's tattoo was also imprinted on the inside of the bag. Anyone else would have assumed they had always been there, but I knew the world of the *Al-Azif* and it was obvious that the words had migrated there from the pages of the book.

Pulling a pen from my pocket, I scratched a symbol of protection into the leather of the satchel that I had learned from the *Necronomicon* during my days as a student at Miskatonic University. Hopefully, that would help contain the book from spreading. I had no doubt that if the words escaped the book that it could be a serious problem.

With that settled, I tossed the satchel onto the floor of the passenger seat and brought my flashlight up to look toward the dark forest.

My light landed on a sign right beside where I had parked, and I shook my head in disbelief.

It read "Ranger Station: 1 Mile."

Ranger Station

The ranger station was a small cabin with a green-painted roof. A roof-covered bulletin board was nailed to outside with fliers and information about the Adirondack Mountains and the park service. I parked the truck and went inside. I was surprised to find a park ranger was inside and awake behind a desk.

Nancy, almost a decade younger than me, was older than the kid sitting in front of me in the ranger uniform. The scrawny ginger started as I came in.

"Hello," I said before he could ask me who I was. "I'm here to look into the disappearances in the mountains." I hooked my thumb in the direction that I came from. "Do you know anything about them?"

"Uh," he was still trying to get over the shock of the evening visit. "Who are you?"

"Andrew Doran," I answered. "My sister went missing about a week ago. What's your name?"

"Joseph, uh, Joe." He seemed confused as he added, "Pahud. Ranger Joe Pahud."

He shook my hand and I repeated what I said when I had entered.

"We've done searches," he answered. "We've combed every inch of those woods. You aren't going to find anything at night that we didn't find during the day."

"Roaches like the dark," I grimaced. . "I might find a lot of things you wouldn't find in the day." I didn't add that I would also be looking for esoteric cultists and they tended to stick to the dark. "I need to know where the caves are, or where any old lodges might be. Places where groups of people might hide."

"What?" Joe asked. He shook his head. "Groups of people? What are you expecting to find out there, Mr. Doran?"

I shook my head at the ranger. "Never mind. Look, I'm going into the woods tonight and I would like some assistance. Can you help me?"

Joe crossed his arms. "Sir, why don't you have a seat on the cot. Maybe take a nap. We can do this first thing in the morning." He held up his hand as I started to speak, halting me so he could continue. "If you go into the woods tonight, you'll get lost and then we'll be spending our days looking for you. Tomorrow we'll go out at first light and you can lead the search if you like. Fresh ideas are always welcome." It was obvious that he had said the last part before as it sounded rehearsed. I'm sure he had said the same thing to my sister.

"I'd welcome a fresh idea," I said, ready to strangle him. "Unfortunately, I think we're dealing with ancient ones."

"You're making no sense, Mr. Doran. Why don't you take that cot?" Joe was getting as annoyed with me as I was with him.

"Did you know Mary Doran?" I asked.

"The school teacher?" He nodded in response. "She was just as crazy about going into those woods as you are, and I told her the same thing. Walking around the forest at night is all sorts of stupid. If you go out there, you're going to get lost and then we're down one more person to help us find the rest of them."

I didn't understand why I had ever trusted that damned book. I turned to leave.

"Thank you for your time," I said over my shoulder. "I need to get out there. I really appreciate all that you're doing here. Keep up the good work."

"Wait," Joe called out. "If I can't stop you from going, take this." He began scribbling something onto a piece of paper that I couldn't see." When he was done, he stood up and came over to me, the paper folded as he handed it to me. "Do you know how to read a map?"

I nodded.

"There's this guy, just north of here," the ranger explained. "He's a kind of hermit. He lives on these mountains and doesn't bother anyone, so we don't bother him. We were going to ask him if he knew anything about the disappearances, but ..." Joe stopped.

"But what?" I asked.

He looked a little embarrassed. "Well, he makes the locals nervous."

I frowned as I took the map from him and looked it over. "That sounds like a suspect to me."

Joe shook his head. "We ruled him out pretty early on. He was in the hospital with a broken leg when the first people started disappearing."

"What's about him makes everyone so nervous?" I asked.

The ranger shrugged. "I don't know. He seems harmless to

me. I think he's an old war hero or something. Someone said he served in the Great War." He walked back to his desk and sat down. "You know how locals get, though. Rumors start spreading and suddenly the lonely man on the hill becomes the crazy old hermit with mystical powers."

"Mystical powers?" My attention spiked when he said that.

"He puts an odd symbol on some of his stuff." Joe zigzagged his finger in the air. "A squiggle of some kind. It makes everyone think he's a witch casting a curse or something. Like I said, rumors have a life of their own."

That sounded like a spell to me. It could be a spell for anything, so I'd have to see it to be sure.

"In my experience, rumors tend to hold a hint to the truth." I held up the map. "Thank you."

"You can thank me by not dying." Joe Pahud waved and returned to his papers on his desk as I left.

I went back to the truck and drove to where I had previously been holding my stakeout. What Ranger Joe didn't know was that I had the power of the void to help me in the dark. The void is the name that I assign to the space between dimensions that tends to bleed through to our own. Those with my talent can harness the energies from that world. Whatever this symbol was that the hermit was using, it was likely to influence the void between our world and the next. That is, if I was right in my assumptions about the hermit.

Sitting in the truck, I looked down at my right wrist where a fat scar crossed it. That scar was a reminder of the last time I had encountered a wizard. It was right after I had met Leo and we were in Lyon, France, attempting to escape Nazi pursuers. We'd taken the catacombs beneath Lyon hoping to slow the soldiers, but the catacombs had secrets of their own, and I had fallen deeper beneath the streets of Lyon. That was where a wizard, whose rotting body implied that he had been stuck down there for at least a century, attempted to hijack my body and take my place in the world above. I managed to fight back through sheer force of will and a modicum of control over my pistol hand. While some in this present time would label me a wizard, I would not have held my own against that ancient thing in the depths of Lyon without luck and my rune-carved pistol. I was able to shoot the thing that hijacked my body and the scar on my wrist was all that remained of the bullet that had given me a chance to turn the tables on the decrepit wizard.

Then again, this hermit might just be a weird old man who liked squiggly lines.

While at the truck, I grabbed the satchel and in the dim light of the cab I saw that the words of the *Al-Azif* had started to bleed onto the outside of the leather bag. The protective symbol I had carved into the satchel didn't seem to be having any effect, as the words had printed directly across it. I didn't have time to worry about it and slung the bag over my shoulder. Reaching in, I grabbed my pistol and shoved it into my waistband along my back. Then I headed for the woods.

Another thing that Ranger Joe didn't know was that the night made it easier to use the magic from the void. I opened my senses as the trees surrounded me and focused on the energies and beings that most men couldn't see.

This was a dangerous tactic that had the potential to drive me mad. It could be argued that it already had. For that reason, I have tried to avoid using the magic provided by our proximity to those foreign worlds. Alien realms and parallel realities weren't meant for normal men to see, and opening my mind's eye to the powers of the universe was dangerous, but it was a risk I had to take for Mary.

My mind interpreted what it saw as a purple haze with the creatures from nearby universes floating through it. In this vision, the real world was transparent as I peered through it and into the next. Surrounding me were creatures that my mind struggled to define. Some of them were familiar to me, large caterpillar-looking beasts wiggling through the air without wings to guide them. Others were entirely new to me, blinking in and out of existence as if their entire lives were only peeking in from yet another universe. What caught my attention, though, were the creatures that were gathered near to, and beneath, the ground.

They were insect-like creatures and, unlike the rest of the beasts from beyond the veil, they moved in tight groups, migrating in the same direction. They were headed toward the area on the ranger's map where he'd marked the location of the hermit's cabin.

The problem with monsters is that they tend to notice you when you notice them. The larger of the creatures began to drift in my direction as I followed along their path.

I decided that if I kept moving , the bigger, slower creature wouldn't catch up with me right away. If it did, it might devour my sanity, but that wouldn't be a problem if I kept moving.

As I tried to watch the obstacles in both worlds at once, I noticed a pulsing of energy radiating from the satchel. It didn't seem foreign to the otherworldly environment, but was instead a component of it, like a harmonic vibration. Even through the satchel, it looked as though the book was woven into the very fabric of space. The *Al-Azif* was more a part of this reality than it was of mine.

I stared at the bag longer than I had intended. It was distracting me from my path, and I dragged my attention from it. The thing was almost hypnotic. I looked around and discovered that I had drifted from the path being woven by the insect creatures. I concentrated, and after a moment was back on track, but the larger thing that had trailed behind had managed to catch up with me. Up close, it looked like a large, floating crab with a worm-like body and insect wings. The wings didn't flap but remained open as it moved through space.

I turned and ran after the other creatures, following them up the nearest hill. They showed no deviation in their path, and I had already kept my mind open to the veil for too long. If I stepped fully back into the real world, the worm-crab thing would be unable to reach me.

Before I could return my sight to my own reality, something crashed into me from the left. It was big, man sized and heavy. I turned to see what had attacked and immediately wished I had not. It looked like a many-armed snake. In place of its head was a gaping maw with a sharp proboscis that kept darting in and out trying to impale me.

As we rolled, I managed to grab my pistol from where it rested against my back. It glowed with an alien light in that other place. I pressed the gun to the snake monster's head, but it twisted, hitting my arm and sending the gun flying into the darkness. It lunged for me again, pinning me to the ground and darting to bite my face.

Instinctively, I barked a spell I had learned a long time before. I'd never thought I would need it, as it only worked behind the veil, a place that I preferred not to linger. The words had barely left my mouth when the beast exploded into a million alien parts.

I rocked backward from the explosion, skidding across the dirt and pine needles. Something struck me in the back of the head and the world went dark.

The smell was the first thing that I was aware of when I woke up. It was a mix of rot and dirt that reminded me of a freshly dug grave. Opening my eyes, I saw the sun had risen and snow was falling lightly onto my face. It took me a moment to realize that something was wrong. It had only been just past dusk when I had fought the snake beast. If the sun was up, I had been unconscious the entire night. The only benefit to seeing the sun and a mostly gray sky was that I had woken up on the right side of the veil. Blacking out like that, without actively closing the sight, had disastrous potentials that I managed to avoid.

A loud snort startled me into full consciousness and I bolted upright. Five feet from me was the satchel and a lanky-looking gray creature pawing at it. My first thought was that it was a sickly Wendigo. Upon further examination, I realized that the creature was an emaciated black bear. Unlike normal black bears that were around 300 pounds of fat and muscle, this was a thin thing that looked like someone had taken a poorly treated bear skin and draped it over a skeleton. Large patches of hair were missing, and lesions were randomly spread across its torso.

I reached for the pistol before remembering that I had lost it during the fight with the snake thing. I cast my eyes around in search for the gun but didn't see it anywhere nearby. A stick caught my attention nearby and I grabbed it as I stood up.

There were no illusions in my mind about whether I could sneak up on this creature. Whatever it was, it was something less than a bear and more than dead. Dead things tended to be stronger than their living counterparts and I was aware of the irony that I intended to attack whatever it was with a stick.

Being a damned fool was on my curriculum vitae between dean and archaeologist.

I lunged at the bear-thing, jabbing with the stick toward his wide flank. If I was correct and this was a reanimated corpse, this wouldn't have much effect other than to puncture the bear's side, but if I was wrong and this was a sick, yet alive, animal, this could have been a killing blow.

The emaciated creature spun, swung its paw in a backhanded arc that connected with my makeshift weapon. The stick disintegrated in my hands and I only barely managed to duck as the same paw shifted directions and struck at me. The smell of rot and—something else—was worse the closer I got.

I hit the ground hard, sliding through the snow as the thing simply let gravity draw it to the ground, toppling toward me. Either the bear, or whatever was animating it, was clever. I only barely managed to roll out from under it. It landed directly where my slide had taken me, but just a second behind. The satchel was within my reach and I scooped it up, jumped to my feet and ran.

A normal black bear can move swiftly, and this beast was certainly not normal. I spun to face it as it came at me, raising my hand and grabbing for the power of the veil. I pushed it out and toward the bear.

Nothing happened. The veil was there, but my ability to touch it had been drained. I was spiritually exhausted. The dead bear slammed into me. The satchel flew from my hands as I bounced off a tree trunk. Before I could land, I was batted by the beast again, then pinned to the snow-packed earth.

Whatever this creature was, it wasn't thinking like a bear. Black bears were generally peaceful animals in that they only attacked when they felt threatened, and when they felt threatened, they attacked with their paws. A solid swing from the paw of a bear could take off a person's face like a hot knife through butter.

This thing wasn't using its paws offensively at all. One paw was being used to pin me down, and the other seemed to have a mind of its own as it stretched away from me and toward where the satchel had fallen.

If this creature's attention hadn't been divided, I would already be dead. Instead, I was able to use all my strength to keep the bear-thing's snapping jaws at bay. I grasped at its neck with both of my hands and pressed upward with all my strength, but I quickly realized that it wasn't only my spiritual powers that had been exhausted.

As my executioner's teeth inched closer to my face and the rotting stench seemed to soak through my flesh, I noticed that the bear's eyes were clouded over. Between its eyes was a nickel-sized hole that was caked with dry blood. If the dead bear-thing's hair hadn't been falling off, I wouldn't have ever noticed it.

Its jaws got closer, and I turned my head away to avoid losing my face. That's when I saw my pistol. If I released my hold on its throat to reach for it, the bear would eat my face, but if I was quick enough…

Something slammed into the side of the dead thing's head. It jerked to the side and shuddered before collapsing on me with the entirety of its weight. As emaciated as the creature was, I didn't have the strength to just push it off of me.

I wasn't about to die by suffocation, though, and I struggled to get free. I'd managed to move enough to realize that with time I could get out from under the thing when a voice stopped me in my tracks.

"Before I help you out from under that," said a man about twenty years my senior, wearing a red flannel jacket and a broad-brimmed hat, kneeling near my head, "would you mind telling me what you're doing with this thirty-eight?" He held up my pistol with one finger through the trigger guard. "It isn't much of a hunting rifle, is it?"

"I don't know," I grunted. "If I could have kept my hands on it, it might have taken this thing out."

Small talk was evidently over. As he stood, he put my pistol in his belt and I noticed that he had a longbow slung over his shoulder. "Who are you and what do you want in my woods?"

"Andrew Doran," I replied. It was getting harder to breathe, as if the monster was gaining in mass. "I'm looking for my sister."

His face shifted from business to empathy. "They got the school teacher then, did they?"

I nodded, but mostly because I couldn't take a breath anymore. Realizing I couldn't breathe, the hunter came over and helped me get out from under the twice-dead bear. It wasn't until then that I saw the arrow sticking out of the back of the thing's head. The man handed me my pistol as he stuck out his hand. I shook it.

"I'm sorry to hear about your sister, Mr. Doran. I'm assuming that dumb kid playing at being a ranger sent you up here?"

"You mean Pahud?" I nodded. "Yes. He told me that if I wanted to find my sister and couldn't wait for a search party to help me that I should try and find the local ghost story. Are you the hermit I'm looking for?"

"Donny Bear," he waved his hand at the bear. "Mind grabbing my arrow for me? I'll get your bag." He stomped through the snow in the direction that my tussle had carried me.

This was getting more convoluted by the second. The message from the *Al-Azif* drifted to the forefront of my memory and I wasn't sure if I should trust this man or not. The book, or Booth, whoever that was, had told me to trust Bear, but did it mean the creature that just tried to kill me or Donny? I would have thought on it more, but as I put my foot on the side of the bear's head and pulled out the arrow, I saw something that distracted me from my thoughts.

Through the hole that the arrow had made, I could see something moving inside the bear's head. Before I could take a closer look, Donny was back at my side and handing me my bag.

"The woods have been more dangerous than usual, lately," he said as he looked down at the bear.

"You've seen more things with this … affliction?"

Donny nodded. "There are more of them every day." He

took the arrow from me and slapped it against the side of his leg. "A deer that looked like this broke my leg. That was the first one that I saw. Since then, I can't move around these woods without coming across some sick animal."

I squatted down by the dead thing and looked for the first mark I had seen when I was underneath its snapping jaws.

The hole that the arrow had made was under what was left of the creature's fur. I slid th flap of skin aside to get a better look and saw movement. There wasn't enough light to see what it was, but I had a suspicion.

"What are you looking at?" Bear asked me.

I pointed at the first hole. "It looks like you weren't the first one to shoot him."

Bear shook his head. "The crazy ones all have that hole. Somebody lobotomized them or something."

Drawing my pistol, I replied, "Or somebody put something in there."

The blast from my pistol broke the morning silence as the top of the bear's head exploded. Donny cussed, taking a step back, but we stared at the result of the damage.

Thousands of thumb-sized ants crawled out of the gaping hole that my gun had made. Bear and I jumped back as the bugs scattered into the woods.

"What the hell was that?" the older hunter asked.

"I don't know, for sure," I said. "I think it has something to do with the disappearances."

Bear shook his head. "Ants like that aren't from around here."

"Not this time of year, either," I added.

As the ants disappeared into the trees, I realized that the creature hadn't been alive at all when I had fought it. This thing had been a re-animated corpse. Running into things like this was my line of work, but I didn't want to shock Donny. This was something that normal men didn't see.

I turned him from the corpse, but he pulled away from me and started prodding it with the arrow.

"Don't try to coddle me, boy," he snapped without looking over his shoulder. The ants had mostly cleared out, and Donny was poking around inside its skull. "I fought in the Great War before this one. I've seen things that'd make you shit bricks, so save that crap for someone else." When I didn't respond to that, he asked, "You think the ants were controlling the bear?"

"Yes," I said absently as I noticed the marks on the tip of his arrow. "The bear was dead, but I don't know if the ants killed it first or if they found it. More importantly," I pointed at his arrow, "what's that symbol on your broadhead?"

Instead of handing me the arrow so that I could look at it more closely, Donny twisted and jabbed the end at me threateningly. "Never mind that."

I leapt back, but he stood his ground and kept the arrow aimed at me like a sword. "Who the hell are you, Andrew Doran?"

"I told you," I explained. "I'm looking for my sister."

"That's not what I mean." The arrow's tip moved closer to my throat. "Dancing corpses don't make you flinch, and your pistol has symbols of its own."

"I'm an anthropologist who studies the occult, and I'm also the dean of Miskatonic University, in Massachusetts." I nodded toward the decomposing monster. "I've seen things like that before."

Bear eyed me for a second more before flipping the arrow in his hand and handing it to me, fletching first. I took it as he started to march toward the east. The symbol carved into the tip of the arrow was an almost artistic squiggle with specific angles and turns. To the untrained eye it was just a mark on the blade. I sensed that it was a rune, or sigil of power, but I had never seen anything like it before.

As I caught up with Bear, he explained.

"After the War ended, I decided to stay in Europe. I was young and wanted to see what I had fought so hard for. I took odd jobs for different people and worked my way across Europe." He took the arrow from me and put it into his quiver. "I learned that symbol while on a job in Norwood, London. I worked for a man named Cross and he believed in being prepared, whether you believed in magic or not. He made me and a big man he was working with practice this symbol until we knew it better than our own names." He stopped and sighed. "There were bugs then, too." Bear turned to face me. "The dead things never came to my home, but they were everywhere around it. The only thing that made that home special is that I had carved that symbol into some trees outside."

"Are you referring to Captain Cross?" I asked, certain that I knew the man that he referred to. "He deals in antique and rare books?"

Bear frowned. "You know him?"

I had worked with and against Cross on many occasions. "Professional hazard. We've met a few times." I didn't want to dwell on Cross, but knew that if the man knew anything, it was about the magic of old books. Bear's words could be trusted.

"So," I picked up the story for him, "when you realized the symbol was keeping them away, it wasn't hard to figure out that it might kill them."

Bear returned to marching through the snow. "I don't know about kill them. They're dead already, aren't they?" He shrugged. "I think it shuts off whatever is controlling them."

"Where are we going?" I asked.

"My cabin is a mile from here. I figured we should resupply before we go after your sister."

"Go after my sister? You know where she is?"

Bear shook his head. "No, I don't know where she is, but I can maybe guess." He pointed south. "If people are hiding anywhere near here, then they have to be in the caves to the south." He shot me a glance. "Do you know what we're looking for?"

Bear was already proving to be an invaluable resource, so I decided to let him know the little information that I had. "I think the people we're looking for are cultists. A group of people who worship an ancient book."

"The *Al-Azif*?" A somber look came to Bear's face. He saw my look of surprise and added, "With insects everywhere, and the fact that my marks work on them, it had to be the *Al-Azif*. That was the book Cross was hunting back in Norwood."

Concern flooded my mind. What forces were working together to keep the *Al-Azif* in Donny Bear's life? Or what forces were working to put him in my path, a man who had the means to fight back?

Caverns

Bear's home in the Adirondack Mountains was a one-room log cabin, the four corners of which were almost perfectly equidistant pine trees. There was only a small clearing in the front that showed the snow-covered remains of a campfire, and one log nailed between two more pines where Bear hung any game he killed with his bow. In the back of the cabin was a much smaller version of the one-room living quarters—obviously, Bear's outhouse. Finally, I had an answer to that age-old adage about bears in the woods.

The squiggle that marked Bear's arrows was everywhere, and as we entered the area they protected, a weight lifted from my shoulders that I hadn't realized had been there. I felt safe.

The entire place looked almost majestic with the morning light cutting through the hills and touching the top of the roof.

"I can see why someone might choose to live like this," I said honestly. "It's beautiful."

Bear nodded as we reached the front door. We entered, and he hung his bow on the wall.

"That's part of it. I grew up in these woods, part of a big logging family. All that I ever wanted was to get out and see the world.. A smile flickered briefly across his face but was quickly erased by the memories that followed. "Then I did. I saw evil things, long before Cross showed me that book. Dark things that only one man can do to another. After that, I stayed in Europe to try and see some of the good things man could do, and maybe help them recover. By the time I came back here, this was all I wanted. We spend our whole lives trying to find Heaven, just to see that we had it the whole time."

The cabin had a small fireplace, a table, and a bed. Next to the bed was a large trunk with a lantern on top. Bear's life distilled to one room. On the table was a plate and fork at one end, while on the other were arrows in various stages of assembly.

Bear grabbed an old army backpack from beside the trunk,

made from canvas with long pockets on each side of the main section. Removing the lantern, he opened the trunk and started pulling out various things and putting them into the pack.

I only had the satchel, my gun, and my ammo, so I reloaded the pistol at the table. As I did, I noticed that while my pistol was covered in the magical runes that gave it the ability to damage things from beyond the veil, it didn't have the one that marked everything in Bear's world.

He came over to the table with his backpack and slammed it down before taking a seat to work on the unfinished arrows. As he did, his eyes drifted to my satchel. It was open, since I had been grabbing ammo from it.

Bear suddenly jumped to his feet, the chair falling behind him.

"What the hell is that doing here?"

He was pointing at my satchel and I saw that the *Al-Azif* had been peeking out of it.

I didn't want Bear to threaten me with another arrow, so I made no movement toward the bag.

"Whatever group has been causing the disappearances— Mary, my sister—thought that the book was their end goal. I brought it with me because I might need it to get those people back."

Bear's voice was only barely above a whisper. "You can't trade it for those people."

I shook my head, agreeing with him. "No, I can't, but I might need to convince them that I will. I can't do that without the *Al-Azif.*"

He deflated as the tension left his shoulders. He didn't relax entirely, but it was enough that I felt safe again. As he righted his chair, he pointed at the bag. "Your mark isn't working. The words are escaping."

I looked down at the satchel and saw that Bear was right. The protective symbol from the *Necronomicon* that I had carved into the satchel's leather had become covered with more of that dark style of writing that seemed to move within the book. Bear grabbed the bag and began carving his symbol into it.

"That's the most powerful protective symbol that I know,"

I said as he worked. "Why does your symbol work, while mine doesn't?"

Bear didn't look up from his work as he answered. "Cross said he learned the symbol from a dead page of the *Al-Azif.* He thought it worked like heads on spikes outside of a castle. The living pages of the *Al-Azif* see it and turn around, seeing only death."

"Living pages?" I asked, surprised by how this hermit in the woods seemed to know so much more about an occult book in my library than I did. "What do you know about the *Al-Azif*?"

"Not as much as you're hoping I do." He resumed working his arrows as he spoke. "I was only the driver, but the book had Cross and his hired man on edge. They said it was somehow alive and had something to do with bugs. He had a lot of wild stories about that thing, but I don't know if they were all true. All I know for sure is that wherever that book goes, nightmares and death follow."

I took another look at my pistol and all of the useless runes covering it. This gun wasn't going to be enough during whatever battle was ahead of us.

"Do you have anything else that I can use," I held up my gun, "just in case this isn't enough?"

Bear reached behind his back and pulled out a large knife, flipped it, and handed it to me handle first. "I'll want that back."

Taking the knife, I nodded and thanked him. It was a large hunting knife with Bear's marking carved into the blade on each side.

I nodded toward the backpack. "What's in there?"

"Some food, water, and tools," Bear answered. "We don't know what state these folks might be in when we find them."

I nodded, appreciative.

Bear wasn't a wizard, as many of the locals thought. He was just incredibly resourceful.

"That all you're bringing?" I said, referencing his bow.

Bear stood, putting his newly made arrows into the quiver slung over his back with the others. "I've used guns, but at the end of the day it comes down to trust. I stopped trusting guns before the War ended." He took his bow from where he had hung it near the door. "I trust my bow. Besides," he added, "it's easier to carve that mark on arrows than bullets."

I slid the knife into my belt and slung the satchel over my shoulder. Bear wasn't wearing his bow across his chest like he had been when I met him, and I didn't see any point in putting away my pistol. We were packing light, and I didn't want to waste time getting it out in an emergency.

We started back into the woods, and although it was still early in the morning, the woods seemed to darken as we left Bear's camp. He led us east, explaining that the caves weren't far. As we walked, he nocked an arrow and kept a slow but steady pace. I was doing much the same, keeping both hands on my pistol as I marched behind him, keeping my eyes to the hills.

We were hunting cultists, an act that Bear was familiar with, and a quarry that I was familiar with.

We'd made it about a mile from Bear's cabin when he held up his hand, stopping me in my tracks. I tried to open my senses to the power of the veil, but it was distant, and my spirit was still exhausted from earlier. There was something wrong about the area, but that's all that I could sense. Instead, I tried to focus and listen for what had made Bear stop moving.

That's when I heard it—the background noise that I might not have noticed if he hadn't stopped us.

The forest was alive with the sound of insects. Rustling and cricket noises like loud static.

"Aren't bugs supposed to go to sleep or something in the winter?" Bear whispered to me.

I nodded. "Most of them go dormant, I think." I paused and tried to reach out to the power behind the veil again. "It's the magic from the *Al-Azif*. These cultists don't have the book, but you don't need the Bible to know how to pray. They're using the magic to try and keep us away."

No sooner had I said this, Bear spun, drew his bow and aimed it toward the trees. I turned and brought up my pistol, looking where he aimed. In the tree was a large crow staring down at us.

"Something is wrong with that bird," Bear whispered.

I stared, squinting to see what Bear might have noticed. That's when I saw it. The bird was shuddering and shaking, much like Adam Mitchell had. As I watched, I noticed that it also had a small spot of blood on the side of the head. I was sure that it was another hole.

"The crow is like the bear was," I explained. "Dead."

Three more birds landed near the first on the same tree. I turned slowly and saw that all of the trees nearby and some patches of snow on the ground were starting to fill with various types of birds all suffering from the same affliction. The eerie scene worsened when, as one, the birds all opened their mouths in soundless shrieks.

"Suggestions?" Bear asked.

I shrugged. "Run?"

Bear nodded. "Run."

I fired on the first bird, vaporizing its head. Before I had cocked the hammer again on my pistol, Bear had already shot two others with his special arrows. The rest took that as their cue and flew at us as one.

We turned and ran. Bear didn't bother with his bow and I didn't bother aiming as I fired over my shoulder.

"How much farther to the caves?" I shouted.

"Not far," Bear grunted.

A bird hit me in the center of my back and I tumbled to the ground. More landed on me, pecking and scratching. An arrow took two of them at once and suddenly Bear was swinging his bow like a club, getting the re-animated corpses off me. They dove at his face, and he suffered a deep scratch to his cheek. The blood soaked into his beard.

Struggling to my feet, I worked on getting the birds off Bear as he alternated between shooting at them and swinging his bow. I pulled the knife that he had given me and began grabbing the birds off of him and stabbing them as they pecked at my hands.

Then, just when the fight looked like it was hopeless, the birds were suddenly gone.

Bear and I stood, panting and covered in blood, both ours and that of the birds. Even worse, insects crawled all over us.

We took our time brushing them off and making sure they were gone before taking stock of our location.

"Why'd they leave?" Bear asked.

I shook my head and removed a bird from one of his arrows, handing it back to him. "I have no idea."

We collected as many of Bear's arrows as we could and surveyed the scene again. That was when I noticed the caves.

"I'm guessing we're here?" I asked, turning to Bear. His eyes weren't turned toward the caves but toward my side.

I looked down and saw the satchel, its flap open, and realized why the birds had left.

"They have the *Al-Azif*," I said.

Bear cussed and stomped in a circle for a minute. After he felt that he had raged long enough, he walked to the cave entrance and peered into the darkness.

"They're definitely down there," he said as I stepped up to him.

"What makes you say that?" I asked.

"There's light," he paused and tilted his head, "and the insects are louder down there."

I reloaded my pistol. "Nothing's changed. We're getting the people back, and we're leaving here with the *Al-Azif*."

Bear nodded, but his mind was elsewhere. He slung his bow over his shoulder and drew another knife that I didn't know he'd had. He spun me around and started digging into the backpack. When he was done, he had two angled military flashlights. He clipped one to his shirt and handed me the other. Without saying another word, he led the charge into the cave.

I left the gun and the knife in my belt and walked with the flashlight aimed ahead of me and to the side of Bear. I didn't want to fire the gun in the close confines of the cave unless I had to. The angled floor was slick, and we moved slowly It led down and into the Earth. As we traveled deeper, the caves became warmer, more so than any natural ground heat would have provided. I had a feeling that it had something to do with the insects.

We traveled like that for about five minutes before we could make out a new noise beyond the chirping of insects. Someone was chanting.

We followed the chanting for what seemed like a hundred feet or deeper into the ground and we came to the entrance to a large cavern. A slow moving stream of water ran through the center of it. On each side were campsites and people covered in tattoos. A quick count estimaged fifteen men and women. They were gathered in two groups, one on each side of the stream, and chanting in unison around small fires.

Bear pointed to where the stream left the cavern on the opposite side from us. Another tattooed cultist exited that cave and joined his companions.

I nodded, understanding. The people we were looking for would probably be in that direction.

There were too many cultists between us and the outlet for us to make our way directly through them. Besides, we were still unsure what kind of power they might wield from the *Al-Azif*. They had already shown a means of controlling a horde of woodland creatures; we didn't want to see what they could do to living men.

I signaled to Bear that we should go one at a time. The cavern was awash in shadows. The campfires did not cast much light near the walls, and the tents added shadows of their own. Bear nodded and took off, assuming the role of leader. I nervously watched as he timed his movements, stepping behind tents, and slipping through shadows when those nearest him looked away. After what seemed like forever, Bear entered the mouth of the stream outlet and gave a sharp nod, indicating that it was my turn to move.

Bear had moved with a practiced grace that left no sound in his wake. I didn't know where he had learned that skill, but it was something that I didn't have faith that I could mimic. Instead, I took off my boots and tied them together, slinging them over my neck. The removed shoes allowed me to move silently on the cold and wet stone.

I stepped out from behind our hiding spot near the entrance of the cave and moved as quietly as I could toward the first tent on the far right. I followed the same path that Bear had taken and stuck to the shadows as closely as he had, my bare feet making no sound as I moved slowly across the cavern.

Finally, I stood behind the last tent with nothing between Bear and myself, but the cultists chanting had ended, and they were returning to their individual camps.

Bear was well hidden, but two couples were moving directly toward me. I couldn't move without drawing their attention. Even when they stepped into their canvas tents, they would be close enough to hear me shuffling behind.

Seeing my dilemma, Bear unslung his bow and twisted so that he was barely out of the lit cavern. He was visible, but only if you were looking for him. No one was watching as he drew back the bow and launched an arrow at where we had been hiding.

The arrow sailed silently across the cavern before hitting just beyond where we had hidden and shattering against the stone walls, the pieces clattering loudly.

Every cultist's head snapped in that direction. I ran to Bear and down the smaller tunnel as they started yelling for someone to check out that direction. The arrow would let them know that we were in the caves. We had to move quickly.

We ran down the tunnel, the light behind us fading as the light ahead of us grew stronger. As we rounded a corner in the tunnel, we saw that the light wasn't coming from a fire, but from a type of insect that I didn't recognize. They crawled on the walls, covering every inch, but they glowed like fireflies. Their radiance was brighter than the fires had been, and Bear and I both flinched as they came into sight.

As our eyes adjusted, we saw that the insects lit up what could only be described as cocoons near the walls. There were at least a dozen of them lining the long tunnel. The cocoons were a mixture of thick webbing and some sort of mucous excretion and each was at least as large as a man. I pulled out the knife that Bear had given me and cut open the nearest cocoon at head height.

Inside was a sight from my nightmares. Bear gasped, but didn't look away, instead pulling his knife and opening the next one down. Directly in front of me was the face of another person, an elderly woman. Her eyes were wide and vacant and her skin was gray with decay. In the middle of her forehead was another hole with dried blood around it.

Bear shook his head as he opened the next cocoon and that told me two things. The first was that the person was dead and that we couldn't help them. The second was that it wasn't Mary. I was awash in a mix of terror and relief.

We tried to be quick about it but checking each of the cocoons was slow work. We watched for signs of cultists coming down the tunnel, but as we finished cutting open the last cocoon, there were still no cultists in sight.

And none of the cocoons held Mary.

A sudden cry from farther down the tunnel caught our attention, so Bear and I followed it. As we rounded another turn in the tunnel, we came to a much smaller cavern than the first, this one also lit by those bright bugs. The cavern itself was only about the size of my office back at Miskatonic University.

While the walls glowed, the floor of the smaller cavern crawled. Large black things that looked like beetles of some kind stood between us and a clear section of the floor where my sister crouched.

"Mary!" I said, breaking the silence that had been with us so long. Mary glanced up . The circle the bugs made around her didn't seem to be closing, but they kept her contained, and she seemed reluctant, even with our presence, to take her eyes off of them.

"Andrew?" She sounded surprised. "How did you find me?" As soon as she asked, she shook her head. "Never mind. Help me. These things are going to eat me."

"Did they kill the rest?" Bear asked.

Mary nodded, curiosity crossing her face as she noticed him for the first time. "Mr. Bear?"

Bear drew an arrow and looked around for something to shoot. I figured that his idea was to use his arrows to repel some of the bugs and make a path between us and Mary, but the floor was stone and the arrows would shatter or bounce. I had a different idea.

I pulled the satchel off and held it by the strap in front of me, letting the carved marking that Bear had made point forward. Almost instantly, the bugs parted by several feet and Bear and I made our way toward my sister. I had become a twisted Moses parting the dark and evil sea to bring my sister to freedom.

I passed the bag to Bear and pulled my sister into a hug. Only in my arms did I notice that she smelled like she hadn't showered in a week, which she obviously hadn't. She also felt weak in my hands as if they hadn't been feeding her much. This hadn't been a pleasure kidnapping. Mary had been starved and treated poorly.

My already boiling rage only burned hotter. I was going to kill every damned *Al-Azif* cultist in the Adirondack Mountains.

"Mary," I said as we pulled apart, "I'm so sorry about Mom." It was something that I should have said years ago. I stuttered to find the right words, but that was all that I could think to say as she hugged me again.

"I never blamed you for that. She made her choices." She pulled away and shook Bear's hand. "Thank you both for coming. We need to get out of here."

I shook my head. "Not yet." I took the satchel back from Bear and turned back toward where we had come. "They have the *Al-Azif*. We need to get it back."

Mary surprised me with a smack to the back of my head. "You brought the book with you?"

I shrugged sheepishly. "I thought I might need to trade it for you."

"Idiot," was all she said to that.

All three of us pulled together closely and walked forward with the satchel in front of us stepping out of the cavern and into the cocoon-riddled tunnel.

As we reached the first bend in the tunnel, Bear drew an arrow but didn't let go. I was much slower to notice the passage was full of cultists with knives.

Bear lowered his bow as one of the cultists stepped forward, with words seemingly tattooed over all her visible skin. I recognized the style of writing as that from the *Al-Azif*.

Instead of a long knife like her companions, she held a torn sheet of paper.

A page from the book.

Callisto

The cultists took us back to the large cavern after disarming Bear and me. The woman with the tattoos and the page from the *Al-Azif* watched us the entire time. They didn't need to tie us up or threaten us with the knives after they took my satchel. Instead, the insects that we had just freed Mary from continued to follow and surround us. This close to the cultists, I could see that many of them had the small hole in their head. Just like Adam Mitchell. They probably had the word "more" tattooed on them somewhere as well.

The cultists had all become whatever this tattooed woman thought of as more. Maybe it was more than their station in life, or maybe it meant part of whatever hive mind this odd religion had created.

"Mr. Doran," the tattooed cultist turned to me as we were taking positions around the stream at the center of the first cavern. "Thank you for bringing me the *Al-Azif*. As I am sure that you are aware, that book is a most holy relic to us."

"Doctor," I said.

"Really?" Mary shook her head. "You want to do this now?"

"What?" the cultist asked, confused. "Doctor?"

"It's Doctor Doran," I explained irritably. "I didn't spend years at the most cursed school on the East Coast so that uneducated zealots could call me 'Mister.'"

"You're ridiculous," Mary mumbled.

Donny Bear shook his head. "Great, now they won't mess up your headstone."

"I apologize, Dr. Doran," the tattooed woman said. "My name is Patricia Evans. My friends call me Pat and my followers call me 'Her Holiness.'"

"We'll stick with Patricia, thanks," I replied.

Patricia nodded, "Not that it matters. With the book we can finally finish our greatwork. Your time with us will not be long."

"Why?" Mary asked. "Are you going to let us go?"

Patricia smirked. "No, I'm going to feed you to Vhourvath."

The name was unfamiliar to me, so I asked, "Who's Vhourvath?"

Patricia smiled, "Vhourvath is from beyond our world." She held up the page of the *Al-Azif*. "He speaks to us through the words of the *Al-Azif*." She lowered her gaze to the stream. Several cultists gathered around us. "Through the words of the *Al-Azif*, Vhourvath, of the fourth moon of Jupiter and leader of the Ixtol, has guided us into creating a door for him."

The mention of Jupiter's fourth moon, Callisto, triggered a memory from my time with Karl Jansky during a brief and very alcohol-fueled stint at the University of Oklahoma. Karl had turned his time there into a lucrative career using radio waves to study the cosmos, and he had a unique theory regarding the moons of Jupiter.

"Vhourvath is an insect philosopher from Callisto?" I asked.

"How dare you sully his name," Patricia spat. "He is no mere philosopher, but a god, speaking to us from across the stars."

I shook my head, "He lied to you. He's a large bug. What does he want?"

Patricia pulled the *Al-Azif*, the entire book, from beneath her robes. "He wishes to grace us with his presence."

Understanding dawned on me. "He wants to come here?"

"We shall be graced by his Holiness and together we shall end the wars that plague this world as he brings us peace."

The cultists all repeated the word "peace" in unison.

"What is she talking about, Andy?" Mary asked me.

"She's deluded," I shouted, to be heard over the chanting that was increasing in volume. "The insect philosophers of Callisto have long sought a new home but have no resources to leave their planet. They've obviously figured out how to talk to these idiots. They aren't coming here to bring religious order, they are coming here to rule, subjugate, and devour our planet like an enormous plague of locusts."

"We can't let them do that." My sister's attention was suddenly drawn to the middle of the stream.

I looked to where her gaze was directed and saw something that looked like one of those previous cocoons, but it was pulsing. It was as large as we were, but as we watched, it seemed to grow.

The cultists chanted, Patricia opened the *Al-Azif* and began to read from whatever text appeared. I didn't recognize the words, but I also wasn't paying attention. Instead, I was looking toward the nearest cultist and trying to decide if he was close enough to grab and disarm.

Before I could decide, Bear moved. While I had been planning to attack the nearest cultist, Bear had grabbed him, and was grappling with the robed figure, there was a sudden flash of the cultist's blade and then a gurgling noise that I only barely heard over the chanting. The cultist fell to the ground, dead, and the bugs moved toward Bear to avenge their fallen acolyte. Bear spun and dropped to the ground, scattering something across the cavern floor.

Arrowheads. Bear had scattered a handful of his marked arrowheads onto the ground, creating a wide swath of the cavern that the possessed insects would need to cross to reach us.

Those arrowheads weren't easy to make and along with his surplus, Bear had obviously been collecting the special arrowheads that had broken off during hunts and travels through the woods. While they had taken his arrows and his bow, the cultists hadn't thought to take a small bag filled with stone and metal points.

As the bugs retreated, Mary and I were suddenly free. I spun and punched the cultist nearest to me in the nose. My fist ached, but I didn't stop. For all I knew, this was the man who had kidnapped my sister.

My third punch saw him fall back and bounce his head roughly off the floor. He had been carrying my pistol and the knife that Bear had loaned me. I lunged, grabbed the gun, spun and shot the guard who had grabbed at my sister.

The loud bang stopped everyone's chanting as they saw us breaking free.. I brought up my pistol and pulled Mary behind me as they surrounded us. Somewhere in the fight, Bear had found his bow and quiver and was backing up to us with his bow aimed at whichever cultist dared to take a step closer to us.

"You're too late," Patricia said with a melody in her voice. "Vhourvath has arrived."

Everyone in the cavern turned to the cocoon in the stream as something started to claw its way out of it. A horse-sized insect, very similar to a praying mantis but with three eyes and a bulging brain mass on the back of its head, clawed its way from the cocoon. Except that I knew now that it wasn't a cocoon so much as a portal to Jupiter's moon, Callisto. Vhourvath's mandibles clacked and clicked as it freed itself from the webbing and mucous. It stepped toward Patricia and let out a roar and she smiled up at her god.

Vhourvath's brain sac exploded as my bullet tore through it. He fell on top of Patricia as she screamed. As the cultists helped her up, I shouted at Bear to protect Mary and then I ran at the portal to Callisto.

As I approached, it began pulsing again, heralding the arrival of the rest of it's swarm. The Adirondack Mountains were minutes away from being Ground Zero for the largest plague of locusts to attack the Earth since biblical times.

I knelt to the cocoon like gateway, and as the head of one of those damned insect philosophers began to push through, I slammed Bear's knife down through the sides of the cocoon, driving it into the clay beneath the water.. The blade glowed red with heat almost instantly as the symbol carved into it fought against the power behind the portal—the *Al-Azif.*

With an almost silent "whoompf" of air, the cocoon collapsed on itself and the portal was closed.

I spun back toward my companions and saw that Bear was firing arrow after arrow in the fastest and most accurate display of archery skill that I had ever seen. Cultists were falling and, in some cases, exploding into a shower of new insects. Patricia had freed herself and was already trying to chant new words from the *Al-Azif.*

Raising my gun, I shot myself a path back to the hermit and my sister.

"Bear!" I shouted over the ever-deafening reverberation of the gunfire. "Shoot the *Al-Azif!*"

He looked at me with something behind his eyes. Confusion maybe, or something else. It wasn't a lack of confidence, as I had seen Bear hit smaller targets than the book that had been moving.

"It's the only way to stop all of this!" I tried to calm whatever was behind his eyes. "Shoot the damn book!"

He frowned and raised his bow. Bear didn't hesitate as he drew back and shot, seeming not even to aim.

The arrow, marked with the symbol that fought the powers of that ancient text, sailed over the heads of the cultists before finding its home in the book and through the flesh of Patricia's hand.

Every single cultist fell to the ground immediately. All, that is, except for Patricia.

Her Holiness screamed in both terror and pain as the words bled from the *Al-Azif* and onto her flesh. In the poor lighting, I could only barely make out the "ink" of the book as it bled down the length of Patricia and into the stream. As the words passed over her flesh, they took away the tattoos that covered her body, but they didn't do it politely. Lengths of flesh were torn from her body with each word until her entire form was overrun with insects and devoured before us. Both Mary and I turned away, but Bear watched as the priestess of the Cult of the Insect Philosophers of the Fourth Moon of Jupiter was torn apart by the very book that she worshiped.

The insects that had been guarding us scattered deeper into the mountain, and as Patricia's final screams echoed around the cave, I knew that this fight was over.

It was time to go home.

Donny Bear helped Mary and me get back to my truck, but he was silent the entire walk back.

On the march through the snow, we came across a lot of the undead birds, finally dead. There were also a lot of other dead animals, scattered throughout the woods. It wouldn't be long before the forest claimed their corpses.

My sister was cold and hungry. I needed to get her back to her home and maybe spend a week or so catching up with her. I loved my sister, and I should never have let a rift form between us.

Before I climbed into the truck, I turned to Donny and thanked him.

"I couldn't have done any of this without you." I nodded toward my sister. "She's alive because of you."

He nodded slowly, his mind somewhere else. "A lot are still dead. I'll lead Ranger Joe to the cave." He shrugged, saying, "Maybe I'll tell him what happened."

I agreed, knowing well that when people were confronted with the truth they rarely reacted well. "I'll leave that decision to you." I reached into my coat and pulled out a business card. It had my name with a direct number for my secretary, Carol. I had a direct number as well, but I was rarely in the office. "If you ever need anything, call this number and tell her your name. She'll make sure I get the message." I smiled. "At least one more powerful tome has been destroyed. It's not usually that easy."

Bear's brow furrowed as he took the business card. "I wouldn't be so certain of that."

Fear lanced through my chest. "What do you mean?"

"Another old story," he said, but his voice implied something darker. "When Cross was hunting the book, he said that it can't be destroyed. That the words just migrate to new pages."

That's what we had seen when the words had bled onto the priestess. They were tearing her skin to make new pages. The next book would be from the flesh of a believer.

"I don't know that we stopped the book or that giant mantis thing," Bear explained. "I think we just postponed it."

I shook his hand and as I climbed into the truck, I said, "At least we live to fight another day."

He nodded and waved to Mary as I pulled the truck onto the road and pulled away.

The ride was mostly quiet, until we were almost to Mary's home.

Sitting up straighter, my sister said, "Andy, I don't blame you for what happened to Mom."

Our mother had been consumed by the evils that I had been studying. Even with my sister's forgiveness, I had a hard time forgiving myself. "Thank you, Mary," I replied. It was still a subject I didn't like revisiting. "Can we just not talk about it? I don't think I'm ready."

Mary nodded but didn't look at me. "That's alright with me, but there's something you should know."

I had spent most of the drive worried about where the *Al-Azif* might show up next, but suddenly it was the furthest thing from my mind.

"What?" I asked.

Mary looked me in the eye as we parked in her driveway. "I think I know where Dad is."

Our father had disappeared not long after our mother's accident. Mary and I both believed that he had been driven mad by his loss. While Mary thought our father had just decided to disappear, I believed that he was following in Mom's interests and looking for a a way to revive his wife. Either way, I thought he must have died years before.

"You know where he is?" I asked, my voice barely a whisper.

Mary nodded and pulled a folded-envelope from her pocket and handed it to me.

I unfolded it and saw the return address.

If this was to be believed, our father was alive and living in Arkham Sanitarium in Arkham, Massachusetts.

Our long-lost father was locked up in our home town, and if I was ever going to stop the Germans from getting the *Book of Eibon*, he was going to have to stay there for the time being.

COCKROACH SUCKERS

By David Niall Wilson

Near the Great Dismal Swamp, everything grows. Bugs thrive. Plants barely hesitate between frost and full, pollen-bearing bloom. A warm winter week can produce things that should sleep until summer. It's in the earth. Birth, rebirth, and death.

Whatever grows must decompose. That is truth. As the sun set in a splash of deep violet and dark purple above the tree line, Jasper Winslow was contemplating that truth. He was rocking slowly in an ancient pressed back chair, watching the road crumble and brushing flies from his sweat-slicked brow.

Jasper wasn't an old man, but he was no pup. He'd been running his father's farm pretty much on his own since he turned twenty, and he'd been selling the excess produce at this out-of-the-way, run-down stand for just as long. The boards were gray, warped, and without a sign of peeling paint left to indicate they'd ever been white. The swamp was a ways down the road and across a field, but its creeping, encroaching presence worked its way closer every year. The road had nearly washed out in the last flood, and only a dump truck or two of gravel and half-a-dozen lazy state highway workers had prevented it.

In the opposite direction, spitting up a shower of dust and stone in its wake, a pickup truck turned off the freeway, bouncing and weaving down the two-lane gravel road. The back of the truck was covered with a blue tarp that flapped in the breeze. Something poked out from beneath that tarp, but it was still too far away for Jasper to see. The truck was Bobby Lee's, a grimy green-colored Ford as old as Methuselah and twice as cantankerous. Whitish smoke billowed from the tailpipe, and the truck listed heavily to the left, obviously struggling under an unfamiliar load.

Jasper reached down to his left, flipped up the lid on a rusted old metal cooler, fished in the ice and water until he found a beer, and pulled it free. He twisted off the top, slammed the cooler closed with a practiced motion, and leaned back again. He drained a third of the bottle in one quick drag, then sat, resting it on the bulky expanse of his belly, and watched Bobby Lee park.

The truck wheezed, gasped, and died with the rumble of an engine that doesn't want to quit running, despite its dubious ability to do so. The belch of smoke that erupted from Bobby Lee's pipes was so reminiscent of a giant fart that Jasper broke into a grin.

"You runnin' that thing on beans?" he hollered, not getting up, but raising a hand in greeting. Bobby Lee was Jasper's best friend in the world, but it was hot, and Jasper Winslow rose for no man, once he'd started rocking.

Bobby Lee clambered down from the driver's seat, slammed the door without looking back and grinned. "Got one a' them nitro bottles up front," he said, nodding. "Filled it with Hall-a PENYAS just yesterday. You ought to see her run when I punch that chili button."

Jasper laughed. With an uncharacteristic flash of energy, he opened the cooler again, grabbed a second cold beer, and flipped it through the air. Bobby Lee caught it neatly, brought the bottle to the brim of his faded Catfish Hunter baseball cap with a flourish that resembled a salute, and twisted off the top.

"I just bet," Jasper commented. "Day you waste a Hall-a Penya on that truck is the day I quit drinking."

Both of them laughed at that.

"What you got in the truck, Bobby Lee?" Jasper asked, eyeing the oddly draped tarp and the still-listing rear end of the truck. "Some sorta tractor?"

Bobby Lee grinned. He took another pull on his beer, and

then shook his head. "Nope. I got me a gold mine, is what. I got the answer to all our problems." He sipped his beer and his grin widened.

Jasper frowned. When he frowned, his brow furrowed, and the expression never ceased to widen Bobby Lee's grin.

"Don't think *too* hard," Bobby Lee advised. "I know you've been conservin' that gray matter all these years—be a shame to waste it now."

Jasper considered getting up. Bobby Lee needed his ass kicked, and there wasn't anyone else around to take up his slack, but for the moment, he held his peace. He was rocking, and that was important. So was the beer, and it was only half empty.

"What's in the truck?" he asked again. This time, his eyes narrowed, and his voice had taken on a cold, empty tone.

Bobby Lee watched him a moment longer, still chuckling, then he spoke.

"You still got that old tin shed you had stored behind your mom's place?" he asked, ignoring Jasper's question. "You know, the one you never put together?"

"I got it," Jasper answered. "So what? What's in the fucking *truck*, asshole?"

Bobby Lee hesitated a little less this time, but his smile had darkened. "Hold your horses," he said finally, "and I'll show you. You don't have to be an asshole about it—I'm lettin' you in on a good thing."

Jasper just rocked. He was one step closer to rising from the chair and doing what had to be done, but he let it ride a last time.

Bobby drained his beer, tossed the bottle aside and turned back to his truck with a curse. "Ought to just leave you here and keep it for myself," he growled. When he got no response, his shoulders sagged, just enough to be perceptible, and he stepped to the truck. There were three ties holding the tarp in place on the near side. Bobby undid them quickly. Then he stepped to the back of the truck, gripped the blue plastic tightly, and with a flourish, he yanked it free.

Jasper stopped rocking. He drained his beer, reached around

to set it on the cooler, let go of it and missed by six inches. He gripped the arms of his chair tightly, half rising. "What the f..."

What rose from the bed of the truck took his breath away. Jasper fell back with a thump, setting the rocker in motion again and nearly tipping over backward. He gasped, tried to speak, fell silent, and gasped again. Without thinking, he reached down and retrieved another beer. It was half gone when Bobby Lee, grinning again, stepped closer, leaned down, and winked.

"What do you think of her? She's somethin', ain't she?" he said.

Jasper gulped more beer, rocked forward, and gained his feet. He staggered forward, reached out a hand to steady himself against the truck, and then reached up to run his hand over polished wood that literally swam with tiny intricate detail and what appeared to be words, or letters, or symbols. Who knew? Who the fuck knew and who *cared*?

"It's a ... double-D goddam COCKROACH," he pronounced in amazement.

"The world's largest," Bobby Lee agreed, cackling. "Ain't she a beaut? I picked her up down at the flea market. They tried three weeks to sell her, but nobody knew what they was lookin' at."

"They didn't know it was a cockroach?" Jasper turned, his face a wrinkled map of confusion. "How they hell could they not know that? The fucking thing's seven foot tall, Bobby."

It was all of that. Rising so that its antennae floated above the cab of the truck, the gigantic wooden vermin leaned to its left, apparently off-balance, making the truck list crazily. The detail was amazing, like some sort of ART or something. Jasper scratched his head and tilted his hat back to facilitate the motion. Who in HELL would go to that kind of trouble for a goddam cockroach?

"She's an antique," Bobby continued. "Feller said he didn't know how old it was. Picked it up at an Indian camp about ten years ago. Had her in his barn ever since, but his wife said it had ta go. They don't make a Raid can big enough, so here she is."

Bobby was still grinning. Jasper was still frowning.

"But," Jasper formed both thoughts and words carefully, and

this one was a corker. Nothing in his experience had prepared him for it, and so he had to figure it out, one word at a time. "Why?"

"Why what?" Bobby asked. "Why did his wife want him to get rid of her, or why aren't there giant Raid cans?"

Bobby had sense enough to back up at this, raising his hands and laughing.

"Easy, hoss," he said. "Hear me out. You ever been out west? I have. I traveled out to Kansas once with my Pa. There's some mountains over there where … well, anyway, I went there. You know what we saw along that highway?"

"Fields?" Jasper guessed, trying to follow.

"We saw fields, for sure," Bobby grinned, "but there was something else. We saw the world's largest prairie dog. We saw the biggest ball of string ever, and we saw the footprints of dinosaurs, preserved in the mud. Every time we saw one of them things, you know what we had to do? We had to pay. You know what Pa said every time, just as we left? He said we was suckers. Didn't stop him from wanting to see the world's largest sausage link, or from payin', but he knew. I know too. That ain't a cockroach, ol' buddy. That's a goldmine."

Jasper was still staring up at the wooden monstrosity. Its eyes glittered in the sunlight, polished and seeming to glare down at him from their cocked, off-kilter angle.

"What the fuck are you talkin' about, Bobby? It's a damned roach. A BIG roach, no mistakin' that, but still a roach. A goddam, filthy, infest-your-house-and-eat-your-chicken roach. Where's the money in that? Hell, anyone sees it now, they won't buy my fruit."

"That's your problem, Jasper," Bobby said with true sorrow in his voice. "You ain't got the VISION. That's why I'm here—why I'm gonna share this good fortune with you. I'll tell you what we're gonna do."

Jasper listened, staring up at the roach, a tickling, creeping sensation transiting his spine as he did. He didn't like it. The damned wood was slimy to the touch, and no wood that wasn't growing mold should feel that way.

"We're gonna get that damn shed of yours," Bobby went on,

"and we're gonna set it up right out yonder." He pointed to the back of the produce stand. "We're gonna put ol' Papa Roach here inside, and then we're gonna make some signs. All up and down 17 we'll have advertisements: 'Ten miles to the World's Largest Cockroach', 'Don't MISS THIS—5 Miles to the Vermin from HELL', '1 Mile to Go—Exit 16A—Produce and souvenirs'. You get it?"

Jasper didn't. He was still staring at the roach.

Bobby leaned in close, whispering conspiratorially in his friend's ear. "It's simple, Jasper. We sell tickets. Folks stop to see, buy a ticket, maybe buy some tomatoes and some corn, and they drive on. They won't be able to help themselves."

"You have got to be fucking kidding," Jasper said, turning to meet Bobby's earnest gaze. "I mean, who would PAY to see … THAT?"

"They won't see it," Bobby said. "Not right off. It will be in the shed. That's the key. And the answer is simple. We make our money," Bobby looked around, as if there were someone to see him, or to overhear a great secret, "off suckers. *Cockroach* suckers."

There were no words for how Jasper felt at that moment, so he turned away, sort of tripped back to his chair, and reached for another beer. "Cockroach suckers," he muttered. "Jesus fucking Christ on a Popsicle stick."

Bobby Lee trailed after him, reaching in to get his own beer this time, and Jasper didn't stop him. There was plenty of beer, and it took too much effort to think and yell at the same time.

"You really believe," Jasper said at last, "that folks'll pay good, hard-earned money to see the world's largest cockroach?"

Bobby Lee's grin was full wattage again. "I know they will, partner. I know they will. Hell, if I didn't OWN it, I'd rather see the thing myself than the world's largest link sausage, and I paid for that."

"How long you think it'll take us to get that tin shed up?" Jasper asked.

"Not more'n a day," Bobby Lee speculated, getting serious. "I helped my Pap put one up in his yard last spring. Not much to it, once you get started."

Jasper nodded, and the nod worked itself naturally into a

slow rock. He stared up at the truck and met the multi-faceted gaze of Martha Stewart's worst nightmare steadily. He wanted to tell Bobby Lee to take the thing and hit the trail. It was a damn-fool idea. He knew it, and Bobby Lee should know it, but... damned if it didn't sound as if it might actually work.

"Shit," Jasper muttered.

Bobby Lee let out a whoop, knowing he'd won.

"You be here first thing in the morning," Jasper growled. "Be ready to work, no hangover. If we're a' goin' to do this, we're a' goin' to do it quick. I still got fields to plow, and produce to get in. If I let it go, we won't have a thing to sell except tickets, and I doubt that's gonna work out too well."

"I'll be here," Bobby Lee promised. Then he turned back to the truck and grabbed the ties on the tarp, pulling them tight and cinching them to the truck bed.

Once the huge bug was covered, Jasper felt a little better. There was something in the smooth, wooden surface of the thing's eyes that was unnerving. He knew it was silly, but that didn't change a thing.

"Damn thing gives me the willies," he said, reaching for another beer and staring at the blue-draped figure.

"Hope it gives everyone the willies," Bobby Lee commented. He reached into the cooler and fished out another beer for himself. "I'll have this one more, then I'm gonna hit the road. SmackDown is on tonight, and directly after that I'll be gettin' me some shuteye. I feel destiny callin'."

"That ain't destiny," Jasper chuckled, "it's indigestion from all them Hall-a-Penyas you *ain't* feedin' to your truck."

The two laughed and drank their beer in silence. Both of them kept giving the truck sidelong glances, but neither of them mentioned the thing in the back again. Not much later, Bobby Lee climbed in behind the wheel and, honking like an idiot, backed up in a cloud of dust and trundled his huge cargo off down the dirt road toward the highway. Jasper cleared his produce, locked what he could in his makeshift office, and stacked the rest in the back of his truck. He didn't have far to go. Two backroads turns and he'd be on his own road, tucked back up in close to the swamp.

Just before he left, he hefted his cooler onto the tailgate of the truck and slid it in, closing up behind it. He glanced at the road, thought about it for about ten seconds, then grabbed a last beer "for the road" and hopped in behind the wheel. He wasn't likely to meet one of North Carolina's finest between the stand and his home, but by his way of thinking, he was drunk enough already to get the ticket. No reason to deny himself a pleasant drive by leaving all the beer in back.

A white tail of dust and gravel spitting out behind him, Jasper gunned the truck into the growing twilight.

When Jasper pulled up in front of his stand the next morning, he saw Bobby Lee's truck already parked over to one side. There was no sign of his buddy, but around back of the shack, dust was rising, like there was a herd of something rushing past. Jasper parked, hopped down from his truck, and started around the side of the building to see what was what.

He stopped at the corner and stared. Bobby Lee was going to town on the ground behind the stand with a rake, clearing away brambles and bushes like there was no tomorrow. He'd already cleared a space about twice as big as the metal building in the back of Jasper's truck would need, and that ground was bare, scraped even, and squared off with perfect edges like Jasper had never seen.

"Bobby!" he called out. "Bobby Lee what in HELL are you doin'?"

At first, Bobby didn't seem to hear him, just kept right on a rakin' and shuffling around that rectangular patch of cleared ground. Jasper leaned down, picked up a rock and whipped it through the air to collide with the seat of Bobby Lee's pants. That got his attention.

"Wha..." Bobby Lee whirled, his rake held high in a comical parody of a martial arts stance. Then he saw Jasper.

"I said," Jasper repeated, "what in HELL are you doin'?"

"Just wanted to get me an early start, that's all," Bobby Lee said, grinning sheepishly. "I stayed up kinda late last night. Guess I talked a bit too much about her," he cocked his head in the direction of the wooden behemoth still tarp-covered in the back of his pickup truck. "Irma got tired of it and chased me out. I slept in the truck until the sun came up, then I came here and got started."

Jasper blinked, glanced down at the ground, and at the rake in his friend's hand, then back up to Bobby Lee's eyes. "Just how much coffee you had, Bobby?" he asked at last. "I ain't seen that much work out of you in the last year, and you don't even look like you broke a sweat yet."

Bobby Lee glanced down at the ground as if noticing the cleared patch for the first time. He leaned on the rake, reached to his back pocket for the bandanna tucked into his hip pocket and brushed it across his face. It was more out of habit than necessity. Jasper could see the man was as cool and fresh as if he'd just gotten up after a long night's sleep.

"Hell of a job," Jasper commented. "Gonna make settin' up a durn site easier."

Bobby Lee nodded. Now that he'd stopped working and started seeing what he'd been doing, he'd taken on a sort of glazed expression. He heard Jasper fine but didn't seem to really be paying any attention to him. He was looking at the earth he'd cleared, and glancing up now and then at the truck, as if there was something he couldn't quite make sense of.

"We have to put her here first," Bobby Lee said at last, tossing his rake aside. "I ain't seen the door of that shed, but I'm betting it's not big enough to take her in through. I brought us some pallets I had out back of my place to keep her out of the dirt."

Jasper blinked. He hadn't thought about it, but damned if Bobby Lee wasn't right. They'd have to build the shed around that thing, and even then it was going to come close. The peaked roof of the shed would top out at around eight feet in height, and the roach ran over seven. Jasper shook his head.

"We're damn fools, is what we are," he commented, turning away. "Damn fools."

Bobby Lee didn't answer. He was already headed toward his truck, the tarp, and the giant wooden body beneath. While Jasper unpacked his own truck, setting up the tomatoes and beans in neat rows on the bench out in front of his stand, Bobby unfurled the tarp, rolled it, and tossed it to one side. Then he got in behind the wheel of his truck and very slowly backed it toward the space he'd cleared, being careful not to catch the edge of his tailgate on the corner of the produce stand.

Jasper paid him no mind. He knew there'd be a short rush on the vegetables just before noon, and he needed to get them out and in place to be inspected, detected and selected, as his ol' Pap had used to say. No time for cockroach nonsense, nor for Bobby Lee, if it came to it. That boy needed any help, he'd have to holler for it.

That call never came. Jasper plunked down into his old rocker, kicked up his boots like he'd done a thousand times before, and started rocking. Mrs. Tefft dropped by on her way back from dropping her kids at school and picked up two pounds of fresh tomatoes. Edna Johnson came by for her regular order of green beans and potatoes, and Sheriff Ben Grouse pulled up in his cruiser to grab a small basket of strawberries for his Missus. Jasper never charged the sheriff for small things like the strawberries, and in return Jasper never got charged with anything himself. Like drunk driving or illegal parking. Or running a produce stand without a business license. Things in the country had a way of working themselves out.

All that while, Bobby Lee was out of sight back behind the stand. None of Jasper's customers commented on it, though Sheriff Grouse eyed Bobby's old pickup suspiciously while he perused the strawberries.

A couple of times Bobby Lee walked past to Jasper's truck, grabbed parts of the shed out of its long, corrugated box, and headed back out of sight, but he didn't say a word. He was moving fast and he kept his head down, mumbling to himself all the time. Jasper figured it for cursing, but the one time Bobby Lee came close enough for his friend to hear, all that came across was some sort of rhythmic mumbo jumbo.

"What you doin', Bobby Lee?" Jasper called after him. "Takin' up that rap music?"

Bobby Lee didn't answer, and Jasper wasn't inclined to raise himself out of his seat and follow after to insist on it. Truth be told, he didn't rightly care what Bobby Lee was sayin' as long as he didn't say "Come on back and help me, Jasper."

The noon rush passed, and Jasper was popping the top on his second beer of the afternoon when he finally started to feel guilty. Bobby Lee had been working quietly all morning long, since before Jasper himself had even arrived, and not a finger had been raised to help him. It was true that Jasper had provided the land, the shed, and all the moral support a fella could want, but it was also true that he'd agreed to be part of this cockamamie project. The least he could do was make a solid effort to pitch in and do his part.

Besides, the pile of shed parts still left in the truck was getting pretty small, and Jasper was beginning to wonder just what the hell Bobby Lee was doing back there. They'd agreed to move the cockroach into the cleared spot first, and then build the shed, but it seemed like Bobby Lee had changed his mind somewhere along the way and just started building. Hell, from the banging and clanking Jasper had heard, the damn thing must have been just about finished, and that was a job. Jasper had built one just like it out back of his house for storing lawn tools and making home brew.

Shifting his weight forward, he sat up, drained his beer, reached with practiced ease into the cooler and brought out two more. Then, with a long, drawn-out burp, he stood and headed around back of the stand.

For the second time that day, Jasper Winslow stopped dead in his tracks. He felt the bottle in his left hand slipping free and gripped it very suddenly, stumbling back. Bobby Lee's truck stood off to the side again, but it was empty. The damned roach was nowhere to be seen and standing smack-dab in the center of that cleared plot of land, the shed had taken shape. More than that, it was perfect. Jasper had had two cousins and his old lady helping, and he had not managed to get his shed up in near the time or manner that Bobby Lee had done this one by himself.

Bobby Lee was nowhere to be seen, and Jasper, taking a deep breath for courage, stepped forward to the door, slid it aside, and stepped inside. The building's interior was shadowed. There were no windows, and even the sunlight that slipped in behind him through the door did little. Jasper stepped forward, blinking, and ran smack into something hard after the second step. Something jabbed his cheek hard, something smooth and cool. Something sharp.

"Damn!" he grunted, stepping back. "Bobby? You in here? What in hell did you DO?"

There was no reply, but Jasper heard the murmur of voices near the rear of the shed. He reached out with one hand, letting the beer bottle crack gently into the side wall of the shed, and followed the left wall around, being careful not to move too fast, in case any more of the damned cockroach's double-D goddamned appendages felt inclined to give him a whack.

About halfway back, Jasper stopped. The shed had gone deathly cold. And quiet. The shadows, which shouldn't have been very deep in a building with open eaves and the front door open wide, clung to him, blocking his vision. The mumble of voices had shifted to more of a drone, like a bunch of midge flies hovering over the swamp. The tone rose and fell in a steady, hypnotic pattern, but there was no sign of Bobby.

Jasper turned and edged his way back toward the front. He had a big halogen search light in the back of his truck he used for deer spotting. That would light this place up and show him what was what.

Thing was, the farther he slid along the wall toward where he knew that door had to be, the farther it seemed he still had to go. He saw the cleared dirt outside, plain as day, but his breath was coming in short bursts, and he knew, without seeing it, that it was shooting out of his mouth like fog. It was cold enough Jasper felt the frost that suddenly coated the beers he held, and the burn of the cold glass against his skin. His toes were numb, and each step he took toward the door, and the light, was an effort he wasn't sure he felt like making.

Then the sound stopped. A hand fell heavily on Jasper's shoulder and he screamed, jumping back against the pressed metal wall so hard it dented. He gripped the beers so tightly he wondered if they might shatter.

The shed had grown lighter. Bobby Lee stood in front of him, holding out a hand for one of the beers.

Jasper teetered. He leaned heavily on the wall, despite knowing full well it had been erected by the grinning idiot standing before him in about half the time the job should have taken. It held.

"Hell, Jasper, what's wrong with you?" Bobby Lee asked. "You look like you've seen a ghost. Or maybe," Bobby grinned, turning and raising a hand to the wooden monstrosity behind him, "a giant cock-a-roach?"

Jasper heaved off the wall, lurched to the door, and stumbled out into the late afternoon light. He took in several deep breaths, and then turned back. All he saw was Bobby, sipping on his beer and staring back at him. The shed behind Bobby's back had no special characteristics, beyond being extremely well-constructed. There was no way to penetrate the shadowed interior from where Jasper stood, but he heard no soft voices and he saw no deeper-than-normal shadows. The air was warm, moist, and filled with mosquitoes.

Jasper shook his head. He glanced down and noticed he was still holding his unopened beer. With a quick twist, he opened it and tossed down half the bottle.

"Maybe you've been sittin' out in the sun too long, Jasper," Bobby Lee commented. "You don't look so good."

"You didn't see, or hear, or feel anything wrong in there?" Jasper asked, eyeing his friend suspiciously.

"Like what?" Bobby Lee scratched his head and took a draw from his beer. "I was in the back, tyin' down the straps to hold that big old money-makin' baby in place. I didn't see or hear a thing."

"I don't reckon you want to tell me how you got that thing out of your truck, neither," Jasper observed, his eyes narrowing.

Bobby Lee never blinked. "I backed her up and used the winch. How in hell did you think I got her *in* the truck, Jasper? I ain't no Superman."

Jasper blinked. He hadn't expected such a simple answer, and if he could've gotten his body to contort to the right shape, he'd have kicked himself in the ass for not thinking of it.

"Is there somethin' wrong, Jasper?" Bobby Lee asked.

Jasper turned away and lurched back toward his chair, and his beer. He didn't say a thing until he was seated once more in his old rocker, staring out at the dying sun and route 17 passing in the distance. He reached for another beer, tossed another one to Bobby, and closed his eyes, leaning back.

"So," he said at last. "Just when did you expect we would start drawing in these 'Cockroach Suckers,'" he asked.

Bobby was grinning when he opened his eyes, and the two talked well into the evening, watching the sun dip deep orange behind the line of trees that bordered the swamp. Finally, when the last of the beers had been emptied, Jasper rose shakily and headed for his truck. He left the produce baskets as they stood and grimaced at the expected tirade when he reached home without them, drunk. Didn't matter. For once, Jasper was convinced that Bobby Lee might border on human intelligence, and might actually, God forbid, be right about something. They were going to make them a pile of money, and it was going to start the very next day.

Bobby Lee stood beside Jasper's truck and helped him up into the seat, slamming the door for his friend.

"I'll see you tomorrow, partner," Bobby said. "Bright and early."

"You done a piece of work today, Bobby," Jasper replied. "Maybe you should sleep in a bit. Won't be any good tomorrow if you're all worn out or hung over."

Bobby winked at him, and something in that gesture, something sparking deep in his friend's eye, sent a cold a shiver through the air, and set the murmur of distant voices caroming off his skull and ricocheting about his mind.

"Don't you worry about me," Bobby said, his voice low. "I'll be here, ready to rock."

Jasper turned the key in the ignition and brought his old truck to life. He punched down on the gas and shot out of the small gravel lot onto the feeder road without a word. He was shaking, and his skin was coated in sweat.

"Damn beer," he whispered, gunning his engine and praying not to see a cop.

Bobby Lee stood, watching his partner depart, and then turned back. He didn't head for his own truck but slid through the door of the metal shed and pulled it tightly closed behind him. Moments later, the night filled with the drone of a thousand mosquitoes, or the grating crackle of cicadas in season. The blood-red sun drenched the skyline and melted to black.

Jasper saw the signs before he was within five miles of his stand. The first one was simple, square and white, black lettering.

"LOOK—5 MILES"

Then they got progressively larger, and more explicit, as he moved along 17. Jasper didn't take 17 very often, but this morning he'd had to restock his beer cooler in Elizabeth City, so he'd come in the popular route—the way his customers would come in.

"DON'T MISS OUT"

"3 ½ MILES TO YOUR WORST NIGHTMARE"

"2 MILES—THE WORLDS LARGEST AND HARDEST TO KILL"

"ONLY ONE MILE, TURN IN ON LEFT"

"½ MILE TO WORLD'S LARGEST COCKROACH! TURN NOW!"

This last sign was subtitled with the words "Fresh fruit and produce, inquire within."

Jasper turned down the side road and gunned his engine, spinning his tires and shooting dust and gravel into the air so thick he couldn't see the road behind him. He saw that even the dirt road itself hadn't escaped the signs. There were small ones and large ones, some proclaiming TOMATOES and others with large brown roach feelers raised high and eyes bugged out, staring at the road.

When he pulled up in front of his stand, he saw that there was a walkway, flat river stones set into the loose dirt of the field, running around back of the produce stand. A huge white wooden finger pointed the way around the corner toward the shed in back. Jasper climbed down out of his truck, slammed the door in case by some miracle Bobby Lee hadn't heard him, and followed where that finger pointed.

The shed was transformed. Sometime in the night, Bobby Lee had brought in paint and turned the drab, beige-colored pressed metal into a gleaming, multi-colored monstrosity. The base was black, but there was orange trim, and there were pictures, cockroaches running this way and that, little roach motels in pastel, Miami-Florida sorta colors, and to the right of the door a large can of bug spray with feet, holding a finger to its button and spraying toward the entrance.

Jasper's jaw dropped, and his legs turned to rubber, but before he could collapse to the newly-lain stone walk, Bobby Lee hurried out the door of the shed and grabbed him by the arm, steadying him. Jasper gaped at his friend, who was wearing a button-down shirt, a clean pair of black pants, a damned *belt*.

"Wha..." Jasper never got it out.

"Mornin' partner!" Bobby Lee said. "I did a little sprucin' up, seein' as how this was our first day in business, and all."

"Sprucin'... but..."

Bobby Lee cut him off again. "Don't you worry about it, partner. I didn't expect you to be here to help. I just got the bug, you know? Get it? GET IT?"

Bobby Lee was shaking him, and Jasper wished it would stop. He couldn't decide whether he more wanted to collapse to the ground or puke, and the shaking wasn't helping him with the decision. Then Bobby whirled back toward the front of the produce stand, supporting Jasper by the grip on his arm, and led him to his rocker.

"You don't worry 'bout a thing, Jasper," Bobby said. "Any customers show up, you send 'em around back to me. I'll handle it from there. You stay up here, sell the fruit, smile at the people, and watch out for ol' Sheriff Grouse. I expect we'll see him before the day's out. I got his paperwork all finished and signed in my truck, but I figgered I'd let him have the satisfaction of figurin' he's got us by the balls before I showed it to him."

Mention of the sheriff broke Jasper out of his fog.

"What papers? What did you do, Bobby Lee? Why would the sheriff..."

"Well, you don't think he'll drive down 17 and miss those signs, do you?" Bobby Lee asked, keeping his voice low and slow, like he was talking to a recalcitrant mule. "I tried to get as many out there as I could. Got to rememberin' those signs for the biggest ball of string I was tellin' you about, and just let my imagination go, you know?"

"When did you sleep?" Jasper asked finally. "My God, Bobby Lee, where did you learn to paint like that ..." Jasper waved his hand back in the general direction of the shed and its not-quite-dry murals, "over yonder? And where in HELL did you get a button-down shirt that has all the buttons?"

Bobby Lee's grin never faded.

"I feel like a new man," Jasper, he said. "I feel like this has been my destiny, you know? Everyone has to find them a place in life, and I reckon I walked into mine when I hit that flea market the other day."

"You was born to rip off suckers on a giant wooden cockroach display?" Jasper asked, trying to sort it all out in his head. "That what you're sayin', Bobby Lee? You tellin' me your momma raised you and fed you and tried to put you through school just so's you could build a home for a giant bug?"

Bobby Lee blinked. Just for a moment, Jasper thought he might be getting through, and then the light in Bobby Lee's eyes faded out, and blinked on again, high beams flashing.

"That's exactly what I'm sayin', I guess," he replied. "You just send them folks around to see me," he added, "and don't forget to sell them their ticket first."

Jasper glanced down to where Bobby's gaze had strayed and noticed a big roll of paper tickets on the old wood table next to his cooler. The tickets said $5 ADMIT ONE. Jasper shook his head. He was about to comment further when Bobby Lee abruptly turned on his heel and marched back around the corner to his shed. Jasper thought about following to press whatever point was forming in his mind, but something made him sit tight. He didn't want to go into that shed again. He didn't know why, would have denied the sensation altogether if confronted with it, but there it was. He remembered those voices. He remembered the chill, the dampness, and the way his steps had slowed as if he were wading through butter.

Jasper got up, set to work putting out his produce and clearing away what he'd left behind the night before. He pointedly ignored the walkway leading behind his stand—until the people started coming.

Over the next week, the produce stand became something of a sensation. It seemed like everyone from the Outer Banks and Kitty Hawk to Raleigh and Durham had heard the news. There was a new roadside attraction, and they were flocking to it in droves. Jasper's small garden had proven unable to keep up with the sudden demand for fresh tomatoes and strawberries, and Bobby Lee worked straight through one weekend to get pavers in to create a real parking lot. The drive coming in from 17, which had been nothing more than a gravel and dirt side-road, more discouraging than inviting to anything with wheels, had been resurfaced by the county, who were quick to see what the new attraction was doing for the tourist trade and local businesses.

The white signs on the freeway had been replaced by a longer series that ran up and down route 17 and onto some of the bisecting and intersecting roads with exits. In the middle of the bypass on the way to Virginia, there was a huge black sign with dripping green letters proclaiming:

STRAIGHT FROM THE DEPTHS OF THE GREAT DISMAL SWAMP. NO KITCHEN IS SAFE—NO TRASH CAN IS SACRED. SHE'S BIG—SHE'S THE BIGGEST DURNED COCKROACH IN THE WORLD—18 Miles, South 17. FRESH PRODUCE—T-SHIRTS—SOUVENIRS—PEANUTS.

The sign featured a giant, comical bug crawling over the top of the letters, huge antennae blocking the long, flat view of cotton fields beyond. It was only one of many signs, and it wasn't kidding about a bit of it. Racks of t-shirts lined the front of the parking lot. The produce stand itself had grown, incorporating a double-wide trailer with siding that housed vats and bins of rubber and plastic cockroaches and giant mosquitoes, rubber snakes, and bumper stickers that said, "I Saw it and Lived" and other such things. Jasper's mind was whirling so fast from one new thing to the next that he nearly forgot the shed out back, and what lay within.

He sat out front every day, watching them, curious coming and sort of dazed and glazed going. They bought the shirts, the produce, bags of peanuts, and handfuls of rubber bugs. Jasper had never had so much money in his life, and, for once there didn't seem to be a legal reason he couldn't keep it.

But as things settled into a rhythm, and he had some time to sit and watch, little things began to itch at him. Bobby Lee, for one thing. The man never slept. As far as Jasper could tell, Bobby Lee had not slept a wink since the first day he'd brought the damned cockroach to the stand. It didn't show. Bobby Lee was always smiling, always moving, working, and scheming. The shed out back had grown a foundation of concrete blocks that raised it a good four feet higher off the ground, for instance, and it had happened, seemingly, overnight. There was no sign that Bobby Lee had hired the work done, or that anyone else had an idea how it might have happened, but the next morning Bobby Lee was as fresh as a daisy and ready for anything. So he said.

Jasper had seen the difference the minute he pulled into his reserved spot at the front of the lot. There had already been three families in from Raleigh, waiting for the cockroach exhibit to open, parked in the lot. The shed, which should have been, as always, hidden by the structure of the produce stand itself, was clearly visible, rising into the sky to a height it should not have attained. Jasper had nearly run over a stand full of t-shirts staring at it.

Ignoring the calls and questions of the customers, waiting on him to open, he ran around the corner to the shed. Bobby Lee stepped quickly through door, as if he'd been waiting for his partner to arrive, smiling broadly and waving at the new foundation with a flourish of one brawny arm.

"Well, what do you think? I got to worryin' over hurricanes and the like, thought I might get 'er fixed into the ground a little more permanently."

Jasper stared up at the ludicrously tall structure and frowned. His mind was framing all sorts of questions, most of them starting with the words "How in the HELL," but none of them would quite make the journey to his lips. He stepped toward the doorway and reached around to where he knew the light switch was mounted on the wall, but before he could flick it, Bobby Lee grabbed him by the arm.

"You might not want to do that," Bobby Lee said softly.

The touch of Bobby Lee's hand on his arm was cold. Where their skin met felt like ice had been packed in under Jasper's skin. He heard the scuttling of what his mind conjured into a mound of thousands of crustaceous, squirming bodies. He stared into the shadowed interior of the shed, and more tiny glittering pinpoints of light than the stars in a cloudless summer's night sky winked back at him—then were gone. Something huge and hulking centered the shed, larger than the cockroach itself could possibly be, twelve, maybe fifteen feet in the air, instead of seven. The interior of that shed had a cold draft, and the scent of the place was dank and sweet with rot. Like the swamp.

Jasper reeled from the stench, yanking his arm free of Bobby Lee's grip. His partner was still smiling, but the smile was brittle, and for the first time Jasper looked deeper into his friend's eyes. They were bright, far too bright to be natural. His skin was sun-dried to the point of being leathery—or even papery. And the cold.

"You mainlining ice, Bobby Lee?" Jasper whispered. "What the hell is wrong with you—and—with that place?"

"Not a thing, Jasper," Bobby Lee said. His voice was as normal and pleasant as ever, but there was no mistaking the way he moved in front of the shed door. It was a sidewise sort of shuffle. Like a scuttling bug, or a man working his arms and legs via strings, like a puppet. Too fast, but sort of clumsy and "wrong".

"You go back out front and send those folks in," Bobby Lee said softly. "We don't want to disappoint them."

Jasper turned, remembering the customers gathered at the edge of the parking lot for the first time since he'd rounded the corner. He stepped back, started to say something, then turned and fled to the front—to his chair, and his beer, and the line of folks already stretching halfway around the parking lot, all of them wanting a glimpse of that damned giant cockroach.

Jasper wondered if they felt it. He wondered if they smelled the stench, and heard the scuttling feet—the soft, chitinous voices that never stopped speaking or chirping or chanting or whatever-the-hell they were doing. Maybe he was just losing it. Bobby Lee had sure done him a good turn, letting him in on this deal, and one thing was certain—there was no shortage of cockroach suckers in the world. No sir.

Jasper grabbed the roll of tickets and began doling them out, five dollars a pop, to bright, eager-faced kids and tolerant parents, young couples on long vacations and truckloads of rednecks in for a quick laugh. He only paid them half a mind, but one family caught his eye.

They pulled up in a brand-new SUV, the kind with a million features, such as a Blu-ray player in back and OnStar up front. Mother, father, a boy of maybe thirteen in a black t-shirt with the center of his lower lip pierced and his hair spiked like a damned purple and green porcupine, and the girls. They were twin girls, probably eighteen or nineteen, tall and long-legged with matched honey-colored hair and short skirts. Jasper couldn't have missed them if he tried, and despite his need to vend tickets to the next twenty people in line and price t-shirts for another fifteen visitors on their way out, he managed to keep an eye on them until they wound around the corner and out of site toward the shed.

For the next half hour or so, Jasper was too busy to think about them, and that was a tribute to how hard he was working, because there was absolutely NOTHING Jasper loved better than a cute set of twins. He liked to watch TV Land on cable so he could catch the old Doublemint Girls commercials. It wasn't until that family was winding their way back out, the boy selecting a truly disgusting plastic roach souvenir, and the mother laughingly holding one of the "I Survived the Great Dismal Swamp" t-shirts across her breasts and winking at her husband, that Jasper remembered them at all.

It was later in the afternoon, and Jasper scanned the diminishing crowd quickly for the twins. They were nowhere to be seen, and he grew almost frantic, staring out over the thinning traffic in the small parking lot to see if he'd somehow missed their trek back to the SUV. There was no one visible inside the vehicle, and the rest of the family seemed oblivious. They laughed and joked a little—or the parents did. The boy jammed a pair of headphones onto his head, cranked the volume on some sort of expensive portable MP3 player, and zoned out.

They walked away as a group, straight to the SUV, opened the doors, and got in.

Jasper stepped away from his counter, holding up a hand to those waiting on him to give him a moment. He stepped to the corner of the stand and glanced around at the shed. Bobby Lee was there, grinning and waving at him, but there was no sign of the girls. Jasper frowned. He turned to scan the SUV again, but its taillights were already disappearing out the feeder road toward 17.

"What the hell?" he muttered. He turned back to the counter and went through the motions for the next twenty minutes or so, ushering the last of the crowds out and away. Jasper carefully counted out the day's proceeds, which were phenomenal, and packed the bills away into the bank bag he'd taken to carrying in a lock box beneath the seat of his truck. When the shirt racks had been wheeled inside, and the tiny remnants of the day's fresh produce had been stored for the night, he locked up carefully.

He stepped to the corner of the building, as he did every night, and called out to Bobby Lee.

"You done for the night, Bobby?"

"Just about," Bobby called back. His voice floated out from the interior of the shed, and for a moment, Jasper stared. There was no light on inside, and it was growing dark outside. The shadows inside had to be deeper still.

Jasper shook his head and turned, walking deliberately to his truck. He had no intention of going home, but he had a plan, and it involved Bobby Lee watching him leave the parking lot, so he drove on out the feeder road and turned right on 17 toward Elizabeth City. He figured it wouldn't take him more than five or six beers and a shot or two to be ready to come back.

The hulking signs leading toward the world's largest cockroach loomed over the ditches and crossroads of Highway 17 as Jasper passed them, winding his way slowly back toward the stand, and the shed, and what lay within. He had no intention of turning onto the feeder road; that would be too obvious. Jasper had been running his produce stand for a lot of years, and he knew more than one way in, and out. He passed the main road and went about half a mile until a paved road bisected the highway. It bore the same name as a thousand North Carolina roads, Dead End, but he paid that no mind, other than to hope it was just a name, and would not prove prophetic.

The road wound back in along lines of trees that bordered fields outlined by even rows of cotton. Jasper drove slowly and carefully, keeping his engine as quiet as possible. He turned left onto a dirt track and followed the rutted, poorly kept road deeper into the trees. The road grew progressively worse, and it wasn't long before he found a place to pull the truck in under the overhanging branches and off the road. He parked and popped the top on another beer as he stared off into the darkness across the cotton field.

He could make out the imposing shadow of the impossibly tall shack from where he sat. The odd shape of the building reminded him of a giant outhouse, and he chuckled, downing the beer in quick gulps and reaching for another. Made sense, he reckoned, that a giant roach would end up in a giant outhouse. He wondered why he'd never noticed it before.

When the second beer had been sucked dry, he got out, tossed the can in the back of his truck, and stood, getting his bearings. It was still a quarter of a mile through the cotton to the shed, but as long as he was quiet, he was sure he could sneak up on the place. He saw Bobby Lee's truck, and there was a dim glow seeping out along the roof line, and near the bottom of the building. Whatever it was Bobby Lee had going on in that place, it was going on now, and Jasper aimed to see it for himself. If Bobby Lee was holding out on him, partying with those twins and such, Jasper aimed to be part of that, too. If it was something else…he shivered deep inside.

"Partners," he muttered to himself, "is partners."

The moonlight was bright, bathing the back of the shed in cold, white illumination. Though it was unseasonably warm, the closer Jasper came to the back of the building, the colder it grew. By the time he broke free of the cotton and into the area Bobby Lee had raked clear that first day, his teeth were chattering, and he threw his nearly empty beer can behind him, curling his arms around his chest.

"What the hell?" he said to no one in particular.

Moving quietly, he worked his way around the shed on the left side, hesitating as he drew near the corner. He pressed close to the shed, and where his arm brushed the corrugated metal, something rippled over his skin. There was a stench, like rotted vegetation, or some sort of hot mud, but there was no heat. Jasper's heart danced like a bug on a magnifying glass, and for a moment, with the blood rushing to his head, he thought he'd pass out. Then he steadied himself, regretting instantly the contact with the building this required.

The walls vibrated, and the vibration translated to sound in his head. The sound was a drone, as though there were a million mosquitoes humming inside, or the wings of a host of wasps beating against the far side of the wall. Jasper closed his eyes, caught his breath, and in that instant, he saw them, clinging to one another, climbing and grasping and bobbing with black-gold-black-striped stingers primed, dripping poison. And he heard... words.

There were no words he knew or understood—except that on some very deep level, he did.

He opened his eyes with a start and pulled away from the wall.

"Jesus Jumpin' Jehosephat Christ," he whispered. Each syllable of the words came out in a separate gasp.

He wavered between continuing around the corner and turning to run and never look back, moving on to Virginia, or Maryland, and starting over. Then he thought of Bobby Lee. He remembered long, lazy afternoons fishing, hard days on his daddy's farm, Bobby Lee at his side, working until they fell down in the dirt exhausted and then washing it all off with a garden hose to start over and do it again. He couldn't leave Bobby Lee in there, even if Bobby Lee WANTED to be in there.

"Wish I'd brought some bug spray," he muttered, and turned the corner of the shed, moving stealthily toward the sliding door in front.

A sickly, greenish glow seeped out through the doorway. It reminded Jasper of the glow sticks they sold at summer carnivals, or the glow-in-the-dark stars he'd hung on his ceiling as a boy. The droning was louder now, and it covered a wide range of tones—deep and resonant to high-pitched and ear-splitting. Jasper pulled a wad of tissue out of his pocket, hoped it wasn't too dirty, and wadded rolls of it in each ear, blocking as much of the sound as possible.

He thought he recognized two recurring words... *"Al-Azif"*—he'd heard—felt?—them when he'd leaned on the building outside. Thinking about them brought him a memory of his first glance at the Double-D Goddammed cock-a-roach in the back of Bobby's truck. Words, symbols, that rippled across that slimy surface... like they were moving. Had the thing been talking to him, even then? Was it talking to Bobby?

He stared at the door, trying to think of a compelling enough reason to turn tail and run, but he couldn't shake the thought of Bobby Lee, and those crawling, touching, stinging bugs.

"Ah, hell," he said softly. Before he could change his mind, he stepped inside.

If the air had been cold outside the shed, inside it was frigid. There were lights, but they were soft and green, and buried in the corners near the rear of the building. Jasper couldn't see a thing except the huge, vaguely defined silhouette of the giant wooden cockroach. The greenish glow shimmered around the edges of it like the silver lining on a cloud gone rotten. And that was another thing. The stench was horrible. Every breath had weight, as if he were breathing liquid, or some sort of thick gas, rather than air.

The droning pounded in Jasper's head, and thinking became difficult. Gritting his teeth, he skirted the side wall of the shed, pulling as far away from the statue on its wood pallet base as possible without coming into contact with the wall to his left. He didn't want a repeat encounter with the vibration. As he moved through the cloying shadows, he concentrated on an image of Bobby Lee's smiling face, and whenever that started to fade into the sound and stink, or threatened to be rattled out of his head by his chattering teeth, he thought about those twins.

It was the longest walk of Jasper's life. He knew the length and breadth of the shed; he'd bought the damned thing in the garden department at Handy-Mart himself. Sure, the walls were taller than they'd been, and it was a little harder to walk in this air than it had been last time he'd been inside, but it should have been a ten-step, twelve at the max, journey from the front to the back, and though he couldn't string two thoughts together in a line, he knew he should have already run smack into the back wall. Except, he didn't.

The sound and shadows closed in behind him then, and he saw that the glow was concentrated near the rear of the cockroach and down low. He headed in that direction, sweeping his gaze to the right and left, looking for any sign of Bobby Lee, or the twins, or whatever the hell was making that fucking NOISE... but he saw nothing. Nothing but the glow, and as he drew near to it, he felt a scream bubbling up through his chest that he only barely managed to bite off, clamping his lip tightly between his teeth and grinding. He tasted blood, but it didn't matter. Somehow, he knew that the last thing he wanted in this place, at this moment, was to draw attention.

What he saw was a small pile of glowing orbs. They were roughly the shape of a baseball, and there were dozens of them, clinging in a wet, sticky mass and coated in slimy ichor. Among them, tiny shapes squirmed and crawled, some flitting a few inches through the air but unable—quite—to break free of the mass, plopping wetly back into the others to crawl and tug at the sticky fluid, and then trying to break free once more. Jasper stared, mesmerized. It took a few moments to realize that the droning had increased in volume, and that it was moving.

Breaking his gaze free of the crawling mass at his feet, Jasper glanced up sharply. He couldn't see anything, but he could hear it, and moments later, he felt it as well. The air whirled, driving the image of a tornado like a spike into his brain. He still saw nothing, but his mind formed the images he couldn't bring into focus, and he knew they were there. He didn't know if they were mosquitoes, or wasps, hornets, or something... else. It didn't matter. They were circling, faster and faster, but they were not coming closer. Something else was.

He saw Bobby Lee's shadowed form step from the shadows, moving slowly and deliberately, as he himself had been moving since stepping into the place, only differently. Jasper wanted to turn, run, and be done with it, but he stood his ground. Licking his dry lips, he tried to speak, but the words came out in a rasping whisper.

"Bobby?" he whispered. "Bobby, what..."

Then Bobby was close enough to be seen in the dim, green glow of the orbs, or eggs, or whatever the hell they were, and Jasper nearly fell. His knees, solid and strong a moment before, had taken on the consistency of jelly, and the only thing that kept him from losing a perfectly good six-pack of beer was the thought of those—things—crawling among the scraps and bits and drinking his beer as they fought free... and joined the swarm overhead.

Bobby was awash in tiny bodies. It was impossible to tell what they were, what color, what size, as there were too many. They coated him like a second skin, moving and chittering, squirming and lifting tiny antennae and proboscises to search and test, looking for—what?

"Jas...per" Bobby Lee croaked. He couldn't speak clearly. When he opened his mouth they crawled out slowly, sliding over and around one another as they crossed his lips, and curled back up over his ears to join the rest.

Jasper wanted to vomit, but he held it. Bobby Lee's eyes were clear and bright. Maybe too bright, but there was no alarm in them. No panic. The insects, roaches, wasps, whatever they were, shimmered over him in waves, but he stood, staring calmly into Jasper's wondering gaze.

"Wha..." Jasper stopped. He didn't want to ask a question. He knew Bobby Lee would answer, but he didn't want to witness the filling and emptying of his friend's mouth a second time if he could help it. Instead of speaking, he shrugged, backing away a step.

Bobby Lee nodded toward the huge wooden cockroach, and stepped forward, laying a hand across the bottom segment of one huge mandible. Jasper stepped back, but something in Bobby Lee's expression held him steady.

Without speaking, Bobby Lee reached into his pocket and pulled something free. A moment later, as Bobby Lee flicked his thumb to free the blade, Jasper saw that it was a Buck knife.

Without hesitation, Bobby Lee took a slice off the statue. Jasper watched the splinter of wood float to the floor and followed Bobby Lee's pointing finger to the spot where he'd cut it free.

The wood only coated what lay beneath. It was smooth, as the wood had been smooth, but darker. Bobby Lee gestured for Jasper to step closer, and, not knowing what else to do, unless it was to run, Jasper complied. Bobby grabbed his wrist, and for a moment, that was nearly the end of it. The bugs crawling and shifting and seething over Bobby Lee's arm reached out feelers and legs, pinchers and proboscises to the new flesh Jasper offered. He tried to yank free, but Bobby Lee held tight. In a moment, it didn't matter.

As Bobby Lee pressed Jasper's hand to the cut in the wood, something shot out from within. It was hard and sharp, round and hollow, and it plunged into Jasper's hand without hesitation. His body spasmed, and he tried to jerk free, but it was too late. He felt his pulse through the palm of his hand, felt whatever it was that had pierced him probing deeper, sucking with incredible force at that small puncture in his hand.

The things that coated Bobby Lee were moving up Jasper's arm, but he couldn't spare them any attention. He was trying to scream and unable to free himself of the muscle-contracting spasm of pain long enough to force the air from his lungs.

Then it stopped. Jasper staggered back, grabbing his wounded hand in the other and then releasing it to swat at the bugs, brushing them from his arm, waiting for the bites and stings that never came, and backing away again. Bobby Lee looked as if he would speak again, despite the danger of the insects swarming his throat, but at that moment, Jasper struck his back on the wall, pressing tightly into the metal and its constant, droning vibration, and the need for speech was erased.

Thoughts flowed in a steady progression through Jasper's mind. He saw things, strange, impossible things. He saw stars, gleaming in the sky. He saw cylinders of sleek, shining metal, gleaming and shooting at impossible speeds among those stars. He saw explosions of fire and light, like a Fourth of July gone mad and he felt the waves of pain as explosions followed the flight.

He saw masses of people and mounds of insects. He saw the giant roach, not solid and carved, but skittering about a mountain slope. He saw stone pillars and a temple, and he saw the people, kneeling, coated in shimmering sheets of exoskeletal motion, kneeling in an ocean of insects.

A man—no, a priest—stood near the top of the tallest mound, a huge book open in his arms. A single shaft of light snaked from the stars above to strike the pages as the man read, slowly, his voice a drone that blended with those of the insects swarming around him. Jasper opened his mouth... whispered... *Al-Azif.*

He saw the swamp, crazily recognizing the fishing hole he and Bobby Lee had been visiting since they were kids. He saw the muck and the rising water, moss and scum, the slither of snakes, and the great crash of gator tails, and always, over and over, the passing of sun to moon to sun, until, finally, he saw a fishing pole and a red and white bobber, rising and falling in the grip of a soft swell on the surface of a still pool. The line grew taut and the pole bent. Whatever it was, it was huge, and there were droplets of water running up and down the line ... or ... not water. The droplets moved up, not down, and Jasper saw them reach the pole and continue coming. They moved in a solid, lightning-fast strike up the line and down the bamboo and onto the hands and arms that waited. Onto Bobby Lee, who stood on the bank, staring stupidly as they invaded his flesh, taking him before he could cast the pole away and dropping him to his knees on the bank of that swampy lake.

Then the statue rose, hung up on Bobby's line and dripping swamp mud and putrid, rotting vegetation. No way Bobby Lee was pulling it free of that mire, but he was connected to it, and as more and more of the insects, or whatever they were, coated his skin, he rose unsteadily to his feet, shook his head as if freeing it from something, and watched in wonder.

Then the statue was on the bank, no clear view of how this had come to be, only that it was. Bobby Lee was wiping it down with rags, spraying it with some sort of bottled detergent, and clearing away every indication that it had ever come within a foot of the swamp. Cleaning and wiping and polishing, he brought it to the sheen that Jasper had first noted, and then, turning, he walked away.

The next image was Bobby Lee's truck and somehow, impossibly, the statue was in the back. Bobby Lee was covering it with the blue tarp and fastening it carefully to the hooks up and down either side of the truck's bed.

And then the vision faded. The connection between Jasper and the swarming, droning horde was broken. Jasper turned and walked out of the shed. He didn't look back. When he was out in the fresh, cool air of the evening, he turned around the corner of the shed and moved toward the parking lot. He plopped into his old rocker, closed his eyes, laid his head back, and sat very, very still. A few moments later, he heard the crunch of Bobby Lee's feet on the walk, and he looked up. There were no bugs. Jasper glanced to the side, but realized too late the cooler wasn't there. No beer.

"It's not what you think," Bobby Lee said softly.

"I don't think a damn thing," Jasper replied. "I saw what I saw. Where are they, crawling under your shirt, down your damned pants?"

"They're in there with *her,*" Bobby Lee said. His voice was still calm. "They never come out of the shed."

"Not just them, neither," Jasper shot back. "I know them twins never come out, Bobby. What did it do, suck them inside like it tried to do to me?"

"No," Bobby Lee said. Then he chuckled.

Jasper snapped his chin from his chest and glared at his friend. "What in HELL are you laughing at? Them girls is gone, and no tellin' how many others, and you stand there grinnin' like a damn fool."

Bobby Lee was actually laughing, and it pissed Jasper off. He rose to his feet and cocked his arm back. "You shut up, Bobby Lee, or giant double-D Goddamned cockroach or not, I'm gonna SHUT you up."

Bobby Lee was still laughing, but he held up his hands in surrender, backing off.

"It ain't that, Jasper," he managed to say at last. "There ain't nothin' wrong with them twins. They's waitin' at the Eagle and

Anchor back in Hertford for us. You thought she was EATIN' 'em?"

Jasper's arm fell to his side, and he frowned.

"What the hell are you talking about?" he asked at last. "What do you MEAN they's waitin' on us?"

"Just what I said," Bobby Lee chuckled. "She don't eat folks, Jasper, she just likes to have us near. Those others, the little ones? They only come out at night. That shed is like her temple, now. You saw the temple."

"I saw a bunch of naked folks kneeling in a lake of bugs, too," Jasper countered.

"Well, she has a right to feel wanted, don't she?" Bobby Lee said. He was almost whining. "I mean, she DID bring all them folks in here, just like she said, and she DID help me build that shed, then build 'er up again. She's even talkin' 'bout havin' me bring in river rocks and do it right."

"What do you get for all that?" Jasper asked. "You ain't been home in a month. I know, cuz I talked to your old lady just yesterday. She isn't sorry to see you go, but ... why?"

"Them twins isn't the first to stay at the Eagle and Anchor, Jasper. They won't be the last, neither. Those girls, they'll be back, too. Ever' last one of 'em has felt her touch, and she calls 'em back. For me. There was a book, once. She told me about it. It was destroyed, but she managed to suck enough of the words into her children we might could rewrite it. Bring it back..."

Jasper's mind reeled. Already he was daydreaming of those twins, their honey hair and wide eyes. In the background of those dreams, he could see a stone building rising from the cotton to challenge the sky. He saw cars lined up like soldiers in a huge lot, bright neon signs and banners flapping in the wind.

"Waitin' for us now, you say?" he asked softly.

Bobby Lee nodded. There was a flicker of greenish light around the corner of the produce stand, and then the night went dark. Jasper closed his eyes, and in that darkness, he felt antennae flicking in the night breeze, seeking him, yearning for the salt of his sweat and the heat of his skin. Seeking communion.

"Thank the Lord," he said at last, turning toward Bobby Lee's truck and walking away, "for all them cockroach suckers."

"Amen," Bobby Lee added, grinning.

Above, the stars shone brightly, and Jasper could have sworn, as Bobby Lee pulled out of the parking lot, that the brilliant spots of light re-arranged themselves into a new shape. A constellation he could believe in. Popping the top on the beer Bobby handed him, Jasper saluted the sky, tracing the lines of stars with his graze and grinning.

"Look, Bobby Lee," he said softly. "Ain't that constellation The Twins?"

THE LAST PAGE

A CTHULHU ARMAGGEDON ADVENTURE

By. C.T. Phipps

"So, you have a magic book?" I said, leaning back in my wooden stool and looking at my cards.

Two aces, two eights.

All black.

The Dead Man's Hand.

Well, there was also a Queen of Hearts, but no one knew what the last card held by Wild Bill Hickock had been when he was shot in the back by Jack McCall. It was a story that wasn't really told anymore. Not many people had much to say about the Wild West of the 19th century since humanity had largely ended in the 21st.

The previous twenty thousand years of human history seemed like a distant dream, a fanciful lie told children. No one could even conceive of a time before the Rising, when the Great Old Ones stalked the Earth and mankind were the insects that crawled on the surface of its face.

My name was John Henry Booth and I was a survivor living on a dying world. I wasn't human, not anymore, and I was considered insane by the standards of my own shapeshifting twisted race. I preferred to live as a human being, wearing their form like a suit of clothes, than give into the alien timeless inhumanity that was my birthright. It was a constant daily struggle, though, that ate away at my consciousness. Eventually, I knew the monster inside me would win and I'd fly off to distant stars with the human I'd been as immaterial as a forgotten dream. In the meantime, though, I owned a bar that doubled as the town brothel. I was also the local sheriff.

"Not just *a* magic book," Owen Jones said, his face flush with drink and his breath smelling of rotting flesh. He was a Wastelander with weathered leathery features, bad teeth, and stringy white hair. He wasn't a local and apparently had made a lengthy journey from Canada irradiated ice lands to the New England deserts. *The* magic book, the *Al-Azif.* That may not make much sense to you—"

"It's the book the *Necronomicon* was created from. Supposedly, the Mad Arab had a vision of the book and copied its contents out into his more famous work," I interrupted, throwing in half my pot on this hand. The cards weren't especially good, but Owen couldn't afford it and I was ready to end tonight.

I'd pegged Owen as trouble as soon as he'd come in here hours ago, accompanied by a young slave girl. New Ulthar was a free town but no one was willing to raise their guns to him either. The girl also didn't seem ready to abandon the man either. Life was hellish enough that some accepted life as property if it meant surviving another day. There was also an aura of the unnatural about Owen, even more so than most Wastelanders, that made me think he was a threat to my people. It looked like I was right. I was glad I'd lured him into this card game as it meant I'd kept him out of whatever trouble he might have otherwise caused.

Owen narrowed his eyes. "You know a lot for a local."

"You have no idea," I said, giving a bitter chuckle.

Owen huffed then looked back at his cards. "Nice establishment you got here."

"It's a hellhole but it's my hellhole," I said, simply.

The Wages of Sin catered to travelers between Kingston, the University, and New Arkham. I'd killed the man who'd previously owned the place and taken over the business. Property rights weren't a thing people cared too much about in this corner of the Wasteland, and the man I'd killed was an asshole. Really, people had been more concerned at the possibility of the place shutting its doors than anything else.

The Wages of Sin wasn't particularly different from other similar establishments in this corner of the world. It had a piano in one corner, a bar, tables, and a second story where the women, and one man, conducted their business. I also owned the hotel next door, or more precisely, my wife did, since Mercury was far savvier at business. Generally, the rougher sorts plied their trades here and the more genteel costumers availed themselves of theirs. It wasn't a great retirement for a man who'd literally saved the world, but I supposed I'd only delayed the inevitable.

"It seems I'm a little short," Owen said, frowning. "I'm still willing to play, though."

"Do you have anything I'd want?" I asked, deliberately proving him.

Owen looked upstairs. "Your madam took my slave girl up to her quarters. I think that's worth something since you're using my property."

Owen assumed Mercury, my wife, had taken his slave to bed. Instead, Mercury was finding out everything she could about him. His girl didn't seem to want to go with our earlier, hidden, questions but that might not be the case once her options were explained to her. Either way, I didn't like slavers and was happy to put two bullets in the back of his head to get his property's freedom.

"What's her name?" I asked.

"Asenath," Owen said, as if the name was somehow offensive to him. "She comes from around here. I never did find out how she got all the way up in Canada but she's the reason I'm on this crazy mission."

"Really?" I asked.

I had to wonder at the sort of circumstances that could compel a young woman to depart across the hostile New England Wasteland to the equally horrifying desolate Canadian Badlands. When I was a New Arkham Ranger, I'd once made the perilous journey but it had taken an entire year. I'd lost two of my team during the trek as well.

"Yeah," Owen grinned. "But the rest of the story requires you covering the bet. What was your name, Booth?"

Owen poured himself another whisky, coughing hideously

and only covering his mouth after he'd sprayed a few droplets of blood and blackish phlegm onto the table. He could have spit in the floor. It irritated me he was belittling me, but I'd dealt with far worse in my time. When you faced down a rampaging shoggoth with nothing more than a pair of magic pistols, humans became an annoyance at worst.

"My friends call me John," I said, holding my cards close. I'd pegged him for trouble the moment he'd come in. Most trouble the locals could deal with—if it was human. The alternative? Not so much. In this world, you came to deal with the supernatural the same way you did famine or flood—you did your best to survive it and move on. I had additional advantages being not entirely human myself.

I took a moment to look at my "guest" more closely, taking in elements I hadn't properly considered before. Owen looked about seventy with a long white beard and a bald head. He wore a thick pair of denim overalls over a cotton shirt, his arms had a fetid green tinge. Sometimes, I saw movement inside his jeans when he breathed, as if something was swimming inside him.

The warm human face he wore seemed oddly placed, as if he'd somehow sewn it on. No one else had noticed that he probably wasn't entirely human, either, but I knew that creatures who wanted to fit in had ways of making sure their prey didn't notice. It was more reason to make sure he didn't leave my little town alive.

"I see, John," Owen said, misunderstanding my meaning.

"I didn't say we were friends," I said, pulling out a cigar from my pocket and lightning it. Tobacco was rare these days but there were lots of strange plants you could smoke if you weren't too concerned about your sanity. I'd sacrificed that on the altar of truth a long time back.

Owen narrowed his eyes and reached down to his pocket, possibly going for a gun. Despite the fact he was more corpse than man, he'd drunk hard liquor all night. "I have some emergency gold but I'd rather not touch it. Still—"

I chose my next words carefully. I wasn't interested in gold or silver and his words about the *Al-Azif* were probably bragging but, if true, made him infinitely more dangerous than just another slaver. Inhuman or not. "Why don't you tell me your story and show me the book. I'll consider that covering the bet."

Owen paused, and I knew I had him. He was human enough to still love the inherent dance of lies and greed that was gambling. "Alright."

He moved his hand from his pocket to the bag on the ground by his foot and picked up a book that, to my human eyes, looked like an old leather-bound volume with paper pages. If it had been written during the heyday of Medieval Arab culture, it would have been composed of different materials than the modernized thing in his hands. Luckily I could see with more than the fleshy orbs I'd been born with.

My 'Eyes of Yog-Sothoth' saw that the volume was a living piece of the Dreamlands. It was a glowing collection of thoughts and ideas that was more akin to a rift in the fabric of time than a mere book. It shone and whispered to anyone with the Sight, issuing promises and seeking a way in—a way to possess. The power behind it trying to enter a mortal mind was a bit like an atomic bomb being used to remove a stump. It was a thing beyond the pathetic lifeforms that had evolved on this third rock from the sun.

"Interesting," I said, understating matters. "Two pair."

"Three of a kind," Owen said. "I guess we'll be continuing to play."

"For now," I said. "You still owe me a tale."

"How do you figure?" Owen asked, looking ready to get while the getting was good. He'd picked up on the fact I wasn't another Wastelander and he'd perhaps said too much about his prize.

"Your luck is changing, and you don't want me to leave," I said, guessing he was as addicted to talking about himself as playing cards. Either would work, though. "Long journeys need cash and supplies."

"Deal the cards and I'll tell you everything," Owen said. "Centuries ago, my slave's ancestor, Andrew Doran, was a fool who actually thought he could fight the horrors beyond. Foolishness, I know, because I understand that the humans are the aberration, not the monsters. He discovered that this volume was actually a reliquary, all that remained of an insectoid race called the Nameless Ones."

"The Nameless Ones?" I asked, dealing the next hand.

"They don't speak English, jackass," Owen said, sounding more than a little drunk. Which surprised me. I had thought that he was probably a walking corpse, animated by something eldritch, or some remnant of old magic, rather than a man. "The Nameless Ones were things born in the darkness of space from the same fungus that spawned the dreaded Mi-Go from Yuggoth. The two races split long ago and came to worship different gods. The Yuggoth worshiped Yog-Sothoth and science, while the Nameless Ones venerated Nyarlathotep and the debased cults of great Kai-too-loo. The Yuggoth took refuge on Pluto and the asteroid belt past it. The Ixtol, as close as their name for themselves could be pronounced by human mouths, settled on what we call Callisto."

"Not very nameless then, are they?"

"Do you want to hear the story or not?"

"So, the Yuggoths were the Catholics and the Ixtol the Protestants."

I personally didn't see the need to differentiate religion like that. Yog-Sothoth, Cthulhu, and Nyarlathtotep were all real, and existed in the physical world. Debating the worship between them was a bit like choosing to worship gravity or space. I wasn't about to tell him to shut up, though, since this was potentially worthwhile information.

Assuming he wasn't making it all up.

"If you want to humanize them that way. Personally, I've got enough of them in me to know they're monsters through and through."

"You might want to keep your voice down," I said, tossing in my bet. "There's places where saying things like that will get you burned alive. Places like this one."

In fact, the citizens of New Ulthar were surprisingly tolerant of the strange and unusual as long as they kept it to themselves. There were Deep Ones, glamoured ghouls, cultists, Catholics, Jews, psychics, and sorcerers among its modest population.

Hidden temples, unnatural ancestry, and foul rituals were all things kept indoors. I'd been invited to two orgies and a cannibal feast in the last month, the latter's hosts insisting it had been arranged without innocent deaths.

"Right," Owen said, looking bored with my warning. "Eventually, the Nameless Ones encountered a malignant being, the spawn of Yog-Sothoth with a mortal, that destroyed their civilization. Their immortal prophet-god, a wizard king named Vhourvath, summoned all the peoples of Callisto, and then devoured them. They became this book, which hurtled itself into space and eventually landed on Earth. It has sought the time and means to release its people into this world ever since."

"It picked a poor planet to avoid being eaten on," I said, dryly. "You'd also think it would have succeeded by now if it was a real threat."

Despite my attitude I was interested in hearing what he had to say. There were more weird tales in this world than even a quasi-immortal like myself could ever hear. That didn't mean I didn't want to hear as many of them as I could, though. It was, Ironically, one of the ways I kept myself human.

Owen shrugged and raised his bet. "Supposedly, it almost did during the 1940s."

"What happened then?"

"Andrew Doran killed Vhourvath. Shot him dead."

I laughed then matched his bet. "So, the millions of years-old monster's plan to preserve themselves was a failure because of a human with a gun?"

I'd heard of Andrew Doran from the files in New Arkham's military base. He'd been something of an adventurer archaeologist and occult detective back in an age before humanity had learned that the supernatural was real—the hard way. No one knew what had happened to him past the Second Great War, which seemed a silly name for it, but there were legends that he'd fought Jack Parsons and the Selfosophy cult in the Fifties before ascending to another dimension. It was hardly the strangest fate I'd heard for a wizard but a somewhat anticlimactic end for a man who'd stood up to Dagon and lived.

"A bit," Owen admitted. "Vhourvath had to teach much of

humanity the secrets of the occult to create the glyphs, wards, and science necessary to resurrect his kind. Without Vhourvath's consciousness to direct the hive-mind of the Nameless Ones, however. they were a shadow of themselves. Barely more powerful than humans, even if they *were* still immortal. The book's magic became wild and unpredictable. It got stolen from Miskatonic University by another cult sometime in the late 20th century. Apparently, that was a problem in those days. "The TDS or Terra Defense Service, a dreadful secret society, researched ways to destroy it, and discovered a way, but only when the stars aligned properly."

"When was that supposed to happen?"

"After the end of the world."

I hadn't heard of the TDS but there had been many people who had tried to fight the Mythos before the Rising, with varying results. Some of them like the late Elizabeth Dee, had left their journals behind, while most had simply died or gone insane with little to show for their efforts. Maybe they had delayed the Rising for a time or maybe it had appeared on time when the stars were right, as impossible to oppose as the seasons. That didn't mean their struggle had no meaning but it did mean it was an existential one. To fight the chaos of the universe was a choice made knowing it was impossible like Sisyphus rolling his boulder up the hills of Hades, knowing it would roll back down immediately after it reached the top.

"So now." I looked at my cards. It was another Dead Man's Hand with clubs instead of spades, which made me wonder if the deck was stacked.

"Yes."

"The TDS were a nasty group of people," Owen admitted. "Wanted to wipe out everything nonhuman, which would have included you and me."

"I don't know what you're talking about," I said, looking at him.

"Sure, you don't," Owen said. "In any case, I might not look it but I'm over a century old. I was born before the Rising."

"Who told you that you don't look it?" I asked, being more insulting than I had to be.

Thankfully, Owen let the jibe slide and just smiled. "I was an occult book dealer before the end of the world. I knew enough to prepare for the end. While others stocked up on canned goods and ammunition, I took the book away from one of the TDS' last members, a gibbering-insane lunatic living in a Southern Gothic mansion untouched by the apocalypse. I used its power to live like a king. Perhaps you've heard of the Golden City of Halifax?"

"They say everyone there is immortal, beautiful, and that there are no children born or living."

Owen didn't respond to that. "Yes, well, we all make mistakes."

I didn't discard any of my cards. "So, what are you doing with the book now?"

Owen's eyes went blurry as he seemed to disappear into his own thoughts. Eventually, he spoke. "For the longest time, I did not think there was any evil act I could not perform in the name of pleasure and power. The book was a hungry god and I fed it many lives. There were, however, things even I would not do to fulfill its needs, and now I am going to destroy it. My slave and I are going to take it to Sentinel Hill where it can be fed to The Thing That Waits."

"You could give it a name, like Bob or something," I said.

Owen glared at me. "Call."

I laid my cards on the table.

Owen had nothing and growled, before pushing the chips across to me. "I think I'm done playing poker. I'll just fetch my slave and get going."

I guessed it was as good a in his hands that made from pipe time as any to shoot the man and rob him of the *Al-Azif* but, I admitted, I didn't want to. Slaver or not, the man had traveled all the way down here in order to destroy an evil that had imperiled the world. I decided I would kill him quickly rather than drawing it out as I did with most slavers. I was tempted to even give him a chance to leave peacefully. The thing was I didn't trust anyone to destroy objects of power like that but me. Even if I hadn't known about its existence nearby until a few minutes prior.

"She's a bit occupied right now," I said, looking up to the

second story.

I'd caught a glimpse of Asenath earlier. She was pretty as a picture and seemed a lot sharper than her owner. I would have liked to have consulted Mercury to get a bit more information but, instead, moved my hand underneath the table toward my gun. I hoped whatever gods Owen believed in would be more merciful to him than I was about to be.

"That's not my problem," Owen hissed, right before his head exploded.

No exaggeration, Owen's head detonated like a watermelon struck by a shotgun blast. His skull shattered. I watched in fascination as his brain matter splattered across the table. It was alive with hundreds of disgusting, still-living alien insects that had formed a colony inside him. The thing was, I hadn't been the one to shoot him. No, the round that had ended him had come from another's hand.

That was unexpected.

I drew my gun and swung around, scanning the room. A tall man, maybe six foot nine, stood in the door. A heavy duster covered his clothes. He looked like a mummified corpse in dirty clothing. He had no eyes, but a pair of centipedes stuck out of the empty sockets, making screaming sounds at a volume their bodies should have been far too small to possess. Long stringy white hair clung to the back of his scalp. There was also a handcrafted rifle in his hands that was made from pipe and carved wood.

The sudden appearance of the supernatural and violence caused the expected reaction. Panic. Most humans had either learned to pray, or to run away from the monsters when they found them. Neither reaction helped, though those who ran tended to die tired. My clientele was not the usual mix. Instead of running, they opened fire, heading for windows and doors and throwing everything they had at the undead intruder as they went. Dozens of bullets struck the creature, but they had no more effect than if they'd been fired into a wooden post.

The thing ignored the attacks and headed straight for me. I saw he was going for the book. I was tempted to grab the thing and make a run for it but changed my mind. I grabbed

Owen's bottle of whisky, damn near hundred-proof, and hurled it against the creature's head. The tumbler shattered and soaked the creature good. I flicked my cigar at it, and the whisky blazed, turning the thing into a walking torch.

That pissed it off.

Burning with no sign of pain or agony, it raised its rifle and aimed it at me. "You meddle with things you do not understand, Timeless One." It said in a dry, rattling voice.

"That I do," I said. I fired an orihalcum bullet into its head. Deep One gold was not of this Earth. It was often useful against trans-dimensional beings. It blew the creature to bits, splattering me with anti-climatic gore.

I blinked. "Huh."

That was when I saw a chocolate-skinned teenage girl grab the book and make a run for the swinging doors.

Asenath.

"Dammit!" I shouted.

I was out of my seat, across the floor, and out the door within seconds. I moved faster than a normal human, though it wasn't very impressive compared to some of the other things I could do.

"Get away from me!" Asenath said, turning around to punch me. She held a piece of broken glass in her hand, and it might have killed me, but I was faster. I grabbed her throat and squeezed, and her arm went limp.

"Owen is dead," I said, grabbing the book from her hands.

I almost immediately fell over. There was power in those pages and I didn't have to be a wizard or psychic to know it came from the Great Old Ones. Just holding it caused me to hear insects crawling on the surface of my consciousness, whispering the secrets of a dead world.

"Give that back!" Asenath shouted. "I'll call the sheriff!"

"I am the sheriff," I said, absently. "Mayor too. Mercury is the town doctor and brothel owner, like Doc Holliday."

"It was Wyatt Earp and his brother James who owned a brothel. Holliday was a dentist," Asenath growled.

I blinked, surprised at her knowledge. "Your owner said that you were taking this to Sentinel Hill to destroy it."

"That's not your concern!" Asenath hissed. "That book is dangerous! People are looking for it."

"People are a relative term," I said, my voice low and threatening. "Who is after them?"

Asenath stopped struggling. "The Cult of the Insect—"

"Stop," I said, letting her go. "You don't have to say any more."

The Cult of the Insect was one of the many religions, once secretive and kept underground that had emerged after the Rising to become the dominate faiths of humanity. I'd seen no sign of the Great Old Ones ever paying attention to the rites invoked in their name, but plenty of atrocities had been perpetrated by their followers. The Cult of the Insect was one of the worst, spreading disease and misery indiscriminately, because they believed they would be spared the wrath of the unfathomable aliens who ruled over the Earth. Crazy, but they were also possessed of real. Real enough to send a man made of maggots after me. If they were linked to the *Al-Azif,* then that explained quite a few things. Mind you, I probably should have made that connection earlier.

"I need that book," Asenath said.

"You wouldn't get within ten miles of Sentinel Hill. It's across the Great Barrier Desert, past the Dunwych tribe, and through the Forest of Lies."

"Forest of Lies? Really?" Asenath asked, keeping her eyes squarely on the book.

"I didn't name it," I said, putting the book in the pocket of my shirt. "Nothing gets named anything normal anymore. I thought you were a local."

"I am," Asenath said. "Just not...recently."

"Uh huh," I said, trying to figure out what she meant by that.

"How are you holding the book?" Asenath asked.

"It's called a pocket."

"The book can't be held by humans," she said. "It burns the flesh of anyone not consecrated to the cult."

"I don't recall that from the legends I've heard of the book."

"Because I put that curse on it a few months ago in order

to make it harder for the cult to retrieve it." Asenath spit on the ground. "It is evil, a thing of chaos. It warps and changes reality to better torture the living. If you're holding it, you're something less than human."

"Or more," I said.

Moments later, my partner, Mercury, came running down. She was dressed in a pair of denim jeans and a cotton shirt. There was a blood stain on her shirt and she was carrying a pistol.

"Asenath, I told you to stay put," Mercury said, looking at me. "What the hell happened?"

"I could ask the same."

"Cultists," Mercury said, making a sour face. "I managed to shoot two of them. The third collapsed into a bunch of bugs."

"Did you squish them?" I asked.

"I paid Gino the drunk to do it," Mercury said, shrugging. "He sang *La Cucaracha* the entire time as he danced on them in his boots."

Good ol' Gino.

"It's the Insect cultists," Asenath said, looking at Mercury. "Do you know this thing?"

I was really starting to dislike this girl.

"John is more or less human," Mercury said defensively.

"It's the less I'm worried about," Asenath said, looking disgusted. "I had to deal with that monster, the human kind, for months. I pretended to be his obedient slave, played on his insecurities, and convinced him he could find redemption by taking it to be destroyed. We're almost there. This could be the end of something terrible."

I looked down at her. "That's a lot of work for a young woman."

"I'm older than I look," Asenath said, simply. "Listen, I told my story to your friend. I trust her. She gave me the sign."

I raised an eyebrow. "The sign?"

"The sign of the University," Mercury said, simply. "She's one of their agents."

I grimaced, not at all happy with this revelation. Centuries ago, Miskatonic University had been the only place on Earth to do serious research on the occult horrors of the Great Old Ones. Some poor foolish souls had even tried to oppose them, though that was like trying to put out a forest fire with a teacup full of water. In the end, they'd failed to save the world and now existed as a depraved pseudo-religious sect that had made alliances with the Yith and with Mi-Go. Sometimes they did things that benefited the world, and others they poked things better left alone with an obvious stick.

"John, we have to help her destroy the *Al-Azif*," Mercury said, her tone brooking no argument.

"It's a book," I said, knowing in my heart that it was so much more. I heard it whisper that it could restore my humanity, make me stronger than any other man alive, or allow me to build a refuge for humanity in the Dreamlands. These were all reflections of my most heart-felt wishes. There was also something old, malevolent, and hungry in the book's pages— which weren't pages at all, but more of a mirage covering a pit of flesh-eating scarabs.

"The *Al-Azif* was injured by my ancestor," Asenath said, looking around the town to see if anyone was paying attention. She needn't have bothered. The people who lived in the tiny watering hole built around the Wages of Sin, charitably named New Ulthar, didn't care a lick about anyone but themselves. Really, the only thing they did seem to care about was no one hurt the ridiculous number of stray cats that lived around the town. One poor asshole had thrown a horseshoe at one that was eyeing his sandwich, only to end up flayed alive by something in the night. It was why I always bought a pitcher of milk for them every month.

"Injured?" I asked.

Asenath nodded. "Once it contained a whole race of aliens trying to survive. I don't know how but the book was like a whole other universe."

"Dreams are real and contain as much space as they need," Mercury said, as if this was some sort of profound statement. Then again, I'd physically visited the Dreamlands and seen friends killed in them. Witches had a different perspective on the world and Mercury knew the foul tongues of long dead races who could mold reality with their minds.

"My ancestor killed the wizard-god at the heart of it," Asenath said. "The people inside were consumed by the terrible things the Nameless Ones summoned and bound to create their ark. What's left is a hungry vortex that is fueled by the deranged ramblings of an entire race's echo. A thing that, unleashed, would kill the whole of humanity with its dying scream."

I blinked. "Mercury, where would you put that on our scale of 'humanity-is-fucked o-meter'?"

"Five, five-and-a-half?" Mercury suggested.

"Sounds about right."

Asenath stared between us. "Are you not taking this seriously?"

"Lady, you have no idea the kind of unfathomable horrific shit we have been neck deep in for the past few years," I said, thinking about how unbearable the cost of trying to do some good in this world had been.

The most terrible truth I'd encountered as a New Arkham Ranger turned lawman was not that the world was a godless, soulless, place where humanity was an unimportant speck of bacteria. It was the world was a god-filled, soulful place, where humanity was an unimportant speck of bacteria. Mankind was not just insects buzzing against the face of beings infinitely their superior, but things those superior being's pets liked to eat.

Things like me.

"We'll help you," Mercury said, blinking. "One less relic of a dead world won't make a difference. Humanity is already going extinct. This might delay it for a few more days, weeks, or even centuries."

I thought, considering it was an object of power, that keeping it might save a portion of mankind, but I wasn't about to tell my partner that. Mercury and I disagreed on several things. One of them was the best way to try to make sure humanity's legacy didn't completely disappear. Mercury wanted to try and save humanity, as futile as that effort might be. We—no---they were ill-equipped as a race to continue living in a world that Dread Cthulhu had terraformed into something closer to the primordial Earth his people found palatable.

Evolution had passed humanity by and the only way now to survive was to adapt. If mankind was to survive, then we had to become more like the Great Old Ones, wild, free, and immortal. My children and I could pass on our genetics and bond with mankind to create something new. To be as the race that was my genetic heritage and had sent their own ark to Earth to preserve—perhaps as fruitlessly as the creators of the *Al-Azif* had.

Instead of making that argument, I simply nodded. "You're right. The book has to be destroyed."

I wondered if, in a million years, the next race of Earth would look back on that moment and say, "*Yeah, that guy could have saved his mate's species, but ended up letting it be destroyed so he could continue to sleep with her. This is where Darwinism failed.*"

Asenath nodded. "Thank you, both of you. I guess I'll have to trust you."

"You really have no choice. You have no money, horse, car, or thing to barter. Any man or woman who wants to take you as a slave outside these borders would and could."

"I can take care of myself," Asenath said, dangerously.

Mercury punched her in the face.

Asenath hit the ground then felt her nose. "What the hell!?"

"Concise argument," I said, applauding her debate skills.

"Do what we say and stay behind us," Mercury said. "We've been across the New England Wasteland many times."

"I know the Dunwych," I said, not entirely happy to think about going back into their territory. "They aren't fond of me but they're not our enemies either. We'll have to keep the book secret if we want to make it to Sentinel Hill alive."

I was understating the difficulty. Sentinel Hill was one of the holy sites of tribal worshippers of the Great Old Ones. The Dunwych were descendants of a rural town and the refugees it had taken in that had degenerated into barbarism. They were among the most ruthless of all of humanity's survivors, and some of the most occult savvy. Not that humanity's knowledge of the truth of reality amounted to anything more than a thimble full of water from an ocean of madness.

"Then we should get going," Asenath said, her voice

containing the barest hint of panic. "If the Cult of the Insect have found us, they'll stop at nothing to destroy us."

"We can handle—"

That was when the entirety of New Ulthar shook with an earthquake. The ground rumbled, and buildings began collapsing around us. People ran in every direction. It turned toward the Western edge of town, which was visible from the middle, and I saw a huge cloud of dirt flying into the air. A hideous, crawling thing emerged beneath it, rising above the buildings as if there was no end to its body.

The thing could not be fully perceived by human eyes or understood by human brains. They filled in images with something that resembled a dragon, a squid, and a centipede crossed together. My eyes were artificial, a product of my shapeshifting, but they still saw the horrible image of a monster. The rest of my vision, saw a thing that spanned six dimensions, time, and space.

The creature had been summoned through some foul sorcery I did not recognize. I knew, in some primordial genetic memory of the alien that sired me that it was an eater of worlds. The only thing preventing it from destroying the continent where I stood was its ability to manifest only the tip of its presence into this world. The fools in the Cult of the Insect had brought oblivion to the world in hopes of acquiring something that would allow them to do the same.

"A Tunneler!" Mercury shouted, misidentifying the creature as one of the primordial things that dwelled in the dark corners of the Earth. "John you need to kill it!"

I looked back at Mercury like she was insane.

"They can't be allowed to have the book!" Asenath said, missing that this was every bit as horrid a threat.

I realized we had no choice. It was seeking the *Al-Azif,* and the book pulsed like it had a heartbeat, craving to join itself to the monster. It wished to be devoured and merge its essence, to tear apart reality for a dozen galaxies width. The creature could resurrect its dead race across every micro-second of its life and have them live together in a chaos where nothing ever died but, at the same time did not exist. It offered that insane joy and peculiar immortality to humanity as well.

"No," I said, staring at it. "I'm not going to let you do that."

So, I opened the book and set my will against it.

That was a profoundly stupid idea.

I opened the *Al-Azif* and focused. I hoped that there was something inside the object powerful enough to beat back the Horror Below (as I'd instantly named the thing in a poetic flourish). Unfortunately, no sooner had I opened the book than my mind was assaulted by the THINGS inside.

The *Al-Azif* was not a book, any more than a Venus fly trap was a safe place for a bug to land. It was a device designed to absorb the consciousness and information of those poor souls who opened it, to tear the dream stuff that forged realities in other layers of reality, and then build a new home for a long-extinct race. The creatures within no longer had a central focusing consciousness but were a soup of a million lesser things. They were a mindless horde of hungry otherworldly consciousnesses lashing out and begging for release.

The thing was, I quickly realized, if you could provide the book with lives, you could use it for a little while before you were completely consumed. I was recognized the trap at a glance. I felt the chaotic hungry creatures within reaching into my mind with invisible tendrils to plant their parasite. They would never be able to work as one but even one of their lesser castes could outthink a "mere" human and live again through their bodies. They thought I was a potential victim to replace the body of and give another of their race a form to live through.

This was a mistake.

If I was a human being, save perhaps one of those exceptional, deranged individuals like Randolph Carter or Titus Crow, I would have been obliterated outright. I was not, though, but a beast every bit as terrifying that chose to wear human skin. In that, I was every bit as insane as any human confronted with the unknowable horror of the unknown. It also meant my mind was not so easily obligated or cast aside. Instead, I reached into the book's pages, crossing five or six dimensional boundaries.

And I fed.

It was only as I tore at and feasted on the creature within that

I remembered the billions of years my species has dominated their own corner of the galaxy. That the creatures around me, obscene and mammalian, ape-like things barely evolved from protoplasm, were nothing but mayflies unworthy of the least consideration. Breeding stock that I could create a newer, better, race from the ruins of.

NO!

I was not going to allow myself to go sane. To abandon the truth of the reality: that I was anything but a human being, a part of the terrible horrific things that dominated creation. I preferred to be a tiny immaterial thing for as long as I could manage it. I stopped feasting, having barely tasted the power within, and slammed the book shut. I turned; opened my mouth and unleashed a column of flame made of a hundred eldritch energies that tore into the Horror Below. It wailed, hissed, and thrashed before collapsing to the ground into a puddle of other-dimensional matter that should not exist in this reality but was real enough that it would probably kill whoever stepped on that spot for decades.

I'd have to put up a sign or something.

"John!" Mercury shouted, running to my side.

"What did you see?" I asked, hoping the spell remained.

Mercury was one of the few people who had ever seen the face of Great Cthulhu and lived. She'd also had her sanity completely shattered by the psychic backlash and been driven to catatonia. I'd erased her memory of the event, violating her mind in the process, then bound magics to make sure she could never see the true face of the horror about us. They translated, theoretically, into terrible but explicable monsters. A dragon could kill you, after all, but it would not leave you gibbering mad.

Ironically, the greatest effect of my betrayal was the fact that Mercury possessed the power to make invocations and spells to the Great Old Ones that had cost more experienced wizards their sanity. I'd seen her cast the winds of Ithaqua, summon tentacles of Zul'Cthonic, and speak words of Azathoth without any danger to her mind. Weirdly, her body too showed no signs of the strains that channeling energies of ancient foulnesses usually required. Looking past her, I saw fifteen dead and burning corpses of Insect cultists. They'd apparently not been content to leave my fate to the Horror Below but had tried to ambush us as I used the book, only to be shredded by my lover's spells. This was turning into a bloody, bloody night.

"You throwing a fireball at the Tunneler," Mercury said, taking a deep breath. "What else?"

"I see."

"That's not what happened," Asenath said, coming up behind her. "*What are you?*"

"The person who is going to take you to Sentinel Hill."

Asenath looked at me with hate in her eyes. She clearly had enough sensitivity to know I wasn't human, was one of the things that threatened humanity by my very existence, but I didn't care.

"And if I refuse?" Asenath asked.

"Then I'll shoot you," Mercury said.

"Wait, what?" Asenath asked, doing a double take.

"This is a partnership, tenderfoot, and you helped lead a monster to our home," Mercury said, having already drawn her gun. "Just how many cultists are after us and how many more are we likely to encounter on the way to New Dunwych?"

Asenath looked down. "The Cult of the Insect has an entire city in Halifax."

"I like Canadians," Mercury muttered. "The kingdoms up there are pretty hardy."

"This is not a normal kingdom," Asenath said. "The Golden City's residents wear the skins of human beings and cover themselves with glamour but are nothing more than colonies of insects bound to human souls. It is a rebirth of the Nameless City cleansed by the Yith millennia ago. It was the original goal of the Ixtol, but without their leader, they are a shadow of what they once were. The residents depend on the *Al-Azif* to provide them with their immortality as well as power their dreadful machines."

"I thought Owen owned it."

"Owen is one of them or was one of them," Asenath corrected herself. "I can be most persuasive."

"Oh?" Mercury asked. "What did you do?"

"I cast a spell that warped his mind and made him think it was a good idea to destroy it," Asenath said.

"Ah," I said, nodding.

I thought of the irony of the Callisto people. They had sacrificed everything to create their dreadful artifact and now it was providing immortality to a bunch of depraved humans. The Cult of the Insect wasn't purely the creatures of Callisto if Owen was any indication but an unholy fusion of them with humans. Creatures like me.

"So, we're likely to face more of them," I muttered.

"Yes," Asenath said.

"Great," I said, looking over at Mercury. "I suppose we should get the hell out of town and try to divert their attention."

"So, you're robbing me and taking over my quest?" Asenath asked.

"Try and keep up," Mercury said, frowning. "Yes. Because, again, you brought this horror to our doorstep."

It occurred to me how ridiculous the coincidence must have been that she could come to our little town and find us out of all the survivors of humanity. That's when it clicked for me and I felt remarkably stupid.

"She's manipulating us, Mercury."

"What?" Mercury said, confused.

"She knew we were here. She directed Owen—"

"Balthazar," Asenath said. "His name was Balthazar. He was a horrible person but easily led about by his groin."

"So, you came here deliberately?" Mercury said. "Son of a bitch."

"I thought the famous witch here would help me," Asenath said, looking at Mercury. "I didn't know I'd also have to deal with her demon."

"Yes, well, if you're dealing with witches then you should be expecting to also deal with demons," Mercury said, dryly.

"Famous witch?" I asked, looking down at her.

"I do have a life beyond you," Mercury said, her voice lowering. "There's things I do not understand that I do not perceive the way other people do. I don't yet know what's happened to me, what makes me different, but there are things that I can do that you cannot."

I lowered my head. "True, Mercury. You are a powerful dreamer and that will benefit you. Still, I don't like being lied to or manipulated."

Asenath's eyes flashed a dangerous intelligence. "All I want is to destroy the book. When it is gone, there will be one less threat to the world. The Golden City will collapse, and its horde of ancient bug-ridden liches will vanish. That's all that matters."

Somehow, I doubted that. "Then I suggest we get moving."

"That's the first sensible thing you've said tonight," Mercury said, never taking her gun off Asenath, though she visibly relaxed.

Around us, the people of New Ulthar went back to their nightly routines. The deaths of probably a half-dozen townsfolk and the arrival of an enormous monster was not so uncommon as to mean a serious disruption in their evening.

I could not ride a horse; animals aside from cats could not stand me. We ended up piling into one of the few functioning motor vehicles in town. I'd purchased the ramshackle composite from a caravanner who wanted to leave the lifestyle of transporting goods from New Arkham to Kingsport. I didn't use it much and there had been a dozen attempts to steal the thing over the years, but the solar powered machine took us across the Great Barrier Desert past hordes of D'toan giant centipedes, each the size of houses, and the half-real Pyramids of Gah'nak.

Once humankind had held uncontested dominion over the Earth's surface, but their supremacy was an illusion even then. The ghouls had ruled the tunnels beneath their cities, and the Deep Ones had slumbered in dimensional pockets hidden within the ocean's many trenches. Cultists had venerated Great Cthulhu and the inner circles of many religions had been warped by secret worship of the Things Which Should Not Be. When the Rising had occurred, mad prophets and would-be despots had claimed the Gods Below would reward their faithful. If so, it had been only the reward of being eaten first and avoiding the horror to come. Even humanity's sister races like the Tcho-Tcho or satyr-like Leng had died in droves as their hidden fortresses were overwhelmed by the screams of the Great Old

Ones awakening.

There were perhaps one in a hundred of the human beings left that had existed a century prior, and that estimation was generous. Many of the survivors of mankind were no longer strictly what could be referred to as human. I was on the far end of things, despite my delusion that I was as human as any other man, but even people like Mercury had elements wholly different from what existed before. Asenath's desire to destroy the Nameless Ones of Halifax made me wonder if she was driven by a desire to save humanity from another dangerous threat, or whether it was pure hatred of the Other. But what *was* the other when the mirror held only an enemy?

I had plenty of time for such thoughts during the eight-hour drive to New Dunwych. The Dunwych were a powerful tribal empire that stretched from the radioactive jungles of time lost Maine to the haunted rivers of Providence. They were a fierce and savage people who had fully embraced the insanity of the new world, which perhaps made them the only sane ones left.

"So, what is your story, Asenath?" I asked, looking back at the slave girl who seemed so familiar with things she should not know.

"I told you, I'm from Miskatonic University. I'm a descendant of the Doran line," Asenath said, giving a smile that did not quite reach her eyes. She was sitting in the back of our composite vehicle as a cloud of dust followed its exhaust.

"I don't recall Doran having any family," I said, keeping my eye on the rear-view mirror.

"Perhaps I'm the descendant of Harold Stubbs then, the famous London investigator, or Albert Wilmarth," Asenath said, dismissing us. "Maybe I'm just some poor waif they managed to pick up at one of the slaver's auctions. Does it matter? I lived, I learned, and I am here now."

There was something about her demeanor that put me in the mind of someone far older than her apparent nineteen years. The way she spoke was also more cultured than someone born in this savage age. Even Mercury, who had been educated as a doctor in a city state, had a coarser and more practical way of speaking. There was also something about her cold dead eyes that put me in mind of a snake. I could not see the interior of human's souls, though, and she seemed to have nothing of the Otherworld about her. Whatever she was, she was human.

Such as that was.

"Why all the questions, John? We're the ones who robbed her, after all," Mercury said, looking at Asenath with a longing gaze. She was an attractive girl and it seemed that her cover story of wanting to lie with her earlier hadn't entirely been a fiction.

"Clearly, I am in the wrong," I said, sarcastically before bringing the vehicle to a stop. It was not because of the conversation but because we had arrived.

Sentinel Hill was far into the territory of the Dunwych, surrounded by miles of dense forest that grew along the edge of the Great Barrier Desert. The Dunwych built their homes along the coast in tree-houses, cabins, and cottages nearby. The craggy peak was a place of religious worship for the tribals and had numerous stone temples surrounding it. The smoke from sacrifices accompanied the droning alien music of things not quite human summoned to pass their wisdom on to the natives. The Forest of Lies, as it was known, was full of traps and places of execution for the tribals' enemies.

"Do you think they're going to let us pass?" Mercury asked.

I shrugged. "Only one way to find out."

As I probably should have anticipated, Mercury, Asenath, and I were led to the sacrificial altar to die.

"Great job negotiating, John," Mercury said, her arms tied before her as she was pushed by a rifle-toting Dunwych.

The three of us were ascending the Path of Skulls, a rocky path up the side of Sentinel Hill. The road was lined with spears, each adorned with a human skull. So, it was an apropos name. The Dunwych wore white chalk on their faces and carried ancient but well-maintained weapons from before the Rising.

There were close to a hundred of them and they knew exactly who we were and as what we carried. Unfortunately, they seemed to have very different ideas about what to do with the book than we did. We were all naked, our hands tied before us, the *Al-Azif* confiscated and held by a white-haired albino priestess with unnatural cat-like yellow eyes wearing only a loin cloth and bloody tattoos. It was like something out of a lurid Pre-Rising motion picture. I could rip free of normal bonds easily enough, but there were sorceries in the ropes that kept me from acting.

"Hey, we got here, didn't we?" I replied, less worried than I should have been.

"Yeah, that's a real comfort, John," Mercury muttered.

"I hate you all," Asenath said.

"They want the book's power," I said, looking at them. I spoke the Dunwych language and had been listening to them discuss it for the past half-hour.

"Can they take it?" Mercury asked.

"What do you think?" I asked, relying on her knowledge of the subject more than mine.

"No," Asenath said. "They do not know how to bind the energies within. They will unleash a horde of millions of hungry insects. They will devour this existence and leave only an empty dead world before turning on one another."

"How do you know that?" Mercury asked.

"I read," Asenath said.

"What would you do with it?" I asked, trying to trip her up.

"Find a way off this rock," Asenath said, pausing. "If I wasn't destroying it, I mean."

"Of course," I said.

Our destination was the stone circle at the top of Sentinel Hill. It was eight stone pillars around a ninth rock that was stained with dried blood, viscera, and disgusting fluids excreted upon hundreds of deaths. We were forced to our knees before the high priestess and I debated transforming into something else. I wanted to wait until just the right moment, though.

"The blood of these humans will sanctify the book and provide us with the power of the Ones Above. Long ago, Abdul Al'Hazred was enlightened—" the priestess started a rather irritating speech that I had no interest in hearing. In her right hand was an obsidian dagger that glowed with unearthly power, though I was likely the only one to see it.

Before I could rip her head off, it exploded from a rifle shot and I hit the ground. Mercury forced Asenath down as well. The air filled with bullets as century-old jeeps that had been refurbished and reengineered so many times they barely resembled their own origins drove up the side of the hill. Insect cultists fired machine guns and rifles from their seats.

I tried to shift but found I could not, which made me realize my plan to get us here might not have been the best one. There was something woven into the rope that prevented the change.

Mercury grabbed the obsidian knife and cut my bonds before turning the dagger on her own.

"Help me!" hissed Asenath.

Mercury tossed her the knife as Asenath freed herself.

All around us, the Dunwych were getting massacred as the ground erupted with swarms of flesh-eating scarabs that stripped their bodies clean in seconds. Two D'toan giant centipedes emerged as well, throwing the Dunwych charge to the ground.

"Do your thing, John!" Mercury shouted. "I'll start the summoning!"

"You got..." I didn't get to respond because I was promptly stabbed in the side by Asenath.

The blade passed through my skin and into five or six dimensions, causing pain the like of which I hadn't experienced in a long time. The obsidian was not actually volcanic glass but the talon of something that bore some surface resemblance. I collapsed, feeling like I was being eaten away from the insides.

"Dammit," I muttered, clutching my side. "I should have seen that coming."

Asenath then punched Mercury in the face, grabbing the *Al-Azif* from the priestess' corpse. She spoke with a thicker, deeper voice that seemed to blend genders. "Thank you, John, Mercury, I couldn't have done it without you."

For a moment, I saw her glow. It looked like an amorphous sexless humanoid thing was puppeteering her body. Whoever Asenath was, she wasn't a nineteen-year-old girl. She was someone far older, perhaps a Deep One or human wizard, wearing their skin as you might a pair of clothes.

"I take it you're not actually Andrew Doran's descendant," I muttered, bleeding worse than any other time since I'd discovered I wasn't human. "Is Asenath even your name?"

"Oh, this body is and no, it's my daughter's name," Asenath said, her voice becoming an old man's. "She consulted with the ghosts that haunted Kingsport's oldest cemeteries and found me. It's not the first time I've worn a woman's body and I admit having grown comfortable with them. I'd recommend you try it if you weren't about to end with this wretched planet."

A swarm of flesh-eating beetles fell upon us, only for Mercury to make a Ward of the Elder Sign in the air, flames forming an inverted pentagram the size of a building that disintegrated the beetles in a shower of flame. It also bought us time, preventing the rest of the Cult of the Insect from reaching us. The symbol terrified me, and I and would have fled immediately, if not for the fact I was badly wounded.

"What do you hope to accomplish?" I said, searching the ground for a weapon. I was injured but hoped Asenath, whatever her real name was, didn't realize I still had a monster's strength within me.

"I will summon the son of Yog-Sothoth, the brother of Wilbur Whateley, and bring back that which was banished here centuries ago. A creature that was meant to open the door and be both the key and the gate for his father."

"The apocalypse has already happened!" I snapped, angrily. "What possible good could that do?"

"As this world lays dying, I will use the *Al-Azif*'s energy to power a binding spell that will let me control the Monster of Sentinel Hill. It will carry me across the universes so that I may visit an Earth where the Old Ones never awoke or don't even exist! A place I can live a blessed life as a man or woman free from this miserable hellhole. I'll even settle for living a loop of the last hundred years of mankind."

"You'll destroy the world to escape to an alternate reality?" I asked, finding no weapon worth using.

"Yes!" Azenath shouted, a glowing circle of fire circling around her and preventing either of us from moving forward.

I'd heard some crazy over the years, but this took the cake.

Then again, was it truly crazy or merely evil? Good and evil were things the Great Old Ones' ilk were beyond but I believed in them as a human concept. Yet, I found myself not able to judge her either. Not completely. This was a dying world and whatever man or woman was unforunate enoug to live on it was resigning themselves to oblivion. There were infinite worlds out there with infinite varieties of beings, I'd caught glimpse of them while traveling the Dreamlands.

Was it truly such a deranged idea to escape this shell of a world and seek out a place where human kindness was not so strange a concept? The answer was yes if the cost was unleashing the horror of an Outer Gods' spawn upon the rest of mankind. A mass murdering cultist was not going to be someone who could escape the Wasteland's horrors. No, they would simply bring it with them. It was why I could never leave this world. I was part of its nightmares now.

"Fuck you," I finally said.

Asenath shrugged and assumed a space next to the altar. "Goodbye. This is a mercy killing if that's any comfort."

It wasn't.

Asenath muttered words in an inhuman tongue that surrounded her in a glowing field that would serve as a barrier between humans and monsters both.

"Sorry, John, I'm a terrible judge of character," Mercury said, turning around and rushing to my side.

"You are," I said, feeling the life drain out of me.

Mercury turned around and started casting an invocation to Shub-Niggurath to heal my injuries. The agony of this was exquisite, but it drove the hideous otherworldly poison from my body. My blood was already on the ground, though and had joined with that of the dozens of Dunwych warriors now serving as bait to the hungry thing on the other side.

"Ia Vhourvath! Ia Hastur! Ia Cthugha! I invoke thee in the name of the Outer Gods! I compel thee to bring forth he who has been trapped in a moment of time in this place! I offer the spirits of Callisto to you! I offer thee beings so that you may feed and be free!" Asenath cackled. "I compel you to come and bind thee in the name of thy father, in the name of the Crawling

Chaos, and the name of Azathoth!"

It was all mumbo jumbo, but powerful mumbo jumbo. The words were not what was important but the will, the dreaming power of the mind behind them. Asenath was clearly a powerful sorceress, perhaps even more powerful than Mercury, and had a source of inexhaustible magic empowering her.

"Do not commit this insanity!" I shouted, helplessly. "This world still has people on it! Millions of lives who still matter."

"The only life that matters to me, is mine!" Asenath hissed. "I would not expect a brainwashed servitor of Yog-Sothoth to understand!"

The sky swirled and a thing that human eyes could not see but that my own began to descend. It was made of possibilities and ate time. Trust me when I say it was not something you wanted tocomprehend. It was, however, a creature with a shared partial humanity. It had a mother, a brother, a grandfather, and a tie to this world that Miskatonic wizards had ignored. It was my kin.

So, I did something very stupid and asked for its help. "She is trying to kill this world! Your mother and brother's world! It is becoming a place where you can live freely but it will destroy everything here that matters! I will free you from your prison, friend, and let you sail through time. I ask you to rid me of this troublesome priestess, first."

The creature listened to my words and understood. I don't think Asenath ever considered it was born of this planet and human enough to care. It was, however, despite being trapped between dimensions. Sentinel Hill shuddered and shook as the creature resisted the spell of the pitiful mind trying to bind it.

"I have the power!" Asenath called, holding up the book. "I am in control! The power of the *Al-Azif* compels you!"

Mercury shot it out of her hands with her revolver, the defensive spells the girl had cast not applying to the book itself.

Asenath looked horrified, and Wilbur Whately's brother promptly ate her. It then began to feast on the *Al-Azif*, devouring millions of souls and endless possibilities into itself. It became more solid and powerful, becoming a gestalt of the race that once had been, and might be again. The cultists outside Mercury's ward screamed and melted into the ground as their source of power evaporated.

Wilbur's brother escaped the prison he'd been placed in and vanished into the time stream, satisfied and now more akin to his father than the humans he'd left behind. Mercury invoked several powers to protect herself from possession by Asenath's ghost, but I suspected it was now part of something infinitely larger.

For a moment, I saw Wilbur's brother follow the timeline of the *Al-Azif* into the past. It set free the creature that Abdul Al'Hazred attempted to summon and followed the *Al-Azif* back to its homeworld of Callisto. I tried to send a message telepathically down through the timeline, linking my mind to the book, but only briefly was able to touch minds with those in the past. Ironically, including Andrew Doran. To my horror, I saw the planet and its peoples destroyed by the ever fatter and more powerful time-wyrm that had been born of a human woman giving birth to Yog-Sothoth's spawn. The Callisto people might have been able to use sorcery to save themselves but, ironically, had created a Mobius strip that guaranteed their own destruction. I'd been party to a genocide on a planetary scale but the monster inside me did not care and the human on the outside could not understand the whole. I simply shook away the image and turned back to join those still-living on this world.

"So, did we win?" Mercury asked.

"Yeah," I said, blinking. "I think we did."

"Good," Mercury said. "That damned book has caused way too much trouble over the years."

THE LAUGHING SKULL

By. C.T. Phipps

I was amused by the final fate of the *Al-Azif*, as well as disappointed. Even as I sat on the desk of my author, a half-finished story in his typewriter, I couldn't help but think the *Al-Azif*'s story was one of missed opportunities.

The source of unfathomable alien wisdom being destroyed did not surprise me. Vhourvath had been an arrogant fool and it had ultimately proved to be his undoing. Unfortunately, its history was not of spreading the glories of Great Cthulhu, Yog-Sothoth, and other beings across the Earth. It was not a legacy of bringing destruction to great empires and laying waste to the feeble excuse for civilization that mankind had constructed.

Instead, the history of the *Al-Azif* was nothing more than a series of adventurers like the kind Robert E. Howard and Clark Ashton Smith wrote about. Ignorant savages, including one who was an alien himself, struggling to protect humanity from a destiny that was impossible to avert.

In truth, the discovery that humanity survived the rise of the Great Old Ones left me disquieted. I had thought they would be annihilated by the time depicted in the final story, but they seemed to have eked out an existence in the shadow of eldritch gods. Perhaps they would eventually go extinct or give in to the wild magics I had helped foster in them, but it would not happen without self-styled adventurers like the kind I'd seen resisting it.

Pity.

The fact the *Al-Azif* had led to a stable time loop was

something I decided I would ponder for the next couple of centuries. I had already decided I would educate my author in the secrets of the occult. Secrets far beyond the tidbits I'd placed in his dreams to excite the imagination and spread the glories of the Great Old Ones among the masses.

I would make him a sorcerer who would bring about an early rise of the monsters in his fantasies and thwart the future I'd seen. It would be my spite to the pathetic Yith who had set this bizarre story in motion. Perhaps I would even seize his body and wear it like a robe.

Yes, his latent talents would make that possible. I was tired of my cursed half-life and while it had taken centuries, I had fed from the dreams and wills of many users. There was another World War coming soon, and while human lives were like flickering candles, it would be a bonfire of death, more than enough to achieve my goals.

Howard walked into the room. "Sonia, I'm going to go for a walk. I must have fallen asleep on the couch. I had the most exciting dreams."

"More monsters?"

"More like people who fight them. I might actually let the humans win next time."

"Really?" a bemused female voice spoke from the other room.

"Nah," Howard said, laughing. "Who would want to read that?"

Howard grabbed his coat and passed by me without a second thought. I was already envisioning the terrible things I would make him do to his loved ones to break down his will when Sonia entered the room. There was something different about the Jewish woman and if I had lungs, I would have choked on my next breath.

Her eyes were now crystal blue.

A voice I hadn't heard in millennia spoke from her mind. *It is time to close the loop, Abdul.*

No, I have so much more to learn! I hissed, finding the words ridiculous even as they left my mind. Death cared for no man.

Not even me.

You have been permitted to know how the story ends, the Yith woman said. *It is only fair given how well you have served us.*

Could I have done differently? I asked, pondering how events might have achieved different results.

No, the Yith woman replied. *Then you would not have been you.*

I tried to think of some incantation, secret, or plea that would preserve my immortal life. Instead, I thought of the *Al-Azif* and all the terrible wonders it had opened my mind to. Then I laughed, letting mental peals of insane cackling fill the room.

The Yith woman then picked me up off the desk and hurled me into the wall. The last thing I heard before the shattering unmade my existence was the sound of buzzing insects. I didn't have time to fully ponder what that meant before darkness swallowed me.

Perhaps the ending was not so neatly writte—

Curious about other Crossroad Press books?
Stop by our site:
http://store.crossroadpress.com
We offer quality writing
in digital, audio, and print formats.

Enter the code FIRSTBOOK
to get 20% off your first order from our store!
Stop by today!

www.ingramcontent.com/pod-product-compliance
Lightning Source LLC
Chambersburg PA
CBHW060413180626
46817CB00007B/2567